The Doom Assigned
King Richard III in Victory

By

Richard Unwin

Let if flame or fade, and the war roll down like a wind,
We have proved we have hearts in a cause, we are noble still,
And myself have awaked, as it seems, to the better mind;
It is better to fight for the good than to rail at the ill;
I have felt with my native land, I am one with my kind,
I embrace the purpose of God, and the doom assigned.

Alfred Lord Tennyson

By the Same Author

The Laurence the Armourer Series:

On Summer Seas – The Fighting Plantagenets
A Wilderness of Sea – The Rise of King Richard III
The Roaring Tide – A Tale of High Treason

Other Books:

Who Wrote Marlowe – Christopher Marlowe Exposed
Ironmaster – A Brief History of John Wilkinson

Web Site - www.quoadultra.net

Copyright © Richard Unwin June 2015

All rights reserved. No part of this publication may be reproduced, stored in a retrieval system or transmitted in any form, or by any means, electronic mechanical, photocopying, recording, or otherwise, without the prior permission of the copyright holder.

THE DOOM ASSIGNED........1

1 – RICARDUS VICTOR 7

2 – HERE BE DRAGONS 30

3 – THE FUGITIVES......................................56

4 – NEMESIS 77

5 - THE SIEGE OF PEMBROKE CASTLE 95

6 – THE WORD OF CHIRON.................................118

7 – TRIAL AND RETRIBUTION 142

8 - THE PORTUGUESE MARRIAGE 163

9 – THE KING'S BRIDE............................188

10 – A PERILOUS SEA 216

11 – SAINT GEORGE FOR ENGLAND...............237

12 – THE KING'S JUDGEMENT 256

13 – LORD OF THE MANOR 282

14 – THE ASSASSINS 310

15 - SETTLED IN BLOOD 338

EPILOGUE - ENGLAND PRESENT DAY 366

1 – Ricardus Victor

"They run, my lord; they run!" cried Robert de la Halle excitedly, pointing with his sword. The man lying on the ground waved away the physician attending his wounds and lifted his head to gaze out over the battlefield. Another of his squires rushed to kneel behind him to lend support as he struggled to rise. Across the Redemore Plain large groups of men were milling around in what appeared to be confusion, yet to the practised eye of the wounded knight he could see some of them were breaking free, while the banners of the king's army could be made out as being the pursuers.

"I see the colours of Sir William Stanley there," gasped the knight in astonishment. "They seem to be chasing after Oxford's men?"

"Yes, my lord," shouted another of his squires, "Sir William charged in on the king's side to overwhelm the Tudor. I saw the Tudor banner go down as the King drove his men into the ring of steel about him. Those around Tudor rallied for a few minutes then Sir William attacked. I saw the Tudor colours go down a second time and after that all was confusion."

"There! There is the king!" called Robert directing their attention to where a wheeling column of knights had mounted their horses and were circling, clearly surveying the confused field. The royal standard was flying there amongst them and in the fore the figure of the king, mounted on a fresh white horse with his standard bearer beside him flying his banner of the white boar. It clearly displayed the cross of St. George before a murrey and blue tail embroidered with white roses. They looked to where the king could be seen with those of his remaining household knights standing up in his saddle, clearly searching the field.

Robert squinted as he gazed in the bright sunlight that illuminated the plain. "I cannot see any sign of the Tudor," he called out. "I suppose he lies somewhere among the dead – the king will have made short work of him that's for sure."

Men were running in all directions. He could see where a host of French mercenaries, part of the defeated Tudor army, were being chased and cut down by English knights. Some of these, he noted in surprise, were the earl of Northumberland's men. They had taken no part in the battle but were now enthusiastic in the rout.

"Can you see anything of lord Thomas Stanley," growled his master, struggling to his feet and looking towards Market Bosworth where he knew lord Stanley's considerable army was lurking.

"Nothing, my lord. Think you he will attack?" said Robert curiously.

"Not now," came the faint reply. The knight was clearly struggling to get his breath. "He has left it too late. Had he been in the field, the Tudor might have had the protection of his army rather than expose himself with a small force as he did. Things would have been different then and we would not have had so easy a victory."

"Not so easy a victory as that, my lord," muttered Robert in a subdued voice while signing himself. Word had come early in the battle that the knight's father, John Howard the duke of Norfolk was killed when attacking the centre of the earl of Oxford's army, part of the Tudor invasion force. His son and heir, Thomas Howard, earl of Surrey had come close to suffering the same fate had not his squire, Robert de la Halle got to him with a fresh horse and managed to help him mount to spur clear. Earl Thomas had been struck in the shoulder by the hammer side of a war axe, dislocating his shoulder and possibly damaging his collarbone. The man at arms with the war axe was after ransom and intended to disable the earl rather than kill him. He was despatched by a crossbow quarrel fired by Robert, who, seeing the danger to his lord, had forced his way through the press of men around the earl with a horse. Early in the action, earl Thomas' men were being forced back by the weight of Oxford's attack and it became apparent that the earl must get clear in order to rally his men. It was at this point in the battle that Henry Tudor appeared with a small force, isolated at the rear of the field. King Richard, seeing an opportunity to finish the battle by taking down the Tudor, mounted up along with his household knights and charged at his enemy.

For a few minutes the attack on earl Thomas' men had slackened letting Robert and the other squires get him clear. It was then Sir William Stanley made up his mind and lent his considerable force to the king. Earl Thomas had expressed shock when he observed the Stanley charge. Until that moment Sir William had kept his army out of the fight. He was suspected, along with his brother, of dubious loyalty to the king, if not outright treason. Lord Strange, the son and heir of lord Thomas Stanley was a prisoner in King Richard's pavilion as surety for his father's loyalty. Lord Thomas Stanley, Henry Tudor's father-in-law, though as a vassal was called to battle by King Richard, sent word to the king that he cared little as he had other sons. This prompted George Stanley, lord Strange, to hurl an accusation at his uncle William declaring he too was in collusion with Henry Tudor. Indeed, the king had declared Sir William traitor in the day before the battle. Thus all English commanders were wary of both Stanley brothers and watched their respective armies in the half-expectation they might join with Tudor. Lord Stanley had six thousand men just out of sight of the Redemore Plain, but Sir William Stanley had three thousand in the field, passively watching until the king's heroic charge when, seeing the Tudor banner fall, Sir William decided to join in the battle for the king.

Suspicious at the duplicity of the Stanley clan, earl Thomas thought Sir William was indeed going to the aid of the Tudor and so too did the men of the king's household knights. All became confused until it was realised Sir William's men were fighting with the halberdiers that surrounded Henry Tudor and were there to help rid the land of the invader. The Tudor contingent was soon overwhelmed by the fury of the king's attack, and the additional weight of the Stanley force finally broke them. It seemed then that the Tudor must have gone down with his men; few of them would be likely to get away. When Oxford's men saw the Tudor banner go down for the second time and the royal standard remaining aloft, they knew the day was lost and began to run. Most of them were foreign mercenaries and they understood there would be little mercy for them at the hands of a triumphant and angry English army.

There were but few Englishmen with the Tudor, his army being a hotchpotch of French, Breton and treasonable Welsh, all with a long history of enmity with the English. They had dared to challenge the rightful king of England with a dubious nobody at their head. Henry Tudor, a descendant of the bastard Beauforts and a Welsh yeoman was the best claimant that the House of Lancaster could trawl up. His mother, Margaret Beaufort, Lady Stanley now she was married to her third husband Lord Stanley, had encouraged in him a morbid desire to wear the crown of England. Away to the west could just be seen the Welsh army under Rhys-ap-Thomas. They seemed to be attempting a strategic withdrawal, though once the mercenaries had been dealt with the English would turn on them, and now that Northumberland had decided to enter the field, albeit after the real fighting had died away, they might soon be overwhelmed and cut down too.

"The day is ours, my lord," declared Robert triumphantly.

"Aye, it seems so," returned the earl, the glint of triumph in his eyes tempered by the sadness in his voice as he thought on his personal loss.

They watched as the king raised his sword and whirled it victoriously above his head as he gathered his men around him. He cantered off towards his pavilions where he would receive the reports of his commanders to discover who lived and who had died. There were but a few familiar banners streaming around and behind him as many of his best knights had fallen in the mêlée around Henry Tudor in the minutes before Sir William Stanley came to the rescue. One banner that had not been there before the battle was that of Sir William himself who, riding close by his sovereign, was already about the business of ingratiating himself with a victorious King Richard the Third.

* * *

King Richard's pavilion was buzzing with men-at-arms as bees around their skep. The king had not yet issued orders regarding the capture of prisoners and there were few nobles in Tudor's defunct army to attract the hope for ransom. The only one of note was John de Vere, thirteenth earl of Oxford and the Lancastrian's principal general. Word was that he had fallen in the rout and was killed. This had not been a civil war, as those former battles in England were between the contending houses of York and Lancaster, but a foreign invasion. There were few Englishmen with the Tudor and those with him were mostly dead or captured. It had been the final Lancastrian attempt at the English Crown. The man who was their candidate for king was but a bastard claimant and now he was finished there could hardly be more. Any foreign mercenaries that were caught were being summarily despatched in revenge for the disturbance their invasion had caused the realm. Many were fleeing for their lives into the countryside hoping to make it to the coast where they could take ship back across the narrow seas to France. The Redemore plain was now clear of fighting and only the cries of the wounded could be heard. Scavengers were coming into the field from the surrounding fields and villages, stripping the dead of anything of value and sending to their God any wounded enemies unable to flee. King Richard had commanded that the wounded of his own army be taken care of and the dead conveyed to Dadlington Church nearby for burial in the churchyard there.

Robert de la Halle approached the king's camp carrying a list of the dead and wounded of earl Thomas' men. He took his place in the queue of squires there on the same business, sent by their lords while they attended upon the king. Earl Thomas was lying in his own pavilion, having difficulty with breathing, the wound to his shoulder having become unbearably painful due to the probing of his physician. In talking with his companion squires, Robert soon discovered that although there were many dead, matters would have been far worse had it not been for the king's precipitate action in attacking Henry Tudor when he did.

It had been a brave charge against the advice of his captains. Indeed, after Norfolk's death the king was advised to withdraw to fight another day. Everyone knew the risk of using cavalry against pikes, and eighteen foot long pikes were what surrounded and protected the Tudor, who seems not to have done any fighting for himself. However, the pikes were hastily deployed and too few. They did not have sufficient men-at-arms in support to dispose of any knight that managed to get by them. Once the pike wall collapsed, then French halberdiers closed around Henry Tudor to protect him. The king's men were his best knights and they almost succeeded in getting to the Tudor when Sir William burst suddenly upon them. In the suspicion and confusion before it was realised Sir William was actually there to support the king, Henry Tudor had disappeared. Where he was now was a matter for much speculation among the king's soldiers but few thought he would remain undiscovered for long.

When his turn came to present his account, Robert recognised the notary who was in charge of the clerical scribes that sat within his pavilion scratching the record for presentation to the king. He was a Dominican friar as denoted by his white habit, which was covered over by a distinctive black cloak with peaked hood, giving his order the name of black friars. Normally attached to the household of the now deceased duke of Norfolk, he had regularly attended upon earl Thomas with messages from the earl's father, John Howard. The friar's robes disguised a meagre frame that remained scrawny in spite of his renowned appetite, an appetite that extended to sampling the delights in a certain house near to the duke of Norfolk's main residence of Framlingham castle, a house familiar to the duke's squires who went there for instruction in those skills that might better fit them for their future, and more legitimate, amours. Fra Dominic, it was said, owned a share of it along with his bishop though he was never seen there. It was common knowledge that some of the new and fairer ladies went discreetly to his chambers in the nearby castle so he could approve them and assess them for their best price. Fra Dominic frowned at him then gave Robert a nod of recognition as he presented his list. The friar looked over the details then made a note of the numbers in a parchment on the table before passing the scrip, which also contained the names of those nobles who were dead or wounded, to a clerk for scribing into the permanent record.

He appraised the young man in front of him. He saw a youth of fourteen years well clad in armour of somewhat better quality than most squires though he was too young to have been given a position in the front line of battle. He would have remained behind his lord's lance ready to serve him with fresh arms and horses should he require them. Tall and muscular for his age, wisps of black hair could just be seen escaping from under the brim of his armet, a fine headpiece fitted with a visor that was now raised to show his face. Bright eyes gleamed with youthful exuberance, the residue of excitement induced by the recently won battle. At his belt he carried an arming sword and also a scabbard with a murderer, a long dagger. This, he knew, had been the lad's first experience of real fighting though the youth was one of the earl of Surrey's favourite squires. Already the friar knew it had been Robert de la Halle who had saved the earl from further harm. Unusually for a youth who aspired to become a man-at-arms, he practised shooting with the crossbow and it had been his use of that weapon which had rescued his lord.

"Your father would speak with you, by my lord of Surrey's leave," he squeaked hoarsely. "He is somewhere close to the king, I think." Robert supposed his hoarseness was, no doubt, due to the cloying fumes of incense that fogged the air in the castle chapel. He began to cough and waved Robert impatiently away. The friar seemed to be stricken with some debilitating illness and when he walked, breathed badly and needed the aid of a staff.

His father was not difficult to find although Robert did have to force his way through the press of soldiery that surrounded the king's pavilion. This brought him a few rough shoves and indignant glares, but eventually he managed to get within visible distance of his father. Laurence de la Halle, the king's armourer was standing near to King Richard, examining the king's battle helm. It looked to be somewhat battered but intact. The golden crown that encircled it had a deep cut but was otherwise unscathed. The armourer's own helm, a barbute, lay on a side table where Robert could see it had suffered a large dent. It seemed his father had been in the thick of the fighting. King Richard had his hands over his ears and his eyes screwed shut in protest at the clamour of his remaining captains and courtiers who were all eager for attention and ready with advice. Among those standing close by the king he recognised William Catesby the lawyer and Sir William Stanley. With Catesby was the forlorn figure of lord Strange, George Stanley, still with his head on his shoulders. Obviously King Richard had not carried out his threat to decapitate him unless his father lord Thomas joined battle against the Tudor. Robert called to his father. The armourer lifted his head at the sound of his son's voice and grinned widely when he spotted him in the crowd. Assuring himself the king was occupied for the moment, he placed the royal armet by his own barbute and indicated they should step to one side to talk together.

Laurence de la Halle was clad as a fighting knight although, as the king's armourer he would normally have remained with the other armourers among the baggage wagons until the battle was decided. Robert wondered at his appearance; his surcoat, displaying the murrey and blue colours of York and emblazoned with King Richard's personal badge of the White Boar, was cut and torn. Mud was encrusted here and there and a track of dried blood traced out his facial scar down his right cheek, obviously emanating from a head wound. His eyes were thus directed upwards to a patch of matted hair and blood. Robert noticed that though his father's arming sword still hung at his belt, the dagger he habitually carried was missing from its scabbard. Laurence too, swiftly examined the appearance of his son for signs of injury, and finding none offered his arms. The two embraced for a moment, each glad the other had come through the ordeal of battle in one piece and still standing.

"My prayers to St. Barbara were answered," declared Laurence, referring to the intercession of his personal saint, the patron of armourers. "I expect your own to the Virgin and your mother were as effective." Laurence had instructed his son to pray to the Virgin and ask the blessing of his mother in the expectation the two would protect him in the conflict. Robert's mother had died some years before of the sweating sickness at Gloucester where his father had his main business.

"I think St. Barbara might have blinked in distraction for a moment, seeing as your barbute has suffered a severe blow?" Robert gave a nod towards the table where his father's helmet lay beside that of the king.

"I came within a strike of the Tudor," enthused Laurence smiting his right hand into his left. "The king would have had him too, were it not for the intervention of Sir William Stanley. King Richard chopped down Sir William Brandon, Tudor's standard-bearer, and was about to finish off the Tudor himself when Stanley appeared. We thought he was coming in on the side of the Tudor and his grace was swept away from his quarry in the confusion before we sorted out who was attacking who. I saw a chance and went for the Tudor as he stood helpless in the centre of his men. The wretch must have shit himself as I came at him. Unfortunately, the tide of battle swept me aside and the bastard Tudor too. The last I saw of him he was mounting a horse brought to him by one of his closest knights and after that I was busy fighting free of the press around the Tudor position and lost him. I was unhorsed and had to walk from the field."

"But what were you doing there in the first place?" asked Robert. "You should have remained with the baggage seeing as you are a skilled artisan, not a man-at-arms."

"I believe I was riding to extricate you from the onslaught of the earl of Oxford. The king was informed of the death of the duke of Norfolk in the centre of the battle and I knew you were with the earl of Surrey on Norfolk's right flank. The king ordered Northumberland to attack Oxford's right flank to relieve the pressure but Henry Percy refused to move his army, saying he was watching Sir William Stanley for suspected treachery, so the king decided he would mount up and do the job himself. I joined him, intending to do something to come to your aid. It was then the king spotted the Tudor with but a few men around him at the back of the field. He ordered a charge with just his own household knights to support him and I was caught up with them."

"And when did you receive the blow that almost split your head?"

"No idea." Laurence gazed at his son with concern. "I hear you were engaged in the fighting too," he said with a mixture of concern and pride.

"I was following the advice you gave me before the battle, father, and kept close to the horses. When my lord of Surrey was felled I reached for the crossbow at my saddle and shot down his enemy. Then I mounted the courser and taking another of my lord's mounts, brought it to him. I had to dismount to help get him into the saddle then remount and we were both able to retire from the fray. It must have been most desperate in the fight around the Tudor, too?"

"Aye, and the king lost many of his best knights and truest friends. I am beginning to wonder what he will do now. His most faithful supporters are mostly killed and those of dubious loyalty still live." Laurence tugged at his short black beard musing on the residual politics. Robert noticed the scar that ran down his right cheek seemed deeper than usual. It was encrusted with blood from his head wound, almost invisible rather than as normal, showing white against the weathered tan of his face. It was the result of a close shave with a war axe. He got it in the service of the duke of Gloucester, the present King Richard and shortly after Robert himself had been the means whereby the younger son of King Edward was extracted secretly out of the Tower of London and taken to safety.

"Yes, Sir William Stanley might yet ingratiate himself after being accused of treason," said Robert. "I wonder how his brother my lord Thomas Stanley will fare. His army is still over Bosworth way and he refused to come to the aid of the king. The earl of Northumberland has a few questions to answer too. He only came into the field after the Tudor's men began to run."

"Yes," mused Laurence. "The battle is won but the mess it has left in its wake is to be cleared up. I cannot see how the king can get himself entirely free. There are yet many threats to him, perhaps more than before?"

"How can that be, father?"

"Let it be for now," came the reply. "We shall bide our time and perhaps consult with your grandfather Cornelius. He has a nose for such things. For now let us watch this . . ." Laurence hardly needed to direct his son's attention to what was about to occur as the tumult associated with it was hardly something that could be missed. A blast of clarions announced the coming of Henry Percy, fourth earl of Northumberland. The earl arrived apparently hoping the grandness of his entrance would somehow impress his king. Fifty or so men-at-arms, then his personal herald and squires of the body preceded him. King Richard raised his hand for silence as the earl walked between his men and swept him an elegant bow. Percy was still clad in full harness with a surcoat displaying the emblems of his house, blue and gold lions quartered with a trio of luces. The earl removed his armet and knelt bare-headed before the king.

"You make a brave show, Northumberland," snarled King Richard contemptuously. He appeared to be holding himself in check. Perhaps he was considering the trouble that the infamous Plantagenet rage had caused him in the past. The soldier in him at this delicate time, when there were still foes in the field, needed to preserve calm. Henry Percy knelt white faced, in fear of his life. Everyone there remembered how the king, when duke of Gloucester, dealt with the vacillating Lord Hastings, and that lord, friend and companion to his brother King Edward the Fourth, had been Richard's chief supporter until then. Hastings had been summarily beheaded on a block of scrap wood in the Tower of London without trial or preamble. His crime had been disloyalty rather than outright treason but Richard's anger had nevertheless seen him off. Lord Thomas Stanley had been part of the conspiracy against Gloucester at that time but, somehow, had escaped the duke's wrath. It was unlikely that would happen a second time, not once King Richard had him in his charge. "It is regrettable that so brave a show could not be granted us when we commanded you during the battle. Your soldiers were bold enough in the rout, I observed."

Robert and Laurence detected an uncomfortable stirring among the men in Northumberland's contingent. It seemed they felt some shame at their perceived lack of valour.

"My lord king," cried Henry Percy as if in anguish. "Your grace himself declared Sir William Stanley a traitor. He has three thousand men with him. I was poised to intervene should he have attacked your army. It would have been irresponsible of me to turn my back on him!"

"Your grace, I object," came a furious shout. Sir William Stanley exploded out from the press of soldiers around the king, his face contorted with rage. "It was I who came to your aid." Sir William stretched out his arm and pointed an accusing finger at the earl who continued to gaze directly into the face of the king. "As I recall, Northumberland - you made no attempt to stop me when I moved to support my king though you dare tell us you suspected my loyalty to his grace. If that were so then why did you remain an observer merely?"

"A good question, Sir William," replied King Richard turning a stern eye upon Henry Percy. "Perhaps my cousin Northumberland might explain?"

"My l-lord king," stammered Percy, "I saw the Tudor banner go down and considered it would be more prudent to destroy the enemy as they disintegrated to prevent them reforming." Henry Percy reddened as he realised how lame his excuses were sounding.

Sir William Stanley grinned triumphantly, relishing the diversion of embarrassing questioning to Henry Percy rather than himself. "Well, seeing as his grace's army considerably outnumbered the Tudor's that was unlikely," he snapped.

Northumberland, shaking with a combination of dread and suppressed ire clamped a hand around the pommel of his sword, displaying his fury at Sir William's insinuation. "Battles have been lost ere now by underestimating an enemy," he growled. "That is why King Henry the Fifth of famous memory ordered the killing of his prisoners at Agincourt. They were numerous enough, should they rally, to overwhelm his victorious army."

"Enough!" shouted King Richard. "We will not dispute the matter now. My lord Northumberland, you will take your army and march to where Lord Stanley is still hovering, near Market Bosworth I am informed, and take him in charge. He has six thousand men with him. If he resists with his host then you can demonstrate your martial valour, as you should have done earlier and use your army to take him by force. In any case I would have you disperse his men back to their homes. As for lord Thomas Stanley – arrest him in our name and take him to London. Lodge him in the Tower to await our pleasure. Now, get you from our sight. We would rather consult with men who fought with us and who are *proved* worthy of trust." The king raised the earl who glared briefly at Sir William before stamping away to do the king's bidding.

"Just look there," said Laurence quietly in Robert's ear. "Sir William Stanley can hardly contain his delight at the discomfiture of Northumberland. Already he is calculating which of the earl's lands might be forfeit to the crown and thus available as reward for the man who had ridden with his men to rescue the king. Then there are the lands of his brother, lord Stanley. He owns most of the north-west of England including the Isle of Man. For his part, Sir William owns much of Cheshire, which places him nicely to take over his brother's demesnes should lord Thomas suffer attainder.

"Is that likely?" asked Robert. "Attainder, one of the penalties for high treason he knew, meant the loss of all lord Stanley's lands and affected the inheritance rights of his heirs too."

"Assuredly," answered his father, "and probably his life will be forfeit too."

As the earl of Northumberland left the pavilion he was almost knocked over by the stumbling intrusion of another knight who everyone recognised as the king's man, viscount Lovell. King Richard's face lit up with joy at the approach of his friend.

"My lord Lovell," he cried in delight. "I was informed you were lost!" The king's relief at sight of his friend alive was palpable. Until this moment all those with him, excepting perhaps Catesby, and Laurence de la Halle his personal armourer, were not entirely trustworthy. Those who had been his closest friends and advisors lay in the mud and marshland of the Redemore Plain.

Viscount Lovell fell to his knees in exhaustion at the king's feet. King Richard signalled to a convenient man-at-arms to help Lovell remove his helm. The knight shook his head to loosen his long fair hair.

"I was after the Tudor, your grace," he gasped, "otherwise I would have sent word and come to your side." King Richard's face darkened and he stooped to look closely at his friend.

"You have him?"

"Alas no, your grace. I thought so at first: I chased after him with a few of my men and caught up with him. We managed to cut down the men in his escort and captured he who we thought was

Henry Tudor. When we removed his helm it turned out to be a decoy. The Tudor has escaped us and rides, we believe, to join with Rhys-ap-Thomas. It is as we suspected, your grace. Tudor had an escape rout planned, back the way he came it seems."

"The decoy – what information did you manage to extract from him."

"Nothing, your grace. The man knew nothing other than to ride north, away from the field. We slit his throat and left him for the scavengers."

"He was told to ride north, you say," mused the king. He paced the floor of his pavilion for a few minutes in deep thought. His squires and courtiers scatted away from his path. "If the decoy was riding north then it is likely the Tudor will head west towards Wales where he believes he has free passage. The news of our victory will travel behind him so he is unlikely to be impeded."

"Then we need to send news of your victory before so that any who shelter him will know they be committing treason against your grace's crown," said Lovell. "It is possible he is travelling with the army of Rhys-ap-Thomas and thus his progress into Wales will be slow."

"Yes and we shall send into Wales using our fleet to get word along the coast to stop the Tudor taking ship. He must not escape us after all the trouble we have taken in getting him to invade our realm and thus rid ourselves of his arrant ambition." The king turned on Sir William and fixed him with a dreadful stare.

"Sir William," commanded the king, "you will take your men and join with my army in the destruction of the Welsh under Rhys-ap-Thomas who is withdrawing into Wales. He should have stopped Henry Tudor before he came into England and instead treacherously joined with him against our crown of England. If the Tudor is with him then we want him alive. I believe you have already had discourse with the traitor ere now. Your familiarity with him should give you something to talk about as you bring him to the Tower. There is lodging enough for him there beside his father-in-law. As for Rhys-ap-Thomas, you will bring me his head. It will serve as decoration in London. I have no use for any other part of him."

Sir William flushed and staggered back clearly discomfited to be sent thus from the king's presence. He had been counting on continually ingratiating himself hoping that his recent prevarications and clandestine meetings with the Tudor faction might be forgotten, or at least forgiven. It was clear the King was not about to unconditionally pardon anyone who previously had been tardy in support of his crown. If he proved unable to bring Henry Tudor to the king, then Fortune might frown severely upon Sir William Stanley.

Laurence smiled in satisfaction at the king's words and again whispered into Robert's ear. "Sir William now realises it will take more than outrageous sycophancy to overcome his reputation for vacillating loyalty, though, to be fair, until recently he has been a fervent supporter of the house of York." Laurence looked over to the king and then gripped his son's arm. "Stand to – the king beckons me and I believe you are included in the invitation."

Viscount Lovell was the only one around the king who displayed pleasure at the approach of the master armourer and his son. The other courtiers clamouring for his attention, realising there was soon to be much alteration in the government of England, were impatient to get the ear of the king to obtain advantage. The presence of an artisan craftsman impeded any progress they might make in that regard. Laurence pulled his son down beside him as he knelt before the king.

"You may rise, master armourer. I am pleased to inform you that my harness stood the test of battle very well. Had it not been for the strength of my helm I would have taken serious injury as you can see." The king pointed to the gash in the gold crown of his armet on the table beside him.

"Thank you, your grace," responded Laurence. "I hope all harness that I make will serve as well."

"There will be reward coming to you," smiled the king as he turned his attention to the young man beside his armourer. "I take it this is Robert de la Halle?" Robert glowed with pride that the king actually knew his name, particularly at a time like this when the shouts and cries that were the remnants of battle clamoured all around.

"It is, your grace," replied Laurence proudly. King Richard looked fondly on the youth and spoke directly to him.

"I remember well the role you played in getting our nephew Richard free of the Tower of London," said the king. "Sir James Tyrell spoke highly of you too. It was a pity that some time later you managed to find yourself imprisoned for a while, and your father was fortunate in getting you out. Still, here we all are." The king opened his arms to indicate those close to him, his faithful followers. "I hear your lord the earl of Surrey is injured?"

"He is, your grace," replied Robert tremulously. "He took a heavy blow to his left shoulder and has difficulty breathing and in using his arm."

"I wish you to convey to him our grief at the death of his father, the duke of Norfolk. Jockey Norfolk was a good friend of York as well as to us and served our house faithfully and loyally. I believe that his son might fill some of the void his father has left in our realm of England. Tell him we know how to thank those who fought with us this day."

"I will, most gladly your grace."

"We have lost some good friends this day," lamented viscount Lovell. "Happily the earl of Surrey is not among them."

"Just so," agreed the king, "but our secretary John Kendall is killed and our dear Robert Percy. Brackenbury went down too and Richard Ratcliffe. I have yet to receive the full toll of dead and injured. "By God's blood the Tudor will suffer for this day when I have him," cursed the king, his mood changing instantly. It was a characteristic that those close to him knew and many had reason to fear.

* * *

By the time the king's men had found the body of the earl of Oxford he was already stripped naked by the scavengers that roamed the battlefield. King Richard instructed that his body be brought to Leicester. The king had retired there to lick his wounds and decide what to do now that the threat of the Tudor invasion no longer lay over his reign like a dark cloud. Thomas Howard was recovered sufficiently in the few hours before the evening of the twenty-second of August 1485 to mount his horse and, accompanied by his lance, those men-at-arms comprising his immediate household knights, his squires and body servants, escorted the dead earl of Oxford into the town. Oxford's body was slung over a horse and Robert, who rode immediately behind, noted how his head bumped ignominiously on the parapets of the bridge over the River Soar. He felt some disgust at how humiliation wounds had been inflicted on the earl's buttocks by English soldiers in revenge for his temerity in attacking their king and disturbing his realm of England. Oxford had lost his helm in the battle and all his fatal injuries had been to his head. King Richard had ordered the earl be taken to the Abbey of the Grey Friars at Leicester and interred respectfully beneath the entrance to the choir, as befitted his rank. The king had denied him burial at his castle of Hedingham seeing as he was attainted as a traitor and his lands forfeit to the crown. There was no point in sending him there. Soon those demesnes would belong to another.

After leaving the body of the earl of Oxford with the Abbey

fathers, earl Thomas presented himself before the king who was lodged at the Guildhall. The aftermath of a battle always presented logistical and political problems even though the victor was the legitimate monarch. Government would continue as before, but policy advisors around the king would now change. His best and most trusted supporters were mostly dead and new ones must be sought out to fill the void. Moreover, certain magnates in the realm with great power had demonstrated their lack of support for his crown and must have their positions in the scheme of things reviewed. Then there were those who had gone so far as to give surreptitious support to the Tudor. Principal among these was lord Thomas Stanley, one of the most powerful magnates in England. Rumour had it that he had surrendered to the earl of Northumberland who was at this moment bringing him before the king to explain himself.

Robert entered the guildhall at Leicester in the train of the earl of Surrey. Most were still clad in full harness in case there was to be any further fighting, though the chance of that seemed to have faded quickly now the invaders were all dispersed and there were no Tudor supporters in Leicester. They all knelt as the earl made obeisance before the king who alone had removed his harness and robed in purple trimmed with ermine, was seated at one end of the hall. The cloth of state had been draped over a seat on a low dais to serve as a throne. Hovering obsequiously close beside King Richard was William Catesby, and a weary viscount Lovell stood behind the king, content at merely observing the gathering in the hall. The same notary that Robert had spoken to earlier, Fra Dominic, was serving as the king's secretary because John Kendall, his previous secretary was killed having accompanied the king in his madcap charge at Henry Tudor.

Before King Richard could speak to the earl of Surrey a commotion near the far door drew the attention of everyone there. Surrey hurriedly indicated to his men to stand aside as the earl of Northumberland entered with an armed escort between which slouched a contrite lord Thomas Stanley. The air in the hall became still and mood of those present pregnant with expectation. The king's eyes flashed fire for a fraction of a second before fading to a slow burn, his face set as stone where the mason had carved disgust in every line. Torches had been lit in the sconces around the walls and even the flames that flickered brightly seemed to steady. Through the tall lancet windows of the hall, the daylight was fading into night; a circumstance that fitted the current moment seeing as one of England's most luminous nobles was approaching his shadowy nemesis. Northumberland knelt before the king, who immediately raised him with an impatient wave, never taking his eyes from the abject figure of lord Stanley.

"Lord Thomas Stanley, your grace," drawled Northumberland observing the necessary protocol even though all knew the man who now staggered forward then threw himself upon the rushes on the floor before the king. He spread his arms as if an oblate before the cross of Our Lord. The king gazed down on him with contempt for a while then gestured to Northumberland.

"Get my lord Stanley to his feet, Northumberland. He seems to have lost the use of his limbs and I would see his face." Northumberland commanded two of his men-at-arms to drag lord Stanley upright. Stanley held out his arms in supplication to the king.

"Your grace," he cried piteously, "I have been much misunderstood. I am no traitor, sire."

"No traitor, you say," drawled King Richard scornfully. "I see you in full harness. It seems you came to the field intending to join battle, but for whom, I wonder? My realm was under attack from a foreign invader, yet you held your men back rather than support your king. Northumberland here did much the same but managed to move his men eventually, even if only to chase away the vanquished host of Henry Tudor, your son-in-law." The king paused to let the significance of his words strike home. "Even my threat to deprive you of your son and heir couldn't move you. Your brother, on the other hand, at least acted for me even though he came to battle rather late."

Thomas Stanley suddenly stood erect at the mention of his brother. The old practiced arrogance of a high noble flared up in him, then subsided. He opened his mouth to speak but then thought better of it. Eventually he managed a few words, uttered with grim bitterness.

"My brother is his own man and his intervention on your side was not how it now seems," he murmured.

The king's eyes glittered as he pondered this remark. The muscles in his jaw were pronounced, showing he was clamping his jaws tightly to prevent hasty speech. Slowly the muscles in his face relaxed as he gained control of his temper.

"Your brother is even now chasing after your son-in-law who, should you have done your duty to your king, would never have considered his bastard claim to our throne let alone act upon it. We shall have him soon and then the matter of treason amongst those formerly of our court will be dealt with. You, sir, were our Lord

High Constable and carried the mace of your office at our coronation. We made you steward of our household with lands and wealth granted by us and power enough except you would have more!"

"It was his mother who wanted more, your grace," cried lord Stanley without thinking. "Henry Tudor is but a creature of her ambition. I held my men back, sire and would not take the field against you." The king snorted in derision.

"His mother!" spat the king. "The woman is your wife and under house arrest for past plottings. See where my mercy has led? She should have been burned for a witch years ago. Margaret Stanley is held at your manor of Lathom in Lancashire, unless you have released her. She shall be brought to trial also." King Richard lanced the treasonous baron with his eyes. "Henry Tudor a creature of her ambition! Yours too it would seem. I ordered you to keep her away from intrigue; instead you have joined with her. Don't think I am unaware of your scheming, nor hers for that matter. Your family have ever been dissemblers – and don't try to deny it. I recall my father telling me of your conduct at the battle of Blore Heath, or rather the nearest you got to it. King Henry the sixth expected you by your word to come to his aid. You remained six miles away for three days and failed to join battle, watching while the earl of Salisbury defeated the Lancastrians. Afterwards you had the temerity to send Salisbury your congratulations!" The king's voice rose in pitch, verging on hysteria and he gripped the arms of his chair half rising from it as if he would hurl himself at lord Stanley. He paused and settled himself back into his seat, determined not to lose his temper. "You got away with it that time but the sands of time do not drain in their glass for ever, when the glass must be turned to flow in the opposite direction. That being so I am content to let the law take its course." King Richard flapped a hand at the earl of Northumberland. "Take my lord Stanley, under close armed guard to the Tower of London. Lord Stanley tried to get out some speech, but the panic that welled up in him prevented anything other than a strangled gurgle as the guard took him away.

Robert, who had been observing this from among the earl of Surrey's men was much affected by the look of horror in the eyes of lord Stanley as he was dragged from the presence of the king. So abject was the lord that Robert could not help feeling some pity for him, wrenched from his position as one of the country's greatest magnates to a prison cell. Was lord Stanley powerful enough to escape a traitor's death? Robert could hardly imagine so high a noble brought so low. He carefully shoved himself closer the better to hear what was being said. Northumberland remained behind, waiting to speak some more with the king, his face set grimly.

"Your grace, there is someone here you might like to hear. He is a captain in lord Stanley's army and I believe you should hear him."

"Another traitor. How many more? I suppose I must get used to hearing their pleas ere this business is finished."

"This one is no traitor, your grace, rather a loyal subject whom it is necessary for you to hear."

The king leaned back in his chair and considered Northumberland's words with interest.

"Then bring him forward and we shall hear him. It will be a pleasant change from the mewling cries of traitors."

Northumberland gestured for his men to stand back while a fellow, clad in the plain armour of a yeoman stepped hesitantly forward. He fell on his knees before the king, his head bowed. Richard frowned. Protocol demanded a raised head so the king could see the expression in a subject's face, but this fellow, unschooled in courtly procedures was not to know that and was clearly overwhelmed.

"Get yourself to your feet, good man, and stop your trembling. An honest Englishman has nothing to fear standing before this king, if you are indeed honest, which we think you might be seeing as my lord Northumberland has vouched for you."

"My lord king," stuttered the yeoman. "I am your most loyal subject and so too was my brother. He was a yeoman and captain of his men, called by your royal commission of array to come to your aid."

"Was?" said the king. "Is he no longer in the world? We think he could not have been killed in lord Stanley's host."

"Indeed he was, dread king, killed by order of lord Stanley."

"Killed? Why was he killed?"

"For treason, sire. He was hanged."

"Then if he was guilty of treason he got off lightly, being hanged merely. Are you here to tell us lord Stanley is a merciful man?"

"My lord king, my brother was hanged for refusing to obey the order to join with the invader."

King Richard stiffened with shock. "You mean lord Stanley actually ordered his army to support the Tudor?" he gasped.

"He did, dread king, and the order spread great alarm among us. We were commanded to add weight to the earl of Oxford's men and destroy the centre of your grace's army. Until then we thought we were there to fight a foreign invader. We had no idea who he was, but French, Bretons and Welsh have ever been at enmity with us

English; there were Scots with the invader, too. The thought of joining with them against our king was unthinkable. My brother was one of the first to disobey the order; there were a dozen or so others hanged with him."

"Yet nobody in the Stanley army moved against us?"

"None, my lord king. The deaths of our captains stirred the men and lord Stanley was lucky he wasn't dragged down and hanged himself." The man's eyes suddenly opened wide in fear as he realised he had just informed the king that he was describing the rebellion of a subject against his liege lord. He began to tremble as he witnessed a host of emotions chasing across the king's face. Presently King Richard, realising the effect his expression was having on his subject, let his features soften reassuringly.

"Your name, good yeoman?"

"John Warren, my liege."

"And your brother who was hanged?"

"Daniel Warren, sire."

"Has he family?"

"He has, my lord king; a wife and five children. He leases land from the estates of my lord Stanley in Lancashire. I live there too, with my wife and three children."

"You will, therefore, take over the landholding?"

"I suppose I shall sire, unless lord Stanley turns us off."

"Then, John Warren, give your name and details to master Catesby, just here," Catesby stepped forward intent on the king's instructions. "Catesby, secure this man's rights to his brother's former lease holding and give him payment for his service to us." Catesby nodded his understanding and beckoned one of his scribes who would make a note of the king's wishes. King Richard looked to his new secretary. "Fra Dominic, take down this man's story and any others you think might serve for evidence at the trial for treason of lord Thomas Stanley." The king turned his eyes upon the yeoman. "Many thanks to you, John Warren, and to your companions. Please assure them they will suffer no retribution for being among lord Stanley's army. You may go."

John Warren scrambled unsteadily to his feet and paused, shuffling his feet as if there was more he could tell. King Richard noted his recalcitrance.

"Stay – is there something more you can tell us?"

"There is, dread king," said the yeoman, his voice shaking.

"Then speak, man."

"It is just that - not all in lord Stanley's army were loyal, my lord king. There were some among his army, those that willingly hanged my brother, who would have betrayed you."

King Richard leaned forward, his eyes blazing with a mixture of curiosity and fury. This was a king whose personal motto was *Loyaultie Me Lie* – Loyalty Binds Me, a precept he rigidly held to and expected in others.

"Who?"

"Those of the household of lady Stanley, your grace. They were firmly on the Lancastrian – the Tudor side. Most of us took little notice of them until arrayed into battle order, when they were given the command of the army under lord Stanley. They had his authority over our own captains. They took horse back into Lancashire immediately after the battle."

King Richard sat back to consider the import of this information. He turned his attention to Northumberland.

"This business is deeper than we first thought. We are too angry now to think properly upon it."

"Indeed, my lord king," said Northumberland, "it appears your common people are loyal, but others who would command them are traitors. The lady Stanley has long schemed against your house. We should take her up closely and investigate the depths of her plotting."

The king nodded then leant on the right arm of his chair while resting his chin upon his hand. His eyes searched the room and came to light upon a certain knight standing close to where Robert was. He was distinctive in black armour and Robert was already curious about him.

"Sir Ralph de Assheton," called the king his face suddenly alight with decision. "The knight stepped forward and swept a low bow of obeisance. "Though you are our Lieutenant at the Tower of London, and Vice-Constable of England yet we have need of you elsewhere. You are a northern knight and familiar with the county of Lancashire. Take a body of men and get you to Lathom. Arrest the woman Margaret Stanley and bring her to London. Also, question those of her household and arrest any that you think might be in league with her against our throne of England."

"I shall, most willingly, your grace," said Sir Ralph.

"My lord Surrey," said the king turning to the earl. "Send some of your own men with Sir Ralph. If, as our yeoman John Warren tells us there are men of authority in Lancashire who would corrupt our countrymen, there may be some resistance."

"Very good, your grace," replied Surrey.

"For our part, on the morrow we shall retire to Nottingham and, once we have all the reports of our captains, from there to London."

***

"You will need other protection than hard steel," declared Laurence the armourer to his son Robert. "There are dark forces at work where you are bound." He was responding to the news that his son Robert was to go with Sir Ralph de Assheton as one of the earl of Surrey's contingent into Lancashire.

"The lady Stanley, you mean, father?"

"She is part of it. She pretends great piety, but never be fooled. It is common for some to hide behind the shield of Holy Church yet be in league with the devil. You must always remember that she has been working against a king anointed by God's church and a full blood prince to promote her son, whose claim is so distant as to be beyond the visible horizon. I am sure that Northumberland will bring him to condign punishment any day now. That being so, whatever lady Stanley is, she cannot be an instrument of God's will; the woman has ever been deceitful."

Robert knew the source of his father's opinion. In the house of his grandfather, the apothecary Cornelius Quirke lived an old crone named Mother Malkin who hailed from Lancashire. She was a cunning woman skilled in the preparation of simples and cures for the sick. Not only that, but she was the associate of dubious astrologers and necromancers. It was she, along with her acquaintance Peter Otteler, a blind potter and finder of objects and people, who by his dark magic had located him when imprisoned in London and allowed his father to arrange his escape. Robert's imprisonment had been part of one of lady Stanley's plots to discover the whereabouts of the lost prince, the lord bastard, Richard of York. For sure the bastard youth would not have lived long after lady Stanley had discovered where he was hidden, and Robert, too, would likely have lost his life. Cornelius Quirke had married as his second wife a woman named Anna Thorne, whose first husband had been hanged for treason in the reign of Edward the Fourth. She it was who had brought Mother Malkin along with her, the two previously being camp followers dragged along by his father after he first came into England with the invading army of King Edward.

There was some mystery regarding Laurence de la Halle and the woman Anna Thorne, which he had not quite worked out. She brought a son with her, Philip, a youth just a year older than himself and who was currently taking up the study of medicine. The two got along fairly well, due perhaps to the considerable differences in temperament between them.

"I shall pray daily to my patron, Saint Adrian," declared Robert. His choice of patron was satisfactory in every way – the patron of soldiers, Adrian was depicted in church art holding a sword and with an anvil at his feet. The association with his family, artisan armourers, could not have been more explicit. His father nodded sombrely and touched his own talisman, a silver reliquary containing filings from the nail that had pierced Christ's feet on the cross. It was suspended around his neck by a silver chain.

Yes, he is fit for your prayers," said Laurence approvingly. "Make sure you are shriven whenever you have the opportunity in Lancashire. There are forces there that work on an unrepentant soul, ever looking to bring about its destruction."

"Where exactly is Lathom?" asked Robert.

"It is close to the coastal town of Liverpool," replied his father, "near a place named Knowsley. You will have to cross the whole county to get there."

"Is it not strange that the lord Stanley should have his main residence so far from London and the court?"

"Yes, I suppose it is inconvenient for him, though he does have a house in London too. Lathom, and the vast lands associated with it, came to him from his father and grandfather though the origins of the family go back as far as the twelfth century, I believe. I have learned that one John Stanley married Isabel Lathom whose father was the owner of what are now the Stanley lands. She was not his heir, it must be said. All this happened almost exactly one hundred years ago. John Stanley was but a Master Forrester in the Wirral, a peninsular to be found in that region. John Stanley was also a soldier who had come to the attention of King Richard the Second. By a complicated set of events, involving the unexpected deaths of several associated family members, the couple, through Isabel, became the inheritors of those present lands now the Stanley demesnes in the north west of England."

"Not unlike the circumstances surrounding the present king and his family. He too finds himself the inheritor of a kingdom where the sudden and unexpected deaths of his brothers, amid spectacular circumstance propelled him to the throne."

"Yes," mused Laurence, "there is a divinity that shapes our ends, rough hew them how we will."

"I think you should write some of this down, father. It might be useful in later times, just as what you are telling me now is to us today."

Laurence shrugged and gave a grin. "There are certainly a few interesting stories regarding the early lives of the Stanley's and the Lathom's. One involves the substitution of a child for an illegitimate one of Isabel's father Thomas Lathom, an unfortunate man whose wife left him in old age to live adulterously with one Roger de Fazakerly at Knowsley. It seems this child was discovered below an eagle's eyrie and that Isabel's' father and her mother took him in and accepted him as their heir. The story is, of course, apocryphal and has little substance yet the Lathom family in later years adopted the Eagle and Child as their crest. You might find the tale of the Eagle and Child is preserved in certain inn signs of the region."

"From your descriptions of the county of Lancashire, I hope we shall be able to secure lady Stanley quickly and be out of there."

"I hope so too," replied Laurence. "With the devil at your back you should make good time home."

2 – Here Be Dragons

Events were moving fast, which sometimes confused the older knights around King Richard the Third of England, but not so much those of fewer years, such as Robert de la Halle. His problem, due to his being but a little into his fifteenth year, was ignorance of great affairs, yet once appraised of the facts, easily assimilated them into his mind. His father, a native Breton, or so he insisted even though his mother, Robert's paternal grandmother was English, was firmly loyal to King Richard, essential seeing that Laurence de la Halle was the king's personal armourer. His maternal grandfather, one Cornelius Quirke, was an English apothecary in London, which trade served as a cover for his clandestine operations as a spymaster for the house of York. This meant that Robert was English by blood with some Breton roots he had no reason to be ashamed of, despite the political vacillations and often piratical activities of that nation. It was useful, too, that he was fluent in both the English and French languages. His father had hoped he would follow him in the lucrative trade of artisan armourer but Robert, due partly to his father's involvement with the duke of Gloucester, now King Richard the Third, discovered in himself a love of adventure that could only be satisfied by engaging in chivalric arms.

He had been, if only for a short time, the companion of the elder son of the defunct King Edward the Fourth who was lodged in the royal apartments of the Tower of London for his protection. Unfortunately Edward died prematurely, to the consternation of his uncle the duke of Gloucester, of a recurring affliction he already suffered before moving into the Tower. The Lancastrian element in the country, having discovered rumours of prince Edward's demise, immediately used it to discomfit King Richard, proclaiming that the two boys had been murdered and daring him to produce them alive. Of course, only one still lived and should he be shown to the people, Lancastrian daggers, to prove the lie, would soon shorten his life. This prompted King Richard to get the surviving prince away to safety. Having helped in the removal abroad of this prince, the young noble the lord bastard Richard of York from the Tower of London, Robert persuaded his father to let him enter service as a page with the duke of Norfolk, John Howard. Norfolk later attached him to the household of his son, Thomas Howard, earl of Surrey and there he had risen to become one of the earl's squires.

Today, having been commanded so to do by the earl of Surrey, he was riding in the lance of Sir Ralph de Assheton towards a region of the country he knew little of but had reason to fear. Following was a troop of about fifty men half in the livery of Sir Ralph, a black mullet on a white ground, while the others wore tabards in red with white crosslets, identifying them as being in the service of the earl of Surrey.

Lancashire, he knew, was a frighteningly wild county where witches, wizards and hobgoblins were reputed to thrive. There were deep forests, rocky chasms and vast moorland where dark forces lurked ready to come down on the farms and villages of the region to wreak destruction upon mankind. His father informed him they have their own particular malevolent demons in Lancashire. Boggarts lived there, hidden by day but emerging at night to do mischief if they could get into the houses of men. Cattle would take sick and die, sheep would go down with the murrain and people would become afflicted by illness and disease with no cause other than the malign influence of the devil's own agents. Rivulets that meandered seemingly innocently between the hills, tracing silver tracks in the moonlight and singing over deceptively smooth rocks, seductively concealed the means whereby the unwary might be sucked down into a nearby swamp or an infant drown to the accompaniment of their siren song.

They were crossing even now a stretch of harsh moorland that swept down from the High Peak forest of Derbyshire, through into Cheshire - Longdendale and past the hamlet at Staley where a bridge crossed the River Tame. There was a manor house at Staley occupied by the Staley family, though at the death of Sir Ralph Staley leaving no male heir, his daughter Elizabeth married Thomas Assheton, a renowned alchemist and Sir Ralph Assheton's brother, thus uniting Staley with the de Asshetons. After traversing the bridge they would stop for at least a night at Assheton Hall, where Sir Ralph had his family home. Sir Ralph, he knew, was keen to greet his wife Margaret and thus might easily decide to spend the night by his own fire rather than hurry onwards through the darkness on the king's business. Robert's riding companion, Abel Mostyn, was an ancient; that is a sergeant, in the company of Sir Ralph and was delighted to impart what he imagined to be his extensive knowledge of his master's affairs to the simple youth by his side.

"Keep a sharp eye out for the corn marigold," Abel advised. "Sir Ralph always be on the lookout for the plant and if you can spot one before him you will have a better chance of a place by a warm fire this night."

"Corn marigold?" Robert laughed at the idea.

"I am not jesting," returned the ancient. "The plant is common hereabouts and pernicious. It infests wheat crops and causes them to rot. Sir Ralph levies a heavy fine on any of his tenants who let it grow on his lands."

Robert shrugged and let his gaze wander over the moors looking for a splash of yellow that might betray the presence of the plant.

"I suppose it is a source of income if the plant really is as common as you say."

"That is the way with lords of the manor," stated Abel, his tone betraying nothing of his opinion on the matter. Robert wondered if he resented such practices. Many did, and he had heard mutterings of discontent among the English soldiery in general. Whenever money was extracted by whatever means, mostly on a pretext it was impossible to avoid, such as a pernicious weed that took root in the field, it was no wonder payment would be given grudgingly. Nevertheless in this case, if the weed caused the harvest to fail then it was the poorest people who would starve. Perhaps Sir Ralph was simply ensuring the survival of the wheat crop and thereby his own tenants.

"Is that the hall below us?" queried Robert. The dusk was deepening and they could see where the sloping ground finished at a flat plateau where the outline of a grand residence could just be discerned in the lower far distance and the faint yellow glow of flickering torchlight betrayed its location. They were yet in the parish of Mottram in Longdendale, in the county of Cheshire but would enter Lancashire after they crossed the River Tame, entering the parish of Ashton-under-Lyne.

Sir Ralph, who had been riding in front of his men in his distinctive black harness, suddenly spurred his mount into a gallop, breaking away from the bulk of his soldiers obviously intending to arrive first at his family home. Ancient Mostyn signalled for the rest of the soldiers to spur their mounts after their lord. They cantered through the tiny hamlet of Staley and clattered across the wooden bridge that spanned the River Tame. Robert's spine tingled apprehensively when his turn came to traverse the bridge and he crossed himself before venturing over. Underneath such was a favourite hiding place for a Boggart and it was not unknown for the creature to spook a horse into throwing its rider.

He wondered what other demons he might encounter out here in the wilds of England. Until now he had lived safe from spiritual harm in his father's Gloucester home, or sometimes with his grandfather in London. During his service with the duke of Norfolk he trained within the castle walls at Framlingham. His present liege, the earl of Surrey would now also claim the castle of Framlingham for his home. This was the first time Robert had been on what was, to all intents, a campaign.

The inhabitants of Staley kept to their homes as Sir Ralph de Assheton and his men rode through. Robert wondered at this. In most villages and hamlets of England the people invariably came out of their doors to welcome their lord into his demesnes though they sometimes did so with bad grace. Abel Mostyn had informed him Sir Ralph was generally feared in his own county and he wondered why that might be?

After a mile or so they arrived at Assheton Hall. The manor house was constructed from grey blocks of granite with a pair of round towers at two of its corners. It was not crenellated but had a high wall around to render it defensible should it become necessary to fend off a determined enemy. As Robert arrived with the bulk of the soldiers, Sir Ralph had already dismounted and was embracing a woman, clearly the lady of the manor, surrounded by six or so household servants. Night was falling fast and the torches and cressets that burned in the courtyard were necessary to see to the efficient disposition of the newcomers. As Robert and Abel Mostyn dismounted, a farrier ran from the direction of the stables to take care of the horses. Robert, of course, was responsible for rubbing down and securing the feed of his own mount, as was the ancient Mostyn and his men, but Sir Ralph had his led away by his servant.

That evening Sir Ralph, divested of his black harness and dressed now in a gown of blue velvet trimmed with fox fur, sat with the lady Margaret de Assheton at the high table in the great hall. A huge bright fire blazed in the stone hearth and candles lit the lord of the manor and his wife while the lower tables benefited from the blaze of candles set in freestanding candelabrum placed about the room to illuminate the warm colours of the arras hanging by the walls. The air was heady with the smell of wood smoke mingled with the odour of candles and the viands that were brought into the hall by serving women. There seemed to be few serving men in the household. Robert was wearing a dark brown leather doublet over a white linen shirt and light brown hose. His boots were calf length. On the road he was commanded to wear full harness, as Sir Ralph himself so being able to change, albeit into his travelling clothes, was a comfort.

Sitting by Sir Ralph on his left was the Steward of Longdendale one of whose roles it was to care for the lord's manor in his absence. He was a rough-looking fellow for such an important office. The valley of Longdendale was one of the king's hunting preserves. On the right of lady Margaret sat a friar in the habit of a Franciscan, a beadsman who earlier had blessed the table hurriedly, with a keen eye upon the wine flagon as if it might be spirited away down the table, impatient to set to. Sir Ralph's hounds, a pair of lean grizzled animals lurked expectantly in the rushes before the high table, waiting for any scraps that might be thrown to them. Strange beasts they were with eyes that shone yellow in the flickering lights of the hall. Robert had been allocated a place with two squires, one of whom served Sir Ralph, at the end of the lower table. Ancient Mostyn was with those of his soldiers permitted to dine in the hall. The rest were accommodated in the barns and outhouses of the hall.

William Berry, one of several in Sir Ralph's household was a youth a couple of years older than Robert and who considered himself to rank above him. He was short in the leg and broad in the chest, which made him a formidable fighter. At sixteen though he was just old enough to take his place in the line of battle, however, he had not been so at Bosworth, having been placed to defend the baggage. This rankled, especially when he learned Robert, two years younger, had actually been in the thick of it, and resentment welled up in him. His father was but a minor tenant on Sir Ralph's lands and William had entered service with the knight due more to his useful fighting nature than any claim to rank. Robert's father had no particular rank, yet he was the king's personal armourer and that gave his son a certain status. Moreover, Robert's harness, made for him by his father, was of far better quality than William Berry could afford. To make matters worse between them, Robert's manners were courtly, having been coached by his father who moved in the highest circles, and William's were those of rough yeoman stock. While this hardly concerned Robert yet William felt it keenly. A bully by nature, he had taken to baiting Robert, hoping the younger and lighter youth would respond by attacking him, giving him the opportunity to administer a beating. Robert was not averse to taking him on, but so far had resisted the temptation to do so.

The other squire, John Biggar, was the son of a minor landowner in Norfolk and had been taken into the service of the duke of Norfolk in gratitude for some service his father had done the duke. With the old duke killed in the recent battle he was temporarily masterless and had been placed with Sir Ralph de Assheton while the king confirmed the new duke, almost certain to be John Howard's son earl Thomas, when he would be hopefully taken into the duke's household again. He was of average height and build; no match for the animal strength of William Berry and so had become his factotum as a means of mitigating the thrashings he regularly received from his fellow squire under the pretence of practice at arms.

"We mun mak' do with capon," growled William Berry. "I suppose you would prefer the king's venison?" he said, directing his remark at Robert. He stabbed at a platter containing slices of the white flesh before them on the table.

"Venison becomes tiresome when eaten too often," Robert responded laconically and deliberately to annoy the youth. "Besides, capon is easier to get. You merely wring its neck. Venison must be hunted and therefore the appetite is encouraged and its consumption deserved."

"Then I suppose we mun do without boar too," said Berry, "seeing as the beast be honourably procured bravely by spear in a close encounter, not at distance wi' a machine." This was a clear reference to Robert's skill with the crossbow. "You can down a boar from a safe distance with a crossbow, or a man-at-arms in battle."

John Biggar sniggered at what he presumed was a jest by his companion squire.

"Yet there are no more boars in England, I believe, to test our bravery," answered Robert. He had worked out that one way of dealing with a braggart was to goad him into indiscretion where his temper might cause him to overreach himself.

"The commons, when they are not eating pottage, are reduced to mere butchery of cattle – after rendering them helpless before applying the knife. I see a plate of beef near your elbow. There has been no prowess in its procurement I should think, therefore it is safe for your eating, having come by cart from market." Clearly he was referring to William Berry's position with the baggage during the recent battle. It was akin to touching the nerve of a pugging tooth. Berry stabbed his dagger into the bench just missing Robert's leg.

"Take care Sir Ralph doesn't notice the damage you are doing his property," said Robert with a grim smile. "You might have to pay for it."

"It's you who'll pay," growled Berry menacingly. "I know how to deal with an idle fop such as you, be sure on that!" Nevertheless, he looked apprehensively towards his lord's table to reassure himself his action had not been observed. Sir Ralph was deep in conversation with his wife, who had been overjoyed to discover her husband had survived battle at the king's side when so many others had not. Strictly speaking, Sir Ralph was in dereliction of duty not to proceed more directly to Lathom, but who was there to tell providing the woman Margaret Stanley was in his custody when they returned to London.

Robert arranged a napkin over his left shoulder and took some beef onto his trencher. He washed his fingers in the water contained in a small pewter bowl placed on the table for that purpose and wiped them casually on the napkin. Berry had grudgingly wrenched his dagger point from the bench and took some meat for himself. He was no match for Robert when it came to verbal exchange, but once outside the hall it would be a different matter. He took up a roll of bread and with a menacing glint in his eyes made great show of tearing it to pieces, scattering crumbs over the table.

The meal had turned out to be a pleasant surprise for the soldiers in the small force. It was hastily arranged by lady Margaret in her joy at the presence of her husband. Normally they would have expected nothing more than bread with perhaps a morsel of cheese as a sparse supper. On their way from Leicester, they ate whatever they could get at midday while resting their horses. Soldiers were expert at foraging and took advantage of the produce of farms and villages as they passed through. As soon as the meal was over Sir Ralph got to his feet and conducted his lady to their privy chamber. Everyone else sorted out a place for themselves in the hall.

Berry and John Biggar had no alternative but to follow their lord. As his squires, they would sleep in the corridor near his chamber door. The household retainers had, as was their right, the better places near the fire. Sir Ralph's hounds were rather better lodged finding a place in a corner by the fire where none dared to move them. Robert had an affinity with dogs, yet even he was cautious in getting close to them. They regarded him dispassionately as predators do, their yellow eyes gleaming in the dying firelight, watchful but not hostile. He decided a better place might be in the stables with the horses. There was warm straw there and the heat from the horses tended to keep stables warmer than a draughty hall after the fire had died down. Although it was late August the air had turned cold, here in the foothills of the Pennines and the night would be a cold one. He made his way out of a side door and wended his way towards the stables.

Outside, the wind was rising and soughed around the hall as if calling to whatever lurked in the dark countryside all around. Robert signed himself against any malevolent spirits that might be abroad. He noted the horseshoe nailed to the heavy oak door at the entrance to the stables as a barrier to the Boggart, which creature was known to cause problems with horses unless they be protected by a charm. He clinked the latch of the stables door and stepped inside to be greeted by a farrier with a lantern.

"Who be thee?" he queried with a scowl on his face.

"I am Robert de la Halle with the earl of Surrey's men," Robert replied authoritatively, closing firmly the door behind him. "I shall find a place to sleep here tonight. I believe that is my mount just there." He pointed to his own rouncey. As a squire to the earl his mount was properly stabled with those of the other squires while the mounts of the common soldiers were set free in a paddock nearby. His saddle and saddlebags were placed on pegs fitted into the stall boards. Piled in a corner of the stall was his harness. There too was his crossbow and quiver. The farrier nodded, having already noticed Robert when he was seeing to his mount upon arrival.

"There be some straw for bedding over in 't corner. Tha' con settle there."

Robert clapped the man on the shoulder in thanks and went to the corner the farrier had indicated where a heap of straw was piled ready for making new bedding. He threw his riding mantle over the straw, sat down and began to remove his boots. The farrier hung the lantern on a post in the centre of the stables well away from any burnable material and took himself off to the far end of the building where he had his own straw bed. Robert knelt in the straw and muttered a prayer to Saint Adrian for the success of their mission and to the Virgin for protection against night demons. He lay himself down in the straw, listening to the creaking timbers of the building and the squeak of iron hinges as the wind, like an unseen hand, pushed at the stable door. He listened carefully to the sounds of the horses as they moved peacefully in their stalls. If there were any spirits abroad, he considered, the animals would soon detect them and become agitated. With this thought to comfort him he closed his eyes and drifted off to sleep.

* * *

Robert was not a particularly light sleeper so it must have been his heightened apprehension regarding malevolent night creatures that woke him. He lay with his eyes wide open and listened to the sounds the horses made. Most of them were relaxed, but his own beast seemed disturbed by something. It clopped its hind hooves against the earth floor, a sound muffled by a cushion of straw but loud enough to draw attention. He could feel the hair at the back of his neck begin to rise and his ears twitched as he strained to filter out any sound of something moving that should not be there. The candle in the lantern had burned low and was guttering, ready to go out and gave hardly any light. It was the darkest part of the night, not long before the dawn.

The stall where his horse stood nervously tapping a hoof was in pitch-blackness and it was impossible to discern if anything might be lurking there. Robert forced his fears back as he reasoned that if there was anything there it could not be a demon as the horse, indeed all the horses in the place would take fright. It was probably a rat, or perhaps a cat on the prowl. Then, just as he was about to close his eyes he thought he detected something – a shape that could not be defined, almost as dark as the blackest recesses of the stall, yet there was a sense of movement. The shape moved stealthily across the stable floor towards the door. There was just enough light from the expiring lantern to show the outline of a man. No demon, then, but something foul was afoot for sure. Robert quietly stretched his hand out to feel for his dagger, which was in the scabbard of his belt that he had placed close by him. He closed his fingers around the haft and drew it stealthily from its scabbard.

Suddenly one of the horses must have sensed something and began whickering and stomping around in its stall. This set off the other horses and instantly the whole stables was filled with the sound of disturbed horses. The shadow flitted to the stable door and Robert heard the clink of its latch and the creak of hinges. He leapt to his feet and ran to the door, which had been left ajar. He looked out into the night and thought he saw someone by the hall. The darkness there was absolute and it was impossible to make out whom it had been. He was just about to go after the phantom when he was gripped by a strong hand and pulled back.

"What are ye doing spooking the horses," growled the farrier. The alarmed horses had woken the man and seeing Robert in the doorway he assumed he was the one responsible.

"There was someone here, man," responded Robert urgently, waving his dagger over at the dark hall. "He is over there somewhere." The farrier strained to look but the shadows against the hall were too deep to see anything. To his credit the man accepted Robert's explanation.

"Let us go and see," he whispered. "You go one way, I t'other and we'll have 'im atween us." The pair crept over to the hall and searched about. There was a small door there; the one Robert came through to go to the stable. He tried the handle, but it had been secured from the inside.

"If he has gone in by here then we shall never know who it was," he declared angrily. "We had better look to the horses and see if we can find what was afoot."

Back in the stables the farrier found another lantern, lit it and brought it to where Robert was standing, trying to peer into the stall where his horse was standing, calm now.

"He was lurking around here, you say?" The farrier raised the lantern and shone its light into the stall. Nothing seemed amiss. They kicked the straw around but found nothing.

"Whatever he was about we must have disturbed him," Robert decided, though there was a small voice in his head telling him to take care. The farrier shrugged and handed over the lantern.

"Have another look to be sure," he said, stifling a yawn. "It will soon be dawn anyway and the daylight might reveal more, if there is any more." He shuffled off back to his bed to retrieve what remained of his sleep.

Robert raised the lantern and decided to take one more look. Everything seemed to be as it had been earlier except for one small thing. His saddle bags, which were hanging in the stall seemed to be different – one of them hung higher that the other and he was sure he had arranged them tidily side-by-side. He lifted them down and opened them to see if anything had been taken. He had a shirt in there, and a few items of clothing, but as he rummaged around he felt something solid at the bottom of one. It was metal and when he withdrew it he immediately recognised what it was - the pewter bowl he had dipped his fingers in at table the night before. A sudden wave of apprehension swept over him. This was the property of Sir Ralph de Assheton and finding it here meant it could only have been stolen! Should the bowl be discovered in his saddlebags, or even in the stall of his own horse, then he would be accused of theft and the penalty for such was severe. Even if he escaped with his life it might not be with his anatomy intact, and in any case his life in the service of the earl of Surrey would be over. He felt his legs turn to jelly and leaned against the stall, his mind in a whirl and turning over the bowl with a look of horror at the dreadful implications.

It took him a minute or so, but slowly rational thought returned to him. First, nobody knew the bowl was in his possession, except the person who had put it there and it was apparent now what the shadowy figure had been doing in the stable. William Berry! It must have been him. He had been next to him at the table and the bowl was directly in front of them both. Obviously this was a way of getting back at him for the insults Berry had perceived. He confessed himself surprised. Berry was the sort who would normally settle a score with brute force, yet there would be little chance of that during their present mission. The more he thought on it the more it became obvious who his enemy was; indeed Berry, and his companion squire, John Biggar, were the only possible suspects. However, they would not know he had discovered the plot and thus he had time to retrieve the situation and perhaps secure for himself a condign revenge.

The horses of the two squires were stabled two stalls further down than his own. He looked into their stalls and to his chagrin discovered there were no saddlebags there, only plate harness. Looking along the stable to ensure the farrier was still in his stall, Robert darted into the one of the stalls of the squire's horses and slipped the bowl under the straw behind the breastplate there. It identified the owner as being William Berry. If Berry was innocent then the chances were the bowl would not be missed and they would be well on their way before it was discovered it was missing. On the other hand, he was guessing that the protagonists of the scheme would make sure the bowl was missed and thus searched for, otherwise why place it there? As it had been set before Robert de la Halle on the table, then his belongings would be those searched first. He returned to his straw bed and lay there, unable to sleep until the first light of dawn began to creep under the stable door.

The soldiers had to be content with taking their bread and ale while saddling their mounts ready for the long, fast ride to Lathom. Sir Ralph's serving maids were busily going among the men, handing out their meal and dodging groping hands. Some exchanged lewd comments while the younger girls blushed. Sir Ralph, already clad in his black harness had been the first into the courtyard, along with a dishevelled Steward of Longdendale who looked as if he had been dragged from his bed. He was a stout dark man that scowled at everyone and even spoke gruffly to the knight. Sir Ralph apparently accepted this as being the habit of one used to authority and thus trustworthy in looking to his interests when he was away from his estates on the king's business. At the moment he was saying something to Sir Ralph that was causing the knight's face to redden in fury. Robert was talking with his friend the farrier when a lackey ran up to him and informed him Sir Ralph would speak with him.

He swept Sir Ralph an elegant bow and stood expectantly before him. He could tell by the contained temper of the knight what was coming.

"I hope, master de la Halle, that my hospitality last evening was to your liking?" intoned the knight superciliously.

"It was most generous, my lord," replied Robert as he contrived to maintain an innocent expression.

"I have learned that an object is missing from the table where you were sitting, sir. Have you any idea where it could be. It was a bowl which, I am informed was placed directly in front of you."

"Yes, my lord, I remember – of plain pewter. I have no idea where it could be. It was there I think when I left for the stables."

"Then let us go to the stables and look for it," interrupted the steward, gruffly.

"But my lord," said Robert coolly. "Am I being accused of something?"

"My steward is informed the finger bowl is missing and it can only have been taken by one of my servants or someone who has come along with our expedition. I must clear this up before we move on and I am vexed to the extreme. Come – to the stables."

When they entered the stables, William Berry and John Biggar were already there, feigning surprise at the presence of their master. They had only just strapped him into his harness and were yet to get one another into theirs.

"Remove your horse," commanded the steward. Robert backed his horse from the stall. "Are these yours," said the steward waving a hand at the saddlebags.

"They are, sir," replied Robert seemingly nonplussed. He could not help sneaking a glance at the two squires, both of who were watching in excited expectation.

The steward unceremoniously dumped the contents of the saddlebags onto the floor of the stable. Robert's doublet and hose spilled across the straw along with a shirt and spare breeks. Also was a lump of stale bread – no soldier throws food away when on the road, even if it is stale. The expression on the faces of Berry and Biggar changed to astonishment then puzzlement when nothing was found. If Robert had any doubt as to which it was placed the bowl in his baggage, he had none now. The steward kicked around in the straw but it soon became apparent that wherever the bowl was, it was not in the possession of Robert de la Halle.

"I wonder, my lord why you should think I would take anything from you. I have no need to do so."

Sir Ralph looked with exasperation at the Steward of Longdendale and the steward stood in angry confusion. The two squires whispered together, Berry clearly displeased with Biggar indicating it was probably he who was in the stables last night.

"My lord," said Robert. "Was it merely that the bowl was in front of me that I am suspected of taking it?" Sir Ralph opened his mouth to reply, but the steward got in first.

"We must look to the most obvious first, young sir, and that happened to be you."

"But there were others in reach of the bowl. I was not the only one to dip his fingers in it." He looked deliberately at the two squires and the steward turned his attention to them. Berry opened his mouth in shock at the change in events while Biggar took a guilty step back. The manner of the two squires prompted suspicion in the mind of the steward.

"You are not suggesting one of my own squires has taken it?" gasped Sir Ralph, his face becoming dark.

"Well, no, my lord," said the steward, "but we had better search their stalls too, seeing as we have falsely accused young Robert here; it is the least we can do to preserve fairness."

The steward stepped into the stall vacated by Berry's horse. William Berry stood stony faced. He had nothing to fear regarding the theft, but he was furious that the bowl had mysteriously disappeared from Robert's saddlebag.

"Take up your harness," ordered the steward. Berry obediently took his harness and piece by piece placed it on the floor by his horse. The steward entered the stall and started to kick around half-heartedly in the straw. Suddenly his boot contacted an object and the missing bowl scudded across the floor. William Berry's eyes opened wide in astonishment and he spun his head around to glare at his fellow squire. John Biggar was also shocked. He had placed the bowl in a saddlebag and he knew William Berry's were in the hall with him.

"What have you done," snarled Berry, glaring at Biggar. His companion squire simply gasped as a fish out of water, his mouth working but no sound coming from it. Then, suddenly realising the enormity of what had occurred he turned to Sir Ralph.

"My lord, I know nothing of this," he cried. "Someone has put it there to betray me!"

"Someone certainly put it there," snarled Sir Ralph, his face like thunder. "For sure it did not get from the hall to the stable by itself."

"But it was him," screamed Berry pointing an accusing finger at Robert. "The bowl was right in front of him."

"It was in front of you, too, as I recall your places," replied Sir Ralph. "Do you expect me to believe the bowl got itself from the hall to the stable, then along the stalls to rest within the stall of your own mount? By what agency did that happen? Are there witches abroad?"

"That's it!" responded Berry desperately. "He is a wizard – de la Halle is a wizard. It is the only explanation."

Sir Ralph regarded the assembly trembling with fury. The Steward of Longdendale was watching the faces of the youths when he felt a tug at his sleeve. He looked around and saw a farrier. The man was knuckling his forehead and clearly wanted to speak.

"If it would please you sir, I can tell you of strange happenings last night."

"See, there you are," cried Berry triumphantly. "I told you there was magic involved."

"What can you tell us, man," said the steward looking to see if he had Sir Ralph's attention.

"Last night me and this young gentleman, good sir, we chased off a man who had crept in to the stables secretly. He disappeared through a door into the hall and we lost him. There was no apparent harm done so we went back to our beds, but there was someone here last night about some hidden business and it were no ghost, my lord."

"Then it seems the purpose was to conceal the object we have before us," surmised the steward, glaring accusingly at Berry. The squire backed away trembling with fear as Sir Ralph turned his gaze upon him.

"No! It cannot be, my lord I would never take from you."

"Whatever you have done, William Berry, it was done dishonestly," snapped his master. "I know not what really happened but there is mischief in it and I will not tolerate that among my men. You have tried to place the blame on an innocent man, which smacks of dishonour and that too I despise." He turned to the Steward of Longdendale: "Take up master Berry and see he is held securely until such time as I can return to deal with him. As for now, we are about the king's business and the day is wasting."

Sir Ralph de Assheton stalked angrily from the stables while William Berry, gesticulating and cursing the name of Robert de la Halle, was taken away by the Steward's men. John Biggar, grateful there had been no time to investigate what might have been his part in the scheme, slinked surreptitiously away.

* * *

Lathom house lay luminous, shining white in a hollow, somewhat unusual for the main residence of a Baron, with forest all around. A sandstone tower rose at its centre with a hall attached. Extensions had been built to the hall and the whole was enclosed within a low, crenellated wall. Outside the wall was a moat, which was crossed by a drawbridge at a single point of entry within the walls, protected by a squat guardhouse with portcullis and gates beyond.

"That be the Eagle Tower," said Abel Mostyn to Robert. "The

house was originally that of the Lathom's, brought to the Stanley family by marriage."

Two standards showing the Stanley and the Beaufort arms fluttered on a mast in the centre of the tower. "I expected a castle upon a hill," said Robert. "This is set in low ground with lots of cover around."

"Which goes to show how the king's writ hardly penetrates these regions," responded Abel. "These are Stanley lands and there is nobody close or powerful enough to threaten the Baron."

"Yes, I understand that, which was why King Richard failed to arrest him two years ago when lord Stanley was implicated in the Hastings plot. Having two powerful lords executed at one time was too dreadful to contemplate."

"You are right, young lord, but I think the king could hardly have been worse off than he is now, had he done so."

Robert thrilled when the ancient addressed him as "young lord." He understood it was simply a rhetorical title that amused the old soldier, but nevertheless it raised his spirits.

"Do you think we shall be allowed entry?" asked Robert. "We are but fifty or so and there is a wide moat and drawbridge which, I perceive, is at the moment raised.

"We must wait and see," replied Abel Mostyn. "Sir Ralph be approaching the guardhouse. It will not be long before we have an answer to that question."

They were riding just two horses back from Sir Ralph and his standard bearers, two powerful men-at-arms he had placed either side of him. They were Sir Mortimer de Blanc and Abelard Froisart, soldier sons of minor nobility noted for their fierce martial qualities. In fact, Sir Ralph seemed to have a penchant for employing such men. Robert had the feeling he was already regretting his decision to leave William Berry incarcerated in a local goal when his muscle and naked aggression would be useful right now. Robert had been brought forward to fill the space vacated by William Berry. He preferred, not unreasonable to ride with Abel Mostyn while John Biggar rode sullenly behind. Sir Ralph watched his squires with a suspicious glint in his eye and when he spoke to them it was brusque and cold. Robert, in common with all the men, had a spear to carry and concentrated on making sure he carried it upright so that Sir Ralph's badge could be displayed fluttering at its point. The two men-at-arms carried banners to identify their mission: one was Sir Ralph's arms and the other the Royal Standard, denoting they were here on the king's business.

Sir Ralph de Assheton reigned in his horse before the moat

where the drawbridge had been raised. He was resplendent in his black harness, which Robert had burnished for him a few hours before their arrival. He wore a tall white plume of feathers in his helm and his midnight black destrier snorted and stamped impatiently as his rider contemplated the ramparts of the fortified house.

"Hello the house," he bellowed. "Open in the name of the king!"

They waited for a few moments, listening to the wind in the surrounding trees. Robert was apprehensive at the silence and suspected the forest was filled with hostile eyes. They were here in the clearing before Lathom House with the moat in front and a forest behind. There could not be a more perfect spot for an ambush. He imagined that the casual stirring of the trees by the wind was actually the deployment of a great army positioning itself and merely awaiting an order to attack their pitifully small force. Slowly he reached up and closed the visor over his face as a precaution against an arrow aimed from the defensive walls, whose blank inhuman stare was disconcerting. If there was danger here, Sir Ralph seemed either unaware or unconcerned. The standards in the keep fluttered in the wind, the only sign that there was someone actually living in Lathom House.

"You must open," cried Sir Ralph impatiently. He calmed his destrier and merely sat there upon it, as did they all, in still silence.

Then, suddenly there was movement along a part of the walls and a small figure, a woman by her black voluminous dress, slowly rose into sight. She must have been stepping on some sort of mounting block as most of her could be seen above the protection of the walls, not just her head and shoulders. She was bare headed and her long black hair streamed in the wind, which whipped it around so that she had to pull it deliberately from her face. Robert wondered if there were tears hidden there. He would remember this day – the white walls of Lathom House and the two black figures, one a white plumed knight in full black harness looking up and the other, a writhen, torn scrap of a woman gazing down, her hands clasped before her, standing defiant on the ramparts of her home with a dark green expanse of stagnant water between them. The two remained unmoving as if frozen in time, each contemplating the other. It was strange to Robert how the moment focused on the casual snorting and stamp of impatient horses, the jingle of the rings in their tackle, a creaking of saddle leather, the flapping of the pennons at spear tips and the wind signing its unfathomable signature in the wavelets across the moat.

"You must open to me, madam," cried Sir Ralph, breaking the spell.

"As Eve," called the woman. "Ever the one to be commanded." This seemed to disturb the knight and his destrier, sensing his master's mood, began to jink nervously.

"Fear not, dread lord; I shall open my house to you." She shrank down from sight and immediately a host of soldiers appeared at the walls. Clearly they had been there all the time, commanded to wait out of sight by the mistress of the house. Similarly, men appeared by the gatehouse and the drawbridge began to lower while the portcullis beyond, groaning in its greased stone grooves began to arise.

They cantered across the drawbridge, through the guardhouse portal and into the court before the great keep. Robert felt the skin crawl down his back as he looked about him. Internally this was a house with windows let into the buildings that made up its living accommodation. Kitchens, he noted, were close by but separate, a wise precaution against fire. The lord's main residence would be in the stone keep at the centre. He could not shake off the feeling they were somehow caught in a trap. On the walls were men with halberds and he spied a few archers among them. If there were more of them hidden, Sir Ralph and his men, including Robert de la Halle, would be easy prey gathered together in this confined space.

"Ancient Mostyn!" called Sir Ralph, "Get those men down from the walls and lodge them somewhere safe. They have no further purpose up there. Place some of your men there instead – and close the bridge; we want no nasty surprises emerging from the forest."

Abel Mostyn leapt from his horse and despatched his men to do the knight's bidding. Robert looked to Sir Ralph.

"Sir Mortimer, master Abelard and you squires – dismount and come with me,"

A man dressed in the rich red robes of a chamberlain hurried across the court. He genuflected before Sir Ralph who climbed down from his horse and acknowledged him with a cursory nod.

"If you would follow me, my lord, I shall conduct you to the lady Margaret," he said formally, his face set as stone.

Robert, finally encouraged by what appeared to be safety, raised his visor. Accompanied by John Biggar, he followed Sir Ralph and his standard bearers into the keep. They had to ascend a steep spiral stair but presently they emerged into a spacious hall that encompassed an entire floor of the keep. It was hung with expensive arras depicting hunting scenes and a fire blazed in a fireplace set into the massive wall. Stags horns were mounted at intervals around the plastered walls and Robert recalled that three stags heads were featured in the sinister white bend of the Stanley arms. Above the fireplace was the emblem of the Eagle and Child, the Stanley badge quartered with the three-legged arms of the Isle of Man. Beside them was the emblem of a portcullis, the badge of the Beauforts.

Lady Stanley, born Margaret Beaufort, stood quietly towards the end of the room with four of her serving women, two beside her and two behind. Close by her side was her confessor, a friar of stern mien, plainly accustomed to the arrogant devolved authority of both the church and his aristocratic mistress. Her chamberlain hurried over and stood beside her.

She had arranged her hair to flow around the back of her head and down her front, not as a grand lady, but rather as a woman who wished to present a more abject, though defiant aspect. She was sharp of feature with cold eyes that projected hostility at odds with her otherwise subjugated demeanour. Displayed as she was, her perceived vulnerability demanded chivalric concern from the knight who had been sent to convey her to captivity. Robert, watching from behind Sir Ralph, felt the hopelessness of her position. She was a mature, gentlewoman, in her early forties, rendered captive under the authority of a young knight, Sir Ralph being but twenty-three years of age. The chamber smelled of wood smoke faintly tinged with incense, though it was spoiled for Robert, who was provided with a small measure of reality by the smell of his own sweat within his armour.

"Lady Margaret Stanley," intoned Sir Ralph without the usual courtly preamble, "you are arrested for high treason and will be taken to London where you will be questioned by the king's officers. I think you know me, madam, having been previously at court before your confinement in this house for plotting against the king."

Lady Stanley drew herself up and seemed about to speak except the friar next to her placed a hand upon her arm, which caused her to think better of it. This was the mother of the traitor Henry Tudor. It had been her ambition and his that had brought her and them all to this pass.

"The lady Margaret shall comply with the authority of the king's officers, sir," said the friar officiously. "She asks some time that she might prepare herself and her women for the journey to London."

Sir Ralph considered this for a few moments. Ignoring the friar he turned to lady Margaret. "The day is late so we shall set off tomorrow morning just after first light. You have until then, madam, to prepare for the journey."

"I thank you for your consideration," she replied cynically. "I have four women and six gentlemen who will accompany me, along with Father Simon, here." She nodded towards the friar who bowed his head to her.

"You shall travel with two ladies, madam," responded Sir Ralph and two serving men to tend your horses and wait upon you. The friar will stay here where, no doubt, he has his duty to the household."

This statement served to crack the lady's stern resolve. "I must insist, Sir Knight, that my confessor comes with me. I believe the king himself would not deny me the solace of my ghostly guide." She was visibly trembling, though whether in anger or frustration it was hard to tell. It seemed the only thing that could upset her was the thought of losing her spiritual mentor.

"You are not in a position to demand anything, my lady," said Sir Ralph, noting this chink in her armour.

"But I must have my confessor! You risk the wrath of God to deny me," she snapped angrily, her indomitable spirit rising in her voice.

Sir Ralph glared at her coldly. "I will concede the matter," he decided. "He may travel with you and hear you, but your prayers must be audible to your escort. I will not permit any secret conversation between the two of you. You must wait until we arrive in London before you are shriven."

Lady Margaret and Friar Simon exchanged glances but seemed to accept the knight's stricture.

"Then might I make my confession here and now, in private before we leave?" she said defiantly, raising her head and staring directly into his eyes. "You need have no fear. Anything *secret* that I might have to impart I will have done so before you stamped your way into my house."

"That you may," replied Sir Ralph. With that lady Margaret turned and walked away towards her privy chamber with the friar following while she signalled her ladies to remain behind in the hall. The chamberlain stood as if perplexed.

"You may serve us wine and have ale taken to my men," demanded Sir Ralph. "We shall avail ourselves of my lady's hospitality and eat here." The chamberlain gave a short bow of obedience and snapped his fingers at a couple of servants standing gaping at the side of the hall who hurried to him. He gave them a series of instructions then bowed once more to Sir Ralph.

Sir Ralph turned to Sir Mortimer and Abelard Froisart, his men-at-arms. "See to the needs of the men and ensure the house is secured with our own guard. Disarm the household and see any weapons are locked away somewhere they cannot be got at."

* * *

Robert could not help but feel some sympathy for lady Margaret Stanley. She had come down that morning dressed as he would normally have expected for a lady of her rank and age, except, curiously she was entirely in white, the colour of mourning. Her head was covered with a coif and wrapped under her chin so not a vestige of her black hair was visible. The sharp features of her face were not enhanced by the bitterness of her down-turned mouth. She wore over her dress a dark blue travelling cloak trimmed richly with sable, which was draped over the cruppers of her horse. Robert had not yet attained that experience, which might have informed him feminine wiles were at work when the lady had displayed herself on the battlements of Lathom House, as she had for dramatic effect. Even Sir Ralph had been taken aback then, but soon recovered his wits. Robert, however, could not shake the image of the poor 'lorn woman from his mind. When he was not sympathising with her sad state, he was thinking on her power. Clearly she was a woman to be reckoned with and some niggling fear disturbed his deeper thoughts. He could not bring his qualms to the forefront of his mind, yet there was something and he knew that here in Lancashire there were forces abroad that could be brought into being to rob men of their wits. He was determined to hang onto his and he crossed himself over his heart and muttered a prayer under his breath to the Holy Virgin.

Sir Ralph de Assheton led the way through the pastures of Lancashire, with his two companions. His common soldiers rode either side of the prisoners when the ground permitted and a small party ranged ahead to scout for any possible hazards. Among them, Lady Margaret rode along quietly subdued, with her friar for company on her left hand. Immediately behind were her two women. One was of tender years, about the same age as Robert himself and though she had looked at him with disdain, yet he had experienced a strange thrill of interest in her. The other, though, had engaged his attention for quite another reason. He thought he recognised her and that morning, when they were mounting their horses, she had examined him with some curiosity. She was a few years younger than lady Margaret, perhaps in her late twenties or early thirties. By her complexion she was fair-haired, though he could hardly tell for sure. She was wrapped in a light green

49

travelling cloak for the road and her head was covered with a coif as her mistress. Her eyes were soft brown, something he noticed as she scrutinised him in the court of Lathom House just before they departed.

"Who is that woman in green with the lady Margaret," he asked his companion. John Biggar had been commanded to take his place beside Robert and though he was at first reticent, having still on his conscience his part in William Berry's plot to destroy him, yet when Robert spoke to him courteously, he immediately took the opportunity to ingratiate himself with the youth he had wronged.

"She is the lady Isabella Staunton," he replied.

Robert stiffened at the sound of her name. This was the woman in whose house he had been imprisoned last year. It was part of a plot by lady Stanley's henchman, Sir Reginald Bray, to get his father to reveal the whereabouts of the prince Richard of York. Prince Richard, the younger of the two sons of King Edward the Fourth had been taken to a place of safety on the continent, with his father Laurence's assistance, and Henry Tudor wanted to know where so that he could destroy the one prince who could challenge him for the throne of England, should he manage to defeat King Richard. All that is dust now, but the scars remain. Robert had been plied with drink, then taken and incarcerated in the cellar of this woman's house in London. He had only seen her fleetingly though he suspected his father had some mysterious dealings with her. Somehow, Laurence de la Halle had discovered where he was and rescued him. Ever since, so far as he knew this woman, lady Isabella Staunton, had been sharing Lady Stanley's house arrest.

"Yes, the lady is only just back in the world, having been confined after the birth of her child, a daughter I believe."

"Then she is married? Who is her husband?"

"Oh, Sir Charles Staunton. He died a couple of months ago, of over-excitement it was said. He had been boasting of the fact he had managed to get his wife with child, and he in his dotage. He has been the butt of much jesting since and nobody can work out whose the child actually is, but none will impugn the lady's honour by telling it abroad."

"Tell me, master de la Halle, Robert," said John Biggar, "Have you the impression we are being observed?"

Robert looked about him. They were riding through rough pasture with wild woodlands punctuating the cultivated fields. There were farms and a few hamlets here and there and every now and again a manor. So far as he could tell, the people worked the fields in preparation for the harvest, which was imminent. They had passed by fields of corn, careful not to trample through them as Sir Ralph did not desire to be pestered by irate farmers demanding compensation for damaged crops. They all knew that King Richard kept strict regard for the interests of the common people and a petition to him for damage caused by arrogant nobles trampling down their crops when the country needed the produce, would likely find favour. It was a point of major contention with the nobility, who expected the king to habitually side with them. His attitude had contributed to the lack of enthusiastic response in some of the great lords in the recent call to arms, and acted as an encouragement to the Tudor invader.

"I haven't noticed anything in particular," he replied. This was not quite true. The very county of Lancashire seemed to him pregnant with enchantment, a feeling that was not mitigated by the latter image of lady Margaret Stanley standing defiantly in the rising wind upon the battlements of Lathom House. He wondered had she been holding back those dark forces that might have struck them all down to avoid any further trouble that a charge of witchcraft might bring? If that were so then they were in grave danger out here in the countryside where she might call upon more than mere mortal support.

"Sir Ralph thinks there is," continued John Biggar. "He has half-a-dozen prickers out ahead as a precaution. Remember those who fled lord Stanley's army after the battle? They were Tudor's men and it is likely they brought word to lady Stanley as to the failure of her son's enterprise. She certainly had no need to ask Sir Ralph for news, she already knew."

"Yes, I noticed that," replied Robert, "although it must be said it is simpler to dispatch a single messenger than an armed troop. Such a one would have had at least a day's start ahead of us, probably two. Then, if as you say those Tudor supporters that escaped the aftermath of battle came this way, then they might well yet be here, somewhere close."

The two squires looked around trying to penetrate the thick woodland or spot the glint of polished iron somewhere in the landscape. Robert found himself warming to the presence of John Biggar. He was fairly certain it was he who had planted the bowl in his saddlebags, yet it was probably William Berry who had put him up to it. The youth, though older than Robert by two years, seemed less confident and thus tended to find a companion to attach himself. That had been the brutish William Berry in Sir Ralph's household. Biggar was shorter than Robert by about two inches, standing at five foot nine with a tendency to stoutness, a bodily profile he would no doubt achieve in the fullness of time, should he survive the vicissitudes of fortune as a squire in Sir Ralph's retinue. Clean shaven, the hair on his face being yet too insubstantial to cultivate a beard, he wore his light brown hair cropped under a sallet, the steel of which was brightly burnished. His defence was a mail hauberk with cuirass of plain steel. He wore plate armour on his legs, bare at the back. He carried an arming sword at his belt with a dagger and in common with the rest of them, he held a spear in a mailed fist with Sir Ralph's pennon at its tip. An entertaining companion, his chief amusement was the gathering of gossip, which he passed on without prejudice to anyone who would listen. Robert, having little knowledge of Sir Ralph de Assheton, found this trait most useful, though a small voice in his brain warned him to be careful as to what personal information he divulged.

Ahead of them, Sir Ralph called a halt. The captain of his prickers had ridden up and the two were conversing. Presently the knight signalled for them to come to him. They circled their horses and clustered in a group, Sir Ralph, Sir Mortimer, Abelard Froisart and Ancient Mostyn, who had been leading the prickers and the two squires.

"There is ground ahead that requires caution to traverse," he said, his face set in concentration. "Ancient Mostyn, repeat what you have told me."

"There is a steep sided valley ahead, not a gorge, but steep enough to let an enemy plan an ambush. The sides are littered with rocky outcrops and there is no cover in the bottom."

"Do you suspect an attack?" asked Robert.

"Anything to do with the lord Stanley or his wife is likely to be fraught with treachery," replied Sir Ralph. "These are Stanley lands and it is prudent to consider our progress carefully. Bring up the men and encircle the woman and her servants. That should protect us from the possibility of attack by archers for fear of hitting her. As long as we stay in a tight group we should be safe."

They walked their horses slowly through the valley. It was indeed a good place to stage an attack upon them. Ferns grew up the sides from the shallow valley floor, where a tiny rivulet meandered over a stony bottom. Mosses grew over the boulders that littered the banks and ferns merged with the coarse grass of the upper valley. Single trees grew here and there in the protective crevices of huge rocks seemingly standing like ghostly sentinels as if guarding a dread secret. Anyone looking down on them would see a shape that mimicked the profile of a tadpole having a large round head and body with a thin tail trailing behind.

Soon they came to a narrow pass where the body had to compress and the tail grew longer as a result. Robert wondered whether to drop his visor against the possibility of an arrow in his face, but that would severely limit his vision and right now vigilance was uppermost in his mind. The valley was deathly silent and the absence of bird song was no encouragement to the armed escort of lady Margaret Stanley. Somewhere on the left hand slope a black crow flapped down to land upon a huge rock, then started into flight again as if startled. This served as a signal to the men hidden there.

Suddenly men appeared with what looked like staffs and began levering at some of the rocks. These were readily dislodged and began rolling and bouncing down the valley side. They were aimed at the stragglers of the column, clearly intended to split the escort. In order to protect his men, Sir Ralph had no alternative than to order them to spur their horses forward clear of the danger. They galloped out into wider ground and here arrows began to fly. More men were rising from amongst the ferns and bracken and moving down towards the escort. Sir Ralph ordered his men to close up on lady Margaret, but the bouncing rocks had temporarily disoriented them. One man in front of Robert was caught by a boulder that smashed into the flank of his horse bringing them both screaming to the ground. The soldier's leg was smashed along with the rib cage of his mount.

There was a great deal of confusion around lady Margaret and her servants. These circled their mistress while Sir Ralph tried to establish some order. He had his visor down and Robert dropped his now that arrows were flying. The horses were more vulnerable than the men and already he could hear their screams as the missiles found a soft target. He gripped the sides of his mount with his knees and reached for his crossbow. Fitting the crannequin, he wound back the prod and was reaching into his quiver to extract a quarrel when a huge fellow burst from the bracken in front of him armed with a war axe and launched himself at Sir Ralph who had his back to him as he tried to bring order to the chaos. Robert, as one of his squires had as his first duty to protect his master's back. He hooked the crossbow into his saddle and charged at the giant. Too late the fellow realised the danger and Robert let his horse trample him down. He drew his sword and turned to be sure of his man, but the fellow was trying to crawl away on his elbows, dragging a pair of bloody shattered legs behind him.

There were a dozen archers with the escort and these were replying to the enemy on the slope, a difficult job as the enemy were spread out while the escort was bunched together. A line of halberdiers suddenly arose from the bracken on the right hand slope and charged at the escort. This was getting serious and Sir Ralph, seeing the impossibility of fighting this new threat and guarding his prisoners ordered them to charge out of there. Robert spurred his mount forward, keeping the ladies on his right. Sir Mortimer de Blanc reached for the reins of lady Margaret's mount but failed to get a grip. She urged her horse forward and appeared to be galloping along with the lady Isabella Staunton when the two suddenly rode clear and up the slope of the valley towards some trees. The halberdiers moved forward and split Sir Ralph's force, letting the two women get clear. Robert, being closest to them set off in pursuit, slashing at one halberdier and riding down another. He was able to take advantage of the gap in their line intended to let the women ride through. They were about a hundred yards ahead and without escort he had no doubt he could catch at least lady Margaret and bring her back a prisoner.

He was riding hard up the slope towards the tree line, making hard work of catching the women, they being lighter and well mounted. Then ahead a single mounted man-at-arms rode out from the trees bearing a lance. Robert had thrown down his spear in the fight below and now was confronted by a fighting knight in full harness bearing down on him. He had no defence against a well-aimed lance and this knight looked as though he knew how to use his. He reached down for his crossbow and fitted a quarrel. He would have one chance and he knew if he fired too soon the quarrel would merely bounce of the knight's armour. To be sure of penetration the man would have to be within a few yards and if he missed his aim, or the quarrel failed to penetrate the hardened iron, then he was finished. Robert was the son of an armourer and he knew the temper of fine steel. The knight lowered his lance and aimed it directly at Robert's breastplate. He reined in his horse and sat tight. Raising the crossbow he fired on the upswing just as the knight was bracing himself for the impact of his lance. The quarrel slammed into the centre of his chest. The man cried out in pain as he dropped his lance and threw up his arms. He went over the cantle of his saddle and tumbled over in the grass before lying still. His horse galloped past Robert and continued its riderless course down the valley.

It was obvious the knight would not rise again and so Robert looked after the two women. They were now well ahead of him and he spurred his horse after them, determined to capture at least lady Stanley. She was somewhat ahead of lady Staunton, her blue mantle already disappearing into the fringe of trees while the latter lady took off in another direction. This was clearly a ploy to confuse him, the two women splitting up and no doubt they expected to lose him, then meet up later. He would ignore lady Staunton and get after the woman who the king had ordered to London. Lady Staunton could wait for another day. Lady Margaret had taken a narrow path through the trees, which twisted and turned, slowing down the progress his horse from a gallop to a canter. His heart was pounding in his chest with apprehension. If he failed to catch lady Stanley then his lord would be in dire trouble with the king and some of the opprobrium was sure to rub off on him.

Suddenly, and to his great surprise he burst into a clearing and there, at its centre sitting calmly on her horse, facing away from him was lady Stanley. She sat clad in her blue riding cloak with the hood pulled up, but the whiteness of her gown was just visible where it was blown back during her ride. He pulled up and then trotted cautiously over to her. Surely she had not abandoned the chase this soon? As he approached she turned her horse to face him and dropped the hood. He gasped in shock and disappointment. He was facing the lady Isabella Staunton who was smiling benignly at him. They must have changed riding cloaks and he had been chasing the wrong woman. Wherever lady Stanley was now he had no idea and he would have to content himself in returning with this lady. He was about to reach for the reins of her horse to lead her back when half a dozen archers stepped from the trees, each with an arrow drawn ready to loose at him. At this range they would not miss and the English yew bow could easily pierce his armour. He had failed his master and his king and now he would be shot down in the middle of who knew where, his ambition to rise in the household of the earl of Surrey in ashes.

3 – The Fugitives

Had Robert de la Halle been clubbed and beaten about the head by his captors, he could hardly have been more confused in his brain. Undamaged, but disarmed, he sat his horse in dejection, a condition exacerbated by his hands being tied to his saddle and his legs beneath the horse, which was plodding along after that of lady Isabella Staunton. The archers marched dutifully behind in single file as they made their way through the trees. Why he had not been shot down he could not fathom. Somewhere way behind on the upper slope of the valley where they were ambushed lay an armoured knight with one of Robert's quarrels through his chest. Such armour as the knight wore was expensive so he must have been noble. The deliberate killing of a man of rank could not be lightly forgiven, even if he was acting treasonably. The lady had spoken not a word to him, but ordered him bound to his horse. He had attempted to speak to her but she commanded him to silence.

Soon they emerged from the trees above a fertile valley that stretched away into a hazy distance. Clear of the trees he could get an idea of their heading – westward by the direction of the sun. That, he conjectured, would mean towards the sea. He was hot and uncomfortable in his harness, though he was conditioned to suffer such discomfort, indeed, constant wearing of his iron was an essential part of his training as a man-at-arms, but his inability to move or stretch his limbs made it worse than normal. His sword belt had been removed, of course, though his crossbow remained tied to his saddle. The quiver of arrows had been taken, along with the crannequin used to wind the prod back, thus rendering the weapon useless, it being impossible to draw the steel prod by hand alone. He noticed the lady was leading them circuitously through wooded areas or by high hedgerows as if she was fearful of being observed, which she must have been seeing as she had as her prisoner a young soldier wearing the livery of the earl of Surrey, who had been riding on the king's business.

Presently they came to some cultivated fields where the hovels of those who worked the land could be seen. Smoke was rising from fires and there was the smell of wood smoke in the air. Lady Isabella stopped and beckoned for him to ride up to her side.

"I shall have your bonds cut now, seeing as there is nowhere you could possibly escape to around here. I hope you have enough sense to realise you cannot outride an arrow. You will not be so foolish?"

She nodded at her archers.

"I shall not run just yet, my lady," said Robert coldly, trying to keep any sense of gratitude from his voice while making it plain he would not give his parole willingly.

"I see you have yet to learn that youthful bravado can be costly, but let that pass for now." She indicated to one of her men to cut the bonds, after which they rode on as before.

Ahead a peasant couple with a child, a small boy, stood by the side of the road to let them pass. The woman bobbed a curtsey to lady Isabella while the man tugged at his forelock after clipping the boy around his head teaching him to do the same. It seemed she was known about these parts. This was confirmed when the archers exchanged words with the couple who were curious regarding the young harnessed soldier riding with the lady. He could hear one of the archers growling at them threateningly for enquiring into the lady's business.

As they wound down a low hill a distinct chill enveloped them. The wind came from the west, a sea breeze by the tang of it as it swept across what was a flat expanse of plain. He thought he could see a grey hint of the distant sea. A manor house came into sight and they were heading for it. The manor comprised a single stone tower, which looked to be of two stories with a large crutch hall beside it. Also clustered around were some wood-framed, wattle and daub buildings, a stables and habitation for servants. As they approached Robert could see it had a low circuit wall protected by a surrounding moat. There was a flimsy-seeming drawbridge over which he rode after lady Staunton. Young as he was, Robert was used to examining military architecture and he could tell that this device was merely for access, and to keep casual felons out rather than sustain a determined attack. The thought encouraged him. If Sir Ralph happened this way, or any of the king's men, then there would be no problem in getting him out – providing they knew he was here, and if he could remain alive.

* * *

The evening brought even more surprise. The last time he had enjoyed this lady's hospitality he had languished in a cellar without light or heat. True, he had been fed and given small ale to drink once a day, but that was all. He had no idea how he would have fared if his father had failed to discover his whereabouts and got him free. Now he was sitting by a good fire dressed in his travelling clothes taken from his saddlebags, a good linen shirt and fine leather doublet and woollen hose. His feet were clad in his own boots. Once divested of his iron and mail haubergeon, they were welcome rather than his gambeson, or arming jacket to which his iron was normally tied. That had been taken and deposited in a corner of the hall.

They were sitting in a partitioned part of the ground floor of the tower. It was a neat, sparsely furnished space with fresh rushes strewn on an earth floor mixed with sprigs of rosemary. In the attached crutch hall, on the other side of the door that opened into the hall were the men who had captured him, drinking ale and talking quietly to some others who were already there. It seemed as if the place was serving as some sort of barracks. Robert estimated twenty men, yeomen called to arms by the look of them from their farms. Why were they gathered here? Surely they should now be dispersed back to their homes?

Beside Robert and the lady Isabella was a table with the remains of a meal, a simple one of pottage, bread and cheese. There were apples, too, no doubt from the gardens of the manor. They were not alone in the chamber. Lady Staunton had an elderly manservant and a pair of serving maids to hand. Also, in one corner was a crib where a small baby lay overlooked by a woman who, by her loose dress front and ample bosom, was a wet nurse. He remembered John Biggar informing him lady Staunton had recently been delivered of a daughter, so this must be the babe. Perhaps the presence of the infant was what had prompted the lady to come home rather than ride off after lady Margaret Stanley? Strange, though - the lady seemed to have command of the men.

"I must say you cut a fine figure, young sir," said lady Staunton admiringly. "You are your father's son right enough, though without his collection of scars - yet." She smiled into his eyes causing him to colour up.

"I wonder I did not acquire any this day," he replied to hide his confusion. "How is it I am being treated as a guest rather than a prisoner? Do you hope for ransom?" Indeed, ransom was the only reason Robert could think of for the woman's strange behaviour.

"Ransom - as an alternative to the services of a necromancer? I seem to remember your father used one to find you when you were my husband's guest in London."

She was referring to Peter Otteler, a blind potter who also had a reputation as a *finder*. His grandfather's servant had aided Otteler, one Mother Malkin whom he knew hailed from these parts and was suspected by his father, Laurence de la Halle, of witchcraft. That was almost a year ago now and Sir Charles was dead, but according to his father, his widow was the one who had worked out the scheme to capture him to get his father to reveal where the young prince Richard of York was hidden. She was a committed Lancastrian and her husband a tenant on the Stanley demesnes as testified by their proximity to Ormskirk and Lathom House, their Baronial seat.

"I think you will find the necromancer could only deploy his art in the city of London," she giggled and took a sip of wine from the silver goblet she held in a beringed hand. The other hand played with a lock of her light brown hair, which she wore confined simply by a cap and frontlet where the edge above her forehead was embroidered with white roses. She had changed into a green woollen gown with tied-on sleeves slashed to show a yellow silk shift beneath. "His peculiar skills will have no effect in these lands."

Robert looked down into the bowl of a similar goblet, clasping it with both hands as if in defence.

"Well, madam, you will have to let me go some time. I am on the king's service and your cause is lost. What purpose do you have in holding me? It cannot be to prevent me chasing after lady Stanley. Apart from the fact I have no idea where she is, I am sure Sir Ralph de Assheton will soon have her again without my aid. He has the king's warrant to raise men. If necessary he can raise all Lancashire to find her."

"I am sure that is what he is doing right now," replied the lady with an amused smile. Robert regarded her with a puzzled frown.

"What I cannot understand is, why did you wait until you were on the road before attempting to break free? That ambush was obviously planned and you were quite ready for it. It seems to me an unnecessary risk to take, especially when you must have had word of King Richard's victory well before we arrived at Lathom House." A dark cloud seemed to pass over lady Staunton's face at this statement. She considered his words carefully before replying.

"There was purpose in it," she said quietly. "You need not know the reason."

"That is not good enough, my lady," he responded impertinently. "You had decided on your escape precisely and whatever plan you devised worked perfectly, except I managed to follow after you. Why am I not lying in the dirt with an arrow through my body? Your archers had me completely at their mercy."

"Be careful how you speak to me!" she snarled, her features instantly changing to display a darker side. Slowly her face softened to her previous aspect of feminine softness. "Let us just say I owe you your life for your father's sake, seeing as it was I who deceived him and caused his innocent son to be caught up and imprisoned."

"But my father is committed to the service of King Richard, your declared enemy as am I," he persisted. You are the creature of Margaret Stanley. In chasing you I shot down a knight, a high noble by his harness. He wore no livery to identify him, but he wasn't a yeoman, that's for sure."

"He was one of my lady Margaret's men and if she learns you were the one to destroy him your life would be short indeed. As things stand now, you will remain here until the present problem is resolved, then I shall have you conducted back to your companions."

"Present problem?" laughed Robert with the confident arrogance of youth. "I think King Richard has resolved whatever problem there might have been. The Tudor cause is finished once and for all. I think your objective was to get lady Stanley away and that you have done, though I have no doubt she will soon be caught again. You would better make your peace with the king if you can. He is known to treat women kindly. You stand in danger of losing all you possess as it is."

"You know little of the world, young sir," she responded with a patronising smile. "Consider the cause of Henry Tudor; he has spent many years in exile and never doubted he would one day become King of England. He attempted an invasion last year and was only defeated in his landing by bad weather. Even today, defeated in battle he has escaped and his cause continues. Fortunes may change in a moment. Just think of your own king, as Richard duke of Gloucester - not so long ago there were five between him and the throne. Then, one brother is attainted and executed, disqualifying his son and heir from the succession. Suddenly, as if by divine judgement, his older brother, King Edward dies unexpectedly and his two sons declared bastards. Today Richard sits there, having divested himself of all opposition."

"By your description of events according to the judgement of God, seeing as all would have been prevented had Edward lived a few years longer."

Lady Isabel frowned at him in annoyance. "You might make a better lawyer than a man-at-arms, I believe, once you are grown," she responded cynically.

"I may not know the politics of the world as well as you, my lady, yet I can work out that the people of England, knowing nothing of this Tudor, will not depose a full blood king for the sake of a bastard claimant who must needs raise foreign mercenaries to fight for him. Why, Henry Tudor has never fought a battle except the recent fiasco and I am informed he tried to run before he even came to the field. I think, should he succeed in getting away, there will be no more appetite for financing such a wretch by France or any of the continental monarchs."

A flash of anger passed over lady Isabella's face as this barb seemed to strike home. Robert felt somewhat surprised at this; perhaps he had voiced those doubts that she already considered for herself. Her confidence must be low after the decisive defeat that the Tudor cause had suffered. He wondered how she could think the Lancastrian cause otherwise than defunct, indeed why was she so committed to it in the first place.

"Forgive me, my lady," he said. "It is rude of me to taunt you thus when you have saved me from death and provided me with your gracious hospitality." His father had taught him that chivalry was an important attribute at court and a lady would expect to be treated so. "I think you would be well advised, even by so simple a lawyer as I, to beg forgiveness of the King. He is ever gentle towards women."

"What!" she cried angrily, "beg forgiveness of a son of York – I shall never be reconciled to that house." The manservant came to stand behind her chair, glowering at Robert. The lady calmed herself and looked over her shoulder. "Have no fear, Hubert, there is no danger to me from this fellow." The man Hubert nodded and stood back, but remained watchful, a hand on the hilt of the dagger at his belt.

Robert became flustered at her outburst of anger. Like all attractive women, her beauty was somehow enhanced by it and this acted upon his youth by intimidating him into confusion.

"Forgive me, madam, if I have upset you. I can see you must have suffered loss in the wars, but so have many in the House of York. His grace the King lost his own father and a brother at the battle of Wakefield. My own liege, the earl of Surrey – his father was killed in the battle but a few days ago. Indeed, my own father came close to losing his life." At this latter remark lady Isabella flashed a look of alarm, which she covered up by feigning curiosity.

"You father actually fought in the battle?"

"He did, my lady. He was caught up in King Richard's charge upon the Tudor position. He thought he was riding to my aid in earl Surrey's army when the King diverted his attention."

"But he is unharmed, you say?"

"Except for a scalp wound."

"Ha!" she exclaimed, returning to her previous sociable attitude. "Another scar to add to his collection." Her gaze swept over Robert with a curious interest. "I will tell you why I hate the Yorkists. My mother was murdered by York – the duke of Clarence to be precise, or at least by his order.

"Murdered?"

"Aye – she was executed on a trumped-up charge of witchcraft, judicially murdered. The duke of Clarence commanded the jury, his own tenants, to pronounce her guilty and she was hanged the same day."

"What was her name," he asked. He was surprised at the alacrity in which the sentence was carried out. Her mother must have been a formidable witch.

"Ankarette Twynho," she replied, and leaned back in her chair regarding him as if expecting him to know who the woman was.

"Ankarette Twynho, I seem to recall that name?"

"So you should. It was one of the greatest scandals of King Edward's reign and it led to Clarence's ruin, which is the only good thing that came from the business."

"I seem to recall my father speaking of the matter. He was scandalised, too as I remember. Didn't Clarence accuse her of poisoning his wife?"

"That he did. His duchess was named Isabelle, one of the two Neville sisters, daughters of the defunct Kingmaker; the other as you know, Anne Neville, was married to Richard, now calling himself King of England. *She* was certainly cursed, living just a few months to enjoy the title of Queen and her only brat dead before her. Another case of divine intervention I believe." She took a deep draught of wine from her goblet and looked at him as if demanding sympathy.

Robert was lost for words. So lady Isabella's maiden name was Twynho? Everyone knew about the tragedy of Isabelle Neville, who died shortly after giving birth to a sickly babe that preceded her into the grave. The duke of Clarence was thus left with two children, one a girl named Margaret and a boy named Edward. These two are safely in the keeping of King Richard at Sandal Castle, north of the city of York. It was said the boy Edward was simple minded and still remained under the attainder of his father, who was executed for treason against his own brother King Edward. It had been Clarence's ambition, coupled with the loss of his duchess that provoked the madness that brought him to his doom. Had he been more stable and lived just a few more years, then George duke of Clarence would be King of England today, not his brother Richard. Clarence, too, would have declared bastard the two sons of King Edward the Fourth, seeing as Edward had not been properly married to his queen, Elizabeth Wydville.

"I see now, my lady, why you hate the House of York, but in mitigation – pardon my *lawyer's* talk – King Edward, who was furious when he discovered how his brother had taken the law into his own hands, did overturn your mother's conviction and condemned the actions of the duke of Clarence."

"Yes, I know that, but my family had to petition him hard to clear my mother of a charge of witchcraft, and it does not compensate the distress my mother suffered, a kind and tender-hearted woman who was dragged away from her family home and summarily hanged on the public gibbet at Warwick to the disgust of the people there. Even the hangman had the grace to beg her pardon beforehand. The only person at Edward's court to offer genuine remorse for the business was my lady Stanley. It was she who arranged my marriage to Sir Charles Staunton, knowing he was old and not long for the world, so that I could inherit his wealth at some time and thus obtain an income of my own. You followers of Dickon," he noted how she could not bear to refer to Richard as King, "are fond of proclaiming loyalty as a chivalric attribute – well, the same goes for me. Lady Margaret offered real help and sympathy when I was most in need of it and I shall not betray her."

"Which makes your treatment of me more curious than ever?" He decided it was prudent not to mention that lady Margaret Stanley's motive in promoting the girl Isabelle Twynho's interest might not have been the product of a tender heart.

"I am not a callous woman," she replied, "and your father is Breton, not particularly tied to the House of York, certainly not by blood. He has a misplaced loyalty that is all, though when he gives it he remains true, as do I. You have said he condemned the circumstances of my mother's death after he learned of it. Loyalty does not divest him of compassion, it would appear."

Robert mused on this assessment of his father's character. He was not convinced the lady had it quite right, though in all the essentials that mattered, he supposed she had.

"In any case, there is something else," she said gazing directly into his eyes. "We have talked of fortune, and this is a strange region – things happen in Lancashire which may not always be the product of chance."

"I do not understand," he replied.

"There were many men with Sir Ralph de Assheton and particularly one of them happened to be you. Why do you suppose that was?"

"By command of my liege lord, the earl of Surrey."

"Though you are but a boy, a fine one I will admit, but yet a

63

boy." Robert bridled at this. Aware of his youth, yet he did not regard himself as a boy, but as a young man. "Of all those in my lady's escort, you were the only one that happened to break free and chase after us. You even managed, by the fortune of your having a crossbow with you, to bring down a fully armoured knight. The subterfuge in the changing of cloaks between us resulted in you chasing after one who you thought was lady Margaret Stanley. It was a simple trick and I hardly think you would have fallen for it had your reason been intact."

"*Your* reasoning defeats me, my lady."

"I am merely pointing out that what you believe to be chance has some purpose you have yet to discover. It cannot be mere chance you are here and I can prove it to you."

"Then kindly do so, my lady. I am burning with curiosity as to your meaning." Robert was indeed becoming consumed with curiosity. If the lady was suggesting some witchcraft was at work, then she was confounding the injustice of her own mother's execution on that very charge.

Lady Isabella Staunton stood and waited while Robert put down his wine goblet and scrambled to his feet.

"Come here," she beckoned and walked over to the crib, waving away the wet nurse who had been watching and listening to their conversation. "Get you hence," she commanded the woman. "Attend in another place until I call you." The woman, disappointment written large in her face, took herself off. Lady Staunton gazed down on the infant sleeping peacefully, swaddled tightly in the crib. She turned to Robert and indicated she wished him to look upon the babe.

"Behold, your sister!"

* * *

Robert was too shocked to speak. His mind, not for the first time in his dealings with this woman, was a mass of confusion. Lady Isabella merely stood in contemplation with the hint of a wry smile at her lips. He looked between her and the babe.

"How can this be?" he managed to get out at last.

"I see your father has not informed you as to the nature of the diversion I used to gain his attention while you were abducted. The child was conceived in a chamber of the White Boar Inn, at Westminster."

"I wonder that your husband kept you," he snorted, hardly knowing how to respond to her revelation.

"Sir Charles was too conceited to imagine that the child could be any other than his own. He boasted about his prowess – he had more than seventy years in credit with God - until two months ago when he succumbed to a fever. It was a simple matter to let him think that his pathetic fumbling had managed to get me with child."

Suddenly there was a commotion in the hall beyond the chamber. The man Hubert, who had been standing at a respectful distance, went to find out what was happening. He returned a few moments later.

"Riders are approaching, my lady," he reported. It is dusk and we cannot make out their livery. The gates are already shut and I have ordered the bridge to be raised.

"How many are there?" she asked.

"There are a dozen of them, unless there be more following."

Robert felt a frisson of elation. This could be a detachment of Sir Ralph's men. If so, soon the forced hospitality of lady Isabella Staunton would be at an end. She noticed his flush of excitement.

"I wouldn't get too optimistic, master de la Halle. You don't understand," she sighed. "This whole region is disturbed, and my lord Stanley's men have people everywhere."

"Yes, I know they tried to intimidate good Englishmen into attacking their anointed king at Redemore. I have no doubt they will fail in that here too when the extent of the king's victory is realised. Their lord will not be so for much longer either, I think."

A man-at-arms came to the door and Hubert went to him. "It is my lord the earl of Richmond and his mother," he said upon returning to his mistress. He spoke matter-of-factly as if that were no surprise. Not so the young squire.

"Henry Tudor!" gasped Robert. "How can this be – the king's men are chasing him through Wales?" A wave of trepidation swept all other thoughts from his mind. *The lady Stanley with him?*

"Quickly, lower the bridge and open our gates," commanded Isabella. Hubert hurried away to do her bidding. "You must be hidden somewhere if we are to avoid you being killed, which will be your fate should lady Margaret clap her eyes on you," she said turning to Robert. "I will have you secure in the kitchen. There is a larder there with a stout door. If you have any sense you will remain quiet until my lord of Richmond has travelled on." She hurried to the door and called two of her serving men, telling them what to do with Robert and to keep silent about it. The two surly fellows were clearly unhappy with the task and grabbed him by the arms to march him out of the chamber. The kitchens were in the courtyard of the house in a separate building and he was half pushed, half dragged

65

across the intervening space. He heard the clatter of hooves and the snort of horses as a troop of armoured knights cantered through the gates. It was nearly dark now and he could not tell which was the treacherous Tudor but his mother, lady Margaret was unmistakable, being the only woman with them.

Soon he found himself locked within the larder of the kitchen. At least, he mused, he would not starve to death if he should remain here for any length of time. That was unlikely. Lady Staunton had let slip the Tudor was to travel onwards; indeed he would have to. If he remained here he would be taken before long. He was beginning to understand why the lady Margaret had remained at Lathom rather than get herself away. She must have been waiting the arrival of her son, except Sir Ralph de Assheton got there first to arrest her. None of them thought the Tudor would be this far north. It also accounted for the presence of the knight he had shot down. He must have organised the ambush to get the women free, which means those Tudor stalwarts who fled from the battle would be here too.

His immediate thought was of escape, indeed, it was necessary to alert Sir Ralph as to the Tudors' whereabouts. He looked around for a way out, but except for the door into the kitchen there was none. The building was of timber filled with wattle and daub and he could hear the sounds of soldiery beyond the one wall on the courtyard side. It was dark in the larder so his hearing was enhanced and he placed an ear against the daub. There were muffled sounds of male voices beyond but he was unable to make out their speech. He felt around and found a loose portion of daub and pulled it away to expose the wattle beneath. Now the sounds were clearer but distant. He thought he could detect the sound of a female voice and by the raucous response of the men and the clash of what sounded like metal cups he reckoned that the lady had sent a maid with ale to assuage their thirst. He could hear shouts and the clink of armour while the newcomers were being accommodated. This was a small manor house and not all would spend the night in the hall. The Tudor was a hunted man and needed a watchful guard about him. Once it was realised he had gone north the hunt for him would become intense and King Richard would be as desperate to capture him as the Tudor was to escape. He realised that unless he could get free and disclose the whereabouts of the fugitives, they were likely to get clean away. Where, he had no idea, but out of England for sure.

Robert pressed his head against the wall and listened, straining to catch any scrap of information as to the Tudor escape plan. He caught snatches of conversation, lewd jests mainly at the expense of the serving maids who were seeing to their needs. Clearly some of the men interpreted need as more than just food and drink. One of them had a maid and brought her close to the wall where he was listening on the other side. He thought he had seen a lean-to against the wall and it seemed the man had brought the maid there for some intimacy. From the sounds of it, she had come, if not willingly then resignedly. Soon the sounds of lust could be heard and the wall vibrated and shook. The woman cried out as if in distress, though Robert's experiences of females did not fit him to know whether it was with distress, pleasure or pain. All went silent for a few moments and only the sound of scuffling could be detected, then the loud bellow of a man's voice. An argument ensued and he caught the name Beaufort and someone in authority shouting at the man to wait until after the Pile of Foundray. Beaufort he knew was the lady Margaret Stanley, Beaufort being her family name, but what or where the Pile of Foundray was he had no idea.

The point of all this was swiftly lost to him as the door to the larder was opened.

"Out you come, fellow," growled a hard male voice. Whoever it was plainly knew he was here so he had no option but to comply with the order. As he came forward he was grabbed by a huge fist and hauled into the kitchen to be tripped and thrown to the ground. The cook and her servants stood with their backs to the wall, watching dispassionately. A kick to his ribs made him curl up protectively. It did him no good. He was gripped by powerful hands and hauled to his feet by two burly fellows. One drove a fist into his midriff causing him to double up and attempt to draw painful draughts of air into his lungs. "That's just a taste to let you know there will be more of the same if you so much as step one inch out of line." This came from a man-at-arms in full harness with a surcoat in the green and white livery of the Tudor. The lady Isabella, in spite of her declared consideration for him being the son of her child's father, had obviously betrayed his location. So much for loyalty – everyone of the Tudor faction, he now realised, was a dissembler of the most base and dishonourable sort.

He was propelled across the courtyard and back into the crutch hall then through the door to the chamber in the tower where the lady of the house had recently entertained him. A tableau of people were grouped together, lady Isabella, standing beside the lady Stanley. The others he didn't recognise. One was a man-at-arms in rich harness, a fighting knight by the look of him, while the other, similarly attired, was much slimmer and wore a sour expression in his thin face. Robert felt, although he had never seen the man, that this was Henry Tudor – he had the same mean and pinched features as his mother. He seemed less a king than his knightly servant beside him. He hardly noticed the rest, soldiers in the livery of the Tudor who stood casually around, regarding him with interest. Lady Isabella's gaze failed to meet his, her eyes cold and dispassionate, while those of lady Stanley seemed to pierce him to his soul. This was the woman who had been the driving force of Tudor ambition, the chief promoter of her son. He had seen her wild on the battlements of Lathom House and witnessed her guile when making her escape from the escort of Sir Ralph de Assheton. The two men who had brought him there stood either side of him.

Robert could not help but be fascinated by the presence of Henry Tudor. This was the man who would be king and yet he did not seem much like a monarch now. The rigours of the road could always be guaranteed to take its toll on a hunted rebel but even making such an allowance, standing beside his men he hardly managed a commanding aspect. He had removed his armet and his reddish brown hair was a tangled mass. A king would have had it brushed immediately but there seemed nobody in his entourage responsible for performing that office. Clad in harness he looked the part of a noble knight, but Robert, who through his father's instruction was used to guessing the build of a man inside his iron, could see that the body within was but a sparse one. He held his arm out to accept a goblet of wine from a servant while regarding Robert with scant interest, but declined to speak. It was his mother who gave tongue.

"So you are the felon that shot down Humphrey Cheney," she hissed, almost as a she-cat. "I remember you at the recent invasion of my house at Lathom. It was a coward's blow that brought down my faithful knight."

"It was not!" snapped Robert. "Rather the knight was a coward riding down with a lance upon what he perceived to be a lightly armed man."

The next moment he was on his knees having been dealt a blow to his head with a mailed fist that had him reeling. One of the men shook him to his feet where he stood, his wits flying about him.

"The boy has not yet learned to control his lip," intoned lady Isabella.

"That is not a matter for long consideration," said lady Stanley. She turned once more to fix Robert with her cold glare. "You are in no place to dispute with me," she continued when she decided he had recovered enough of his wits to understand her words. "As it is we have no time to devise a coward's death for you, merely an ignominious one. Sir Reginald" – she turned her attention to the armoured knight beside her. "See that this fellow is taken and hanged. We are for Scotland and may not tarry."

Hardly hearing the scornful tones of lady Margaret Stanley, Robert turned his gaze on the woman who had betrayed him, the lady Isabella. True, she was a declared enemy but she had given him some expectation that there was at least one on the Tudor side that might someday make her peace with the king. *I am not a callous woman, he recalled her saying.* He looked directly into her eyes and saw nothing there, no compassion, no hope.

"Stay one moment," said the knight. Robert had recognised the name immediately as the man who had helped devise the plot for his abduction last year, with the help of lady Isabella. This was Sir Reginald Bray, lady Stanley's right hand and chief money raiser for the Lancastrian cause. "I am informed you are the spawn of Laurence de la Halle, Dickon's armourer. I can see it in you. The man confounded me once. It shall not happen a second time. There is no wizard here to come to your aid."

"If you would permit, Sir Reginald," said the lady Isabella, "my man Hubert will take care of the business. He would have dispatched him ere now had I not thought to question him. As it is, the wretch, being but a boy, has nothing to tell us as to the whereabouts of Dickon's forces. We need detain him in this world no longer."

"Then see to it, madam," said Sir Reginald, bowing gracefully to her. "We must be swiftly on our way before daybreak and the Scottish border is many miles yet. I must see to my men and horses. These two will assist." He pointed to the two of lady Isabella's men either side of Robert.

Robert's stomach tied itself into a knot with fear at what was about to happen. He did not consider himself a coward, but events had come upon him so quickly that he had no time to prepare himself and terror was written in his face. For a moment he thought he detected a glimmer of sympathy in lady Isabella's features, but she turned from him and waved impatiently for the man Hubert to take him out. Hubert beckoned for the men to bring him along and stalked from the chamber, followed by Robert firmly held between them. Already he could feel his bowels loosen and he struggled not to let them release their contents and add further shame to his reputation. He would try to die bravely, though he doubted himself and at the dread moment feared he might descend into abject hysteria. They hauled him across the courtyard and through the gate then over the drawbridge. Robert wondered where they were taking him. He had expected to be hanged in the courtyard of the house. Probably they were looking for a convenient tree, or was there some other torment in store for him? Sure enough they were approaching a wood that grew close to the house. The moon was full and bright and he could see they were following a rough path that disappeared into the trees. Just before the dark maw where the way entered the wood was a single stark tree, blasted by lightening or dead of some disease, it stood bare and spectral white in the moonlight. Tethered to one of its lower branches was a horse. They would sit him on it and then, when the rope was in place around his neck, walk the animal from under to leave him suspended. He had seen this done in the army of the earl of Surrey.

They stopped before the horse and Hubert turned to face him, his white hair and beard illuminated by moonlight, giving his mien a dark aspect and his eyes black as midnight. Strangely the image of the wizard Merlin came into his mind, whose tale he had read in the stories of King Arthur and his knights. That was the power of the forces abroad in this strange and remote corner of England.

"Here, take this and get you gone," said Hubert, handing him the reins of the horse. Robert's jaw dropped in surprise. The two men released his arms and stepped back.

"I . . .I . . ."

"Never mind blathering boy, get you gone." responded Hubert.

"But what is to happen to me? Am I to be shot down while escaping?" He could not think that this was anything other than a trick.

"You are not to be harmed," he said waving the men further back out of earshot. "The lady Isabella would not have your death on her conscience, besides now that Dickon is firmly on the throne she does not want a charge of murder laid at her door. She has enough to worry about as it is."

"Then why did she betray me to the Tudor?"

"She didn't betray you, it was one of her servants that did that. Some of them were with lord Stanley at the recent battle and are furious he has been arrested on a charge of treason, lady Margaret too. They helped in the ambush that let the two women escape and inadvertently brought you here. My lady told lady Margaret she had been questioning you about the location of the king's men and would have brought you out as entertainment after she had seen to her guests comfort."

Robert breathed a sigh of relief; no less at the knowledge the lady had not betrayed him than for his reprieve from a hanging. He knew lady Isabella was an enemy of the king, but the revelation she had given a child to his father and thus provided him with a sister had begun to endear her to him.

"But what about you?" he asked, suddenly realising that Hubert would have to account for his escape. "How will you escape the wrath of lady Margaret?" He hardly considered his remark, but in referring to the wrath of lady Margaret he failed to understand he was tacitly reducing her son, Henry Tudor, to a minor role in the events that had shaken the realm of England.

"Don't worry yourself on that score, young Robert. I shall report that I had you drowned in the moat and sank your body so that the king's men would never know how you met your end. The lady Isabella will say it was to prevent a charge of murder against her, as I have already explained."

"Then it only remains for me to take my leave," said Robert suddenly regaining a modicum of bravado.

Hubert unbuckled the belt he wore around his waist along with the sword and dagger it supported.

"Here are your weapons." They were indeed Robert's own sword and dagger. In his terror he had not noticed that Hubert had them with him. "We shall keep your crossbow for you to retrieve if we are all lucky enough to survive the next few months. Ride carefully away from here and at first light spur due south as fast as you can," advised Hubert. That will take you directly towards the king's men. The Tudor's will not know to send after you and anyway they are riding in another direction."

"Be sure to thank lady Isabella for me." He mounted the horse which was provided with a saddle and tackle.

"I shall, young sir," replied Hubert. "God speed and keep you safe from harm." With that he turned away and shooed the two men with him back towards the manor house. Robert pulled the head of the horse around and walked it into the shadow of the trees. He would have to go carefully in the dark wood, but once clear and in the morning light, he would indeed spur south, eager to find Sir Ralph de Assheton and report to him the unrealised appearance of Henry Tudor with his mother here in the north and their intent of getting into Scotland. There, he knew, James the third, King of the Scots, ever at enmity with England and allied with France, would be certain to grant sanctuary. So far as he knew King Richard was searching for the Tudor in Wales. Robert was the only one who knew where the fugitives actually were and where they were bound. Thinking on this, it became vital that he find Sir Ralph as soon as possible. If the Tudors managed to get away he would also need to seek sanctuary if he were to avoid King Richard's wrath.

* * *

Robert had been forced to give up his passage through the trees due to the absolute darkness of the night. Already his face bore cuts from the lashings of invisible branches. Besides, the noises of the forest conjured visions of goblins and the fairy folk who everyone knew flitted amongst the countryside at night. He tied the reins of his horse to a convenient tree and huddled down at its base, his eyes frantically trying to penetrate the dark and unable to sleep. He must have dozed in spite of his fears for he was woken by the dawn chorus, the chirping of birds and the first light resolving the whispering blackness into the visible branches of trees. This did little to comfort him, but it did prompt him to mount his horse and continue on his way. He emerged from the woodland just as full daylight was resolving the countryside into a wilderness of gorse and broom, *planta gesta*, a sprig of which was the badge of the Plantagenets. The breeze sweeping across the land from the sea had swept away any clinging mist and already the sky was showing blue with hardly a cloud in sight.

Somewhere in the distance he thought he caught the mere glint of light, the early rising sun catching perhaps the polished armour of a fully harnessed knight. That, at least, was his fancy and he turned his horse's head in that direction, southwest as he reckoned. He had ridden for some time and he began to think he was deceived. In fact, he was lost, having no clear idea where he was except it was somewhere in the wilds of Lancashire. Suddenly a band of bowmen ran from the cover of some gorse and, bows drawn, confronted him. Another; a man-at-arms stood with them.

"Halt and state your business," he demanded. Robert wondered if he had fallen foul of an outlaw gang, of which there were many about the country. Then he noticed the man-at-arms was wearing the livery of Sir Ralph de Assheton.

"I am Robert de la Halle, squire to his grace the earl of Surrey and attached to the house of your lord. Do you not recognise me. The man-at-arms strode forward while the bowmen remained as they were, arrows at full draw. He gazed up at Robert and then the two recognised each other.

"Relax your bows," he commanded his men. "He is indeed one of us." The man was ancient Mostyn. "We thought you lost to us. It seems you have had a change of clothes since last we rode together. Where is your harness?"

"It is a long story, but I must speak with Sir Ralph right away. I have found Henry Tudor!"

Ancient Mostyn took a pace back in surprise. "Tudor! Here! Not his mother?"

"Aye, his mother too. There is not a moment to lose if we are to take him. He is riding post haste to Scotland."

Sir Ralph was as incredulous as the ancient Mostyn. He had increased his contingent to over one hundred men in his hunt for lady Stanley, but had no inkling that Henry Tudor had come this way. The whole region of Lancashire was now aware that Thomas Stanley was arraigned for treason and that the Lancastrian cause had once again been defeated, this time definitively. That was not to say residual support in lord Stanley's home county would not conspire to get his wife, lady Margaret out of England. That were ever the danger, but the idea her son was also in the region put a different completion on the whole business. He could not be allowed to get away, that was for sure.

"Towards Scotland, you say?" growled Sir Ralph. They were camped a few miles north of Liverpool and Robert knelt before Sir Ralph to give his report. Ancient Mostyn was there along with Sir Mortimer and master Abelard. Robert had learned from Abel Mostyn that after lady Margaret's escape Sir Ralph had figured she would head for Stanley Tower, a fortified edifice at Liverpool where the Stanley's stored produce from the Isle of Man before distributing it throughout the kingdom. It was the perfect place to take ship for France or anywhere, Scotland perhaps, and his scouts had informed Sir Ralph that the lady was heading there. They heard from local inhabitants that she had fled back north once she realised Sir Ralph occupied the Stanley Tower. It now seemed likely she had planned to meet her son there, too.

"Lady Staunton was surprised when lady Stanley and Henry Tudor turned up at her manor," said Robert. "I do not think they were expected. She seemed to be intent on ensuring lady Stanley, her mistress, had due time to escape. There were a few armed men there, the residue of those used to plot her escape, but there was no general feeling of expectation."

"I hardly think you are one to venture an opinion," drawled Sir Ralph cynically. "If you could fall for a simple trick as an exchange of cloaks between two women then hare off after the wrong one, not to mention managing to get captured by her and losing your weapons and harness . . ." he let the rebuke lie while Robert lowered his head to hide the blush in his face.

"The lad's tale of the Tudor making for Scotland makes sense, though," inserted Sir Mortimer. He was a heavy knight of about forty years with a red face and a black moustache. He stood at just five foot six, and was renowned for his ability in battle.

"I can see that," replied Sir Ralph, ignoring Robert who was still kneeling uncomfortably before him. "The king of the Scots will be only too glad to offer Tudor sanctuary and we shall have the problem of extracting him to deal with all over again. It was the king's intent to finish the traitor once and for all."

"Then if we are to catch him before he manages to reach the border, we must leave without delay," advised Sir Mortimer.

"If I might add a word of caution," interrupted master Abelard. He turned to Robert. "Get to your feet, lad." He looked to Sir Ralph who nodded his permission. "You have given an account that describes your escape from capture after being condemned to a hanging by, who was it? Sir Reginald Bray?"

"It was he, sir," said Robert emphatically, with lady Stanley's agreement."

"And he placed you in the hands of lady Staunton's men to carry out the deed?"

"He said he had other more important things to attend, sir – his men and horses."

Abelard looked meaningfully at Sir Ralph. "There is something not quite right here," he said emphatically.

"I can assure you I tell the truth," blurted out Robert, fearing he would be called a dissembler and part of some sort of Stanley duplicity.

"As I understand your tale," continued Abelard, "you were led out of the manor and into a wood nearby where a horse was tethered convenient for your departure?"

"Yes, the lady wished me no harm and wanted to avoid a charge of murder. I believe she will become a faithful subject of the king by renouncing her allegiance to the Stanley's and hopes to resolve the threat to her lands." He could hardly tell them she was the mother of his half-sister and his father's illegitimate daughter. She had managed to get him free and he felt honour bound to repay the debt; besides, he was reporting the whereabouts of Henry Tudor and preserving a lady's honour hardly constituted treason.

"This smells of trickery, Sir Ralph," said Abelard. "The lad is easily duped. Would you have let him out of your sight after he had been told of your plans. You would have hanged him there and then, not delegated it to another not of your own trusting, and this is Sir Reginald Bray we speak of."

"I hear what you say, master Abelard," said Sir Ralph," but the fact is the Tudor would be safe in Scotland and he is already two thirds of the way there. The king is still chasing him in Wales and we are the only ones with a positive sighting. I dare not let the opportunity of bringing him to heel pass by." He turned and gazed out across the countryside, his hand on his chin in deep thought.

Abelard turned once again to Robert. "We know Scotland was mentioned in your hearing, and it is possible that was a ploy to mislead us. Is there anything else you heard that might qualify your information?"

"No, my lord," replied Robert. "I was hidden away in the larder at the back of the kitchen while Henry Tudor entered the manor house. The lady's servants were Stanley sympathisers, which is why my position was betrayed. The lady would have had me safe."

"You could hear nothing – no servant's gossip?"

"No sir, just some men at arms who were on the other side of the wall outside."

"And did they mention Scotland?"

"No, sir, unless Foundray is a place in Scotland."

"Foundray?"

"Yes, the Pile of Foundray – sounds like a castle. There are many castles with strange names in Scotland."

"Foundray!" Sir Ralph shouted out loud – of course, Foundray; now that does make sense." Everyone looked at the knight in astonishment.

"You know of it?" asked Abelard intensely.

"Of course I do – Furness Abbey! The pile of Foundray is a castle on an island off the Furness peninsula. It is where the monks store their produce from the abbey, with I might add, the object of avoiding taxes to the king before shipping them out."

"You think the Tudor will seek sanctuary at Furness Abbey?" asked Sir Mortimer.

"No, the king would have him out of there quick enough. I believe he is headed for the Isle of Man – that is solid Stanley territory, they are the Kings of Man, and from there he can take ship to anywhere he likes. The Pile of Foundray has a deep-water harbour. That is why our young squire here has been fed the wrong information. It might appear to us that Henry Tudor is riding towards Scotland, but once beyond Lancaster he can easily turn aside and head west for the Cartmel peninsula and then on to Furness while our pursuit carries on North to miss him completely."

"What you say makes sense, Sir Ralph," said Abelard. "If the original plan was to leave England from the Stanley Tower at Liverpool, then the vessel they would take could easily sail the few miles north by sea and await them instead at Foundray."

"It all sounds a bit risky to me," intoned Sir Mortimer, lugubriously. "If we ride northwest there is no chance afterwards of catching the Tudor if you are wrong. He will be in Scotland in two days."

"Sir Ralph de Assheton paced the ground outside his pavilion in a turmoil of indecision. Presently he fixed Robert with a cold stare. "The lad has given us a rare chance, perhaps the only one left if we are to catch the Tudor. I believe in his penchant for being duped. We ride for Poulton. The quickest way to the peninsulas is the road across the sands. That is where the Tudor is headed."

4 – Nemesis

For the first time in setting out with Sir Ralph de Assheton and his men, Robert was seriously depressed. He had expected if not a hero's welcome, then at least an accolade for bringing news of the Tudor. After all, until he told his story they were looking merely for lady Margaret Stanley, and in the wrong place, too. Instead he was met with ridicule and the others in the force ribbed him mercilessly. He had not realised that a lot of this was jealousy due to the fact that he was the one who had changed the game from one of woman chasing to the more serious and imperative task of capturing Henry Tudor himself. It didn't help that he was forced to ride a borrowed horse in doublet and hose, having lost his armour. It was a constant reminder of his ignominy and he felt he stood out from his fellows. The only consolation was that Sir Ralph decided he should ride close to him seeing he believed Robert was blessed with some sort of luck, even if the young squire tended towards misinterpretation of events. He might find the opportunity of redeeming himself. John Biggar was the only one who hadn't ridiculed him. Perhaps he was still feeling guilty regarding his part in the earlier prank, which could have had dire consequences for either of them.

He reflected upon how the whole business with the chase after Henry Tudor was a mass of duplicity. It began with the impostor at the battle of Redemore – Robert had not been the only one to be duped in that way. Viscount Lovell had done the same thing, chasing after the wrong man and then misinterpreting, as did the king, the direction the Tudor was actually taking. One thing he was beginning to learn, though, was when to hold his tongue and he decided this defence might not find favour with Sir Ralph.

He wondered if they would ever catch Henry Tudor and his witch of a mother. England was a wild and varied country while Lancashire had more than its fair share of foul spirits to come to the aid of evildoers. Whole armies could, and often did, pass each other by just a few miles, not realising the presence of the other. Some witches in this county had the power to render themselves invisible. He knew that on St. John's Eve one had only to collect at midnight the golden spores of fern, which burst forth in the dawn of the midsummer solstice, then use these to become invisible. He hoped that lady Stanley knew nothing of secrets such as these for if she did, they were likely to pass the Tudor without knowing he was close. Tudor had, he guessed, about twenty in his retinue and they would find it even easier to hide from pursuit than a great army. Of course, they could not remain free for long. Once the king knew they were in Lancashire, he would send his soldiers to root them out. If they could just get to the isle of Foundray they would be away with the vast sea to hide in. He hoped he had heard aright the name Foundray. Sir Ralph recognised it, which reassured him and certainly, now he knew that the Pile of Foundray was a castle with a harbour, he too felt they were on the right track.

Sir Ralph had decided to begin the pursuit from Staunton Manor where they might question the lady Isabella and her servants for more details. Robert feared for her and the child. She had obviously been part of the plot to feed Robert with misinformation and thus was guilty of aiding the escape of the Tudor. She could not have known he had overheard the Tudor's men speaking of Foundray, nor Sir Reginald Bray or he would certainly have been dangled from a gibbet. They were approaching the manor now, at a fast canter. The bridge was down and the gates open. At least there would not be a fight here to make matters worse for the lady.

The house was abandoned. Smoke still curled from the kitchen fires and there were warm embers in the fireplace of the tower chamber where lady Isabella had entertained Robert the day before. The crib was empty. Fortunately, his harness was still there, heaped in the corner where it had been placed. Sir Ralph ordered a quick search of the house, just in case there was anybody there who could be questioned, but there was nobody, the only sign of life being a few hens that clucked in a corner of the courtyard, all other inhabitants, including the horses, had made themselves scarce. Soon even the hens were quiet, having had their necks wrung then stuffed into the saddlebags of the soldiers. While Sir Ralph's men searched the house Robert took the opportunity of getting into his harness. John Biggar helped him strap his cuirass to his body and his armet down at the back where he couldn't reach for himself.

"The lady must have taken a shine to you," said Sir Ralph when he presented himself. "That's valuable harness. I cannot see it being left behind willingly unless by order of the mistress of the house."

"I cannot tell, my lord," replied Robert sheepishly.

"Well, there is nobody here. They will be hiding in the woods or some country hovel I expect. We cannot waste time searching for them; we must be after the Tudor. Sir Mortimer!" The knight stamped over to Sir Ralph. "Which way do we take from here? Have your men examined the horse spoor?"

"Indeed yes, my lord. They head north as we expected. They have a few hours start on us and we must stop to question the people hereabouts for an idea of their direction."

"Then let us get after them. We shall head for Preston and then Lancaster. If we haven't caught them by then we will change horse and set the county astir. That will give us an advantage."

Robert felt much better now he was clad in his iron once again. He had his own sword and dagger and another spear to carry, which he was told had to be paid for seeing as he lost the first one. Abel Mostyn was away with the advance prickers; indeed Sir Ralph had sent him on ahead while they searched Staunton Manor. He rode with John Biggar behind Abelard and Sir Mortimer.

Staunton Manor was situated due west of Ormskirk and the family seat of lord Stanley at Lathom House. Although practically on the sea, there was no port on that part of the Lancashire coast where a sea-going ship could be taken. Liverpool to the south was the nearest and after that Preston to the north. However, Sir Ralph reckoned that the Tudor would keep well clear of Preston, a fortified town where the citizens might capture him to ingratiate themselves with King Richard. Besides, the town stood some way down the Ribble estuary and the narrow passage to the sea was risky, as they would have nowhere to run if one of the king's ships caught them. They would have to skirt Preston then ride north towards Lancaster. There was a road from the fishing village of Poulton just northwest of there across the sands of Morecambe Bay. Once at the Pile of Foundray, they could take ship directly into the Irish Sea with all options open to them. Sir Ralph was convinced this was the Tudor escape route and the Isle of Man their objective. From there they could take ship to Scotland, Ireland, Brittany or France – anywhere they chose and the king's ships would be hard put to find them, let alone take them.

They were riding hard along the main highway to Preston, forcing foot travellers to leap aside and wagons to lurch into the soft going beside the road. There were many shaken fists but none brave enough to impede the thundering progress of nearly two hundred mounted warriors. The weather had been dry for some weeks and there was little in the way of mud to impede them. The same, of course, went for the Tudor. If Henry Tudor and his mother were to make good their escape they would have to travel fast and the main road to the north was their only option. If they deviated into the countryside, then their pursuers would likely get ahead and trap them. Except, of course, after Lancaster. The whole picture would change from there on when they would turn towards Poulton, the starting point of the road across the sands.

They galloped into the town square of Preston where the Mayor and his council, having heard of their approach assembled to meet them. This was Stanley territory and Sir Ralph was mistrustful of any information they might offer him. Many of these men farmed lands owned by lord Stanley and some of them might even have been at the battle of Redemore. Yes, a band of about twenty had passed through the town around the time of the bell for Sext; it was now something after Nones, about four hours then. They could not tell if it was the Tudor or no. Sir Ralph decided not to waste time at Preston and ordered them to ride on.

The sun was getting low as they approached Lancaster. Ahead loomed the massive castle. They would be welcome enough here seeing it was a royal castle and the constable, Sir Roger de Wycke was one of King Richard's loyal men. The town posed a great threat to the Tudors. The castle garrison were king's men and though they had recently been part of the Stanley army, called to arms by him through the king's Commission of Array, they were not treasonable and were probably one of the reasons lord Stanley was unable to attack the king at the battle of Redemore. They were bound to have news of their quarry at Lancaster; they might even find them captive though nobody really believed in that sort of luck.

A white stone cross identified the outer environs of the town where the road forked. The left hand lane led towards the castle while the right hand took the road through the town. The portcullis that protected the gate was up during the day and would only be lowered if the castle should be attacked. The Scots had not raided this far south for some time so it remained up with just the gates closed at night. They rode between the two great crenellated towers, each semi-octagonal and topped by a further tower giving a commanding height of sixty-six feet. There was a niche let into the wall of the gatehouse containing a statue of St. Cuthbert flanked by the royal arms one side and the escutcheon of Lancaster on the other, denoting this as a Crown castle. Robert recognised the northern saint easily because Cuthbert was a favourite of King Richard and thus familiar to anyone who had ever been to his Court.

In the gathering dusk, servants were preparing cressets to contain the night fires ready for lighting in the vast bailey. The keep was to their right set against the north side, a great square edifice as tall as the gatehouse. Sir Roger de Wycke stood in the doorway with a dozen of his men. He was dressed in a scarlet houpelard with a black chaperone on his head, clearly not clad ready for a fight. Sir Ralph drew his destrier up in front of the constable and leapt from the saddle followed by Sir Mortimer and Abelard. The two squires Robert and John joined them and formed up behind Sir Ralph. The rest of the men remained seated on their horses waiting for orders. There were nearly two hundred of them now, due to further men being recruited on the road, yet they all fitted easily into the castle bailey.

Sir Roger recognised the royal arms in the fore banners so he knew here was a knight on the king's business. Neither men had met before but when Sir Ralph introduced himself Sir Roger knew he was facing the Vice Constable of England.

"I see by the calm domestic order of this castle that you have no inkling of why I am here?"

Sir Roger looked apprehensive. He was a tall man with a forked beard under a thin face. Aged around fifty or so he was clearly nervous and wondering if he had committed some misdemeanour. The thought passed through Robert's mind that perhaps he had. "I do not, my lord. I haven't been long home from the recent battle of Redemore. Is it the Scots? We have heard nothing of particular discontent on the border other than the usual raids."

"It is Henry Tudor, Sir Roger – he has today ridden through your town in an attempt to escape the king's rightful retribution!"

Sir Roger's mouth fell agape and he could do little more than splutter. Sir Ralph waited while he calmed himself. "Let us go inside and I will give you the details."

Sir Roger, grateful for the momentary respite that would give him time to collect his wits, conducted the knight into the lower chamber of the castle keep. The men dismounted and the sergeants began looking to the care of the mounts and then their men.

"I thought that Henry Tudor was running into Wales with the king's men at his heels. He should have been captured by now." Sir Roger was sitting with Sir Ralph and Sir Mortimer while Abelard stood beside them. The two squires took their places standing behind Sir Ralph.

"That is what we all believed until coming north to take the lady Margaret Stanley into our keeping," Sir Ralph informed him. "We discovered the Tudor had duped everyone and headed north. At first it appeared he would try for Scotland, but I now have reason to believe he is heading for the Pile of Foundray."

"Across the sands?" said Sir Roger, immediately understanding the situation seeing as the road across the sands was regularly used, with Lancaster being the starting or finishing point. Alternatively, access to the peninsular of Furness involved a long ride north before turning west and then south again.

"That is my belief," said Sir Ralph. "And there is not a moment to lose. He is but a few hours ahead of us and we must chase after him before he gets across to the Furness peninsula and Foundray."

Sir Roger gave a wry smile. "If he is but a few hours in front of you, then we have him. He cannot cross the sands until the tide goes out. It disappears for miles and the crossing can only be made with the assistance of local guides. The road is beset by and must avoid areas of quicksand. We lose men, wagons, and horses year on year – never to be seen again. It alters regularly as does the channel of the River Kent, which runs between and must be crossed at low tide. Tudor cannot go over by night and though the tide will be out by first light, he will have scant time to cross before it returns and when it does, it comes in faster than a horse can run." He beckoned over his Seneschal who had been hovering by, clearly wishing to speak. "Have you any report of an armed party in the town?"

"Indeed, Sir Roger. When I learned of my lord's mission I questioned my guards by the bridge. A party of about twenty armed men in full harness and one woman passed over this afternoon. They declared themselves king's men, though they wore no colours, and brooked no hindrance."

"They didn't think to question them?"

"No, sire. There are many armed men returning from the battle and it seemed of little consequence, besides men in rich harness such as these would not be commanded by a mere common guard."

"Where is the bridge," asked Sir Ralph. "We could not see it as we entered the town."

"You will have taken the lane to the castle when you arrived," said Sir Roger. "Had you taken the right hand lane that would have led you to the bridge, which goes over to the north bank and the road across the sands. Most folk turn east before the bridge following a loop in the river, then north along the main highway towards Carlisle, or beyond into Scotland."

"So the bridge is lightly guarded?"

"Yes, Sir Ralph, just two men usually, as today."

"Well at least we can be assured the Tudor is trying for the sands if he is on the north bank of the river across the bridge."

"It will be necessary for him to begin the crossing before first light if he is to make the other side," said Sir Roger. "As for us, we will need the dawn to locate his actual position so he is likely to start before we can get to him. The bay is a huge expanse."

"You say a guide is needed to cross safely?"

"To cross at all, there is no question of that. No casual stranger to these shores could get even part way. I have seen men trapped and drown in the sands within sight of the shore when the tide comes in."

"How wide are the sands?"

"Nine miles as the bird flies, but the route is not straight: the Tudor must wind his way across nearly twelve miles of sand, fording the track of the River Kent and other obstacles to get to the Furness peninsular."

"Then the answer is simple. I shall dispatch a few men to secure the guides this side, thus preventing any escape."

"It is a good idea, my lord," responded Sir Roger. "The guides are monks from Furness Abbey. They have a small chapel at Poulton, about five miles from here where they assemble for the crossing. Another group will set off from the other side and those guides will remain at Poulton until the next crossing. That is how it works."

"Master de la Halle," said Sir Ralph. "Send for Ancient Mostyn. You will take a detachment of his men and remove the monks from Poulton Chapel."

"Yes, Sir Ralph," replied Robert enthusiastically. "But what if we encounter the Tudor and his men? There are twenty armoured knights with him." Sir Ralph considered this. "Yes, that might cause a problem. However, it is pitch dark and too many men blundering about unknown territory will alert the Tudors and let them slip away. You will have to assess the situation when you get there. At least monitor the Tudor position and direct the rest of us when we arrive at first light. I do not wish to waste time hunting for them."

* * *

Robert wondered if the forces of darkness were at work as they moved, stalking on foot the five miles between Lancaster and Poulton. Any light that the heavens might have provided was obscured by cloud and it was with great difficulty the small troop of eight men moved forward at all. There was a track, used by those who would cross the sands, which was deeply rutted with the passage of wagon wheels. Had it not been for this it would have been impossible to navigate at all and they had probably gone around in circles. Abel Mostyn provided him with a dark lantern that cast just enough light to show the ground at his feet. There is nothing that disorientates the mind more than total blackness. Ancient Mostyn taught him a good trick and they maintained contact between themselves by holding on to a rope he had brought for the purpose. This let them keep close together without the need for speech. The requirement for stealth meant no man could wear armour that might give sound, so all were dressed in doublet and hose and shod with leather boots. Robert had organised with John Biggar to bring up his horse on the morrow, so he would at least be mounted for the capture of the Tudor. He expected to leave any serious fighting to the harnessed knights, though with two hundred men at his back, Sir Ralph could hardly expect to have a battle on his hands.

They knew when they were close to their objective when the light wind brought the tang of the sea and they came upon a small village, which could only be Poulton. The village folk, if they were aware of their presence at all, showed no curiosity and doors remained firmly closed. Soon the going turned to coarse grass, the kind that grows by the seashore and then the dark impression of a stone building. This, Robert reckoned, must be the chapel they were looking for. He stopped then and listened for any sound that might betray human presence.

"If the Tudors be around here, then where is the guard?" whispered Abel Mostyn.

"Perhaps they have moved on already to cross the sands?"

"You heard what Sir Roger said - they will need some light for that and there is none, not so much as a glim. I can't even see the sands of the bay."

"Then let us look into the chapel. If they are in there it is like to be a tight squeeze, by the size of it, and no guard there either."

They moved cautiously to the chapel, a rectangular building of rough stone, but small, similar to a shepherd's hut sufficient for temporary respite from the elements, but not for permanent living. Robert pushed tentatively at the door, which creaked open to reveal an apparently empty void, a condition that was confirmed as they entered with the dark lantern and found it abandoned.

"I would say the Tudors have taken the guide monks away to confound any pursuit," said Robert quietly.

"I think that unless their mounts can dance on air there will be tracks for us to follow," replied Abel. "It is more likely they have moved out onto the sands as the tide went out ready for a quick start at or before dawn."

"Then there is nothing for it but to remain here and await the arrival of Sir Ralph," decided Robert. "He will not be tardy in his arrival and it is a long way across the sands with nowhere to hide."

"For sure, once we have proper sight of the Tudor he is as good as taken," agreed Abel. "Let *us* post a guard and the rest get some sleep. It would be folly to continue stumbling about in the dark on the fringe of Morecambe Bay."

Daybreak came with a feeling of awareness rather than

illumination, as if the sun somewhere above the thick cloud was reluctant to expose the vastness of the bay. The call of seabirds alerted them closely followed by the sound of bells for Prime drifting across the sands from some distant religious house. Before them was slowly revealed the wet sands of the bay stretching away into the distant gloom. Nearby Robert noted a series of sticks, laurel by the sad look of their decaying leaves, protruding from the sand and acting as markers. They strained their eyes, each hoping to be the first to sight their quarry. Robert felt his stomach churn, anxious that the Tudors might be somewhere close and not on the road to Scotland after all. There had been so much deception practised by the traitors that his previous certainty had all but evaporated. It was his dearest wish that he could locate them before Sir Ralph arrived and they could be after them. There came the sound of voices and Robert wondered that Sir Ralph had managed to get here so quickly. It was not yet light and the road from Lancaster was barely visible. Just then a small group of local men came into sight. They stopped and huddled together, clearly fearing these armed men. Each man carried a wickerwork basket over his shoulder. Robert identified that these were fish traps similar to those set in rivers.

"Have no fear, good people," he called to them. "We are here on the king's business and have none with you." At this the men relaxed and one of them stepped forward.

"We are come to set our traps, sir," he said in an accent that Robert could just about understand. He was dressed as the others in a leather jack and breeches that were cut off above the knee. He and those with him were bare of foot.

"Then you must wait until Sir Ralph de Assheton arrives. He will be here shortly. We are in pursuit of the king's enemies who we think might try to cross the sands this morning."

The man looked around. "Where be the guides?"

"We wondered about that," replied Robert. "We believe they have been taken off by the men we are in pursuit of." He thought it best not to state exactly who the quarry were. There was no knowing where local loyalties lay. "Are there any other guides about here?"

"Well sir," replied the man looking at his fellows. "I know the bay enough to lay my traps between here and Cartmel just over there." He pointed to a peninsular that was just emerging from the gloom.

"I think our quarry is headed for the Furness peninsular beyond."

The man shook his head. "I know not the safe way across to Furness. None of us have much business there except to sell the monks our fish, but the guides take them across in their cart."

"Then where would they start from?" asked Robert.

"Why, by here normally. There be the laurels put in the road as a guide, but they only go so far. The sands are ever changing and there is no permanent road. Only the monks know that. They cross daily and can see the way as it changes."

"What is your name, fellow?"

"Caleb Rigge," he replied.

"Then Caleb Rigge my lord will require you to guide us onto the sands. We shall be mounted – do you ride?"

"I can sit a horse well enow," replied Rigge, his brown, weathered face creased worriedly.

"Then you shall have the chance to serve your king this day," he intoned officiously.

As Robert spoke he heard the approach of a large number of horses. Sir Ralph de Assheton was here. The fishermen moved away nervously and placed their backs against the rough stone of the chapel. Only Caleb Rigge remained, restrained by Robert placing a reassuring hand on his shoulder. The men-at-arms stopped with Sir Ralph as he spotted Robert and the other men.

"You have sight of the Tudor?" he demanded.

"Not yet, my lord," Robert replied, but the light is increasing rapidly. Beside him he could feel Rigge trembling at the sight of two hundred mounted knights, each in full harness. If he now understood they were after Henry Tudor he did not display any recognition of the name, but then, Robert knew, not every Englishman had heard of Tudor. They knew the realm had been invaded, that was all. Many hereabouts had gone in the army of lord Stanley to fight for their king, which was all they knew. Of Thomas Stanley's duplicity they understood nothing.

Sir Ralph raised himself in his saddle and gazed out across the sands which were now showing their extent. Somewhere a few miles off was the sea, but for now the sand was empty and bare. The only sound was the trickle of water running in shallow rivulets between low sandbanks and the occasional cry of a bird.

"There!" cried Abel Mostyn. He climbed on to the roof of the chapel and now was pointing excitedly somewhere to the south west. They all turned their gaze in that direction and sure enough they could just make out from the rapidly fading gloom a party of the right number they were looking for well out in the bay.

"That's them!" shouted Sir Ralph. John Biggar rode up to Robert with a horse. Other men had mounts for the rest of Robert's party and a spare for Caleb Rigge, who was looking decidedly fearful, but compelled by the great lord to do his bidding.

"This man will be our guide, Sir Ralph," he said holding onto Rigge's horse with a rope attached to its bridle.

"I need no guide," snarled Sir Ralph as a hunter with his quarry in his sight. "There is the Tudor. We have only to follow his tracks."

"There may be hazards we know not of, my lord. It will do no harm to have someone with knowledge of the sands with us." Sir Ralph glared at him for his temerity in questioning his decision, but then thought of it and nodded his agreement.

"Let us away," he called raising his arm. "The traitor is in my sight and shall be taken within the hour or we perish in the attempt."

Robert was not particularly enthusiastic about perishing in the attempt, but he was taken up in the excitement of the pursuit. Suddenly, Sir Ralph spurred his mount and the whole force trotted out onto the sands of Morecambe Bay. For the first mile they followed the line of the laurel branches because these marked the safe road and in any case pointed them directly towards their quarry. Sir Ralph ordered a gallop but it soon became apparent that this was dangerous as the ground was not even going and there were soft patches that could trip a galloping horse and after a few near mishaps, he ordered them to a gentle canter. They splashed across rivulets and wide flats, hardly gaining on the quarry, which had obviously been keeping a watch for them and were also making fast progress. Soon, though, they could see they were gaining. The monkish guides, Caleb Rigge informed them, rode in a cart, not on horseback and that slowed them.

It seemed to Robert that they were out on a great flat desert, a wet one but with far horizons to the south. To their right was the tip of the Cartmel peninsular and ahead they could make out the shadowy loom of the Furness peninsular. As they rode he had time to reflect on their chances of catching the Tudor in the sands. Even with their relatively slow guides it was likely Tudor would make land first and with that advantage put some considerable distance between them. If there was a ship waiting at the Pile of Foundray then it was certain they would escape and who would want to face the wrath of King Richard. All depended on the distance between the pursuers and the pursued. The sun, as if it was tired of obscuring the scene, out of curiosity burned off the thick cloud and lit up the whole of the bay. Somewhere to the south was a slim glitter of sea, waiting its inevitable hour when it would return to drown the sands and anyone unfortunate enough to remain on them.

As they splashed their way across the Kent channel, their horses wading through water half way up their legs, Caleb Rigge indicated with a look of panic in his eyes that he would speak. Robert slowed to let him ride alongside.

"There is danger ahead with this number of horses," he cried. "It is the thunder of so many hooves – it vibrates the sand and turns it to quicksand. It can change a safe hard way into a soft one instantly."

Robert understood that if such a thing occurred then they would certainly lose their quarry. He splashed his way over to where Sir Ralph was struggling on his mount clear of the steep sides of the channel and onto firm sand.

"My lord, a word!" Sir Ralph detected the urgency in his squire's voice.

"What is it?" he shouted irritably, the difficulty of catching the Tudors uppermost in his mind.

"The sands! We must slow otherwise we may sink and lose our objective." He explained the problem and Sir Ralph halted his men.

"We must break up into individual groups of no more than twenty five. Spread out and we shall cover a greater spread of the sands and have a good chance of speeding our progress." Robert had not thought of that. Fewer horsemen meant less pounding of the sand. Caleb Rigge sidled up to him.

"If we swing somewhat to the south we might have a better chance of making up the distance. The way the guides are taking them is due west, but they must turn south before they reach the Furness side. If we ride south-west we might have a chance of cutting them off."

Sir Ralph had been listening to this exchange and immediately saw the advantage.

"My good fellow," he bellowed, "if what you say is correct and we have our quarry, then you shall profit by your advice." Caleb Rigge brightened up at this and was suddenly fired with enthusiasm. It represented perhaps the one time in his life when a great reward might be paid him. It would set him up for life and he was not the man to let it pass.

"Are you sure of this," muttered Robert quietly. Rigge looked feared but the idea of reward from a great lord had taken root in his mind.

"It is a risk, but if we move with haste we should meet with your quarry before they reach dry land and before the incoming tide makes that side of the bay impassable.

"I shall ride to the south," declared Sir Ralph. "The rest of you split up into your groups and follow the route of the Tudor. By God's grace we shall catch him and stop him. You will then ride up behind and dispose of any who try to escape, but Tudor must be taken alive."

Now they were off across the wet sands, the underlying surface water flying forth in sparkling bursts from the hooves of their horses, the bright morning sun casting coloured coruscations of light, elevating them almost as Mercury's with wings at their heels. Robert, bending over the front of his saddle looked to the right where the Tudors were now situated. He could see white faces under raised visors peering towards them, working out their strategy. There was a cart there and he could see a woman clinging to the sides supported by monks in Cistercian habits. That must be the lady Margaret Stanley and one of those riding by the side would be Henry Tudor. There was a sheen of bright water between them and Caleb Rigge shook his head when he indicated that they might ride across it.

On they rode and now they were actually getting ahead. Soon, according to Caleb Rigge the Tudor must turn towards them or get bogged down in the sands. The rest of Sir Ralph's men were some way back and for the first time Robert realised the task in front of him. There were about twenty or so with Sir Ralph, equal numbers but they were to face desperate men, battled hardened knights who would fight to the death having no other choice. It was by no means certain that the Tudor could be stopped. His entourage merely had to hold them off long enough for he and his mother to get to dry land and then they would be away with nobody to stop them. If that happened, then all that had been fought for at Redemore would be lost and Henry Tudor, while having forfeited credence on the continent of Europe, would still be placed as a political pawn to harass the reign of King Richard. The business could only be resolved by his capture and Sir Ralph de Assheton and the humble squire attached to him by the earl of Surrey would both suffer the ignominy of having the traitor within spitting distance and losing him. Robert had been the one to discover his escape plan. It would be a great distress to him to witness his final escape having got so close to capturing him and thus gaining glory. The thought flitted through Robert's mind that King Richard too had the Tudor within inches of his war axe at Redemore and failed, by circumstance, to finish him, but that argument would hardly do Robert or Sir Ralph much good when they presented their failure at court. Henry Tudor led a charmed life and it was almost as if he had the devil on his shoulder.

Had he once stood on a precipice to be tempted, and succumbed?

If so he might gain the whole world, yet lose his soul and England the worst for the bargain.

Suddenly Sir Ralph raised his arm and reigned in his men.

"They turn and we must have them!"

The Tudor contingent and their attendant cart carrying the guiding monks and lady Stanley had turned to face them and were advancing with dreadful purpose. The armoured knights in his escort spread out in a defensive line with the cart behind. Robert wondered if Henry Tudor was somewhere in the line of armoured men. They wore no livery, having had to travel surreptitiously north through England, but their purpose was clear. They would bar the way of Sir Ralph de Assheton and once he was defeated run a mile ahead of his main force, which was still struggling on its way behind them through the sands.

Suddenly, one of their company broke away and began to ride at the gallop for the Furness peninsular. His route was along their original path but they had turned by instruction of their guides to avoid the danger of the soft sands. The woman in the cart began to scream and called after for him to return. Robert could see the monks in the cart holding her back as she seemed to want to jump from the cart in pursuit.

"That must be Henry Tudor!" screamed Robert, pointing to the rider.

"Another subterfuge," replied Sir Ralph. "We shall prepare to engage those who now are about to charge upon us."

Robert regarded the opposing force and recognised confusion in their ranks.

"My lord, it is Henry Tudor," cried Robert, suddenly sure of himself.

"Then you have my permission to chase after him," said Sir Ralph with a sardonic grin. "Bring me back the head of a Tudor traitor and I shall be happy, but for now we engage with these." He set spurs to his horse and charged with his men across the sands to where the Tudor escort were milling around.

Robert decided he would chase after the lone rider. Caleb Rigge thought it prudent to attend upon him and so the two set off after the rider making pell-mell for the Furness peninsular. The knight didn't get far. Suddenly the front legs of his horse dropped into the sands projecting the rider into space to land flat upon the ground. He scrambled to his feet and immediately sank to his knees in the sand. Behind them they could hear the sounds of battle as the knights collided and the screams of a woman, lady Margaret Stanley, as the monks drew around her as close as they dared in their cart.

"It is Henry Tudor!" exclaimed Robert as he contemplated the wretch embedded in the quicksand.

"He is in full harness, sir," said Caleb Rigge. "It will be hard to pull him free dressed thus."

"And he cannot divest himself of his iron unless he is pulled free," reflected Robert. "It appears we have him firmly our prisoner."

Caleb tugged at Robert's arm to stop him going over to the Tudor. He pressed a foot on the ground at their feet. They could plainly see the sand move as if it were a jelly. "Go no further, sir," said Caleb. "You will sink yourself."

Henry Tudor struggled to free himself and in the few moments they had been there he had already sunk to his waist.

"Help me!" he cried plaintively. His eyes were wide with fear. It was obvious that he had ridden off in a panic in his desperation to escape and now he was in even more trouble. His horse was in a worse state that its erstwhile rider. Not having the sense to remain still, its legs were already deeply embedded in the sand and part of its belly. Eyes white with fear, Robert, realising it would never be pulled free, normally he would draw his dagger and slit its throat to ease its passage out of the world, but he dare not approach the beast. The man stuck in the stand, though, could not be treated so lightly. It was imperative that he was rescued and brought before King Richard.

"How do we get him free," asked Robert. Henry Tudor looked between the two, his eyes wide, pleading for the answer that would save him. Caleb Rigge's response was for the two of them to step back even further for fear of entering the same trap.

"I fear there is not the time," he said, casting an eye at the position of the sun. "The tide is already turned and will soon sweep into the bay. We must be away ourselves, or perish.

Behind them the sounds of battle were fading and looking back they saw the remnants of the Tudor knights with the cart retreating across the sands. Half a dozen knights were fending off the men in Sir Ralph's party and Robert could see Margaret Stanley, her hair streaming in the wind as it had on the battlements of Lathom House waving her arms and being restrained by the monks of Furness Abbey else she would have leapt from the cart and run across the sands to where Henry Tudor lay trapped. She was screaming for the life of her son, firmly embedded in the land of which he would have been king. Henry Tudor saw her being drawn away and all restraint fell from him. He began to scream to be saved until, the remnants of the Tudor rear guard either dead or prisoners, Sir Ralph came up.

The rest of his force had caught up with him and they spread out across the sands, all eyes on the wretch gesticulating wildly and screaming himself hoarse with terror.

"So this is the Tudor, Henry Tudor. It seems to me sir you are well caught."

"Get me free!" cried the wretch, all courtly protocols forgotten.

"Dig him free," commanded Sir Ralph. His men looked at him and each other, wondering how they could do that.

"He will not come free," stated Caleb Rigge. "He is too far gone. See, he is already up to his waist and though he will not sink further for a while yet, the sea will claim him before that."

"No! No! That cannot be," cried Henry Tudor. "I am the earl of Richmond and must present myself before the king." He flapped his arms about. All this achieved was to let him sink further until it became apparent to everyone he would never get out.

"I cannot see that would do you much good other than earn you a reprieve for a few weeks," said Sir Ralph laconically. He had dismounted and now stood at the edge of the soft sands, his hands on his knees looking across at the Tudor. "You are consistent, sir, in running from battle. Twice you ran at Redemore and now you have run again, but this time your luck has run before you and no doubt lies smothered in sand, as you must be."

"No! The King - King Richard will not allow it."

"So you acknowledge him King at last?"

"Yes! Yes! He was ever King. I shall make my obeisance before him; now get me free."

Sir Ralph looked at Caleb Rigge. "You know these sands, fellow. How do we get him free?"

"We cannot, Lord," murmured Caleb tremulously, fearing some sort of retribution. "The tide is already turned and unless we set off at speed, it will engulf us too."

"Is there nothing to be done to free him?"

"No, sire. In fact, when a fellow is caught thus we usually slit his throat to ease his suffering, but we need planks of wood to get to him and we have none. The sea is a terrible executioner."

"I am not a dog to be treated thus," screamed the Tudor. "I am the earl of Richmond and I demand an audience with the king."

"The only thing I can offer you is an audience with your maker," said Sir Ralph coldly.

"Shall I despatch him, my lord," said Sir Mortimer beckoning forward an archer who had been standing by awaiting instructions."

Sir Ralph gazed across into the terrified eyes of the Tudor, who had been struggling even more and was now firmly above his waist in sand. "No, Sir Mortimer. We shall report to the king that Henry Tudor has been put to rest in the land he would claim for his own and that the tide, which is commanded by God in his heaven, has been his judge and executioner."

"No! No! No!" screamed Henry Tudor. "You cannot leave me thus!"

Caleb Rigge tugged at Robert's arm and pointed to the south. Already a patch of water was extending where there had once been dry sand.

"My Lord!" exclaimed Robert. "We must be away or be caught by the tide."

Sir Ralph looked over what had once been sand to see a shining of water. Seabirds were calling and diving for the food the rising tide brought with it. He jerked his eyes towards Caleb Rigge. "We are in your hands, sirrah," he exclaimed. "Which is the way out of here. Caleb Rigge pointed north towards the tip of Cartmel peninsular.

"That is the only way I know, my lord, and we might already be late." The man's voice shook with fear. He knew the dangers of this coast and the effects of the tide and his rising panic did nothing to reassure them.

"Then lead us out of these cursed sands and let us ride." Sir Ralph vaulted into his saddle and Robert, as was the way with squires did the same. It was with some impatience that they waited while Caleb Rigge managed to get a foot into the stirrup and haul himself into the saddle of his mount.

"Don't leave me here," screamed Henry Tudor. "You cannot leave me here!"

"Away," commanded Sir Ralph, giving not a glance towards the man trapped in the sands. If any had cared to turn their gaze to the distant west they would have seen a manic Margaret Stanley tearing and screaming at the skies, her cries mingled with the screeching of the birds that followed the tide while the remnants of her escort dragged her towards the safety of the Furness peninsular.

They galloped north across the sands, racing the incoming tide and not caring if they hit a soft patch or no. Behind them they knew the tide would come after them faster than they could ride. In front of them was a stretch of water that had been dry sand a few minutes ago. Somehow the tide had got before them and, as if there was retribution in its purpose, was trying to cut them off. Caleb led them more to the east where they were able to ford the rapidly deepening water, their horses belly deep before they climbed out onto firm sand. This too would soon be under water and every man looked to

Caleb Rigge as their only saviour. He led them towards a high limestone headland that protruded into Morecambe Bay like the beckoning finger of a giant. Fortunately the low ground around the east of the head was still accessible and it was with great relief and some difficulty that they scrambled over the stones at its base to solid ground above the tide line with the grassed headland sweeping upwards. Thus Humphrey Head, the place where the last wolf in England once lived and had been killed, became their refuge. It was perhaps fitting that another predator, this one who was wont to prey upon the English crown, had been vanquished within sight of it too. For many years after, Robert, whenever he was confronted by a stretch of vast beach, would hear recorded in his mind the terrible cries of Henry Tudor, which howled across the sands unabated until the rising waters of Morecambe Bay poured into his open mouth and stifled the man and his ambitions forever.

5 - The Siege of Pembroke Castle

"I cannot see what the defenders hope to achieve," said Thomas Howard, earl of Surrey. "We must starve them into submission, seeing as the castle is surrounded with no possibility of succour. There is no need to waste a single man, yet it provokes my ire that they should defy us." He was standing just out of bowshot of the great stone gatehouse and walls of Pembroke Castle. With him was a group of knights and their attendants, all regarding the problem before them.

"And the king wishes the castle taken intact," grumbled viscount Francis Lovell. "He has no wish to bear the cost of its rebuilding when he needs it to protect his Welsh possessions once the traitors are removed." Robert de la Halle stood close by his lord, Thomas Howard, gazing up at the great gatehouse and listening with interest to their conversation. He, as the rest of the army was keen for some action. The sky was a troubled grey where dismal clouds threatened rain. A weak morning light somehow caused the white lime-washed walls to take on a surreal glow that proclaimed the defiant inner strength of the fortress.

Inside the castle were the remnants of the mercenaries and traitorous English that had followed Henry Tudor into England from France. With them was the residue of the army gathered together by Rhys ap Thomas. Though called to arms by King Richard, from whom he held his authority in Wales, the Welshman had treasonably sided with Henry Tudor. Most of his men had dispersed and fled back to their homes, but their captains and those Lancastrian zealots amongst them dared not face a feared retribution. Rhys ap Thomas, along with Jasper Tudor, Henry Tudor's uncle had tried to escape by sea from Pembroke but the king managed to get a flotilla of warships there in time to bar their exit along the tidal inlets that protected it. Now they were closely mewed up in the castle, fearing death and holding out in a final act of desperation. The townspeople, having neither the will nor good reason to engage with their king's army, had opened the gates of the town and now the great castle was under siege.

The castle was constructed on a limestone promontory jutting out into the estuary of the Pembroke River, with water on two sides and a massive barbican that protected the gatehouse on the town side. Attackers must take this before getting at the gatehouse proper, behind which were gates with two portcullises and a series of murder holes to discourage anyone attacking there. The gatehouse alone was bigger than many a castle in England. None of this would withstand the iron shot of guns and it would be a simple matter to bring up a few then pound it to rubble. Pembroke castle's position, however, was strategic, which was why King Richard wanted it preserved intact. It was a good place to start from for Ireland, where the Plantagenets were well established and also to control any unrest in this part of Wales or repel invasion from Europe.

Pembroke was not a royal castle; it was under the suzerainty of the Chief Justice of South Wales, William Herbert, the second earl of Pembroke married to Katherine, the bastard daughter of King Richard. He was not in there at this time, being at Raglan Castle, his favoured home. King Henry the Sixth, a monarch not noted for sound judgement, had once granted Henry Tudor's uncle, Jasper Tudor the earldom of Pembroke, but after sharing in the Lancastrian defeat at the Battle of Barnet in 1471 Jasper had retreated here and was besieged. He escaped to France at that time and was now back, though his enterprise to place his nephew Henry on the throne of England was now finally defeated. The necessity for the English Crown to have due regard for security in the region was manifest in the current situation, where some Welsh, albeit not many, had joined the Tudor invasion.

King Richard's first preference had been, according to viscount Lovell, to raze Pembroke Castle to the ground. It was the place where Henry Tudor had been born in 1457 and the former home of lady Margaret Stanley, though she was Margaret Tudor then, having married and shortly after becoming the widow of one Edmund Tudor, a noble of dubious lineage. King Richard, though, was able to contain his wrath for the sake of common sense and thus the edict forbidding the destruction of the fortress had been proclaimed. Indeed, in all the years of rebellion it had never fallen to the Welsh. The original wooden buildings had been pulled down and rebuilt in stone under the supervision of William Marshall in the late 12th century and even the mighty Welsh prince Owain Glendwr had not penetrated its defences, being happy to be paid off in gold rather than attack it. William Marshall had built the massive round dungeon within the inner ward in the year 1200, though no army had managed to get near enough to it to test its great strength. They could see it from where they stood. It towered 75 feet high topped by a dome and its walls were nineteen feet thick. If the traitors were in there it would take some prising to get them out.

Sir William Stanley joined them accompanied by his squires and immediate servants.

"I dislike this business of standing around waiting for the inevitable day when the castle must surrender or starve to death," he complained. "We have six thousand men and eight thousand horses around here all shitting and pissing. The air is foul and soon we shall have camp fever amongst us. The garrison over there will be our deaths without them firing even a single arrow or letting off as much as a pound of powder."

The other nobles shrugged off his comments. They too knew the problems associated with a long siege, but they also realised that William Stanley was eager to get himself back to the Court where he could engage in some serious sycophancy around the king. He was fretting because the expected acclaim for his aid at the Battle of Bosworth, as it was now becoming known, had not been as enthusiastic as he had hoped. Of more import was the weather. It was now the end of October and the problem here at Pembroke was the last task to complete the king's victory after the Battle of Bosworth. The new name had become more convenient as the location could be identified with the small market town situated close by the plain of Redemore where the conflict had actually taken place.

Already the land around Pembroke was churned to mud and the encampments of the soldiers grim and austere. Food was scarce and though some of the townsfolk had been *persuaded* to reveal their secret stores, there was a severe shortage that could only get worse. Foragers were out in the rich surrounding countryside, depriving the local population of their recently harvested winter sustenance and becoming very unpopular. Most were longing for winter quarters. Perhaps the Tudors were hoping they would all retire for the winter? The nobles had quartered themselves comfortably in the town but Pembroke was too small to accommodate an army. Pavilions and canvas shelters were littered across the two sides of the Pembroke River estuary and around the priory to the east. The monks there had secured the priory and kept themselves out of the way until the hoped-for resolution to the siege. The few whores in the town had been hard-worked too, but even they were rationing their services and had become expensive. There had been some plundering and rapes, which the captains had tried, somewhat half-heartedly to control. A few men had been hanged as examples, but to little effect.

"The king will not tolerate much more delay," said viscount Lovell.

"Then let him come and take the castle himself," responded earl Thomas irritably.

"The personal presence of his grace the king would have a better chance of resolving the impasse," contributed Sir William. "After all, he has created it. Once the garrison have sight of his royal standard, backed by his person, they will likely surrender."

"Perhaps you would care to tell him that yourself?" said Lovell. It was well known that the two men did not get on. Viscount Lovell was a long-time friend of the king while Sir William Stanley, who had been a consummate courtier around the throne of King Edward the Fourth, had some way to go to gain the complete confidence of King Richard the Third.

"I would not have to, my lord Lovell, nor you either but for the matter of the king's nuptial arrangements. That is his only study at this time."

"Yes, and it is I who is charged with going to Portugal to escort the Princess Joanna to England when the arrangements are complete," put in earl Thomas, "so I cannot tarry here all winter. The lady intends to be a Spring Bride, I hear."

"We must make parley with the traitors," replied Lovell. "You have assessed the situation aright, lord Thomas. The king has other business than the trials and executions of Rhys ap Thomas and Jasper Tudor. They are, after all, virtual prisoners here."

"Yes, there will be no mercy for Tudor and his supporters. How can we parley when the end of it for them is death?" replied the earl. "A better way would be to work upon the garrison. We can offer to spare them and thus save them from slow starvation, which is sure as things stand. It is curious that there has been no approach to us so far."

"If it were not for the fact of their hopeless position, I would say they are playing for time," offered Sir William. "That is normal when a place is under siege but with the possibility of someone coming to their relief, yet that is not the case here."

"If, as you say, they are playing for time," mused Lovell, "there is probably some sort of escape plan in progress otherwise they would be begging the king for mercy."

Earl Thomas sighed and gazed over at the castle walls as if hoping they would fall down by miracle. "The only way to lift this siege would be an attack upon us by a great invasion force from France or perhaps Brittany, which would be a declaration of war against England. None in Europe would countenance such a thing. The Tudor cause is defunct there as well as in England. The best they can hope for over there is sanctuary and little else. Aid from across the narrow seas is out of the question so what are they plotting?"

"Perhaps we should try to get someone inside?" suggested viscount Lovell. "We could send an offer to parley – a quite reasonable action on our part. I could go as Lord Chamberlain and the king's representative though I cannot offer to deliver them from the process of the king's law."

"Yes, and take along in your retinue - you will be expected to have a party with you - several good pairs of eyes and ears," enthused earl Thomas. "While you are engaged with the traitors, who knows what might be discovered among the servants and garrison soldiers, who must be fearful for their lives?"

Earl Thomas turned towards Robert, who was standing close enough to hear what had been said. "I have just the lad for the task," he grinned wryly. "You, master de la Halle seem to have developed a talent for discovering secret plans." He looked at the other knights. "This is he that discovered the whereabouts of Henry Tudor when the rest of us were casting about in Wales. I do not know if he is merely lucky or a talented subversive, but I recommend we include him with the envoys."

The knights shrugged indifferently. The fact was they were embarrassed that a mere youth should have discovered Henry Tudor where they had failed. It must be admitted the lad was due some credit for doing so but then they wanted the matter put behind them.

"Send forward the heralds," declared viscount Lovell, "and let them trumpet a request for parley. You, master Robert, get you out of your harness and into your plain livery. As for myself, I and my knights shall dress according to my rank. We must make a grand show to the garrison and let them see they defy the authority of the King of England."

* * *

Though they rode honourably under a truce below the raised defences of the gatehouse. Robert could not help but look up at the murder holes where at any moment, should the defenders betray the truce, boiling oil might pour, or cloth-yard shafts of iron tipped arrows drive into them from the arrow slits in the bastions of the massive stone towers. Unscathed, they emerged into the outer ward of the castle, the closing of the portcullis rumbling ominously behind them cutting them off from the outside world. There were twenty of them, viscount Lovell riding in front flanked by his standard bearers, one of his own showing his family emblem of a silver wolf and another displaying the royal arms of England.

Robert, riding in this company was assailed by the symmetry of the campaign. Here was viscount Francis Lovell with his emblem of a wolf, then there was the wolf's lair at Humphrey head, where the last wolf in England was slain and in sight of the place where Henry Tudor had met his nemesis. The wolf killer, John Harrington lay beside Joan his wife in effigy at Cartmel Priory, originally founded by William Marshall, the very knight that had rebuilt Pembroke castle. Some sort of magic was at work here, and he wondered what was waiting for him at the end of the path that was being laid out before him. In one way it comforted him. Whatever lay in store was inevitable and be it his death or his fortune; there was no way he could escape it. At this moment he felt he was at one with the chivalric knights of old, in particular the spirit of the noble William Marshall, whose loyalty to the Crown of England and the early Plantagenet kings was undisputed. He could do no better than to place his trust with the same faith as that knight, and adopt the chivalric creed of a man in whose spirit, by his own recent experiences, he seemed bound to.

Lying before them was the wide expanse of the outer ward. Beyond was the inner curtain wall, protected by a ditch, behind which arose the great crenellated tower of William Marshal's donjon. Archers were assembled along the walls and upon the very roof of the keep. Around the top of the donjon was a wooden *hourd*, an overhanging platform of wood, which had more archers. Robert was reminded that the Welsh longbow had been the principal offensive weapon of the English army for many years and was only now beginning to be superseded by guns. The longbow was still a formidable weapon and deadly in the strict confine of castle walls. No gunpowder weapon small enough to be hand-held could even approach the rate of fire of a Welsh archer and in any case, such guns required a wall hook – a protrusion that let them be placed against a wall to absorb the recoil. He wondered how many of the archers were actually Welsh, seeing as this was an English fortress? In any case, not all Welshmen had turned against their king. Robert supposed that some of those here were intimidated by the two traitors, one of whom, Jasper Tudor, had been until now earl of Pembroke. They had with them the remnants of their rebel Welsh, along with French and Breton mercenaries who could expect only death at the hands of the English.

The huge outer ward was crammed with wooden buildings, huts for the trades such as farrier and smith. Among these were the pavilions and tents of the rebel army. Fletchers were working on the manufacture of arrows while a number of servants were hurrying to and fro. A quartet of men-at-arms was practising at the pells, wooden posts set in the ground against which they were swinging their whalebone practice swords. There was a granary where the open door showed heaps of corn with barrels of apples, beet and turnips outside as if there had been difficulty cramming so much of nature's bounty inside. Against the walls were sheep pens, poultry enclosures and stabling for the horses. The smell of roasting meat drifted across the ward along with that of freshly baked bread. It seemed the harvest had been gathered before the castle was besieged and there would be enough here to sustain the garrison for most of the winter. The sight of all this, of course, was obviously for their benefit. Maybe the provisions were not as extensive as they appeared here, but it was clear the garrison would not starve for many months yet. The men outside the walls would not fare so well as those in the castle when the winter weather came. It was little wonder that Pembroke Castle was so powerful a stronghold.

Ostlers took care of the horses of viscount Lovell and his knights as they dismounted and a man dressed in the finery of a noble stood flanked by two fully harnessed halberdiers before the entrance to the gate into the upper ward. No doubt behind this edifice, the strongest part of the castle, was where the traitors Rhys-ap-Thomas and Jasper Tudor were hiding. Lord Francis, viscount Lovell was dressed in a deep blue mantle trimmed with sable over a houpelard of light green trimmed with gold embroidery around his neck. A chapeau of black adorned his head sporting a medallion of gold with a trio of pearls set into it. The hilts of his arming sword and dagger, which could be seen beneath the opening of his mantle, were richly encrusted with bright jewels. He wore gloves of the finest leather and embroidered with gold and silver thread with jewels stitched in here and there.

"Thomas Brandon!" spat viscount Lovell, as he recognised the man before him. His hatred for one of Henry Tudor's most fervent supporters caused him to momentarily forget the need for diplomacy. This man's brother William Brandon had been the Tudor's standard-bearer at Bosworth, struck down there by the war axe of King Richard himself. Brandon merely bowed his head acknowledging Lovell's presence. He was plainly dressed in a black leather doublet and brown woollen hose. Over he wore a tabard of green and white. Untidy brown hair showed protruding from a bonnet of green wool. He wore a short beard under a thin, hawk-like face. He too was armed with sword and dagger, though these were more businesslike in their plainness. "I see you still wear the Tudor colours," continued Lovell. "Suitable colours for your master, green and white, who is now a rotting corpse, drowned and sucked down somewhere beneath Cartmel sands."

A flicker of horror briefly showed itself in Brandon's face. He knew his master was dead but not, it seemed, the circumstances of his death.

"If you will follow me," he growled contemptuously, his small black eyes glittering with hatred. "You must leave your minions here and come alone."

"That I shall not," declared Lovell firmly. "I am here to parley with men whose word cannot be counted upon. I shall keep my men with me."

Brandon glared at them for a moment, though it seemed he was merely trying to intimidate rather than make a serious demand of them. He shrugged and tramped off into the ward beyond the inner gatehouse, his two men standing to one side while viscount Lovell and his entourage followed after.

Robert positioned himself behind Lovell and his three other esquires. He had been ordered to look for a way of getting among the castle retainers and for this reason he was not wearing the distinctive Norfolk livery and tabard. For that matter, the men with him were plainly clad too, so as not to cause him to stand out from the rest. The two men-at-arms with Brandon fell in behind making it impossible for him to drift away. They marched through the gatehouse where, just ahead through the gateway he could see the inner ward of the castle. To the right was the Great Tower. Brandon led them towards the wooden steps that led upwards to the entrance. Viscount Lovell commanded most of his men to wait at the foot of the stairs while he and his knights, and squires ascended.

The Great Donjon had five floors, though today they were in the lower hall. Behind the doorway was almost a corridor, so thick was the wall and Robert supposed they had been brought here so that the impregnability of the dungeon could be impressed upon Lovell's mind. A great fireplace was ablaze with heaped up logs, the flames of which illuminated the white plastered walls, traced in symmetrical lines to give the impression of ashlar stone cladding and decorated with a vine motif. The few windows were so far inside their tiny orifices that scant light managed its way through and candles were set in stands around the circular wall to provide decent light and, once again, demonstrate the castle's provision to withstand a long siege.

Two men easily identified by their haughty manner as the lords of the castle, stood behind a long table arranged across the front of the fireplace. Standing thus their faces were in part silhouette, giving them the advantage of not showing much facial expression but letting them have full sight of viscount Lovell. The table was laden with cakes and fruit, capons and haunches of meat. Goblets of gold were placed beside wine jugs of fine French pottery. Ranged either side of the two nobles were serving men and around the walls stood armed men in full harness.

One of the nobles was thick-set, clean shaven and bare-headed with long, dark brown hair, going thin on top. He was dressed in a scarlet tunic trimmed with sable, as viscount Lovell, thus proclaiming his rank. The other man, clad in mail as if he expected to fight, with a white surcoat over had a hard-bitten look about him. He wore a short beard and his dark hair was streaked with grey.

"Jasper Tudor," intoned viscount Lovell coldly. The man in scarlet bowed gracefully. The other, then, was Rhys ap Thomas. "I come to plead for your garrison which, I believe, has some men within that are loyal to their king. I do not believe you can remain in this place for long. Your fate is certain, but your men might escape the worst that the king's justice can do."

"Well, I have faced greater perils than the one I find myself in at the moment," replied Jasper arrogantly. "Here we are," he spread his arms wide and looked about him, a triumphant grin in his face. "We are well provisioned and armed. Dickon cannot get at us here without the expenditure of great time and cost. I expect your men to suffer much more than mine. Consider our walls – you will know, I think, that there are numerous garderobes in the walls and towers of Pembroke castle. That means we shall be shitting on those outside the walls to add to their own and breeding camp fever. Our granaries are full of wheat and barley and our larders crammed while you will find scant supply in the country around here. How many do you have keeping us here? Six thousand? I think Dickon will be more than pleased to deal with us once he realises the cost of trying to bring us to heel."

So that is the rebel plan, thought Robert as he listened to the scornful tones of Jasper Tudor. He was gambling on the tendency of King Richard to deal mercifully with his enemies. After Buckingham's rebellion there were few rebels executed and some, in particular Rhys ap Thomas, though admittedly not a participant in that fiasco, were given reward in the hope of keeping them loyal. A vacillating Lord Thomas Stanley had actually been promoted while his wife, Margaret, though attainted for treason, kept her head on her shoulders and her attainted holdings were gifted to her husband. It was now certain such strategy had failed and Robert wondered how the king would proceed from now on. Lord Stanley, he knew, was condemned at last to suffer a traitor's death and the king had awaited the capture of Henry Tudor and these two men to have them dealt with together as a spectacle. Henry Tudor had escaped his personal retribution, but these men could not be allowed to. If they got away, then not a single leader of the rebels, except Thomas Stanley, would have paid the price at law.

"You mistake the resolve of my king," replied Lovell. "He will have you brought before the people you have wronged and make you pay for your treachery. You, Jasper Tudor, are perhaps the less treasonable, being a declared enemy and in that at least honest, but you, Rhys ap Thomas, you must pay the full penalty." The man thus addressed bridled with indignation.

"Why must I be accused particularly; there were many more than me willing to bring down Dickon."

"That is not true," responded Lovell. "There were few that turned against the king, even here in Wales. You were appointed and paid by the king to defend this country from any pernicious invader landing in Wales. Most Welshmen remained loyal. Only you actually joined the Tudor invader. Let me see," mused Lovell, stroking his chin in contemplation. "You declared before the king that your conscience was your bond. I think I can remember your exact and personal words to King Richard: *Whoever ill affected to the state shall dare to land in those parts of Wales where I have any employment under your grace, must resolve with himself to make his entrance and irruption over my belly.* It seems that Henry Tudor did make his entrance over your belly when you lay upon your back and let him step over you. You betrayed your sworn oath to your anointed king and as such are a false and recreant knight who must suffer the full penalty for your most foul treason. Your king," he snarled, pointing an accusing finger, "set you up as the defender of Wales from a foreign invader and gave you sovereignty over the principality. In thanks for his munificence, you let in and joined the most pernicious of his foes. You are a disgrace to chivalry, and to your own countrymen."

Rhys ap Thomas grabbed for the hilt of his sword.

"That's it," snapped viscount Lovell. "Draw your sword and let us engage in combat here in the castle of your ignominy. I repeat, you are a false and recreant traitor and I claim the right to combat that I might beat you to the ground and then have you dragged in chains to London for the entertainment of the mob."

Jasper Tudor, alarm written large in his face clamped a hand over that of Rhys ap Thomas to prevent him drawing. Everyone else in the chamber, those in viscount Lovell's entourage and those about the walls were greatly agitated, hardly knowing how to respond. Francis Lovell had directly challenged a fellow knight, impugned his honour and dared him to fight in single combat to absolve himself, though that would be impossible as the charge of treason would still stand in spite of the outcome of the fight.

"I see there is nothing to be gained by speaking with you further," declared Jasper Tudor, clearly furious at Lovell's temerity in issuing a direct challenge. "You will return to your camp outside these walls and contemplate the ridiculous situation you find yourself in. Should you request a future parley it must be to discuss our safe passage out of here. There is nothing more to be said."

"The very air I breathe in this chamber is tainted with treason," snarled Lovell, matching Jasper Tudor's arrogance. "Take note," he shouted at the men about the walls. "Unless you deliver these two traitors into my hands then there will be no mercy shown to any of you. *They* might entertain hopes of exile – you have nowhere to run. Deliver these two traitors to me and you shall have safe passage back to your homes. See that you tell it to your fellows." With that he turned his back on the two traitors and swept from the chamber.

Having made his declaration of safe passage to the mercenary soldiers about the walls of the tower, viscount Lovell felt it prudent to get out of the castle before their lords realised the insidiousness of what had occurred. Not only the soldiers but certain castle servants too had been privy to the outburst. It was bound to provoke discord among the rebel soldiers in the garrison. Viscount Lovell drew Robert to his side.

"Try to remain behind and encourage the discord I have just sown. The mercenary troops might outnumber the English garrison, but if you can get enough of them to band together in the hope of redemption, then you have my authority to promise they will be proclaimed blameless once the two true traitors and their immediate officers are in chains." Lovell glared at Brandon, who was standing aloof at the door.

This was a dangerous game to play. Robert would be left behind with no defence and should he be unmasked as one of the king's spies, he could expect sudden death. He gazed up at the great tower, built by the man he had adopted as his spiritual mentor, William Marshall. Robert had listened to the challenge laid down by viscount Lovell and he thrilled with pride at its display of valorous chivalry. If Robert de la Halle could find a way of delivering to the king his most treasonable enemies, he would do it.

Viscount Lovell gathered his men together and marched them towards the gate of the inner bailey. Robert considered that he might break away here, as they went through the gate itself. He nudged the esquire in front of him and whispered discreetly.

"As you leave the inner ward, pretend to stumble so as to confuse our progress. I shall try to slip away." The man nodded, having been told of Robert's task. Fortunately, there was a small step at the gate, which let the esquire convincingly stumble and grab hold of his fellows for support. This caused the others in Lovell's entourage to walk into them. There was a lot of loud cursing and in the confusion, Robert, hardly daring to look around, slipped to one side and walked casually along the side of the wall into the outer ward of the castle. He hoped to be taken for one of the castle inhabitants, of which there were several in the vicinity of the gate though if he were spotted he could easily retake his place in Lovell's entourage.

His luck held and soon he was threading his way between the huts of the tradesmen, trying to look as if he belonged there. Normally such an enterprise would fail miserably as everyone in the closeness of a castle would be familiar with the sight of each other; however, viscount Lovell believed that the castle was inhabited not just with English and Welsh soldiers of the garrison, but foreign mercenaries come from the battle, a confusion of men who were unknown to each other. He might not be readily challenged. Robert spoke French, of course, and his father had insisted on him speaking Breton. Hopefully he might find enough loyal men to capture a sally port, or even better the gatehouse and let the besiegers into the castle that way. It was a mad idea but he was fired up by Lovell's magnificent display.

The portcullis at the main gatehouse rumbled shut again, sealing him in the castle while Lovell rode back into the town. He began to look around, watching for any curious man-at-arms or castle servant. All seemed morose in their attitudes. He noticed with some surprise that the archers along the walls had no arrows for their bows. Those behind the walls of the inner ward certainly had. Normally arrows would be supplied in barrels at intervals along the walls with each man having a quiver for his own use, but in the outer ward there was not a single arrow nor quiver in sight. Alerted to this curiosity he examined more closely the castle soldiers and though the ones who by their dress were mercenaries were armed, the rest seemed not to be. Along the walls of the outer ward, on the town side, the bowmen were being watched by armed knights dispersed between every ten or so. It seemed the garrison was not entirely trusted to be on the side of the present occupying lords. The men in the inner ward were clearly watchful of the rest in the outer ward.

He came upon a trio of mercenaries who, by their accents, were French. They were casting dice on a wooden table outside their pavilion. Robert decided it might be a good idea to join them. He would address them in Breton to confuse them, then he would change to French. In that way any deficiency in his accent might be overlooked. He would reverse the same tactic if approached by a Breton. He stood by as if taking an interest in their play. One of the men noticed him and immediately his gaze took in the purse at his belt.

"*Voulez-vous jouer au meurt avec nous?*" he said shrewdly.

"Oh, I do not play," responded Robert in Breton. In fact he did play, along with the other squires in the household of the earl of Surrey, but confident in the duplicity of the average mercenary he assumed an attitude of youthful inexperience.

"*Breton, êtes-vous?*" The Frenchman looked appraisingly at the youth before him and sniffed out a profit.

"*Oui,*" replied Robert switching to French.

"*Se il vous plaît, je vais vous montrer comment gagner.*" He pushed at the other two to make a space. Robert realised the man's offer to teach him how to win at dice might be disingenuous, but it allowed him entry to their company and thus able to explore their attitude to the siege. It also prevented him standing out like a sore thumb amongst the others in the castle.

They cast dice for a few times and, as he expected, Robert won the first few throws. He used the exuberance this generated to chatter excitedly.

"I only hope I shall have the chance to spend my winnings," he tried.

"To be sure," replied his new friend. "There is not much chance of a good spend while we are trapped here." He looked across to one of his companions whose eyes betrayed nothing but Robert lost the next throw.

"Think you there is a way out of here where we might keep our throats from being cut?" asked Robert with feigned apprehension.

"We must trust to the great lords," replied the Frenchman while watching another of his companions as he shook the dice.

"I heard that l'Anglais who has just been in parley has promised a pardon if the garrison hand over our two lords," muttered Robert. "For myself, I care not if that were to happen. I hold as much loyalty to them as they do to me."

The Frenchman looked at him with amused interest while sweeping coins from the table into his hand. "Where in Brittany do you come from?" he asked with no particular curiosity.

"Vannes," replied Robert. Though he had never been there, only ever having travelled with his father to Nantes where his family resided, yet he thought that the Frenchman would be more impressed by someone coming from the capital of Brittany.

"You Bretons have as much love for the English as we French and you are correct. We stand in great jeopardy, but for the moment we are well provisioned and safer than trying to get over the narrow seas with an English fleet in the offing. Come the spring things might change but as an old soldier I understand the benefit of a full belly and shelter over a risky enterprise."

"You are content to maintain the siege, then?"

"Of course. Who knows, our lords might yet extricate us. It is an expensive business laying siege and the English King will want to resolve it."

Obviously this was the message their captains had proclaimed amongst the mercenary soldiers, who were a tough lot used to living from day-to-day and content providing they were well accommodated and fed.

"And you think our lords will resolve it to include our rescue? I might be a youth, but even my limited experience of noble lords does not convince me we shall prosper in what is, after all, a lost cause."

The Frenchman leaned back and regarded him with something of suspicion. "You either have a surprisingly wise head on your shoulders for one of your years, or you have been primed to spout that doctrine," he growled. "Have you been talking to Henri Vasson? He is one of your lot and will be hanged ere the spring if he cannot keep his opinions to himself."

Robert felt a thrill of excitement. Here was the name of someone inside the castle who was less than convinced of the chances that mercenary soldiers might survive the eventual outcome of the siege. "Henri Vasson has a point," he responded, eager to find out more and tacitly confessing to knowing who he was. "He has no reason to trust to the word of our lords, nor have any of you."

"You speak aright," replied the Frenchman, "but you also speak sedition and there are many months between now and the spring. If you want to survive them and escape a hanging, I recommend you keep closer control of your tongue, and that, my young friend, is truly wise advice."

Robert decided it was time to leave this group and opened his purse to stare into it with disappointment. "I have no more coin," he sighed.

"Then you have learned another lesson, my friend. Make sure

you know who you are engaging with before hazarding your fortune – or your life."

Robert wandered off and tried to appear as if he belonged to one of the disparate groups of soldiery that had run there for refuge after the battle. He would have to find a way of attaching himself to one of these - not a simple task. It was all very well moving among them in the overcrowded outer ward of the castle for the moment as most were strangers to each other, but when it came to taking meals, or finding sleeping accommodation, then all would be in their strict order from which he, as an alien would be excluded and thus exposed. He took himself back towards the gatehouse. This was where the bulk of the mercenary soldiers seemed to be. Looking up at its massive bastions, two great turrets flanking the great gate, his heart sank. The inner portcullis was down and the gate closed. Beyond that, he knew was another similar arrangement. He decided that the possibility of getting both gates open and the portcullis raised was too great a task. The men around here were all armed and looked as if they meant business. Those most committed to the Lancastrian cause, and therefore certain to meet death at the hands of the king's army, were the ones who congregated here.

He turned to his left and followed the wall of the outer ward until he came to St. Anne's bastion beyond which was the river. Earl Thomas, who knew something of the layout of this castle, had informed him that this edifice contained a sally port, a gateway from which the garrison could emerge to attack the besiegers before retiring back into the safety of the castle. It was heavily fortified on the outside, but less intimidating from this side, which though it may well be a false hope, encouraged him to have a closer look. If a sally port let men out, it could also be used to get men in providing there were those in the castle willing to open to them. If only he could find this Henri Vasson and sound him out.

Suddenly he found himself taken either side by a pair of tough soldiers and bustled through a doorway of what seemed to be a farriers' workshop. There was an iron anvil by a cold furnace and barrels of horseshoes. Two pairs of hard hands gripping his arms, made it impossible for him to draw neither sword nor dagger. He was thrust forward to where three figures stood in the shadows, the shutters of the building being closed. Just a few slats of weak sunlight filtered through the slim openings in the upper walls where normally smoke and furnace fumes would get out. He was forced to his knees and his arms were released followed by a rasp of steel as the men behind him drew their daggers. He felt the prick of a dagger point behind his left ear and froze, hardly daring to move.

"Let us have no sound from you, my young friend, if you value your life." The English voice came from the larger of the figures in front of him.

"You may stand once you are calm." This from another who spoke in English tinged with a heavy French accent.

He felt the point of cold steel disappear from behind his ear and cautiously got to his feet. His mind was in turmoil. He couldn't make out the figures in front of him and had not yet had sight of the two behind. It was obvious he was in the presence of hard soldiers but were they of the garrison, or mercenaries?

"What are you?" he asked, getting to his feet and mustering as much confidence as his nerve would permit.

"More to the point, my friend – what are you?"

Robert was stupefied for a moment. How should he reply? Should he claim to be of the mercenary army or one of the English. He might defy them and claim to be a squire of earl Thomas Howard and a representative of viscount Lovell. Which of these would find favour and which lead to his death?

"The lad seems confused," continued the voice. "Did you beat him about the pate to addle his wits?"

"No – we were most tender," came the gruff reply from one of those behind him.

"Then let me help you out of your confusion," came the first voice. "You entered the castle, we believe, in the company of the lord viscount Lovell. We didn't notice you at first but when the viscount left I saw you sneak away. You were lucky then. I had you followed and if you had not sat down with those Frenchmen to play dice, then you would have soon been taken as a spy. That was a clever move I must admit, but it only put off your inevitable capture, as you can see. Fortunately, your game-playing gave us time to do something and so we got you out of sight before you could further advertise your presence."

Robert, feeling he was in friendly company began to relax. He permitted himself a feeling of annoyance that he had so easily been detected in the castle, though his heart would not let him quite believe he had been as transparent as this man was making out. Obviously these men were not loyal Lancastrians otherwise he would now be arraigned as a spy with all that such an arrest would entail – torture and eventual death. The surroundings and the manner of these men indicated more of a conspiracy than an arrest.

"I am Robert de la Halle, squire to the earl of Surrey," he decided to inform them. "I am here deliberately to discover the exact state of the garrison. My lords Surrey, Lovell and Sir William

Stanley are aware there must be some men here loyal to the king, but how many? I take it you are among them?" He sensed the men there stiffen and for a moment there was silence.

"Give me some light," said the leading voice at last. "Our thoughts are dark enough. Let us at least have proper sight of each other."

Someone uncovered a dark lantern, which relieved the gloom to reveal the gathering. Of the three figures before him, two were clearly soldiers though dressed in plain brown doublet and hose. Robert stifled a gasp of surprise as he looked upon the third figure, plainly that of a woman and a very attractive one at that. Then, as was the way with youth, his interest was further provoked as he identified the fact that she was young, a maid similar in age to himself. Small and neat, she too was plainly dressed in a white dress covered by a light blue cloak. A white coif covered her hair, which he could see was fair though, in the poor light of the lantern, he could not discern the colour of her eyes. She regarded him with the same curiosity as he did her, boldly appraising him and taking advantage of his subjective position rather than feign the demureness that protocol demanded. The two men behind him moved away and leaned against the wall, watching him with something akin to amusement at their lips. They were soldiers too and Robert noticed that though all the men had belts around their waists, they had only a short dagger apiece - the place where a swords scabbard should hang being vacant.

"I am Sir Hugo Fishacre," said the larger of the two, the Englishman by his accent, "Master at Arms. This is Henri Vasson." If the light had been better, they would have noticed Robert's eyes widen in recognition, but as it was, they seemed not to notice his familiarity with the name. Vasson gave a slight inclination of his head. "And this is lady Alice de Lucy, daughter of Sir Hubert de Lucy, castellan here at Pembroke."

The castellan would be the main authority when the lord, earl William was absent. Robert swept the girl a gallant bow to which she responded with a half-curtsey. Wrenching his attention from the girl he faced Sir Hugo.

"I am at a loss, sir, to understand what is going on here. There are archers on the walls with no arrows for their bows and men-at-arms with no arms, except a few who seem to be in charge."

"You are correct in your observations, young sir," replied Sir Hugo. "The men on the walls are for show and were forced to display themselves there. The actual numbers of bowmen is scant. There may be eighty or so crossbowmen with the mercenaries," Sir

Hugo looked to Henri who nodded in agreement. "The Welsh bowmen originally with the earl of Richmond deserted and returned to their homes before the traitors arrived here. Perhaps I should explain what exactly happened to bring about this unfortunate situation."

"Yes, I believe my lord the earl of Surrey will be glad to hear it. It is ignominious that the Tudor rebels should hold an English castle. His grace the king is furious and finds it an acute embarrassment."

"Which is why the traitors believe he might let them negotiate their way into exile."

"That, I think you will find is impossible," responded Robert.

"Yes, I think so too," agreed Sir Hugo. "The whole purpose of the recent battle was to rid the land of the Tudor threat once and for all. Henry Tudor may have gone, but the few remaining traitors here will not be permitted to escape the king's justice."

"So far as we know, the lady Margaret Stanley is somewhere in France," said Robert. "If the traitors get to her they will soon be about fomenting further plots. We chased her as far as the Pile of Foundray from where she and a few of the Tudor and Stanley retinue took ship. Nothing more is known, though it will not be long before the king's spies in France and Brittany get to know her whereabouts."

Sir Hugo motioned to the two men at the wall to bring out a stool and arrange a few boxes and barrels to serve for seating. Lady Alice was offered the stool, which she promptly sat upon while the rest of them sat in a tight group, the lantern on the anvil in the centre. He placed a man near the door to keep watch, then once they were settled began the story of how the castle was so easily taken.

"Our best English men-at-arms had been ordered by earl William to join with the king's army leaving but a few behind and the castle servants. We retained enough bowmen and gunners to defend the castle along with some mounted men. It was known that Rhys ap Thomas had raised an army but he did that, so we knew, on the authority of the king. Word came to us that the battle had been won by King Richard but the detail was lacking. So it was, that when Rhys ap Thomas turned up at Pembroke with a retinue of armed men we believed he was here as King Richard's Commissioner of Justice in Wales, the position to which the king had appointed him. That he had turned his coat and joined with the Tudor we had no idea. Perhaps we should have been more circumspect seeing as how everyone knew the king had demanded ap Thomas send his son to the Court to guarantee his loyalty, and he had refused to do so, but that is seeing things after the event. As it was, we believed he had the king's authority to enter the castle. It was only then we discovered who the men with him were, Jasper Tudor and a few other English traitors being amongst them. By then it was too late. They moved against us at both gatehouses and took hostage Sir Hubert de Lucy, his wife and the lady Alice here, his daughter. Next they disarmed the garrison and locked away all weapons other than their own. I shall ask the lady Alice to tell you the rest. She knows from her father better than I what the Tudor plans are."

That suited Robert very well indeed. It gave him a genuine excuse to turn all his attention on the lady. He had been listening to Sir Hugo's narrative with interest but all the while the quiet presence of the girl had been drawing his mind as if it were a lodestone seeking the north star. He found he had to swallow hard before he could address her.

"My lady?" was all he managed to say as she turned her eyes upon him. They shone in the reflected light of the lantern and the shadows that played on her face gave her an aura of surreal beauty. As with most young men who were wakening to the charms of female kind, until then he had experienced such beauty only as a delightful residue after waking from a dream. Of course he had observed those beauties that could be seen around the Court and in the houses of the great lords where he had been in attendance upon his lord, the earl Thomas, but those creatures were distant and aloof, with whom he had no business. This girl, however, was here standing in great danger, vulnerable and in desperate need of rescue. He overlooked the fact that there were four other burly men in the place and no doubt her father's men too in the castle who were better placed than he to defend her. Everything he had been taught of the Chivalric code of arms burned within his breast, provoking a desire to serve this lady. How many times had he witnessed a knight at the joust tip his lance to receive a lady's favour and then present it back to her after he had vanquished his opponent, bringing her great honour. These ideas tumbled over in his mind and he had to force himself to concentrate on her words rather than a delicious movement of red lips and the tantalising flicking glimpse of a pink-tipped tongue as she spoke.

". . . so my father had no option than to capitulate."

"My lady," he forced out realising she was actually speaking to him. "I beg your pardon, I missed that."

She fixed her mouth in a straight line of annoyance. "I was saying that when Jasper Tudor pushed his way into our privy chambers with his men, my father had no option other than capitulate."

"Rest assured, he shall pay for that," he replied vehemently.

She sighed with exasperation.

"Perhaps he shall, but for now he has possession of our castle. If I might continue?"

Robert flushed and silently hoped his reddening features would not be noticed in the poor light of the lantern. He smiled weakly at her. She nodded; satisfied she had tamed him at least for the moment. "Rhys ap Thomas had succeeded in tricking his way into the castle. My father was furious, of course, but there was nothing he could do. He decided that the rebels would have to get away from England or be taken and he comforted himself with the belief that they would soon be away and he could organise a chase after them. As you might know, Henry Tudor landed just a few miles from here, at Milford Haven. We thought he might try to occupy this castle then, but he marched off, eager to engage with the king. King Richard, however, learning of this sent ships to patrol the seas about here in case further men came over from France. That is why they were convenient to seal off the exit to the sea from Pembroke while his pursuing army surrounded us on the land side. Thus, their hoped-for escape cut off, the siege began. The rebels forced our own men to populate the castle walls giving the impression the rebel band is actually larger than it is. They were unable to arm them, of course. Imagine having English bowmen on the walls where they could shoot down into the wards of the castle."

"What are the actual rebel numbers?" he managed to ask.

"My father thinks about two hundred and fifty. Too many for us to attack and overwhelm without weapons. There are but fifty men from the garrison and a few servants. When the traitors realised they were trapped here, they changed their strategy. They understand too well the cost of prosecuting a siege. The king would hardly trouble himself when it comes to destroying a castle in France, or anywhere out of England, but this one is important strategically and he would afterwards be faced with the cost of rebuilding it. Then there is the cost of maintaining for months ships and an army large enough to guarantee nobody will escape from here. Along with that comes the diplomatic problem. King Richard is presently negotiating a marriage contract with Princess Joanna of Portugal. Laying siege to one of England's strongest defensive castles hardly raises his personal status and could easily turn him into an object of jest among the monarchs of Europe and even his own nobles. When you think Henry Tudor, the principal in all this is dead and gone, then the idea that the traitors, as smaller fry, might persuade the king to let them go is seductive. It is really their only practical course - it might even turn out so."

Sir Hugo cut in: "It is too early to consider letting them go. The king will take a lot of persuasion and in the aftermath, if there are any more damaging plots coming from rebels in exile, then those who had advised to let them go would likely suffer for it."

"Well, the reciprocal of that is those who can manage to capture the rebels will be richly rewarded," put in Henri Vasson, speaking for the first time. "I know we Bretons have not always seen eye to eye with the English crown, but we are not deadly enemies either, as the French are."

"Typical mercenary thinking," intoned Sir Hugo, "always on the lookout for profit."

"That is so, Sir Hugo, but this business is already ripe for bargaining. We Bretons have our lives to lose if things go awry for us. It seems to me if we can get you out of this impasse there will be much advantage for us all. My men will be paid for their support and thus the enterprise recovered to profit while you will have the gratitude of your victorious king and no doubt rich reward."

"At the moment," gushed Robert, eager to impress the lady Alice, "I am the only one among the loyal English armed with a sword."

"You point being?" said Sir Hugo, his eyebrows raised and a smile at his lips.

"There must be a store of weapons somewhere," he said unabashed. "If we capture it and then distribute arms to master Henri's men, we can overwhelm the rebels."

"Except I have yet to convince my men that their best interests lie with King Richard. Mercenaries do not fare well when caught in a hostile land. Some of them will side with the rebels, seeing as they are the ones indebted to them. Who can say if King Richard will reward or hang them. Such things happen."

"You have the word of my lord the viscount Lovell that they will all be pardoned if they turn in the traitors," declared Robert.

"The word of lords are not to be trusted," snorted Henri Vasson.

Robert was outraged. "My lord Lovell stands next to the king and is a most valorous and chivalrous gentleman," he cried indignantly. "He told me personally that those in the garrison who turned in the traitors would have the king's pardon and be free to return to their homes."

"And was there any declaration of reward?" asked Henri.

"I presume . . ." began Robert.

"Do not presume, young sir. I have had years dealing with kings and nobles. Let me have guarantees of hard coin and sight of it before you presume anything."

"There is some value in what squire Robert is telling us, though," said Sir Hugo. "Suppose we spread a rumour among the mercenaries that Jasper Tudor and Rhys ap Thomas have a secret plan to escape. That would leave their followers trapped here and in desperate straits having nothing to bargain with."

"Yes," enthused Alice, clapping her hands. "Jasper Tudor escaped the last time he was besieged here. It should be a simple matter to recall that and let the rumour grow by itself."

"Then Lovell's offer of a pardon and a return home in exchange for the English traitors might appear their best option," mused Sir Hugo.

"But no other profit," grumbled Henri.

"Yet you will escape with your lives," replied Robert fiercely.

"No, Henri is correct," said Sir Hugo. "It might be better to get hold of the traitors first and then let the mercenary captains bargain their release with the English lords. That way those men can return home with something to show for their adventure. It is more likely they will fall in with our plan if they hear the chink of hard coin, as Henri says. We risk betrayal else."

"There is still the residue of the rebel English to be accounted for. They are too close to the Tudor to escape retribution," reasoned Henri. "I wouldn't reckon on the French contingent either, though if we can secure the English traitors they will probably fall in with us."

"So it will be the Breton men and our own castle guard," added Sir Hugo. "That should bring our strength up to around one hundred and fifty, more if the French join us. That still means we might have up to one hundred armed men to deal with and us English just with our daggers."

"My Bretons are armed, as are the French," growled Henri, "though they have crossbows and we do not. The armoury is locked and closely guarded by the English traitors but they are easily dealt with. We should be able to arm your men, Sir Hugo.

"I can get the castle servants busy spreading the rumour," said Alice. "My father and mother will be only too pleased to help in that."

"I have been wondering about them," said Robert. "Where exactly are they and how have you become separate?"

"Oh, they are held in the solar, a chamber off from the great hall. Strangely, Jasper let them use it."

"What is strange about that?" asked Robert. "Surely even Jasper Tudor would not lodge the castellan and his wife in a prison?"

"Oh, it is just that Jasper Tudor altered the solar chamber some years back for himself when he was earl of Pembroke. There is an oriel window in there ordered by him and a good fireplace. It is also right next to the dungeon tower, which I suppose is intended as a threat."

"Jasper Tudor gallantly let Alice free to serve the needs of her parents," said Sir Hugo. "He rightly figured that she would thus be some sort of surety for their good conduct. If they were to try anything to get free, Alice, their only daughter, would be alone and unprotected in a camp of lecherous mercenaries."

Robert looked at the girl and silently promised himself that he would protect her if anyone threatened to harm her.

"Yes and I must get back to them with their meal otherwise someone will come looking for me. I am expected at the bakery." With that she hurried to the door. The man standing guard there opened it a fraction and looked out. He gave her a nod and opened it just wide enough for her to get through. Robert's heart skipped a beat as she looked back just before the door closed. Was she taking a farewell glance at him as he was of her?

"You, squire Robert must remain here for the time being. These two," said Sir Hugo pointing to the two men, "are farriers and will keep prying eyes away, though you must get out of sight if anyone comes along."

6 – The Word of Chiron

"Shall we open the gates and let the king's army in?" cried Sir Hugo Fishacre above the tumult around the gatehouse of the upper ward of Pembroke Castle.

"No, not yet," replied Henri Vasson. "We must take the rebels first if we are to bargain for their ransom." He was hustling his men with ladders to scale the inner curtain wall, that being the quickest way of getting into the upper ward of the castle. The plan was for the French crossbowmen to keep the walls clear of archers while the Breton mercenaries scaled the ramparts. At the same time there would be an attack by the English contingent at the gatehouse. Though they would not have much in the way of ransom as the mercenaries expected, there was considerable credit in being involved in the taking of the traitors and thus absolving themselves regarding the loss of their castle in the first place.

Robert de la Halle wound the crannequin of his crossbow and, after detaching it, placed a quarrel ready for shooting. He was wearing a mail hauberk over an arming jack, or jupon, as some protection from arrows and attack by light arms but he would have been more comfortable clad in good steel. His own harness was outside the castle with the army of the king, whose captains and generals were still unaware that the English traitors were now under attack in the castle by their erstwhile allies. His only steel protection was on his head, a common chapel de fer borrowed from the castle armoury, as was the rest of his protection.

The scheme for sowing dissent amongst the mercenary army had worked better than he expected. A sniff of possible ransom did the trick with the mercenaries, along with the thought they could get out of here with a full skin and back to their homes before the winter set in. It was unfortunate that the traitors had got wind of it too and promptly shut themselves close in the upper bailey after killing anyone they thought not entirely to be trusted. Even worse, so far as Robert was concerned - they had the castellan, his wife and daughter shut in with them. There were probably a hundred or so armed men left to deal with.

It had been easy to overcome the guards in the outer gatehouse and break open the armoury in there to rearm the English soldiers of the garrison. Next they captured and killed those mercenaries on the walls set there to deceive the town and rearmed the English sentries. Henri Vasson and Sir Hugo Fishacre had taken command of the mercenaries and the English garrison men respectively. Most of the Pembroke men-at-arms had gone off to fight for the king and had not yet returned, being with the king's army surrounding the castle. Sir Hugo was a minor noble and aged, around sixty but still retained his fighting spirit.

"We might turn the castle cannon on the gatehouse," suggested Henri, who was keen to bring the situation to a swift close.

"Premature," responded Sir Hugo. "If we can capture the walls we might be able to cut off the traitors before they shut themselves into the donjon. If we bring down the gates, that is almost certainly what they will do."

Robert knew what the knight meant. They had discussed strategy and Sir Hugo reckoned the traitors would man the walls to keep the mercenary army out and try to hold the upper ward of the castle. Mewing themselves up in the donjon would render them inaccessible certainly, but they would be unable to get out too. It was considered the traitors, Jasper Tudor, Rhys ap Thomas, Brandon and perhaps a few others might, out of desperation, harbour ideas for some sort of escape bid and once in the donjon that would be impossible. In there they would be virtual prisoners and eventually starve to death while little more than a few men on guard could prevent them getting out. The donjon was impregnable but only of practical use where there was the possibility of an army coming to relieve it. If the traitors shut themselves in there, the king simply had to wait while destitution forced their surrender. So it was that both sides were anxious for a quick resolution.

Robert was in agony of mind. The lady Alice was behind those walls and if she was taken into the donjon with the traitors, could not possibly escape starvation with them. On the other hand the traitors were hardened soldiers and ruthless Lancastrians whose cause was lost; leaving her and her parents free was unlikely. In the donjon they would be three more mouths to feed and as such it would be better practice to slit their throats as a last defiant gesture. His heart would have him first on the scaling ladders, fighting his way over the walls and into the upper ward where he would find the lady and strike down anyone who got in his way. Fortunately his head was still in command and he had heard that scaling castle walls was an efficient way to get killed and if he died who would save the lady then? Better leave it to men whose business was war and who had done it before. These were not his soldiers and he had no obligation as a squire at arms to lead them. Nevertheless, let a portion of the wall be captured, be it ever so slight and he would climb up there.

119

Sir Hugo waved the crossbows forward and Robert attached himself to the right flank. They were mostly French and of dubious individual accuracy but hopefully concentrated numbers of crossbow quarrels at one spot would clear the wall there. One of the farriers that had covered for him earlier was to act as his pavis bearer. A pavis was a heavy wooden shield large enough to provide cover for two men, one a crossbowman, who would step from behind it to fire his weapon. This was necessary because he would be well in range of the archers on the castle ramparts and if they were longbow men, their rate of shooting would spell doom for anyone not thus protected. His own weapon was a powerful match for the longbow, whose penetrating power was legendary, but the crossbow required a mechanical wind mechanism, a crannequin, to draw the steel prod. He would duck behind the pavis to do this. Robert was an above average shot with the crossbow and he expected to choose and hit his target rather than fire into a random group.

They had not advanced more than a few paces when the first arrows thumped into their protective pavisade. Keeping behind the pavisade made by closing next to those of the other crossbow men, he looked to where the Bretons were running with the scaling ladders. They had pavises too, smaller ones that gave limited protection and the hail of arrows from the defenders switched to them. This gave the crossbows an opportunity. Half their number stepped from behind their pavisade and loosed off at the men on the walls. This caused a confusion of arrows, some directed at the crossbows and others at the Bretons. Next, while the first men wound up their weapons, the second half of crossbows shot at the defenders adding to their discomfiture. Robert had held his fire, waiting for an appropriate target and soon one presented itself. A bowman stood with the intention of shooting into the mass of Bretons who were struggling to get their ladders up against the walls. He aimed carefully and snapped off a shot, hitting his mark just as the man let fly sufficient to deflect his aim and letting his arrow fly harmlessly away as Robert's missile struck him through his temples. The fire of the bowmen on the walls at this point slackened. There could not have been many of them anyway as the few defenders were spread out thinly along the castle walls.

Now the first ladders were in place and men were already scurrying up like beetles, mounting quickly before the defenders above could recover. The crossbow men as a body loosed a volley at the defenders just visible on crenellated walls as the first of the Bretons reached the top. It was impossible to shoot in support of them at the point of entry where they were being attacked by the defenders, but they might stop reinforcements reaching them. Robert heard the screams of those who had failed to get over the walls and tumbled down to break their bones on the stones below. He could see where the defenders were hurling rocks down upon the climbers. He saw one giant of a man with a great boulder raised above his head about to hurl it down on the ladder men. Instinctively he loosed his next shot and took the man in the chest. The fellow stood there poised for a moment, as if wondering whether to continue with the business or not, then the rock fell upon his own head before he crashed down behind the wall. Soon more men were pouring over the walls, a portion of which had been cleared of defenders and Robert, sighting on a bowman further along who was persisting in firing upon the mounting Bretons, shot him down. It was time, he decided, to get up there himself. He could do no more here and the lady Alice was on the other side of the wall.

He threw down his crossbow and slackening his sword in its scabbard, ran towards the nearest of the ladders. In all his life, Robert would never again be as afraid as he was climbing that ladder. What were they doing coming up behind him and cutting off his retreat? It was filled top to bottom with men and it bent and trembled ominously as he made his way upward. About half way he felt his courage deserting him. Would it be pushed away from the walls and send them all tumbling to their deaths? Would it slip sideways; would stone missiles or arrows pluck him from his precarious hold? With this weight of men it might snap in two plunging them all down, never to rise again. He had looked down many times from high castle walls, but never imagined himself on a precarious ladder full of men and under attack. Never had castle walls seemed so lofty as these at Pembroke. Let a fully armed man come at him with sword or lance. At least he could defend himself but here, halfway he felt between heaven and hell, there was nothing he could do for himself. Once he had seen a wall painting in a church depicting Hell where men were mounting a long ladder to heaven and where foul demons were pulling them off to be tossed down into the flames below. He could not climb down because of those below and those above seemed to him reluctant to get off the ladder. A man fell past, tumbling over and over. Apparently there were still defenders fighting up there. Looking above, he could see nothing other than the legs and arse of the man immediately above him and he seemed to have shit himself.

It was almost like standing beneath a gallows where the executed felons in their last throes were evacuating their bowels.

As he managed to force himself to the top, the ladder at this point became slippery with a mixture of blood and God knows what else. He managed to scramble over the wall and immediately tripped to fall on his face. One of the previous climbers hauled him to his feet and before he could mumble his gratitude, the man was off along the walls. Robert drew his sword, more grateful than he could tell to be on solid stone, and set off along the wall. He had no idea where he was going or what lay in front of him, but whatever it was could not be so bad as climbing that ladder.

At first there seemed to be nobody on which he could exercise his martial skills. What defenders had been there were still on the ramparts, lying in their own blood, some wounded but most already beyond the troubles of this world. He was on the curtain wall by which stood the great donjon. He looked up at the *hourd*, the wooden platform erected to protrude from the ramparts of the tower. It was devoid of men, which was lucky as they were all sitting targets for archers up there. All the rebel soldiers must have been required to man the walls. Ahead, along the wall was the inner gatehouse, which would have a single entry door to let out onto the parapet. He couldn't see that far because of the press of men in front of him. They seemed to have stopped. Immediately he saw the danger. If they were held here for any length of time, the defenders might get archers up on the donjon tower and then things would get very nasty.

"Halberds!" came the cry somewhere ahead. Robert knew none of the mercenaries could scale the walls carrying halberds so this must mean the defenders were so armed. He forced his way through the press of men until he got himself somewhere near the men at the front. Sure enough, half-a-dozen halberdiers in harness held the space in front of the door to the gatehouse. The mercenaries, men who had scaled the walls, had only sword and dagger. The halberdiers were jabbing with their deadly points and threatening death by the razor sharp axe heads of their weapons. All the attackers could do was try to sweep them aside at each lunge, a difficult and dangerous task and already two were lying on the parapet bleeding their lives away. Robert realised that unless these were cleared very quickly, there would be archers above them and then all would be over here. He was similarly armed as the rest of the men, just sword and dagger. They might wait for the French crossbows to scale the walls. They could strap their weapons to their backs leaving both hands free as they scaled the wall, but just a few archers above in the tower could take them out too. He cursed himself for not thinking to do that with the weapon he had been too ready to throw down, but all his thoughts had been the knightly rescue of the Lady Alice where he would save her by his sword.

Suddenly it came to him how to break the impasse. "Here, take these stones," he called to the men nearest to him. At first he was met by scorn and a few blank looks until realisation dawned on them. All along the exposed parapet were collections of stones put there to hurl down on those trying to scale the walls. "Aim for their faces!" Soon a hail of stone missiles rained down upon the halberdiers. They had been fighting with visors raised for better vision and now they snapped them shut but not before one man retired screaming, his face a bloody mess where a stone had struck him. The deluge of stone checked them but the way into the gatehouse was still blocked.

"Their feet! Throw at their feet!" he cried. Though the rebels were well armoured they wore leather boots making their feet vulnerable. A huge Breton lumbered through, a great lump of rock raised above his head. He hurled this and struck the legs of a halberdier, crushing his feet and ankles. Unable to stand, and screaming in agony, his fellows tried to drag him away while his halberd clattered to the ground. Seeing his chance, Robert leapt forward and grabbed it. Two more rebel halberdiers were beaten back, injured by the very stones they had been wont to use on the attackers. As they advanced the men behind slit the throats of the injured enemy to prevent any chance of retaliation. With just two able men to deal with, Robert advanced with the captured halberd, lunging at the remaining rebels as they retreated towards the doorway at the end of the parapet. Right with him were two more Bretons both with captured halberds. The rebels, seeing the mass of determined attackers advancing upon them fled through the open door and attempted to close it. The door was of stout oak and would delay the attackers long enough for the rebels to get archers above them. Robert had been ready for this and stuck the head of his halberd into the doorjamb, preventing its closure. The men behind the door, realising the hopelessness of their position, turned and ran, skittering down the spiral stairs that served the upper part of the gatehouse, their weapons abandoned in flight.

Robert and the men with him found themselves in possession of the lifting mechanism for the portcullis and immediately set about raising it. The gates still provided an obstacle but if they could get down to clear the gatehouse of rebels and open the gates, the upper ward of the castle would then be theirs. There was but one way down from the chamber they were in via a tight spiral staircase. The castle had been deliberately built to hamper attackers and just one man at a time could make a way down and there were sure to be more halberds and possibly crossbows waiting at the bottom. Looking around the chamber, Robert spotted some coils of rope.

"Get those and follow me," he commanded. Though he was but a youth, the men, having no particular leader with them, automatically followed him. He had already proved his worth as a captain on the parapet. French crossbows were now coming up the ladders and looking for targets in the bailey below. "Watch for archers above," be called to their sergeant. Fortunately none had appeared so far. He tied a rope around one of the crenelles of the wall and flung the other end down into the bailey below.

"Do the same with the other rope," he ordered.

There were men-at-arms in the vicinity and Robert ordered the crossbows to cover them as they shinned down. Soon a small but growing group of mercenaries was assembled in the upper bailey with the castle chapel to their left and the great towering mass of the donjon to their right. He knew the chancery and the great hall was beyond the donjon and further round, the solar where he hoped to find the lady Alice. First, though, the gates must be opened.

A party of around twenty men-at-arms ran at them, hoping to prevent the gates being opened. Immediately the Bretons formed a wall to meet them and Robert, his sword at the ready, joined them. He had directed half of the men that had come down the ropes to take the gatehouse. This was a simple matter seeing that the edifice was constructed to prevent attack from the outside. Nevertheless, the defenders there were putting up a brave fight. Fortunately, those Robert and his men were engaging were yeomen, recruited originally under the Commission of Array of King Richard and who had mistakenly thrown in their lot with Henry Tudor. No doubt their liege lord had spun them a line promising great reward from a new Tudor king. Such promises were in tatters and these men, being traitors, would pay the same penalty as their lords. They had little option other than to fight for their lives, yet they lacked the power of those nobles trained for knighthood from youth. Indeed, Robert was one of these. First as a page then as a squire, he trained with his fellows every day, honing his combat skills and developing the muscle necessary to fight for long periods in full harness.

He could feel that power now, in the strength of his sword arm as he beat down the men before him and stabbing when he could with the dagger in his left hand. Yet a mere youth, he found himself a match for much older men. Time and again he would parry a blow then turn and thrust his sword under the guard of an opponent. Three men had already staggered back, wounded by his probing blade. This was his first taste of real combat, where the adversary was determined to kill. At the Battle of Bosworth he had been denied a place in the line of battle, being responsible for the care of spare horses and support for earl Thomas Howard. Here was a fight in earnest. Robert and his men were slowly forcing the attacking rebels back and he felt a flutter of triumph, which was just as suddenly deflated as he saw heavily harnessed knights armed with war axes, flails and maces stamping their way into the field. These were the nobles – Jasper Tudor, Thomas Brandon, Rhys ap Thomas and about twenty others. He knew in an instant he was no match for these men, nor were the Bretons with him. Once they came down on the lightly armed mercenaries a path would be cleared right through their ranks. It would be like scything corn, except Robert and his men were the corn.

He realised their only chance was for the men attacking the gatehouse to open a way where the bulk of the mercenaries could get into the upper bailey and come to their aid. The men with Robert, though seeing the formidable opposition the knights presented were not about to give up on the chance of ransom. Some of them had found halberds and about a dozen of them stood forward determined to stop the knights. Robert, realising his arming sword and dagger were useless against full armour looked desperately around for some other weapon. One of the wounded rebels was lying by the castle wall loosely gripping a gisarme, a weapon similar to a halberd but with a spear point and an axe head below having a spike behind it. It was a long-handled weapon meaning it could be wielded with great force while keeping out of the way of shorter weapons such as a war axe, or mace. A man could burst armour plate with those. Robert's mail and jupon would provide no protection at all. He beat aside with his sword the man's feeble attempts in stabbing at him and wrested the gisarme from his grip. Leaving the man lying weakly against the wall he returned to the fight with the armoured knights.

Already two of the halberdiers were down, one trying to crawl away having been struck by a mace and his shoulder smashed. The other was dead, his helmet cleaved through by a war axe. Robert knew he must not let a knight near enough to do the same to him. He advanced into the front rank and presented the head of the gisarme as he had been trained to do. It was no consolation that his instructors at Framlingham had always managed to get the better of him, but this was for real and the threat of death gave an added impetus coupled with a desire to prove his prowess when, providing he survived, the story was told to the lady Alice. As he pushed his way to the front line Sir Thomas Brandon immediately confronted him. He recognised the device embroidered on his surcoat, his family shield – a barry of argent and gules with a lion rampant in the centre. The lion had a black mullet at its shoulder. This was the man whose brother William had been the Tudor standard bearer at Bosworth, struck down to his death by King Richard.

Brandon came at him without hesitation as if he had recognised his youth and considered him easy prey. Robert was astonished by the weight of the attack. Brandon was wielding a morning star, a wooden shaft with a chain attached and a heavy spiked iron ball at the end. He was whirling it around his head ready to strike at his chosen victim's head. To discourage this, Robert jabbed at Brandon's legs, hoping to trip him. Brandon swung the morning star letting the chain wrap around the haft of the gisarme. This prevented him swinging it, but now Robert's weapon was hopelessly tangled. He felt the raw power of the knight as he hauled him towards him. Brandon's murderer, a long bladed dagger in his left hand would soon find its way into his unprotected face while his own dagger would hardly scratch at Brandon's harness. He let go of the gisarme and stepped back, realising his only chance was flight but loathe to run. The knight angrily shook the gisarme free and let it fall as, swinging the heavy spiked ball menacingly side to side, he stepped towards his victim. Robert drew his arming sword; far too light a weapon to defend against such an opponent. Perhaps he could dodge around until help came?

Suddenly Brandon stopped his advance. The mercenaries either side of Robert were stepping back in orderly retreat while the rebel knights stood still, their weapons hanging loosely by their sides. To his right he caught sight of men running into the field armed with crossbows. His heart leaped with relief as he realised the gates to the outer bailey were now open letting the French mercenaries sweep in. The English knights were helplessly exposed and even the best armour could not withstand penetration by crossbow bolts fired at the distance of a few yards. Robert could feel their dejection even though he had no sight of their faces, which were obscured by the visors of their helms. For them the realisation of defeat, the long adventure in the cause of the traitor Henry Tudor was finally finished. He wondered if they would make one last gallant charge. It would mean their deaths but at least they would go down fighting and retain some small amount of honour. Undoubtedly that is what they would have done had they been faced with knights of similar status, but to be shot down by common crossbowmen, French peasants at that, was something not to be endured. They would throw themselves on the mercy of the king and face whatever judgement he meted out with bravery and dignity.

A passage was cleared through the press of those men that Robert had been fighting alongside and Sir Hugo Fishacre strode through to confront the traitors.

"Throw down your arms, my lords," he commanded. "We shall send for the viscount Lovell to take you into his hands." The bailey became silent and even the cries of the wounded died away. A gust of wind swept a shower of fine drizzle across the field to wet the surcoats of the knights as if nature was contributing a comment of her own on the business. Then, one by one they let their weapons slip from their fingers and permitted themselves to be jostled by the men who took them in charge.

Robert immediately set off towards the solar where the lady Alice was imprisoned with her parents. He ran through the space between the great donjon and the chancery towards the entrance of the solar. He recognised the place by the protruding oriel window high in the wall. His heart skipped a beat as he saw a white face there, gazing out fearfully. If there had been guards on the door there were none there now. He almost wished there had been so he could engage them and thus rescue the lady Alice where she could witness his prowess. Pushing open the oak door, he looked upwards where a flight of steps led to the solar chamber. Taking the steps two at a time, he burst through the solar door, sword in hand ready to take on any remaining guard. His bravado almost cost him his life. A lady stood by a tapestry her hand to her mouth while in front of her on the floor lay a man, a common soldier by his garb, a pool of blood around his head. He felt himself seized from behind and his helmet ripped away. Then a strong grip took his hair and pulled his head back.

"No, Stop! Father. He is no enemy!" The cry came from the lady Alice who was somewhere behind him by the window. Robert felt the pressure of sharp steel at his throat, but the hand that held it remained still. It only needed a quick draw across to slit his throat from ear to ear. It seemed an eternity as the three of them stood there, frozen as in a tableau. "Release him, father," said Alice quietly. "He is the one I told you of, the squire to earl Thomas Howard."

He felt the iron grip relax and he stepped forward and turned to face the man who had held his life in his hands and had returned it to him. Sir Hubert de Lucy was a stout man with the thick upper torso of a fighting knight. He was about forty years old with long brown hair framing a fierce round face that sported a short beard and moustache. He was clad in a red linen doublet and black hose and armed with a short dagger. He held it now out from his body as he regarded the young man in front of him. Robert's rag-tag appearance did little to endear him to the knight.

"That was stupid of you," he growled. "Never barge into a chamber without making sure there is nobody behind the door. There is one who made the same mistake." He pointed to the man on the floor. "I have no idea if he is friend or foe, so I took no chances with him. Now tell me, what is happening outside?"

"We have taken the castle," cried Robert in delight, hoping to impress the lady Alice who, framed with the light of the window behind her, had taken on the aspect of a divine vision. "The traitors are taken prisoner and are to be delivered to my lord the viscount Lovell who commands the king's army."

"And has my lord Lovell himself not taken the castle?" said Sir Hubert incredulously.

"No, Sir Hubert. My lord offered in parley a free pardon to those who would hand the traitors over to him and that is what they have done. We have taken prisoner Jasper Tudor, Rhys ap Thomas and Thomas Brandon along with some others whose livery I do not recognise. Once their ransom is agreed the castle will be opened to the king's army."

"Will it indeed," mused Sir Hubert, sheathing his dagger.

"So our plan to trick the rebels into believing their leaders were planning to escape and leave them to their fate has worked?" lilted the lady Alice.

"It has, my lady," replied Robert. "But not without a hard fight. I had to scale the castle walls to get in then fight my way through to here." Alice gave a gasp and placed her hand over her mouth, her eyes wide and round with wonder.

"Then the ground outside will be littered with the dead and dying to indicate your progress," snorted Sir Hubert wryly.

"Well, most of the action was by the inner gatehouse," he replied somewhat abashed by Sir Hubert's casual tone.

"My lord, shall we get out of this place," interrupted Sir Hubert's lady. "I loved this chamber once, but now my only wish is never to enter it again." She walked over to stand by her daughter. Alice's mother was perhaps a little younger than her husband. Tall and elegant, she was clad in a gown of dark blue embroidered with floral devices in gold. Her skirt had a train but this was pinned up at her back, she having no women with her to take care of it and in any case it displayed a fine fur lining. She wore a hood on her head with a short cape dangling at the back and a turned-up front just revealing a jewelled under-cap over her scraped-back hair.

"Of course, but I think it would be better if you remain here for the time being," replied her husband sternly. "There might still be traitors lurking within the great hall and castle buildings. I shall set …?" He looked the young squire who was seemingly overawed by sight of his women folk – "your name sir?"

Robert was entranced by the appearance of the lady Alice, though had he been more cognisant of female fashion he would have noticed her mother kept the latest and richest fashion for herself while her daughter was dressed as if for the defunct court of King Edward the Fourth, dead these past two years. A hennin, wired and veiled topped a simple bonnet then set at the back of her head giving her an angelic aspect as the veil caught the light from the window. She wore a simple light-blue gown, almost off her shoulders where the low cut front was trimmed with dark fur, accenting the pale whiteness of her skin. Her hair was scraped back and her eyebrows plucked out of existence.

"Oh, Robert de la Halle, at your service." Tearing his gaze from the lady Alice, he remembered to make proper obeisance to the castellan.

"De la Halle – I seem to know that name. Is not your father the king's armourer?"

"He has the honour to be so, sire."

Sir Hubert regarded him coldly. "Then get you off and search out any traitors not yet accounted for then report to me. Is Sir Hugo still with us?"

"He is, Sir Hubert, and taking charge of the prisoners."

"Then I shall join him." With that he waited while the young squire gave the ladies and himself an elegant bow before standing beside the door for the squire to pass through.

Robert commandeered a few mercenaries and with them went through the castle buildings. The servants had taken refuge in the great hall and once assured there was no further danger, were soon about the business of putting the place back into order. One he was assured the castle was devoid of unaccounted for traitors he took the opportunity to return to the solar eager to conduct the lady Alice and her mother to their proper quarters in the mansion by the great hall. Lady Matilda, Alice's mother dismissed Robert as soon as her ladies came to her from the great hall and he had no option other than report to Sir Hubert and Sir Hugo as ordered.

"The chapel," cried Sir Hugo. "Put them in there for now. My lord Lovell will take charge of them presently." There were around eighty rebels left to secure, the rest being either dead or too badly injured to pose a threat. The chapel was beside the gatehouse and could hardly be fortified. The injured rebels were already in there. As for now the fight seemed to have gone out of the principal knights but there was always the chance they would make a break for freedom and placing them in the chapel was likely to get them thinking upon a forthcoming meeting with their God rather than thoughts of resistance.

While the designated guards were hustling the prisoners into the chapel, Sir Hugo looked around and, spying Robert, beckoned him over. "It is time you returned to your liege," Sir Hugo informed him. "Tell him we have the traitors safe and that the mercenaries wish to discuss ransom with my lord Lovell. You know the tale well enough."

"Yes," cut in a new voice. Henri Vasson guessed what instructions were being given to Robert and was keen to make sure it was the right set. "Tell my lord Lovell that we wish to discuss ransom and upon a satisfactory conclusion shall deliver the English traitors into his hands. My men have saved King Richard much time, effort and money. In return, and as already promised, it is only fair they leave here with safe conduct and purses filled with hard coin."

"Rest assured, I shall," said Robert enthusiastically. He had carried out his subversive task beyond what anyone might have hoped for and looked forward to obtaining the recognition and credit he deserved for his contribution. Afterwards he would seek out the lady Alice and boast of his achievement, maybe even win her heart. Her father stood quietly to one side, content to let Sir Hugo dispose of the prisoners and patiently awaiting the arrival of viscount Lovell.

* * *

"Get yourself swilled down and into proper harness," commanded earl Thomas. "I know a man-at-arms is not thought to have performed well unless his horse smells sweeter than he, but now the bulk of the fighting is over I want those close to me without offence to my nostrils."

Robert had astounded earl Thomas and the commanders of the king's army with the news the traitors were taken prisoner. The best they had hoped for was information on numbers so they could work out where best to storm the walls. He explained the expectation for ransom of the mercenaries, most of whom had done the fighting. Viscount Lovell merely nodded at this and then volubly commended Robert on the success of his mission. He would be specially mentioned to the king who, no doubt, would want to reward him. Robert felt a frisson of pleasure at this, failing to notice neither viscount Lovell, nor his own liege, earl Thomas, were making promises of reward from their own purses. Earl Thomas in particular was certain to have the right of succession to his father's title confirmed by the king, making him the second duke of Norfolk. Sir William Stanley took the news as an excuse to leave now that his men were no longer needed to besiege the castle. He would find the king and get himself to the court, still uncertain as to King Richard's mind on his conduct before the Battle of Bosworth. All Robert's thoughts, however, were on this new capacity for boasting to the lady Alice de Lucy. Earl Thomas' command for freshness could only help matters in that respect. He could hardly wait to get into his harness and let her see him in his proper rig rather than the indifferent uniform he had been forced to wear in the castle.

Some little time later, Robert was rather disappointed when ordered to mount up and ride with the other squires behind their lords. They at least greeted him enthusiastically, eager to hear his story. John Biggar was with them and attached himself to Robert, seeing in his success the possibility of influential friendship. Robert had hoped to be permitted to enter the castle in the company of the earl of Surrey, but knightly protocol forbad that, and he had to be content with his position twenty or so behind the leaders. Still, at least he was horsed and not with the men-at-arms on foot. Resplendent in full harness, wearing the colours of the earl of Surrey and bearing a spear with Surrey's pennant at its tip, he entered once more Pembroke castle where the king's knights were assembling in front of the mercenary captains in the lower ward close to the inner gate house.

The remnants of the mercenary army were still in the upper ward where the traitors remained incarcerated in the chapel. Sir Hugo Fishacre was there with Sir Hubert de Lucy. Both were standing directly in front of the mercenaries. Henri Vasson, who had clearly been given the task of greeting and negotiating with the English lords, stood slightly to one side. All got uncomfortably to their knees as Lovell approached flanked by his standard bearers, the muddy ground being wet and glutinous. Behind him the English soldiers poured into the lower ward and spread out, some mounting the walls, others manning the gatehouse having had instructions to take full possession of the castle.

Robert looked about for the lady Alice but as the present business had nothing to do with the women of the castle, she, her mother and a few other ladies was well out of sight. Viscount Lovell, harnessed and mounted on a belligerent black courser that stamped impatiently and tossed its head, looked down and spoke directly to Sir Hubert de Lucy.

"You have your charge returned to you, Sir Hubert," intoned Lovell, "and in no less a condition than that in which it was taken from you, that is – undamaged."

"My lord!" the castellan responded angrily, scrambling unbidden to his feet. "The castle was taken by a subterfuge where lord Rhys ap Thomas, at the time as I thought the king's Commissioner of Justice in South Wales, pretended still to be the king's man. I had no authority to bar him, and no reason too either."

"As I understand it a subterfuge was the means whereby it was retaken," responded Lovell. "Perhaps our future wars may be fought entirely by prattling courtiers and dissemblers rather than with sword and fire. Most economic - there shall be no need then for castle walls, long marches and bloody battles. Should diplomacy be conducted on a chess board and the winning king be proclaimed victor?"

"It is fine for you to jest, my lord Lovell," spat the castellan furiously, his face reddening, "but so far as I can see the only fighting that has been done was by my men while you stood wonderingly beyond the walls." Viscount Lovell froze in his saddle, anger crinkling like splinters of ice in his blue eyes; their fair lashes blinking slowly as he struggled to contain his ire. After a few moments he relaxed and with some effort softened his features.

"You are insolent, Sir Hubert; yet I take your point and I am sure his grace the king shall give that due consideration when you stand before him to give your account. As for now there is some unfinished business here which needs our joint attention. You sir!" Lovell raised his right arm and pointed at Henri Vasson. "I think you command the mercenaries that captured this castle from the rightful occupants." Henri, seeing that Sir Hubert was standing also got to his feet. At this the rest of the men stood. If viscount Lovell was troubled by this discourtesy he declined to comment upon it, being content to fix Henri Vasson with a steely gaze.

"We acted according to the orders of our commanders, my lord. Had we been in your employ we would have done the same for you. As you see, we have saved you the trouble of a protracted siege and now make our obeisance to you and King Richard the Third of England."

Lovell gave a sardonic smile. "The moment that you set foot upon English soil you were under the rule of England's king and laws. By conspiring with traitors against our anointed king you, by default, commit treason. There is no difference between a foreign mercenary in this respect and any other felon that turns against his lawful monarch."

"My lord, that is unreasonable," cried Henri. "Your own king is not averse to using mercenaries – indeed, he is known to be willing to invade France, and even the duchy of Brittany now that the former treaty with his brother King Edward has lapsed. He will need mercenaries then."

"In that event they will, no doubt, be well paid for their service. Such mercenaries who enter the army of our king will have the same protection as the king's own soldiers; but you offered your services to Henry Tudor, a man who had no claim to the throne of England other than his personal ambition. He was a traitor even before he left France along with those English who followed him. Consider the men in the army of Thomas Stanley, the Tudor's father-in-law. He ordered his men to fight on the Tudor side but they, being subjects of their true king, refused to do so. Had they done, merely being under the command of a peer of the realm would not have mitigated a charge of treason."

Henri Vasson began to look nervously about him. He could see where all this was going. Clearly the English lord was not going to offer a payment as reward for the capture of the English traitors without an argument. Nevertheless, Henri's habit as a mercenary was to ensure he was paid and all nobles were reluctant to part with hard coin. Probably this preamble was Lovell's way of conditioning him to expect less than his just desserts. Henri had to admit to himself he was in a bad bargaining position. His men still had the prisoners under guard and yet to be released into the charge of viscount Lovell. If this were a normal situation he could demand either ransom for the prisoners, or declare an intention of taking their lives. That worked only where the opposite side actually wanted them back alive, which was not necessarily the case here. His best hope was that King Richard would want them to stand public trial and their premature deaths would thwart that idea and maybe provoke the king's wrath. It was hardly a strong bargaining position but it was all he had.

"My lord Lovell," intoned Henri as magisterially as he could. "We already have your word that if we hand over the English traitors to you, then we would be free to go. Furthermore, there is the matter of ransom, according to the normal practice of war."

Lovell affected to look to his fellow lords with astonishment. "Ransom – I do not remember saying anything about ransom!"

"My lord," persisted Henri, "your representative, the young squire Robert de la Halle assured us . . ."

"My representative?" responded Lovell. "I would not send a mere squire as my representative - Earl Thomas!" Lovell turned and beckoned the earl forward. The earl nudged his courser into movement and came up beside Lovell. "I believe squire Robert de la Halle is one of yours?"

"Indeed, my lord," replied the earl. "He has conducted himself well in this present business."

"That may be so, yet it seems he has taken rather more upon himself than he is entitled. Bring him here."

Robert, who had been stretching his neck and watching the proceedings with viscount Lovell well out of earshot, felt his heart leap as earl Thomas sent word for him to come forward and join the great lords. His only disappointment was that the lady Alice was not there to witness the certain accolade he was about to have bestowed upon him. It seems he was to take part in the discussions for the release of the traitors, a great honour indeed.

"Dread Lords," he said, inclining his head and making obeisance to viscount Lovell and earl Thomas. He drew himself up, sitting his horse proudly and displaying all the martial vigour he could muster.

"Earl Thomas," drawled Lovell, staring coldly into the eyes of Henri Vasson and ignoring the presence of the young squire. "Do you recall my mentioning anything about paying ransom for the traitors?"

"I do not, my lord," replied the earl.

"Well, they seem to have that impression. Have you any idea where that might have come from?"

"I have not, my lord."

"I am informed by this fellow here," Lovell pointed to Henri Vasson who was standing agape, "that your own squire had mentioned something that might have led the fellow astray in that regard."

Earl Thomas turned to face his squire. "Robert – can you enlighten us as to why our mercenary friend here might believe there is payment for ransom due him?"

Robert felt a tight knot gripping his vitals. He desperately began trying to recall what actually had taken place when he first encountered Henri Vasson. This was not what he expected at all.

"My lords . . ." he stammered. "As I remember, monsieur Vasson assumed there would be ransom and I did not disabuse him.

I reminded him of my lord Lovell's promise that he and his men would have free passage away from here should they hand over the traitors, but nothing more. It was Sir Hugo who suggested that we might secure the traitors first and then let the mercenaries bargain for ransom afterwards."

Sir Hugo glared at Robert then, clearly flustered addressed viscount Lovell.

"It was but a suggestion – I made no promise," spluttered Sir Hugo. "The situation was desperate and I spoke only what was necessary to take the castle."

Robert understood he had made a serious error in bringing Sir Hugo's name into it, but he had been confused by the sudden turn events had taken. Rather than bathing in the adulation of his betters as expected, he was in danger of being blamed for making promises he had not the rank for.

"Yes, yes, I understand, Sir Hugo," said Lovell, never taking his eyes from those of Henri Vasson.

"We have the traitors secure, my lord Lovell," he said. The Breton was beginning to look decidedly nervous and was striving valiantly to gain some measure of control. "We will slit their throats if there be no ransom."

Lovell smiled and lifted his gaze to study a group of men emerging from the gatehouse of the inner ward. Clearly being dragged along were the figures of Jasper Tudor, Rhys ap Thomas and Thomas Brandon. Behind them, roped together in a line were the rest of their men. All were being prodded and shoved by the French mercenaries, crossbowmen who had been relieved of their crossbows and were now lightly armed, but expectant of reward.

"Gather them together," commanded viscount Lovell. The traitors were herded into the centre of the lower ward. "Bring me Jasper Tudor, Rhys ap Thomas and Thomas Brandon." The three leaders were separated from the remnants of their men, dragged along and thrown down in front of Lovell. Robert found himself discomfited by this spectacle. These were great lords, men of long history and renown though they be traitors. All his life he had been in awe of men like these, tough fighting knights, valorous in combat and noble of aspect. They were the epitome of chivalry yet here they were, scrabbling in the mud inside the outer ward of Pembroke castle, trying vainly to recover some aspect of their rank while making obeisance to viscount Lovell, clearly in fear of their lives.

"Fear not, my lords," said Lovell imperiously. "Your time has not yet expired – as for your followers . . ." He raised his right arm and a hundred long-bowmen pushed their way forward through the ranks of the English soldiers. They notched their arrows and leaning into their bows, drew the strings back to their ears. Lovell dropped his arm and a hundred poplar shafts tipped with hardened iron bodkins penetrated deep into the flesh of the pathetic group huddled in the centre of the castle ward. Their screams endured for what seemed to Robert an eternity as shaft after shaft was released into their ranks until a squad of men rushed forward with knives to slit the throats of those still alive. The whole business had taken less than a minute.

A low hum of voices came from the French mercenaries who had herded the traitors. They realised no ransom could be paid on dead men. Not only that, but looking into the eyes of the English bowmen, they were their next target. As a mass they gave a great roar and charged at the bowmen. Few of them reached their ranks before being shot down. Seeing what had happened to the French men the Bretons charged at the English, furious at what they saw as betrayal. All knew they could expect nothing in the way of mercy at the hands of the English lords. Henri Vasson, his face twisted in a combination of rage and disgust was dragged away by a pair of men of the castle garrison.

"My lord," cried Robert in despair. "These men were fighting for us!" Whether he was calling out to earl Thomas of viscount Lovell he hardly cared, but the earl reached over and grabbed him by the arm, almost unhorsing him.

"Get you on foot and clear out this nest of vipers," he snarled. "There is Sir Hugo Fishacre – he knows what to do." Earl Thomas dismounted and waved his men forward." Sir Hugo was advancing on the Breton mercenaries with his own men, those of the Pembroke garrison. Earl Thomas' men formed up in line and joined the advance. Robert, along with John Biggar dismounted along with their lord and stood, as was their duty, by his side. Swords drawn and visors down, they advanced upon the mercenaries. For all their dissolute appearance, the French and Breton mercenaries were hard fighting men and they would not go down easily.

Soon Robert was in the thick of the fighting and there was nothing for it but to kill or be killed. Provoked and outraged, the mercenaries hurled themselves at the English with demonic fury. Robert sensed that even earl Thomas was shocked at the weight of their attack. To his horror, a huge man he thought he recognised as a former comrade among the mercenaries confronted Robert. That made him hesitate for a fraction of a second, which the man took immediate advantage of. He struck at his helm with an arming sword and had it not been for the superior steel crafted by his father, the king's own armourer, he must have fallen then. As it was the blow was deflected throwing the man off balance. He closed with his man and as he had been taught, stabbed with the dagger in his left hand into the armpit of his opponent, which was unprotected with mail. The man screamed out and Robert, stepping back thrust his sword into his open mouth. Wrenching the blade clear he attacked the next who came at him. This man was already wounded and to his later shame, he plunged his sword into him, hardly gaining glory from the death of an already dying man. The blood lust he had heard experienced soldiers speak of was upon him and he joined the deadly work of hacking down those who were now his enemies. Men armed merely with light swords and daggers could not match opponents clad in good harness. Soon there was no more coming at him. With grim surety, the superior numbers and protective armour of the English knights and men-at-arms took its toll of their opponents and soon the few that were left ran, only to be chased and cut down.

Robert, with John Biggar beside him, raised his visor and stood breathing hard in the midst of a bloody field. It was not the field of glory he had envisioned, but one of almost casual slaughter. These men who, a few hours ago he was conversing with companionably, were now lying in their own blood, ignominiously slain when they might have expected to earn a more gallant treatment. Overlying his horror at what had occurred was a feeling of disgrace, that the word of a chivalrous knight as viscount Lovell could be so lightly overturned. Whatever the rules of war might dictate, he felt the mercenaries had earned at least free passage back to their homes. John looked at him and he too had a look of horror in his eyes. Both young men were experiencing the real work of soldiers for the first time. Set battles were rare, but this sort of work only too common.

"I see your sword is properly bloodied," growled Sir Hugo as he rejoined the earl of Surrey and glowered at Robert, the youth who had given Lovell the idea he, Sir Hugo Fishacre, might have promised ransom. "That makes up for your earlier remarks about making promises to the king's enemies. Let it be a lesson to you. Had there been no mention of it then I believe the mercenaries might have got away with their lives."

Robert felt himself shrinking inside his harness. For one thing, Sir Hugo had been content to let the mercenaries think they might be paid. Had that not been the case then they would not have turned against the Tudor men and the castle would still be in a state of siege. What bothered Robert most was viscount Lovell's attitude and that of his own liege lord, the earl of Surrey. Surely a knight's word was bound up in personal honour and this wholly unnecessary slaughter had little to commend it in that respect.

Sir Hugo watched coldly, reading accurately these conflicting emotions as they chased across Robert's face. He noted also the dejection in the features of John Biggar and decided a lesson must be delivered. Reaching out and gripping Robert by the shoulders he gave him a shake and shoved his face close, his fierce visage glowering grimly. "These men," he said waving his sword arm at the bloody field, "would have met this very fate ere now had they been caught running from the battle at Bosworth Field. It was only the chance of holding out within these walls that put off the inevitable hour of their doom. They are invaders of the king's realm led not by a lawful monarch but a traitor lord of little account. No war had been declared. This was not an invasion by a sovereign power at odds with England where heralds make parley between the contenders and look to the niceties of chivalry; it was not even a rebellion, seeing as most of the king's subjects remained loyal. They were nothing more than pirates and outlaws without honour; therefore the rules of chivalry cannot apply to them. Those lords who might make claim to nobility, who have taken knightly vows only to betray them, are taken and will face the king's justice."

"I understand, Sir Hugo," muttered Robert, somewhat abashed and with John Biggar nodding vigorously too. Indeed he understood perfectly, yet unlike the English lords Robert had become personally familiar with some of these men and found them not so much different to Englishmen except for their language. No doubt Sir Hugo was correct so far as the personal honour of lords was concerned, but he was not ready yet to shake off that which had bound him in common humanity to men who had lives much as his own, with families who would never see them again.

"Look to your house, boy," said Sir Hugo pushing him away. The knight grabbed a fistful of Robert's torn surcoat. "See these colours – they represent your proper duty. I see they are torn. That is good. It shows you have been in a fight; continue to fight under your liege lord and leave matters of conscience to your betters." Sir Hugo released him at last and the squire made an attempt to stand erect to cover the dismay his spirit was suffering.

"Squires," called Thomas Howard, "You will attend upon me." The two youths hurried to stand before their liege lord with bowed heads. "Come, we are bound for the great hall. We shall celebrate tonight and on the morrow make for London and the king. Squire Robert - you have done well for a youth and his grace will hear of it."

Robert glowed with pride. It seemed he was not so badly thought on after all. With the exuberance of youth he felt his heart rise as he followed earl Thomas, and once in the great hall - the lady Alice was sure to be there.

They followed the earl through the inner gatehouse and turned left taking a path beyond the great donjon and towards a cluster of buildings over by the north wall of the castle. Robert decided to voice some of his concerns to John to test his opinion on the matter of chivalry, the minds of both youths being imbued with its more prosaic elements.

"I suppose it is as my father once explained it to me," said John. "He illustrated the principle with the story of how the Greek Achilles was educated."

"Yes," mused Robert. "Wasn't he sent by his father into the service of a centaur?" He seemed to remember his early schooling where Achilles' father, Peleus, brought his son to Chiron who accepted him as a scholar and fed him on the innards of lions, wild boar and the marrow-bones of she wolves. The symbolism came to him as if decreed by fate – the boar and the wolf.

"He was," replied John. "The centaur Chiron, half man, half beast – a horse to be precise. The tale serves to show us that man has two facets to his character: the nobility of humankind as bequeathed by the Lord God - but still dependent to some extent on the animal. Consider our present case where the word of a lord is taken, so you think, lightly. There are two ways of fighting – by law or by force. The first is, of course, to be preferred the second being the way of beasts. Where, however, the first becomes inadequate, and again I must state our present case, we must resort to the second. Thus a lord must display components of both man and beast otherwise he cannot function as a lord. If a lord honours his word such that it defeats his cause, then he is no ruler."

"But it is the blatant deceit that I cannot come to terms with," murmured Robert.

"Ah, but a capacity to be deceived is essential to the human condition," replied John with a chuckle, seeing his friend's discomfiture. "Holy Church is built upon such a rock."

"You speak blasphemy," gasped Robert, darting glances right and left to ensure nobody else was in earshot.

"You mistake me," returned John, seemingly unshaken by Robert's dramatic reaction. "I do not speak against Holy Church, but merely to make a theological point. The inherent truth of scripture cannot fail, but mankind, as we have noted, half divine, half beast is bound to have some failings – it is in our nature. Chiron is our tutor just as he was for Achilles; *his* teachings were not a deceit, merely a channel of a truth we cannot escape."

"You would have me believe the hand of God was in the action of lord Lovell when he commanded the destruction of those men back there?"

"In a way it was, such being the prerequisite of stern rule. Never forget, those men just killed will stand before their God with their own sins upon them. It is He who will pronounce upon them, the earthly lord who sent them hence having no further say in the matter."

In spite of his misgivings, Robert found some comfort in what John had just explained to him. He wondered how much of the beast was within his own breast and what portion belonged to God. Not much to God, he presumed as the great hall of Pembroke Castle loomed before them. The thought that the lady Alice was within suppressed his earlier concerns. His martial exploits would be most valuable when presenting himself before the lady, not the theological musings of a monk; indeed, monkish thoughts were the furthest from his mind as he entered the portal of the hall and saw at once the display of nobles arrayed on the dais at the far end. There, to one side, not where his heart would have her in the centre, stood the diminutive form of the lady Alice. He looked down at the torn surcoat and gave it a tug such that the rips and tears of the recent battle were displayed to their best advantage. He noted with satisfaction the few spots of blood that supplemented the bright colours of the Howard arms. Here was a knight returned to his lady, having valorously defeated those who had violated her castle home.

Viscount Lovell was already there with the castellan Sir Hubert and his wife, with Sir Hugo Fishacre by their side. The lady Alice was with the women attendant upon her mother. Earl Thomas approached the dais and made his obeisance to the viscount. Robert, John Biggar and the other squires stood behind their liege lord. Viscount Lovell indicated that the earl should join him on the dais. Presently, viscount Lovell, looking around settled his gaze upon Robert. Beckoning him forward, Robert knelt in front of the noble, his face raised to indicate lack of guile. Though he was looking intently upon his liege lord, his spirit was inclined to the place where the lady Alice stood as a vision of loveliness.

"Squire Robert de la Halle," began viscount Lovell. "You have served well during this business and it is our wish that you present yourself before his grace the king who will, no doubt, be highly entertained with the story of your exploits. You may rise."

Robert clattered to his feet as elegantly as his harness would permit.

"I have merely done my duty as a true liegeman, my lord," he responded formally.

"That may be true, squire Robert," said Lovell with a condescending smile. "Nevertheless, you have the gratitude of Sir Hubert de Lucy and his family whom you have helped deliver from a most embarrassing internment. In particular, the lady Alice has an especial reason to be grateful to you . . ." Roberts heart leapt within his chest, ". . . as does Sir Piers Pellingham, who now has his betrothed lady returned to him!"

7 – Trial and Retribution

"There is something wrong with the boy," grumbled Laurence the armourer to his father-in-law, the London apothecary Cornelius Quirke.

"Not entirely surprising, considering the events he has been involved in and the times we live in," replied the apothecary.

"Yes, I have accounted for that," responded Laurence, tugging pensively at his beard. "Perhaps it is just his age?"

The three were walking towards Guildhall to witness the trials of lord Thomas Stanley, Jasper Tudor, Rhys-ap-Thomas and Thomas Brandon. Robert was trailing disconsolately behind, which was what had provoked his father's remark. Having been granted leave by his liege lord, the earl of Surrey to attend upon his family in London, Robert should have been in high spirits. Surrey was fully engaged in the court proceedings and had no real need of his squire.

Before them was the ornate façade of London's *Hôtel de Ville*, completed forty years earlier in the reign of King Henry the Sixth. It was the place where not three years ago Henry Stafford, the duke of Buckingham had convened a meeting of London citizens to explain the bastardy of the children of King Edward the Fourth and his queen Elizabeth and thus established Richard of Gloucester's inherent right to the English throne. Buckingham soon proved himself a traitor and so King Richard considered it fitting Guildhall should be the place for the trials of what he hoped were the last of such men. They entered through the south porch where a central statue of Christ looked down flanked either side by two others, one a bishop and the other supposedly William the Conqueror. Four statues - female figures, two either side, flanked the porch - one Cornelius identified as an effigy of Queen Phillipa and another the Empress Maud, two women whose past intercessions had benefited the city. Fresh rushes covered the paving of purbeck stone and clear morning sunlight filtered through the windows, some of them blazoned in stained glass displaying the Whittington escutcheon.

Outside the hall the city landscape was bleak, written in black and white as the early snow of winter overlaid the rooftops. Where there were a few trees, snow teetered precariously on black leafless branches. It was sunlight reflecting off a recent thick fall of snow that provided the bright illumination. Inside, the hall was abuzz with conversation and alive with colour. Nobles, aldermen and merchants displayed themselves in the finest cloths and furs according to their rank. The rest of the commons crowded together at the back of the hall, each vying for position where they could see and hear. Robert stood with his father and grandfather in an alcove where they had a good view of the court. At the top end was a dais and chair set in crimson with the cloth of state hung above displaying the Royal Arms of England. Already black robed scribes with ink-stained fingers were sitting on their benches where on the tables before them was a litter of paper and parchment, ink pots, fresh quills and sharp knives for trimming them. Men-at-arms with halberds stood around the interior walls and grouped here and there further soldiers armed and ready should there be any outrage. Few there considered that possibility as the accused men were certainly guilty of treason, but these were unquiet times and men were still wary.

"This will be a short business, I think," said Laurence in Cornelius' ear. The apothecary gave a grunt and shook his head.

"Some think that lord Stanley might try to weasel his way out of the charge, he being the only one of them not actually having taken arms against the king."

"Yet there is the testimony of his captains who were ordered to advance in support of Tudor at Bosworth Field and refused to do so. On top of that there is the business with Catesby. He is already hanged and lucky not to have been quartered, the king being content to grant him an anonymous grave under the scaffold at Smithfield."

"Yes, there is no doubt lord Stanley's road has run out, though he might yet provide us with an entertainment - but you are right, the conviction for treason of William Catesby and lord Stanley's part in it has trampled on his grapes."

Cornelius, being one of King Richard's spymasters had known of Catesby's duplicity before the Field of Bosworth but kept silent then rather than disturb the king's mind before the battle. Laurence too had known of Catesby's treachery and had held his tongue for the same reason. Both remembered the fate of lord Hastings executed by the king for treason. His offence was that Hastings kept to himself knowledge of the Butler pre-contract, where King Edward had secretly contracted a marriage with one Lady Eleanor Butler thus rendering bigamous his subsequent marriage to Elizabeth Wydville. That effectively disqualified any children of the marriage from the succession. In keeping quiet lord Hastings had deprived King Richard his rightful claim to the throne. It was actually Catesby who disclosed the pre-contract to Richard who then called in a reluctant bishop Stillington, seeing it was he who had been its legal witness, to confirm it and thus Stillington became the public face of the business.

Catesby, though, having privately informed Richard of the contract beforehand absolved lord Thomas Stanley from any knowledge of it. That was why lord Stanley escaped Richard's retribution at the time while lord Hastings lost his head. In fact lord Stanley knew of it through Catesby's affiliation with lady Stanley. Her plans required the children of King Edward to be legitimate if her son Henry Tudor was to marry their sister Elizabeth of York. Any progeny from that union would be bastards else. Catesby, in protecting the secret along with the life of lord Stanley, had attempted to insure himself should the Tudor triumph over King Richard leading to the subsequent rise of the Stanley's, lady Margaret being then the new king's mother. He would call in the favour and ingratiate himself in what would be a new reign. As it turned out, Stanley duplicity failed, thanks to the refusal of his army to attack their king. Lord Stanley, in a fit of pique had testified from his prison cell to Catesby's treachery and King Richard, recalling and regretting his too-presumptive order to execute lord Hastings, turned in fury against the lawyer William Catesby who, until then, had been his chief councillor.

"I believe the king, in putting up the four traitors to stand together in one trial hopes to finish the Tudor cause quickly and put it behind him," said Laurence. "That is sensible; there is much to do. He has the arrival of a bride to look forward to and now the Tudor threat is removed the restitution of his surviving nephew, Richard of York, which disposes of the suspicion he murdered him."

"Yes, and the people are behind him, too," replied Cornelius. "I think the realisation that the common folk refused to support the Tudor has had a sobering affect upon him. The same cannot be said for his nobles. Although he has been king for less than three years, yet his new laws have found great favour among the people. It is the nobles who are complaining."

"Yes, Northumberland is under a cloud and Sir William Stanley has yet to gain any promise of reward," mused Laurence. "After this trial the demesnes of his brother will revert to the crown and into the king's gift. I doubt the king would have so powerful a magnate in the north-west again and those lands will most likely be broken up. Will he gift them to Sir William and expand his already extensive Cheshire holdings? I do not think so. Of course, the same goes for Northumberland – he will probably find his influence much reduced in the north-east and the king is already popular there. We stand in danger of more fighting as the nobles squabble over the spoils in the aftermath of the Tudor invasion."

"Not necessarily so," said Cornelius. "The king is thinking that the nobles cannot raise rebellion against him unless they have the will of their people, and recent events have shown the people favour the king. A few more judicious laws here and there will secure his popularity while stripping the nobility of their erstwhile influence."

"Yes, these are interesting times," agreed Laurence, "and look to it - I believe we are about to witness the ending of the old order and the start of a new one."

Both men turned their attention to a doorway at one side of the hall. The prisoners were being brought into the hall to face the king's justice. They had been allowed to present themselves in their best finery. It was perhaps King Richard's way of showing that his law extended to the highest in the land in letting them display thus. Had they been abject and stinking of the prison cell some might have had pity on them, but as it was the king could demonstrate how even the mightiest magnates could be brought before his court should they have the temerity to challenge his authority.

They had probably been manacled while waiting in the vault below Guildhall, but if so, these had been removed. Lord Thomas Stanley was the first out, followed by Thomas Brandon and then Rhys-ap-Thomas. There was a pause before Jasper Tudor came into the hall. At the sight of him a great deal of expletives and cat-calls were hurled out of the throats of the assembled crowd and the halberdiers stepped forward, reminding the people to keep order.

The chair of judgement on the dais, and the two lower ones either side of it remained empty. The trial would be conducted under John de la Pole, earl of Lincoln, the man King Richard had chosen as his heir until such time as he could produce a new one. The charge was to be read by Thomas Howard, earl of Surrey supported by viscount Francis Lovell. If there was anything to mitigate the indicted crimes then the accused were considered erudite enough to speak for themselves. The prisoners were directed by their guards to stand facing the dais. The prisoners stood with their heads high, disdaining the crowd and keeping their own council. A hush of expectation fell upon those present.

Robert de la Halle merely half-heard what his father and grandfather were discussing, immersed in is own thoughts and eyeing them both carefully. He was clad in his court dress, splendid in green and black. The rich materials of his doublet, hose and short mantle were given to him by his father and made up by one of London's most fashionable tailors. Laurence was determined his son would find advancement at the court of King Richard the Third of England and understood the importance of a fine sartorial display.

Little did he realise how his son lamented this finery – wasted, as Robert considered it now that there was no lady Alice de Lucy to impress. Sure, Robert had caught the eye of several young ladies about the court, but none could compare to the ethereal beauty of his lost love. Some had even expressed annoyance when their gentle and flirtatious blandishments were met with cold disdain. He had not realised there could be so much pain in the world. He had felt something akin to what he was feeling now after his mother and two sisters died, but he was much younger then and hadn't fully grasped the extent of his loss. The revelation that the lady Alice de Lucy was betrothed was a blow harder that the greatest buffet he had received in battle. He had been in a daze for hours after her father's declaration at Pembroke Castle and then, when his wits returned he made enquiries regarding the man she was promised to. It turned out he was old enough to be her father. It was not much consolation to realise that the arrangement could not have been a love match, but merely an agreement. Despair gripped him even more tightly when he regarded the expression in the eyes of the lady Alice, who turned upon him a face whose disappointment was a mirror of his own. She thought of him longingly after all, and he, being unschooled in the ways of maidens had stupidly wondered at what seemed to be indifference. He imagined her in her marriage bed, being mauled by a brute and weeping for the gentle hand and consideration of a true lover.

All this was more than he felt he could bear and to make matters worse he was guarding the secret existence of his father's love child. At first he had been at a loss as how to approach the matter. The lady Isabella Staunton had been of the Tudor faction and here in Guildhall, plain enough, was the consequence of such an alliance – trial for treason and a traitor's death at the end of it. The secret also caused him to regard his father surreptitiously and wonder if there were any other brothers or sisters somewhere in the world? He noted how his father looked at his grandfather's wife, Dame Anna. She had some private history with him, he knew. She had come to London with the army of King Edward the Fourth in fourteen seventy-one after he won back his crown and so had his father Laurence. Soon after, Laurence de la Halle, who had some secret business with grandfather Cornelius, met the apothecary's daughter, Robert's mother, and they married within a year. Something more had lurked at the back of his mind, which he had always considered to be curious. Anna was a widow previously married to a man called Thorne, who was hanged on some trumped up charge or other and they had a son, Philip, about the same age as himself. This boy, he realised, had a remarkable resemblance to his father Laurence, being dark haired. This was peculiar in that the woman Anna Thorne was fair-haired. Clearly Philip had not inherited his colouring from his mother. Moreover his father had helped with the expense of sending Philip to Oxford where he was to train as a physician.

Then there was the old woman, a cunning woman who dispensed herbs and potions supplementing those concocted by Cornelius, Mother Malkin by name, who with the help of the necromancer Peter Otteler managed by some dark magic to discover his whereabouts after he had been captured and imprisoned by no less a person than lady Isabella Staunton! Fate, it seemed had a hand in all this and he was at a loss to understand its apparent circularity. He had the feeling that everyone in his life, like the angels of ecclesiastical debate, were dancing impossibly on the head of a pin.

Just then he was broken out from his reverie by the entrance of the court. A door opened and a quartet of ecclesiasticals trooped magisterially into the hall followed by a squad of eight men at arms. The clerics took up their positions at tables set either side of the dais. Next entered with his entourage the stout figure of Thomas Bouchier, Archbishop of Canterbury dressed in scarlet robes and cardinal's hat. His monks arranged themselves to stand before the seats placed along the sides of the walls. A youthful monk who lent him a strong arm to lean on, the archbishop being elderly, at least eighty years old, supported the archbishop. He took his place at the right hand of the still vacant judgement chair.

A taciturn earl of Northumberland came next. Everyone knew why the king had chosen him as a judge. It was to have it forced upon him the penalty for traitors. But for the fact that his men joined the rout of the Tudor army after the battle of Bosworth was won, he might well have been standing with them.

John de la Pole, earl of Lincoln entered to the triumphant flourish of clarions and took his place on the judgement chair. There was a murmur of interest among the commonality. The earl was the son of the king's sister, Elizabeth and her husband the duke of Suffolk. He was King Richard's heir presumptive and even before the battle of Bosworth, had been granted the reversionary rights to the Beaufort estate of lady Margaret Stanley, subject to the life interest of her husband. That husband, lord Thomas Stanley was here on trial for his life and once he was gone the estate would devolve automatically to the earl of Lincoln. It was a clever move by the king to put all the traitors together on trial rather than allow lord Stanley a solo performance. A communal condemnation mitigated suspicion that the king's justice might be influenced by the pecuniary interest of his nephew, John de la Pole.

Lincoln sat on the judgement chair and casually arranged his robes before indicating to the assembly that those who had them might take their seats. He was dressed in a purple robe trimmed with ermine by virtue of his relationship with the king. He had on his head a dark blue velvet hat from under which hung his brown hair. A Yorkist livery collar adorned his shoulders. The features of his face were carefully arranged so as to show no particular emotion except that perhaps a certain arrogance might be discerned by a close observer. Only the earl of Surrey, Thomas Howard and viscount Lovell remained standing and they had in their hands parchments detailing the charges. The commonality naturally stood at the back of the hall and now settled into a concentrated silence.

"Let the charges be read," commanded Lincoln imperiously.

Thomas Howard shook out a parchment and read the charge: "That Jasper Tudor and Thomas Brandon, did invade the realm of England with the intent of destroying her rightful monarch, Richard, by Grace of God King of England, France and Lord of Ireland, and placing a false usurper on his throne. These two, owing by sworn oath knightly and chivalric fealty to the King of England, Richard the Third, did conspire with one Henry Tudor, of bastard stock with no claim or right of kingship, to cause an army of treasonous English and foreign mercenaries to invade and attack the king's realm. Moreover they did incite and encourage the king's subjects to join with them in rebellion, namely Sir Rhys ap Thomas, appointed by King Richard as his Commissioner of Justice in South Wales and lord Thomas Stanley, Baron of England and husband of the woman Margaret, formerly known as Beaufort, Countess of Richmond and mother of the said traitor, Henry Tudor, and that these last two men conspired with Henry Tudor to murder the king and usurp his throne."

"My lord I must protest," cried lord Stanley. "I demand the right to trial separately. I had no part in the Battle at Bosworth Field and did not come to the aid of these men."

"My lord," said viscount Lovell to Lincoln, clearly ready for an outburst of this sort from lord Stanley. "We have sworn testimony that lord Thomas Stanley did meet with the usurper Henry Tudor after he had invaded the realm to conspire the overthrow and death of the king. There is also sworn evidence that at Bosworth lord Stanley commanded his men to attack in support of Henry Tudor. Had it not been for the loyalty of the true Englishmen in his army, there by the king's commission of array as they believed to expel the invader, and who refused to obey the order, he would have attacked the king's army."

Lincoln looked sternly upon lord Stanley. "We will not allow your plea, Baron Stanley. I believe it has already been explained to you that the evidence against you is absolute. There is also the testimony of the traitor William Catesby to implicate you in plots against his grace the king that go back to the beginning of his reign, when he favoured you with high office and which you disdained when called upon to defend his right and your own people against a pernicious invader. Were you to be tried separately it would only serve to consolidate the infamy of your actions. I am not prepared to waste the time of this or any other court to no purpose."

Thomas Stanley, seeing as there was nothing he could say to sway Lincoln's ruling, shook his head angrily and held his tongue. The prisoners beside him stood mute, affecting unconcern while knowing they were guilty as charged and had no defence to offer other than to plead for the king to have mercy upon them – a forlorn hope indeed. Not one of them would offer a reprieve if fortune had been different and they were in the judgement chair.

Robert, who had moved to stand beside his father with the rest of the commons, began to take an interest. "How could a separate trial benefit lord Stanley?" he whispered, "seeing as the man is clearly a traitor along with the others." His father leaned close to explain.

"Prevarication and obfuscation – an old Stanley trick. If lord Stanley were to be tried alone there would be an examination, among other things, of the matter that brought Catesby to his doom and all the dynastic implications it has on the family of the king. Then there are those others in the nobility who, though not accused of treachery might have given some sort of tacit support to the Tudor cause, foolish as it might now seem. The Stanley's have been plotting for years. Such nobles are now firmly allied to the king but if evidence were to be produced that brought suspicion upon their loyalty to the crown, the king or his officers would be forced to respond. Lord Thomas Stanley has so many fingers in so many pots that half the nobility of England could be implicated and the king wishes to consolidate the peace. All will come into line and some things are best let lie. If lord Stanley were to have a day in court, then who knows what might lurk under which stone? Stanley thinks that this being so, he might yet negotiate himself out of the mess he has found himself in. It wouldn't be the first time he has managed to do so. For the sake of the future peace of England, the king will not allow it."

Laurence's words were soon to be confirmed as true while Lincoln conferred with the archbishop Bouchier and Henry Percy, earl of Northumberland. Bouchier affected a pious aspect as he nodded agreement with Lincoln while Northumberland merely shrugged. Some there suspected Henry Percy to have been in secret negotiations with the Tudor and no doubt he would be as keen as the king to silence Thomas Stanley, who was likely to know about it. Was it apprehension at the thought he could have too easily been indicted and lord Stanley might yet speak out as he had with William Catesby? John de la Pole turned his attention at last to the prisoners.

"There is but one sentence possible seeing as the weight of witness is overwhelming, and that is you are guilty of high treason against the majesty of England, her people and her laws." Lincoln curled his lip in distaste then, thinking on the dignity of his office, set his face as flint. "You Thomas Brandon were a henchman of the traitor Henry Tudor and a declared enemy of King Richard; you stand attainted as a traitor. There can be no mercy shown you. Sir Rhys ap Thomas – you were an officer of the English crown and commanded an army tasked with the job of bringing Henry Tudor's army to battle as soon as he landed as it was at Milford Haven. Instead you and certain rebel Welsh joined with the said traitor Henry Tudor and marched with him intending to destroy the king of England; you stand attainted as a traitor. Jasper Tudor – you had been well treated by the king's brother Edward the Fourth and could have enjoyed liberty and freedom amongst the nobility of England and yet you chose exile and enmity. Formerly the earl of Pembroke, you broke your knightly vows and rebelled against your lawful king; you stand attainted as a traitor. Baron Thomas Stanley – you have a long record of failing the English crown when it needed you most. You stand here, one of the most powerful nobles in England and a Knight of the Garter. Having accepted from the hands of King Richard the highest office yet you have deliberately and spitefully betrayed your kinsmen, your knightly vows and your king. You are the worst of all and stand attainted as a traitor."

There was a pause here as the three judges conferred further together.

"There will be much rubbing of hands at court when the sentences are reported," muttered Cornelius to his two companions. "Many a one will be casting an eye over the Stanley lands. An attainder for treason confiscates all his possessions to the crown."

"A waste of energy," said Laurence with a grim smile. "The lands are nominally Lincoln's, though the king may change that. His grace will already have apportioned those estates in his mind, you can be sure. It will be interesting to discover who gets what. But see, here is the sentence."

The earl of Lincoln straightened his back against his chair and spoke.

"Jasper Tudor, Sir Rhys ap Thomas, Thomas Brandon and lord Thomas Stanley - you stand convicted of high treason. The sentence of this court is that you be taken to a place of confinement and from there to a place of execution at a time and place commanded by his grace King Richard the Third. You will be drawn on a hurdle and there hanged and revived, your genitals shall be cut off to symbolise the impossibility of your being able to produce more of your kind; your insides shall be cut out and burned before your faces. Afterwards your heads shall be cut off and your bodies divided into quarters. Those parts of Thomas Brandon will be placed above London Bridge, Lord Stanley's head at Lancaster and the rest at various parts of Lancashire, Sir Rhys ap Thomas' head to Pembroke town gates and the rest to various towns in South Wales. As for Jasper Tudor - your parts will be interred in an unmarked grave beneath the scaffold there to be forgotten along with the cause of your master Henry Tudor. This sentence subject to the confirmation of his grace, the most high and mighty Richard the Third, King of England and France and Lord of Ireland."

"My lords, are we not permitted to speak to the court" cried Rhys ap Thomas.

"You may petition his grace the king," responded Lincoln. "You are in his hands now and afterwards the hands of God. This court has no more to do with you."

The four prisoners affected to regard the court with disdain. All were ashen faced, as anyone would be after having had such dreadful judgement pronounced upon them, though Jasper Tudor seemed the one most unrepentant. Thomas Stanley had a look of incredulity about him. Until this moment he had been confident in his ability to wriggle his way out of trouble but now, denied a separate trial where he might have confused things enough to gain some advantage, he was yet to resign himself to his fate. Rhys ap Thomas, denied the right to appeal the court, was showing signs of horror and no doubt, had the king been present, would have flung himself at his feet and pleaded for his life. Thomas Brandon, a professional soldier had faced death many times and was the one least affected having resigned himself to his fate long before entering Guildhall for trial.

The earl of Lincoln got to his feet and raised the archbishop and the earl of Northumberland, which prompted the guard to take charge of the prisoners and hustle them from the great hall. Archbishop Bouchier stood as if lost until his attendant monk took him by the arm to steady him. Henry Percy, too, seemed confused as if wondering what to do next. He beckoned over his entourage, which surrounded and escorted him from the hall, the other nobles seemingly having nothing to say to him. John de la Pole engaged the archbishop in casual conversation for a few moments as if the proceedings had been those of a manorial court addressing the mundane affairs of the yeomanry. Earl Thomas Howard and viscount Lovell conferred together and gave instructions to the scribes who had been recording the trial.

"I am for the King's court," declared Laurence, "and I suggest you accompany me there, Robert. Your liege lord will precede you, I doubt not, and there is nothing more to be learned here."

"Will there be repercussions, father?" asked Robert. He had been deeply affected by the fall of four great nobles, men who for years had been at the centre of events both in England and on the continent. These ranked with his own liege lord, Thomas Howard, earl of Surrey. When Surrey's father, John, duke of Norfolk had fallen in battle at Bosworth it had been a shock to him, that the man in whose house he trained and who seemed invincible clad in his iron was, in a moment, no more. John Howard, however, had been sixty years of age and so perhaps not in the best fighting trim, but his son, Thomas had been unhorsed and close to being killed also. Since his childhood he had been in awe of these men, not just for the aura of invincibility induced by their harness and manly strength, horsemanship and martial skills, but also the pageantry and colour of the joust, knightly virtue and chivalric code. All this had been severely tested these last few days since the battle of Bosworth. Before then the old order stood, at least in his mind, as the rock on which society was constructed. Now that rock was proving to be riddled with erosion where that which was formerly thought solid suddenly collapsed into dust.

"There will be great changes, to be sure," replied Laurence, "but perhaps not repercussions in the way you might think – ramifications might be a better word."

"Yes," agreed Cornelius, "matters will start to take many branches of uncertain direction should the high nobles be reduced in power, and that I believe is what is in the king's mind. There is some way to go yet before the lees of the last few years settle out. We must watch and listen carefully – consider the earl of Lincoln, highly favoured and loyal at the moment, but should the king produce a male heir on his promised bride . . ?" Cornelius let his words hang there.

Robert, young though he was understood from past events how a noble raised to high expectation might not be willing lightly to relinquish that ambition such expectations tended to generate in his breast. Why, the king's own father was one such. Having struggled to become Regent during the madness of the Lancastrian King Henry the Sixth, he later declared himself the rightful monarch. His reason, however, was the sickness and general unfitness of King Henry to rule England, but the wars that followed all stemmed from that. Eventually, after the death of the duke of York at the Battle of Wakefield, his son Edward defeated King Henry's army at Towton and deposed Henry to usurp the throne, establishing the rule of the house of York once more.

King Richard was not unstable in mind as Henry the Sixth had been, but there were still plenty of possible contenders other than Lincoln. Richard of York, for one, the remaining bastard son of the former king Edward the Fourth. Another with an even stronger claim to the throne than all of them was Edward, earl of Warwick. A mere boy as yet and weak of mind, so it was said, but the son of the attainted duke of Clarence, the king's deceased brother who, had it not been for his attaint, the next in line after King Edward the Fourth with no charge of bastardy to mar his right. If parliament were to overturn that attainder then Clarence's son, Edward, earl of Warwick was King by right, though as a minor unable to rule until his majority. However, unlike his brother King Edward, Richard the Third had won *his* throne not only by legal right but also maintained it in battle so was pretty much unassailable in that respect.

Robert followed after his father and grandfather as they trooped out of Guildhall and into the snowy streets of London. The wind was rising and finding its teeth to nip at faces and any exposed flesh. The early brightness had gone and now snow-laden greenish cloud threatened another fall as they tramped off towards the river where they could cross to Westminster and from there take horse over Lambeth Moor to Windsor where the king was. Robert shivered in the cold. He supposed he would be away soon with earl Thomas to Framlingham where the earl was supervising modifications to the castle started by his father. Living without warmth was something Robert hated at Framlingham castle, the favourite residence of the duke of Norfolk now passed to his son. As a boy he had always been able to get close to a forge in his father Laurence's workshop when the winter chill began to bite. At Framlingham the means of getting warm was to practice at the pell or in trial with one of his fellow squires. He had no easy access to quenching tanks where metal that was being tempered would be plunged – wonderful to wash in rather than having to break through a skin of ice first. His mind turned to think on the state of the poor wretches that had just been condemned. Their habitation would now be a damp cell somewhere in the Tower of London pending their executions. He shivered and pulled his short cloak tightly about his shoulders. For the first time in days he had forgotten his pain at the loss of the lady Alice de Lucy. It would not be long, though, before a warm fire, a bowl of pottage and a hunk of good white bread comforted him sufficiently to let him remember and the pain return.

* * *

Mid December was always a miserable time, made tolerable by the festivities of Yule at the month's end but until then drear and cold. Robert rode in slow procession with his fellow squires behind his grace the duke of Norfolk. The king had confirmed Thomas Howard in his father's title and granted him the same lands and holdings in addition to those he held in his own right. Robert thought on the fortunes of the Howard family and what was a just reward for their faithfulness to the house of York over the recent years.

Thomas Howard was now the second duke and benefited from part of the Mowbray inheritance. Those lands had originally been the property of the previous Mowbray dukes of Norfolk. The last of them, Thomas Mowbray, died with just a daughter to inherit and the dukedom became defunct. King Edward the Fourth had caused his youngest son Richard of Shrewsbury, later to become duke of York to marry the girl, lady Anne Mowbray, duchess of Norfolk, thus gaining her property. Richard of Shrewsbury was but four years of age and Anne five when they were married. John Howard had been the first in line to inherit the dukedom, being directly related to the Mowbray line, but King Edward's not entirely legal manoeuvres deprived him. Nevertheless, he remained true to the house of York, which was why King Richard raised him at last to the title as soon as possible after he became king. The lady Anne died at the age of nine and her child husband along with his brother had been declared illegitimate. Thus the present title, as granted to John Howard, Thomas' father by King Richard when he ascended the throne in fourteen eighty-three, made John Howard the first duke of Norfolk of the new third creation.

Ahead loomed the great Abbey at Westminster, its gothic architecture a dramatic backdrop to the drama soon to be enacted in the open space before the north porch. Its high pointed roof still maintained a few inches of snow, which also lay along the rows of flying buttresses that supported the abbey walls. A platform had been erected to the east where the king and his nobles would sit to witness the executions of the traitors. A hundred yards in front of it was the scaffold and gibbet. Already the braziers had been lit for the incineration of the internal parts of the prisoners. One of these was smoking heavily and some in the crowd that had already gathered coughed and waved their hands to disperse the smoke from their faces. The duke of Norfolk and his men rode between the ranks of halberdiers that kept back the crowd and provided a pathway to the platform. A canopy above a raised dais displayed the royal arms and the king's royal standards, which along with those of his loyal nobles flapped fitfully either side.

The scene was a pageant where apprentices and labourers capered excitedly among the crowd having been granted a holiday for the occasion. The merchants and city officials, lawyers and tradesmen affected a more stoical mien but were as taken up by the excitement as the common folk. The baking trades had been busy having supplied pie men with their wares, which were now being touted among the crowd. Later the ale houses and taverns would be crammed with folk who would argue and express their opinions after the executions and so settle in their minds what they imagined to be great matters concerning the future of the king's realm. This promised to be spectacle indeed. It was not every day that nobles of such distinction were brought collectively to execution. They were the ones who habitually sat in judgement upon everyone else.

Apart from the king himself, the duke of Norfolk was the last of the nobles to arrive. His squires dismounted and ran forward to attend him. Farriers ran up and the squires handed over their horses and the mount of the duke to be led away somewhere close and ready for departure once the dread sentence was completed. Already on the platform was Sir William Stanley and Robert took particular note of him. He was wrapped in a voluminous red mantle with a black chapeau on his head. His face white, drawn and tired as if he hadn't slept for days. The king had insisted he be there even though one of those to die happened to be his brother. Whatever ambitions Sir William had regarding lord Stanley's forfeited lands, he was still his brother. Archbishop Bouchier had been excused attendance by pleading ill health and the damage the cold and damp would do to his frail health. Instead the Abbot of Westminster was there, though the prisoners would ascend the scaffold in the company of lesser priests.

Beside Sir William Stanley stood a nervous looking marquis of Dorset, Thomas Grey. He had gone over to Henry Tudor when exiled in France but then attempted to leave and return to England and King Richard. He had been caught on his flight from Paris where the Tudor was preparing for his invasion of England and *persuaded* to return to the Tudor camp. Henry Tudor, having doubted the marquis' fidelity left him behind when he invaded and this was enough for King Richard to forgive his former indiscretion. The king, however, as with Sir William Stanley, considered it prudent to have him here to witness the fate of those who would betray the king. Perhaps the cruellest command of the king was the presence of George Stanley, lord Stanley's son and the man who was hostage before the battle of Bosworth. His father had cynically stated he had other sons and was content to leave George to the mercy of King Richard. The king had not fulfilled his promise to execute the son but he would have him here to witness his father's death. George Stanley, of course, with his family was now dispossessed of his inheritance being under the attaint of his father.

Robert and the other squires were directed to the sides of the platform charged with keeping an eye on the crowd in case of trouble. Unlike their lord, who was dressed for show, they were all in full harness and had their arming swords and long daggers in scabbards at their belts. Robert found himself beside John Biggar and the two conversed while waiting the arrival of the prisoners before whom the king would come.

"I notice the earl of Northumberland, Henry Percy is conspicuous by his absence," ventured John Biggar. "He had taken himself back to the north of England and though the king sent after him with a command to attend this day, he sent back saying he was unable to get here soon enough and therefore he would have a wasted journey. Having much to do in his demesnes in Northumbria, he must decline."

"That is similar to the ploy he used at Bosworth," replied Robert, "when he claimed he was watching for Stanley treachery and refused to join battle when commanded."

John nodded in agreement. "I wonder whether this is a deliberate flouting of the king's authority or just the product of a man sick at heart. It's hard to tell. The earl has a lot of thinking to do and should that result in him working against the king then there is the possibility of further trouble."

"My grandfather, who is wise in these matters and has the confidence of the king, thinks that as the earl of Northumberland is already isolated at court, he might be ripe for forming treasonable liaisons with others. His lands are close to Scotland and the Scottish king is in league with the French."

"Aye – the *Auld Alliance* as they term it. I agree; there is much material for mischief in the north of England and with the Stanley faction at Lancashire gone, a possible path for invasion."

"But the king, controls the duchy as established from the time of John of Gaunt – a Lancastrian I know, but that still stands. The king needs a reliable lord in control there. Lancashire is a county palatine."

"Yes, so is the county of Durham under the authority of the Prince Bishops who can raise their own army with the purpose of defending England from the Scots. John Sherwood is the present Bishop of Durham and he was appointed without objection the year after our king was crowned, so is probably safe for now. The Archbishop of York, though, is a different case. Thomas Rotherham was one who, in his capacity as Lord Chancellor, aided Elizabeth Wydville in her attempt to deprive King Richard of his crown. It was he who released the Great Seal of England to her and though he later recovered it and handed it over to Archbishop Bouchier, his bungling and distrustful behaviour led to his being replaced as Lord Chancellor."

"And he was imprisoned for a time by King Richard in the Tower of London for his involvement in that business with lord Hastings," mused Robert, "which only leaves the palatinate of Chester and Flint, ruled by the earl of Chester - that is the Prince of Wales and we don't have one of those."

"No," lamented John, "the young prince died last year. Chester has its own legislature and is not subservient to the English parliament. Weakness in the government of these counties palatine would leave the whole of England below the Trent River vulnerable to attack from the north. Sir William Stanley resides at Holt Castle and has extensive lands in Cheshire. For now he too is the king's man and today's proceedings should encourage him to remain so."

"Tenuous, unless Sir William is suitably rewarded for his support," said Robert. "The king has formed the Council of the North sitting at Sandal Castle and ruled over by the earl of Lincoln. That should provide a measure of security."

"Time will tell us that," muttered John. "Look to it, here comes the king."

Clarions sounded as the king rode from Westminster Palace on his favoured white courser, resplendent in his polished armour decorated with the Royal Arms of England and wearing his war crown, the one he displayed in before the battle of Bosworth. Beside him both sides and also clad in full harness rode viscount Francis Lovell and the earl of Lincoln, John de la Pole. Trooping behind them on foot were the men-at-arms of the king's lance, his household knights who were the remains of those that had rode with him at Bosworth. A squire ran forward and offered his back to the king so he could dismount; Lovell and Lincoln being similarly served by their squires. The king and his friends mounted the platform and King Richard placed himself in the seat provided on the dais after which Lovell and Lincoln sat beside him. The men of his retinue formed up before him at the front of the platform.

Suddenly there came a roar of excitement from the crowd. The prisoners must have been taken to Westminster Palace and now a dozen monks paraded following the path traced by the king and his men. Behind them plodded four horses arranged in pairs, each drawing a hurdle where the prisoners were tied head down. The ground was frozen mud and patched with ice and the hurdles groaned and bumped along, shaking their burdens as they went. The prisoners were clad in white woollen shifts, the easier to cut off them when the time came for their ritual disembowelling. Following after were the personal chaplains allowed for each prisoner and guarded by a squad of yeomen swordsmen.

The crowd fell silent as the prisoners were drawn to the foot of the scaffold. Assistant executioners came and cut the bonds that tied them to the hurdles and dragged them to their feet. All four appeared shaken and disorientated by the experience. Their aspect was dishevelled, a far cry from the brave display they had shown at their trials. It was as if the deprivation of their finery had diminished them; that costly cloths and furs were superficial coverings merely and here they stood -presented as they would stand before their God, ready to leave the world as they entered it, with nothing. Perhaps that was the king's intention. The prisoners were directed up the steps of the scaffold, which they were allowed to ascend without brutal enforcement. Once there, the executioners, there were two of them, arranged the prisoners to face the platform where the king sat straight and stern of feature. To the accompaniment of a blast of clarions, a herald stepped forward to address the people.

Chester Herald it was who repeated the judgement handed down by the earl of Lincoln at their trial. After that he read out the sentence of the court which was to be drawn for treason, hanged for causing death of the king's subjects, disembowelled for sacrilege against their anointed king then beheaded and quartered for plotting the king's death. The prisoners had already received the sacrament for the dead from Holy Church and now knelt before their chaplains for a final blessing.

Asked, as was habitual, if any would make a final declaration before their sentences were carried out, only two offered to do so – Rhys ap Thomas and Thomas Stanley. Rhys ap Thomas regretted his mistaken decision to join with the traitor Henry Tudor and cited his Welsh blood and the Tudor's part share in it as having confused his mind. He had not been easily persuaded to join the Tudor and regretted having believed the calumnies against the king's good name that the Lancastrian Tudor factions within England had been falsely spreading for some years. He died a true and loyal subject of the Crown of England and hoped he would find mercy at the hands of a higher power where he believed his true conscience would stand firm at that awful judgement.

Thomas Stanley cited his martial valour in the Scottish campaign of fourteen eighty-two where, fighting loyally for the English Crown of King Edward the Fourth, the king's brother, and alongside the present king when he was duke of Gloucester, he had won back the town of Berwick from the Scots and returned it to English domination. His present condemnation had come about due to his being identified with the plotting of his wife dame Margaret Stanley, once called countess of Richmond and mother of the usurper Henry Tudor. He had ever been faithful to the English crown and his grace King Richard. He had not moved to attack the king at the recent battle of Bosworth and was condemned for the actions of certain of his captains whose loyalty had been to his wife, dame Stanley, and thus attempted to use his soldiers against the king. He stood in the knowledge that his actions would be commendable to God and was content to pass into a higher judgement.

When it became clear that Brampton and Jasper Tudor would not speak, the executioners moved to take up the prisoners and the ladder was settled firmly against the post of the gibbet. Lord Stanley was taken first and his arms pinioned before being forced onto the first rung of the ladder.

"Hold!" came the command of the king. "We would speak." Silence fell over the crowd as if all had been struck dumb. King Richard got to his feet and walked to the edge of the platform, the better to be heard. "There has been much blood spilt in our realm of England due mainly to men such as these," he declaimed above the heads of the crowd. "We are reminded once again of the traitorous duke of Buckingham who was the first of our reign to rebel. He was treated lightly when we ordered that he was not to suffer the full penalty for treason and merely beheaded. It is enough," declared King Richard, "that these men have been taken and condemned by our court and sentenced according to law and proper justice. They are guilty of grievous faults and over many years at that, yet we are disposed to clemency. Though our patience with traitors is all but run out, let there be an end to it with their deaths. We reduce the sentence of our court to one of decapitation, the full penalty for the treason of which they are so foully guilty being rescinded. We are not a vengeful king, but a just one we hope. Be it known that if in future men like this should rise against our realm of England our wrath will be visited upon them in great and dreadful retribution. Executioners, do your duty. Strike off their heads and let us be done."

With a dismissive wave the king turned and took his seat. Those lords in attendance upon him were astounded at his words and looked to each other in confusion, wondering at the king's sudden decision. A low murmur rose from the crowd like the sound of a wasp nest where the insects were astir but not yet ready to swarm. Many were disappointed, being deprived of the spectacle, others relieved at the quality of the king's mercy. The condemned, one by one, and according to rank beginning with lord Stanley followed by Rhys-ap-Thomas submitted meekly to the block where the executioners took it in turns to strike off their heads and afterwards their attendants held them up high, showing the crowd the heads of the traitors. Had there been any residual Lancastrians in the crowd intent on stirring trouble, they were confounded as everyone was intent on discussing the king's declaration of mercy with no thought of fight or rebellion at all. Those constant in their faithfulness to the king were extolling his virtue while those still inclined to take cognisance of the negative rumours of murder associated with him were reduced in their argument.

The mood of the crowd was ecstatic as the king descended the platform and mounted his courser. As he and his entourage walked their horses between the rows of halberdiers, they were acclaimed by the men and women of London cheering themselves hoarse. Caps were being thrown in the air and soon shouts of *God Save the King*, and *Good King Dickon* were heard. This was a triumph for a king who, until then, had been regarded cautiously by Londoners as being a northern lord. There had been no doubt in anyone's mind that the condemned men were traitors and had the full penalty been exacted in all its cruelty, no blame would have been attached to the king. On the other hand, it would have done his unfortunate reputation no good, fed as it was by Lancastrian rumourmongers. Perhaps another battle had been won this day and one with effects reaching further than a mere military victory as at Bosworth?

Behind them, on the scaffold the bodies of the condemned

traitors were being placed in chests to await the king's instructions as to their disposal. The heads would be placed on public view as already directed by the court. Beneath the scaffold spots of crimson found a way between the planking and dripped to melt into the ice beneath while the blood stained water used to flush the scaffold clean spilled over to form a pink slush. The reign of the House of York was won in the snow at the battle of Towton and it seemed the blood that stained the snow then was now finally being washed away.

Robert and John Biggar mounted their horses behind their liege and tagged on to the end of the king's men.

"Kings need to demonstrate not only fitness, but strength if they are to rule well," said Robert to John Biggar. "Our king has shown his people power and mercy. It augers well I think."

"I remember the style of his brother, King Edward." John Biggar talked as if he had experience of that monarch when in fact, as with Robert, he was but a child for the latter part of his reign. His opinion was derived from his father, though he expressed it as if it were the product of his own wisdom. "King Edward was not entirely to be trusted where the law was concerned," he continued. "Rebellion in his reign was stamped out with mass hangings and executions – sever retribution. That was a stern rule yet he did preserve the peace by strength of will, which, it must be said, fell apart when he died."

"Then let us hope King Richard has reclaimed it," responded Robert. "It has been a terrible struggle for him. Little more than two years king and he has had to cope with rebellion, treason and invasion while in the same period he lost first his son and heir, then his wife and queen. Delivering justice as we have just witnessed demonstrates a strength of mind equal to that of his arm in battle, which is formidable."

"I wonder which of the two brothers will prove in the end to be the better monarch? Can England be governed entirely according to her laws, or must we forever have to win our rights by rebellion and force of arms?"

They rode in pensive silence, following the procession of the king. Soon they were in the courtyard of Westminster Palace and looking to the needs of their liege, the duke of Norfolk. Thomas Howard was in ebullient mood having enjoyed the residual accolade of the crowd. The ladies of the court had not been present at the executions and now they gathered around their respective husbands. Thomas Howard had his wife there, lady Elizabeth, a most attractive woman for her age Robert thought, his awakened interest in women developing into a critical eye for feminine beauty. Thomas Howard greeted her with a fond kiss and the two entered the great hall side by side. Robert felt a sudden pang of loneliness wishing that he might have been greeted thus by the lady Alice. That was not to be and the jostling of the other squires and serving men around the duke led him to a side table where there was a copious quantity of wine. The duke looked over his shoulder and seeing Robert near, beckoned him forward.

"Ah, master de la Halle. His grace the king would have a word with you."

8 - The Portuguese Marriage

Robert stood, somewhat perplexed just beyond the door to the side chamber within the Palace of Westminster where the king was consulting with his chief ministers. The chamber was packed and noisy with courtiers, scribes and officials as his liege, the duke of Norfolk pushed his way forward and knelt with raised face before his sovereign. King Richard stood splendidly attired in a white doublet embroidered with heavy gold thread depicting tangles of Yorkist roses. His hose was white silk and his shoes of black leather squared at the toes in the latest fashion. Placed almost casually on a table close by were the various parts of his harness along with the great helm and golden crown. It was with a feeling of some comfort that Robert saw his father close by, ready to take charge of the king's armour. Curiously, Laurence de la Halle seemed to have no idea his son was in the chamber, either that or he was deliberately ignoring his presence. A courtier brought the king a black velvet chapeau, which he waved away, preferring to remain bare headed. He raised the duke of Norfolk and spoke close in his ear whereupon the duke looked across the room and gestured for his squire to come forward.

Robert walked tentatively towards the king hardly daring to think he was the one being called. Perhaps the duke was actually gesturing to some courtier nearby and not to Robert at all. The expression on the face of the duke confirmed that it was indeed Robert de la Halle that was commanded into the immediate presence. He fell to his knees and gazed up at the king, who seemingly cognisant of the effect his command was having on the young squire, smiled at him and raised him with an upward gesture of his right hand. The king turned his attention to someone who had appeared close behind the youth.

"So this is your son, master de la Halle," said the king benignly. Laurence the armourer stepped forward to stand beside his son.

"He is my lord king, and as faithful a servant of your grace as his father."

"Yes," agreed King Richard, "We have good reason to believe he is." The king turned his gaze to Robert. "We wish to listen to your account of the demise of the traitor Henry Tudor," he drawled. "Sir Ralph de Assheton has good opinion of you and we understand that had it not been for your, shall we say adventures, the traitor might have escaped us."

"That is most generous of Sir Ralph, my king," Robert managed to get out. "But truth to tell there was much luck involved too."

"Modesty!" declared the king looking around at his courtiers. "A rare quality. We hear, squire Robert that your luck further sustained you at Pembroke Castle and led to the capture of the recently executed traitors."

"That might be so, my lord king; I wonder at it myself."

"And you also saved our dear friend, Thomas Howard here, at the battle men are now calling the Field of Bosworth," the king swept a hand at the duke standing beside him and smiling at his squire, "even though you were not supposed to be in the line of battle. We consider, young man, that in you we have a most useful subject with great potential."

"I am overwhelmed by your assessment of my character, dread king; but so far I have stumbled along in your service hardly knowing my destination."

"Patience, my young friend, patience. What you have actually demonstrated is that by serving loyally your king you cannot go awry. We shall retire where you can regale us with your adventures. We should say that we were, at first, disturbed by the report of the traitor Henry Tudor's death in the Morecambe sands. We would rather he had been brought to us in chains. Since then we have had time to ponder on the circumstances of his demise. We are now inclined to think the story of his doom, to be sucked down into the sands of the land he would covert, might be more useful to us than the spectacle we have witnessed this day."

So that was what was behind the mercy the king had shown to the traitors, thought Robert, the promulgation of his grace's political policy.

The king left the hall to the chagrin of his courtiers, commanding to attend just Robert, his armourer Laurence, Thomas Howard and one other whom Robert had never seen before. The latter was a young man, perhaps nineteen or so, richly dressed and having something of a familiar look about him that Robert could not quite place. Whoever he was, the king was content to have him attend as they entered a small chamber. The door was guarded on the outside by two halberdiers while attending within were four of the king's personal servants. A good fire blazed in a stone fireplace and there was a table with several chairs. Above the table was a circular candelabrum where fine wax candles flickered brightly in a slight draught and added to the illumination provided by the firelight, there being no windows to provide daylight. King Richard sat at the head of the table while a servant settled him into his seat and placed a goblet of wine beside his right hand.

"Be seated, all of you," said the king waving his arm over the scene. Robert was astounded – only his chief councillors would ever be invited to sit in the presence of the king. He waited while the duke of Norfolk was seated on the king's left, then the strange youth took his place at the king's right hand. Laurence de la Halle, bowing to the king to remind Robert of his manners, seated himself lower down the table and Robert, mimicking his father and with some trepidation, sat opposite him. Servants served wine, after which the king gestured them away to stand by the arras that decorated the walls of the chamber.

"Squire Robert," began the king, "We would hear your tale. Tell us how you discovered the whereabouts in Lancashire of the Tudor traitor when our soldiers were searching for him in Wales. We understand you were captured by a lady?" The king sat back and took a sip of his wine, his dark eyes sparkling in the reflection of firelight, while Robert marshalled his thoughts. He couldn't tell if the king's reference to his capture was a rebuke or that he was merely intrigued.

Robert told him of his chase after two women, one the lady Isabella Staunton and that she had exchanged her mantle with lady Margaret Stanley to deceive him, letting lady Stanley escape. He explained his encounter with the knight and went on to explain how lady Isabella's archers had captured him. He decided to leave out the part regarding her infant, his father being present. Close questioning by the king might expose the babe's true parentage. He thought it best to admit that he had been fed false information and that it was by mere chance he had overheard the location of the Tudor's true destination. King Richard leant forward eagerly as he told how the Tudor, running in fear had found himself trapped in the sands of Morecambe Bay with no possibility of getting out, seeing as how the tide had turned and threatened to drown them all.

"So, Henry Tudor ran away then, and that time brought about his own destruction rather than that of others," crowed King Richard, thumping his fist on the table in delight.

"That was certainly so," agreed Robert, anxious to reinforce the fact that Henry Tudor could not have been extracted due to the ingress of the tide. "Had there been more time we might have got him out and brought him to your grace's justice, but fate decreed otherwise."

"Nevertheless, and cognisant as we are that your involvement was fatalistic rather than deliberate, yet we are all subject to God's will and you responded well, given your years and inexperience. We believe that there is something about you that provokes a natural wisdom irrespective of your youth. You are an adventurer, much like your father who has also served us well." Laurence bowed his head in recognition of the king's compliment. The king leaned back in his chair and took another pull at his wine. Everyone else took the opportunity to sip at their goblets. Robert was surprised at the quality. Wine provided for the consumption of esquires was habitually of much lesser quality and often watered. Most of the time they had to be content with small ale.

"My lord of Norfolk," said the king after a few moments. "We would ask that you release squire Robert to help with a certain task we have in mind. You know that of which we speak?"

"Indeed, my lord king and I release him most willingly," replied Thomas Howard, looking to note the reaction on Robert's face, which was one of astonishment mixed with curiosity.

"Squire Robert," continued the king fixing the object of his attention with a businesslike countenance. "You will be aware that we are shortly to welcome into our realm our betrothed, the Infanta Joanna of Portugal?"

"Yes, dread king – a most virtuous lady I have heard and one who would be welcomed as our queen."

"Ah, you know something of her lineage, then?"

"It is spread abroad she is the direct descendant of John of Gaunt, a Lancastrian it is true, but of direct lineal descent to the English Crown. You will be incorporating the houses of York and Lancaster when you are joined to her."

"Yes – not of the bastard line as the Tudor. We are pleased the match has already found such approval, if approval that be?"

"But yes, my lord king. Everyone celebrates the coming of the Infanta and hopes for the peace that such an alliance would bring, her brother João the second being King of Portugal. I believe the whole of England is behind your grace in this happy match. Moreover, she is known to be most pious and the perfect partner for a king who has himself endowed many a chantry and other benefices across the land."

"Well, recent events have taught us there are those who would despoil our plans. What think you?"

"My . . . my lord king," stammered Robert, "I can hardly advise your grace."

"It is not advice we ask," snapped the king, " We have plenty of that. What we are asking you is what *you* think? Are our plans like to be spoiled?"

"Your Grace, you do me great honour in asking me but, my lord king, I am hardly in a position to comment – your great lords . . ." Robert swept his arm around the room. Duke Thomas stood, his face stoical, that of his father etched with concern and the youth sitting by the king regarding him with interest. "How can I know better than these?"

"Again we say," responded the king, "It is not your advice but your opinion we require." Robert hung his head in dejection. He hardly knew what to say. In these moments all he was aware of was the flickering sounds coming from the great fire and the snap of burning wood. The soughing of the draught seemed almost to be attempting to suck his soul up into the soot of the chimney.

"I believe," said Robert at last, "that there may be some in your kingdom that still plot your destruction, but they have no power now;" he explained hurriedly as if to speak thus might be construed as treason, "not after your grace's victory over Henry Tudor, except . . ."

"Except?" said King Richard, his eyebrows raised in expectation of an answer.

"Things being as they are, your grace, there are a few who are among us that might try to disturb your realm." Robert was thinking of those lords whom the king had elevated and now reduced in that expectation. John de la Pole, earl of Lincoln, the heir presumptive, necessary before Bosworth but now? Where would the disappointment lead too, provoked by a new heir got on a new bride? Edward, earl of Warwick, Clarence's son was a boy who could be manipulated by any number of disaffected nobles and already the earl of Northumberland was brooding in his northern demesnes. Robert had heard that the former duke of York, Richard of York, the younger of the two sons of Edward the Fourth was with his aunt at the court of Burgundy, having been brought out of the obscurity that had until then protected him from Tudor agents. There was a situation ripe for trouble. The lad had no love of his uncle, who had bastardised him.

"King's have enemies, your grace, whose chief food is ambition," he managed to get out at last. He hardly dared tell his deepest fears. King Richard scrutinised his features as if he would strip away his flesh in layers until his very soul were exposed.

"We think we understand you, squire Robert. You are your father's son and a true one both to him and to us. You will know how we prize loyalty?"

"Indeed your grace."

"Can we count upon you, squire Robert de la Halle?"

"By my life, your grace."

"Then by such a simple promise we give you our trust," said the king quietly. Robert thought that the king might have added – *I hope you are worthy?* – yet those words had more power, being unspoken but understood, than the most eloquent declaration he could give. From this moment, Robert de la Halle would be bound to King Richard the Third of England as closely as if they had been brothers.

"You will serve a new master from now, squire Robert," said the king turning uncomfortably in his seat as if his back were stiff and inclining towards the youth by his right hand. "This is our son, the lord bastard John of Pomfret."

Robert, realising with a shock that the familiar features in the face of the youth he had pondered on were those of the king, and remembering his manners, got to his feet almost knocking his chair over in his haste. Approaching the lord bastard, Robert dropped to his knees and looked up at him.

"My lord, I am your most humble servant," he managed to get out.

John of Pomfret smiled pleasantly, stood and bowed to the king, then reaching for Robert's hand, pulled him to his feet.

"Welcome to my service, squire Robert." John of Pomfret had a pleasing tone to his voice, not unlike that of his father in his benign moods.

"Our son is freshly returned from Calais where he has been acting in the post of captain under lord Dinham our lieutenant there," said King Richard. "He is to join with my lord of Norfolk, who is to go into Portugal to escort our betrothed into England. He will need a good pair of eyes and ears as well as a strong arm to watch out for him. We are not aware of any particular threat but there are still those in France who would do us harm and a dangerous sea to cross between Portugal and England, is that not so lord Thomas?"

"There is a possibility, your grace, that the woman dame Stanley might be in France and she has still a few traitors with her. Moreover, several lords of Brittany, have quarrelled with Pierre Landais, the chief minister and it may be she has found shelter with them. Your decision not to look at Anne, the daughter of duke Francis of Brittany as a bride, she being too young, has alienated that country, not surprisingly. It was the place where Henry Tudor spent most of his exile and his cause may have residual sympathy there. Dame Stanley is impotent so far as raising any kind of army against you, but there is the ever-present possibility she might attempt to revenge the deserved death of her son."

"There you have it," declared the king. "Until that woman is located and dealt with there is always the chance she might bring harm to our intended bride who is a lady unschooled in the ways of villainy. We shall let our son John explain fully our reasoning and concern."

* * *

Robert was still a mass of nervous tension. Walking with his new master, John of Pomfret in a quiet corner of Westminster Hall he was only too aware he was in the presence of a member of the royal family, albeit one who could never inherit. The king was soon swallowed up by a mass of clamoring courtiers as he came out of his privy chamber and those with him dispersed into the crowd, while Robert went off with lord John who began to explain why the king was anxious.

"The main reason for the king's concern is that his forthcoming nuptial, which will take place here at Westminster in the spring, might intimidate the Stanley woman into desperate action, having due regard to the terms of the marriage treaty with Portugal."

"You have lost me my lord?" declared Robert. "In all the recent troubles between King Richard and Europe, it has been France and Brittany where the problem lay, not Portugal. I cannot see how dame Stanley would be provoked by the court there of King João the Second. She was disturbed when our king tormented her in the belief he was considering marriage to his niece, Elizabeth, but that was disposed of when the princess of Portugal, as she is known there, agreed to marriage with him."

"I see you are not familiar with the details of the marriage agreement," said lord John paternally, though there was but five years between them. "There are two in England involved in the treaty – my father your king is one, the other is that same Elizabeth of York. She is to marry with Manuel, duke of Beja and cousin of King João with the possibility, mortality being the sad lot of men, of Elizabeth eventually becoming Queen of Portugal should King João die with no heir apparent. He has but one heir, a robust son, Alfonso, and no other."

"A dire prediction, my lord!"

"Considering the past fortunes of the Wydville women, one we might make with some thought of it coming to pass – but I jest, of course." Lord John laughed as he watched consternation chase over Robert's face. "However, seeing as the Stanley woman intended Elizabeth of York for her own son, it is conceivable she will attempt to damage the alliance in some way, or get her followers to do it.

They are few but desperate and spiteful. The king's advisers believe that until they are tracked down and eliminated, they pose a real threat."

"What is the king's relationship with Portugal?" asked Robert. "Until this moment England has been mostly concerned with events in France, Burgundy and Brittany. I know Spain is keen for an alliance with England, too. There are contested lands in France that Spain wants returned to her sovereignty."

"King João has particular ideas on monarchy that has made him unpopular in certain quarters, though he has managed to stamp his will upon his nobles. The situation there is not that much different to ours in England. King João has acted to curtail the power of his nobles and enhance the process of justice for his people. One thing that made him unpopular with his nobles was when he abolished their right to conduct law courts in their own lands. Our King Richard has much sympathy with that idea and he too has seen how powerful nobles can endanger the crown. King João has caused to be executed the most powerful of his nobles, the duke of Braganza, whose wife has fled into exile, a situation not very different to that of Thomas Stanley and *his* wife. Braganza was the chief conspirator against King João, as was lord Stanley against King Richard in England."

"I see," mused Robert. "Then if dame Stanley can manage to find malcontents among the nobles of Portugal then she has much scope for mischief."

"She has indeed," replied lord John. You didn't really think the king had attached you to me as reward, where you might revel in the luxury of the Portuguese court?" he chuckled with amusement. "I am sufficiently high in King Richard's favour for it not to be considered unusual to include me in the nuptial escort, but not of sufficient status to miss me overmuch if I am elsewhere. His grace the duke of Norfolk, on the other hand, will be closely watched and the actions of his squires, too."

"Forgive me, my lord, but I fail to understand my role in this. I shall, of course do my duty towards you but when it comes to intrigue I am apt to become lost."

"I think the king regards you as some sort of talisman," replied lord John. "Sometimes innocence can be more potent than guile, your recent experiences have demonstrated that. Stick to your duty and let us treat the whole as a game, a deadly one it might transpire, but yet a game for all that."

* * *

"Here it is," said John of Pomfret, "my harness. It is your job to keep it in good trim along with your own." Robert pushed and pulled at the iron on its wooden frame.

"It is finely made, my lord," he offered as his opinion.

"It should be. It was made for me by the king's own armourer, your father." Robert had already guessed that but did not want lord John to think him vain in promoting his family. He was slightly apprehensive that he had in his possession a document, instructions regarding some sort of financial transaction, for a certain contact at Lisbon given to him by his grandfather Cornelius. It was in the nature of an investment in trade goods and Robert was to have a share in any profits that might result. Grandfather Cornelius was one of King Richard's most trusted spymasters, who had trade contacts everywhere and used his couriers to carry confidential information all over Europe. Portugal was a rich trading nation having engaged in nautical exploration for decades, beginning with Henry the Navigator, and now reaching towards China and the Indes by sea rather than the long, tedious and costly route by land. They had not succeeded yet, but who could doubt they would some day soon.

"It is not the first arms he made for me," continued lord John. "The very first was a sword and shield, I recall, back home at Middleham Castle. I was but four years of age and though I recall little of those days, yet I have never forgotten the thrill when your father presented them to me. Later as I grew, the king commanded a complete set and this is my latest, made for me when I took the captaincy of Calais."

Robert noted lord John's reference to home being Middleham Castle. That was the place where the king had received his knightly training under the earl of Warwick, the Kingmaker who had fallen foul of Richard's brother, King Edward the Fourth and met his end at the Battle of Barnet. Afterwards, as the duke of Gloucester, Richard had lived happily there with his wife Anne Neville, daughter of the Kingmaker, before being forced south to take the crown when his brother died unexpectedly and Edward's marriage was discovered to be bigamous. John had been born at Pontefract Castle, hence his familiar name. He was also known as John of Gloucester, that being his father's title at his birth.

King Richard had two illegitimate children, as was well known; this one, John and his sister, Katherine, named after her mother. He had no idea who their mother had been and would never ask, it not being his place. All he knew was she was no longer part of the king's life after his marriage to the lady Anne Neville, although he freely acknowledged his bastard children. Robert wondered why lord John called Middleham home when more correctly it should have been Pontefract. Perhaps Middleham was where his fondest memories were? He suspected the same might be said of the king who, since taking the crown, was compelled to spend much of his time in the central and southern regions of his realm.

The two were standing in a cold, cheerless chamber set within the thick walls of the donjon of Dover Castle. Situated on the third floor at the very top, the chamber was lighted by a small window, unshuttered at the moment, giving sight of a steel grey sea flecked with white and the sails of a variety of craft entering or leaving the harbour below. Beyond the outer walls of the castle stretched a green sward that served as pasture between the castle and the great white cliffs that stood as if mocking the kingdom of France, just visible across the narrow seas. The harbour was out of the line of sight from this window, as was the town that served it. Robert and lord John had just returned from supervising the loading of the five ships that would take them on a voyage to Portugal.

The king, as a reward for his good service, had sent Robert some fabrics so he could present himself properly at court and his father Laurence had engaged a tailor to make them into some suitable clothes. These were packed into chests along with lord John's clothes. The steel harness would be packed away too for the voyage, though it might be needed if they were attacked at sea and thus must be kept close during the voyage. Also, if there were knightly entertainment at the Portuguese court, such as a joust, the harness would be required for that.

"We have a perilous sea to cross, my lord," mused Robert as he worked with flint and tinder to strike a flame intended to light the kindling in the fireplace. The chamber was sparsely furnished with a table, two chairs, a truckle bed for the lord bastard two chests and a low stone shelf that served as a place to store their personal weapons and armour. Robert would spend the night wrapped in his travelling cloak before the fire, which, if he could get it alight, would at least be a warm spot.

"The Bay of Biscay," replied lord John. "It is a wild place at best, and after the calends of February until the spring apt to be savage and unpredictable. Hopefully our return voyage will be easier. If it were not for the king being eager for his bride, we might have waited until the end of March before setting sail from England."

"As it is, my lord, there will be courtly protocols to observe once we arrive, which will serve to delay our return and increase the chance of fair weather."

"And a proliferation of pirates to contend with, too." Lord John went over and stood by the window, gazing out over the distant sea. "There is a rat's nest of them out of Le Havre and others out of Brittany. Breton and Spanish pirates infest the Bay of Biscay from Brest to La Coruna."

"Yet they will hardly dare attack five well found and armed vessels such as we have," said Robert before blowing on the tinder where his sparks had provoked it into smoulder. As the tinder burst into flame, he applied it to the kindling in the fireplace and fanned it to a blaze. "We are well gunned, too. His grace the king has seen to that. On our return voyage we shall have ships of Portugal with us and they are the best armed vessels on the seas."

"That may be so, squire Robert, but the sea is unpredictable and should our ships become separated then that is another matter. It is that which the pirates rely on. There will not be an easy passage I warrant. Let us hope that your famous luck will bring us through unscathed."

"I think that prayer might serve us rather better, my lord," Robert replied, fussing with the fire and letting its warmth penetrate his chilled body. He wondered how long he could fan and play with the flames before lord John realised he was doing so to keep the fire to himself for as long as possible. Just then, as if in agreement with Robert's statement, the bells of the castle church began to peal.

"There is a summons if ever there was," chuckled lord John. "I still wonder at your ability to predict what will happen next."

Robert stood back from the fire that was now blazing in the grate. "They ring the office of Nones," he said while reaching into a chest that stood under the window. "Here is your crucifix, my lord." He withdrew an ornate golden crucifix studded with red jewels, which glowed mystically in the flickering firelight and placed it into a niche in the wall. "Fra Maurice will be here shortly. I shall take myself down to the church and make my devotions there." The lord bastard nodded his agreement and positioned the crucifix more to his liking. Fra Maurice was his personal chaplain and the lord bastard would be shriven before taking ship.

He took himself down through the great donjon, politely bowing to Fra Maurice as he passed him on the stair. The priest was a Spaniard who, apart from his native tongue spoke Latin and French fluently but had little English. He was thick-set and short with swarthy features and bright black eyes that flicked everywhere and seemed to miss nothing. Robert had been surprised that he was lord John's chosen confessor particularly when it was known that the king and queen of Spain were discomfited that King Richard had not chosen one of their daughters for a bride. There was some reason, of course. The Infanta Isabel, at fifteen years had good breeding potential but she was promised to the Portuguese heir, a contract which Spain had been trying to dissolve for years. Her mother the queen, in her youth, had been refused by Edward the Fourth in favour of the commoner Elizabeth Wydville. That still rankled with Queen Isabella of Castile and negotiations had foundered. Richard's empathy with King João and the piety of his sister Joanna had greater appeal. King Richard had been happily married to Anne Neville and despite the political urgency for an heir, longed for a female companion he could live fondly with. Joanna, being the same age as Richard and still an attractive maid, was rather mature when it came to child-bearing, and until now had desired and expected to become a nun. Even Robert with his limited experience of such matters understood how delicate a future their union would bring. Unless the couple were able to produce at least one robust male heir, and the king manage to live until that heir's maturity, the field of competition for the English crown would once more open into dispute.

The church of St. Mary in Castro was small and set close to the castle walls. An old tower, the remnants of early Roman construction, was still in use as a campanile with a peal of three bells and connected to the church by a short passage. The squat tower of the church was the same width as the nave but Robert knew there were three altars there dedicated to St. Edmund, St. Edward and more particularly St. Adrian, Robert's own patron and it was before this latter saint that he knelt to pray for a safe voyage and return. His mind drifted off into thoughts of the lady Alice. The excitement of the court and his attachment to the lord bastard, John of Pomfret had dulled her image and he felt he needed to hold it in his mind. He still had fancies that someday she would be free of her elderly husband and provided he could make a way in the world, become somehow deserving of her hand. All this was leading him towards the sin of lust and it was with some difficulty that he forced his thoughts back to his immediate quest. *Vade retro me, Satana.*

Robert had some experience of the sea. When younger he had sailed across to Brittany with his father to visit his family there and found he could tolerate bad weather reasonably well, although he was not entirely free from seasickness. His greatest fear was the sea itself. He was in awe of the power of the waves and, being a soldier, would rather fight on land and chance the strength of his sword arm than stand helplessly on a tossing piece of floating wood. King Richard, though, had been England's admiral under his brother King Edward and along with the first duke of Norfolk, John Howard, regularly sailed the enemy-infested seas around the coast of England. That was a good thing, though. The king, being a sailor himself had ensured his own ships were well found and he was not about to risk the life of his bride with vessels of inferior design or build.

The inside of the church was dim, lit by the light on the north and south sides through a series of double-splayed round-headed windows. Votive candles were all the rest of the illumination. The office of the ninth hour was over yet there was a residual cloying scent of incense and the casual movement of other votaries who passed intermittently from light into darkness as they walked through shafts of sunlight that streamed through the windows. As he got to his feet and turned, he saw John Biggar, who was in the company of a friar. The two seemed to be engaged in a heated argument. Robert stopped by the church door and watched. After a few minutes John Biggar turned and stomped away leaving the friar glowering malevolently after him. John's face was red with anger and failed to notice Robert's presence until his friend tugged at his sleeve. He snatched his arm away and stood back as if he was expecting to be attacked. When he saw who it was he relaxed and taking Robert by the arm ushered him outside.

"What was that about?" asked Robert, fired with curiosity.

"The fellow tried to sell me an indulgence even though he could see I had just been at my devotions." John set his mouth in a hard line, his chin thrust out belligerently.

"But there is nothing to get angry about there – except the price. Was he overcharging for it?"

"Oh, we hadn't got as far as the price. I simply pointed out that Purgatory is a fiction to frighten children and I had no need of his indulgence." Robert stopped in his tracks and took a firm grip of his friend's arm.

"My friend, you mustn't say such things. That is the doctrine of the Lollards and as such makes anyone speaking it liable to a charge of heresy."

"It may be that Lollards disavow Purgatory, but they are by no means the only ones. There are many aspects of Church doctrine that scholars have questioned for years now. The Holy Bible is the only true reference and there is nothing of Purgatory in that book."

"How can you possibly know?" gasped Robert, seriously

concerned for his friend. "You have never read from it. Only the Church may interpret Holy Bible and it is writ in Latin which, if memory serves me right, you have little of."

"There are Bibles in English," was the sullen answer. "Those who have read there can find no mention of Purgatory nor should we be denied our Holy text. Why should I not read of it?"

Robert looked around to see if anyone was in earshot of their conversation. The castle was busy with preparations for the voyage of the king's representatives, notably the duke of Norfolk in whose household John was an esquire, to take much interest in them.

"Look here, you are about to go into Portugal and my lady, the Infanta Joanna is renowned for her piety. In that land they have measures for dealing with heretics that make our own mere burnings appear benevolent. Hold your tongue else you might find it torn out. Such utterances are sure to be picked up on and the king might have something to say on the matter if he learns a heretic is among his delegation."

"The king has a bible in English," responded John petulantly. "When he was crowned king he commanded that his coronation oath be delivered in English. I believe he might not be unsympathetic to new ideas regarding the Church. He is certainly keen to reform common law, and render that in English, too."

"You speak foolishly," growled Robert through gritted teeth. "The king's bride will certainly demand your life if she hears of it, and the king will hardly deny her. Now I want your oath that you will speak no more in this way."

John smiled grimly at his friend. "I cannot give you my oath, but I will give my word that I shall keep my thoughts to myself for the duration of our present business; will that do?"

Robert stepped away and fixed John with a lugubrious expression in his face. "It will have to for now. I have other things to concern me and I have no desire to besmirch my own reputation by speaking for a friend who has been taken up for heresy."

"I should not expect that of you, Robert."

The two squires clasped each other's arms and parted, John back to his duties with the duke of Norfolk and Robert to his with the lord bastard John of Pomfret. As he returned to the chamber in the castle to attend his master, his breast was troubled. He was familiar with the doctrine of the Lollards and their questioning of Holy Church. Like most folk, he could hardly accept the idea that salvation was possible merely by adhering to scripture with no intercession by Church or clergy necessary. If he could not confess his sins to a priest, how could he be absolved of them? The very idea that the bread and wine of the Eucharist was not actually and miraculously transubstantiated into the very body and blood of Christ was incomprehensible to him. He knew folk were generally contemptuous of the Church, where rich prelates kept their wealth to themselves and at the bottom, mendicant friars had to beg a living. People resented having to pay tithes to the church and then pay again to support the beggar clergy. These matters only added to the uncertainty he was beginning to feel was abroad in the world. He could not shake off the feeling that great events were about to break forth. Above the castle the sky was darkening as rain clouds came over from the west. He shuddered as he wrapped his mantle around him, though the tremor he felt in his body was not entirely due to the chill brought by a freshening wind.

* * *

Robert trotted down the gangway of the ship Primrose, one of the vessels which had brought him to Lisbon including the entourages of the lord bastard John of Pomfret and the duke of Norfolk. The duke, John Howard, had been met by a crowd of courtiers that had come down from the *Castelo de São Jorge*, where Moorish crenellations could be seen atop its square walls and towers on the hill above the city. Already they were processing through the town on their way to the royal palace. Robert was dressed in brown doublet and expensive black hose with a short brown mantle worn off one shoulder. A black chapeau with a depending strip of velvet adorned his head. His boots were brown leather turned over at calf length. At his waist was a belt with his arming sword and a long dagger. He was glad to be on solid ground once more. The passage to Lisbon had been rougher than he had anticipated and everyone, lord, courtier and common servant had been sick most of the way. John Howard had fared better than most, but then his father had taken him to sea regularly and he had his sea legs. Even he, though, had succumbed to nausea at one point.

The quay here at the mouth of the River Tagus was busier even than the landings in London, and to Robert it seemed, somewhat cleaner. Unlike London, there was little smell emanating from the city and the clear sunlight lifted his spirits. Strange sights there were here. Not all the owners of the buildings around the harbour had decided whether to let them remain as the former Moorish architects had left them, or replace them with gothic to reflect modern European taste. They were a collection of warehouses and stores interspersed with the businesses of those concerned with seafaring –

rope-maker, sail-maker, carpenter, maps and instrument maker. Officers were here that appointed captains for trade adventures and collected the taxes when they returned with a rich cargo. The harbour itself was alive with vessels, carracks, caravels, galleys, with pinnaces hurrying between, many at anchor and others at the quay loading and unloading trade goods. The city was, to Robert's eye, a delight of colour – its red roofs and white walls glowing in the sun while around the quay were merchants dressed in the finest robes haranguing their servants and labourers.

Suddenly a sight he had never experienced before took him by surprise. A crowd of about two hundred people, each one as black as midnight, were being herded away from the harbour and into the town. Just having come ashore from a trading vessel, there were men, women and children being jostled and shoved by Portuguese who prodded at them with staves to keep them in close company. The children were naked while the men and women were clad simply in loincloths. He had heard of black men, but had never seen one, though he had heard there were a few in London. He knew there were blackamoors in Levant but that was so distant from England he could hardly envision it. These were slaves come from Africa. Those who traded in that commodity had them brought to them at the coast by their tribal chiefs from the hinterland, a place they dared not venture into themselves. Africa was a land of wild beasts, some of which he had seen in the king's menagerie at the Tower of London. It was said that inland were men with no heads and eyes and mouths in their chests. That thought caused him to look closely but he could see nothing that distinguished these from any other human except their colour and some of the Portuguese guards with them were almost as black.

Robert looked about him for his master, the lord John and spied him gathering his servants around him. Fra Maurice was with him, though he seemed to be holding back while he surveyed the city with a slightly disapproving frown. He hurried over before he was missed, shoved himself forward and swept lord John a bow.

"Ah, squire Robert, I was wondering when you would join us."

"I was taken in by the sights of the city, my lord, being a month at sea and glad to be on land again," offered Robert as an excuse.

"Yes, I can see why," said lord John gazing at the sight with green hills rolling away into the distance beyond the city. "Lisbon shows a pretty aspect. Let us away to the palace." He pointed to the castelo on its dominant hill. "Howell!"

"My lord?" One of his servants stepped forward.

"See to the unloading of my chests and bring them up to the

castelo. The rest of you come along. We must catch my lord Norfolk before he reaches the palace." The man Howell bowed and turned back to the ship waving over a couple of loungers, of which there are many on a busy quay, and these two had a donkey cart. Robert wondered if the man would bring his chest along too then reassured himself. His own clothes were placed in the chest containing their harness and the man would hardly leave that behind.

Lord John strode out at a smart pace leaving Fra Maurice puffing some way behind. His attendants were able to keep up and Robert was beckoned forward to walk with him. They left the harbour and wound their way through the narrow streets of the city, which were unpaved but dry and firm. Unlike London, there were no running sewers nor was rubbish piled about. As they climbed upwards, the streets would open here and there into orchards, and gardens heady with the scent of herbs, and bare patches where goats were tethered, then close again into small market squares, covered over in the style of Arab medina. People were everywhere, hurrying about their business and gazing with unabashed and probing curiously at the Englishmen, here to take their Infanta into England to marry with that country's king.

"There is the connection with England," said lord John as the great castle came into view before them. "*Castelo de São Jorge de Lancastre*, the castle of St. George and Lancaster. See the flags flying there. You might think it is to welcome us and that might be, but St. George is as important here as in England."

"Why is Lancaster added to the name?" panted Robert. Just ahead they could see the tail end of the duke of Norfolk's entourage and lord John had quickened his pace to be there with the duke when he entered through the castle portal.

"Why, the castle was named by King João the First of Portugal upon his marriage to Phillipa of Lancaster, daughter of John of Gaunt. Our king's intended bride is a direct descendent of hers and thus the object of much hope for the future of England. Their children will be of unassailable Plantagenet blood. The daughter of King João the First and Phillipa of Lancaster, the Infanta Isabella, married Philip the Good of Burgundy and was the mother of Charles the Bold, recently deceased husband of the present duchess of Burgundy, sister of our King Richard."

Robert marvelled that such a definite royal connection was to be found here, in this strange place. The castle was of a peculiar design and he had enough knowledge of castle construction to see that it was hardly defensible, should it be laid siege by a determined army. Portugal had been under Moorish rule for centuries until the Moors were finally driven out in the year 1147. Much of their architectural influence had been retained though he had heard this castle was now rebuilt as a palace, which explained its lack of military strength.

"There is a story that might entertain you," gasped lord John, himself beginning to feel the effects of his exertions. "See this gate before us?" There was indeed a huge gate with massive doors that, at the moment stood agape.

"I do my lord."

"When the castle was taken from the Moors it was due to the sacrifice of a knight of Portugal, I forget his name. The story goes that seeing the gate open, but in the process of being closed by the Moor defenders, he threw himself into the gap and wedged it open with his own body letting his Christian soldiers get inside, though at the cost of his own life."

"A true Christian knight!"

"Fortunately, today the gate is opened to us," said lord John breathlessly as they entered through the gate and into the castle. Guards either side of the gate stood to attention as the Englishmen passed by. They found themselves in a great square packed with people, soldiers, nobles and knights. At the far side was a huge palace whose walls were pierced with numerous windows, many furnished with ornate stone fretwork to let in light and air while obscuring the inside. A semi-circle of stone steps led upwards to a magnificent doorway set inside pillars carved in a variety of designs. Beside were niches where statues of saints glowed in their coloured robes. St. George slaying the dragon was depicted in stone above the portal. Robert noted with some satisfaction that the dragon was painted red, like the Welsh one and it was the English patron saint with his sword in its throat.

Looking around the square, the other buildings had banners hanging from them, the emblems and badges of the Portuguese nobles who were there to greet their English counterparts. On the towers that interspersed the castle walls were flying alternately the English flag of St. George and the royal arms of Portugal. The latter was a shield of silver with a cross of five blue shields each with five white balls. A red border around the shield had seven golden castles and above was an open golden crown. Six fountains, quartets of porpoise signifying Portugal's maritime interests punctuated the square, spouting from their mouths sparkling water into fanciful scallop shells; but the music of their playing was lost in the general hubbub of the assembled crowd.

There were four cardinals, resplendent in their scarlet robes at the top of the steps waiting to greet their guests. Between them was the bishop of Lisbon, come there from the cathedral of Lisbon, *Se Patriarcal de St. Mary Major*. The archbishop of York, Thomas Rotherham was the first to ascend the steps as was befitting, along with a dozen of his clergy, with the duke of Norfolk immediately behind him. Norfolk had a hundred knights and men-at-arms in his entourage and lord John took his place behind them. He too, had fifty men-at-arms, all there to escort the king's bride to her new land. Robert took his place close behind his lord in the company of his three fellow squires. Following them were more clergy and twenty nuns. The king had sent them as a gesture to comfort and reassure his bride, who he knew had declared her intent to become a nun herself, until her dynastic duty as Infanta of Portugal overrode her personal desire.

After much bowing and exhibition of polite greeting the prominent nobles entered the palace. As they passed through the doors a magnificent hall opened up before them. For some reason Robert looked up and there above him was the most resplendent ceiling, chased in gold and every colour the art of man could devise and there, in the centre, the Royal arms of Portugal. At the far end of the hall two figures stood under the canopy, which itself was a thing of wonder. Here to greet their guests were the king and queen of Portugal. A vast sheet of pale green silk rose above the dais where the royal thrones were set. Behind were the royal arms of King Richard the Third of England, complete with his supporters of two white boars. Beside were displayed the arms of the royal House of Aviz, the arms of Portugal supported each side by angels with resplendent white wings. The bishop of Lisbon and the Archbishop of York bowed to the king who stood before his throne, his queen by his side, then stood to one side as the cardinals made their obeisance. Next the duke of Norfolk came forward and knelt before the king and his queen, Eleanor of Viseu.

"My lord, John Howard, duke of Norfolk," intoned King João. "We are pleased to see you at last. I hear you had a rough passage from England?" King João spoke in courtly French, the duke having no Portuguese though he could manage a little Spanish, if compelled to do so. The whole of this meeting would be conducted in French, the universal language of the nobility.

"Indeed, dread king," replied the duke, "but brought to safe harbour by the Grace of God."

With great curiosity, Robert scrutinised the figures of John the Second of Portugal and his queen. The Portuguese king was of moderate height, inclined to corpulence and wore a short beard that began at his hairline and descended to his chin. His long face had something of a sour expression, as if he had just tasted of a lemon fruit. Dark brown eyes were sunk into his head as if reluctant to show their depths yet with a quality, perhaps exclusive to kings, which seemed to obscure his thoughts while penetrating the soul of a subject. His queen was small and dark of mien, swathed in the finest embroidered silks and resplendent with jewels. Both wore purple mantles trimmed with ermine.

King João raised the duke while his queen looked on, smiling benignly. The king presented his ministers to the duke who, in turn, presented his own, beginning formally with the lord John of Gloucester. King João invited the duke of Norfolk to sit beside him on the dais while his queen sat on his other side. Arranged either side of the thrones were other chairs for lord John, the cardinals, the Archbishop of York and the Bishop of Lisbon. Everyone else stood with those of highest rank nearest to the dais. Robert found himself somewhere to one side behind a courtier of low stature which permitted a view of the monarchs. There was, of course, one person missing; the Infanta Joanna - and everyone waited eagerly for her entrance.

She came preceded by the gentle music of lutes and viols. A troop of minstrels came into the hall behind which walked a dozen ladies dressed modestly in plain black satin with saffron over-gowns trimmed with sable. Their heads were covered with black bonnets dressed with lace and they held Psalters in their hands. The Infanta Joanna followed, splendidly attired in brown silk showing through a surplice of fine white lace. On her head she wore a coronet richly encrusted with jewels. Her face was similar to her brother the king, being full with large cheeks and a small pert mouth turned down at the corners giving her an air of petulance. She could have been beautiful had it not been for her lugubrious expression. Her dress had a long train, somewhat old-fashioned now, requiring two ladies to carry it with a further six trailing behind.

Robert, gazing at her over the heads of the courtiers in front of him, thought she had the aspect of a plump Margaret Stanley, perhaps her antithesis in feature seeing as that woman was lean and sour of face. He knew she was pious and had it not been for the requirements of the alliance with England, would have entered by preference a convent of Dominican nuns. Still, she could have presented a more pleasant mien rather than the reluctant fatalism written in her face. Her only concession to the occasion was the magnificent coronet, and Robert suspected she had been instructed to wear it rather than its portage being her own choice – but this was speculation and it might be the Infanta would prove a loving and comforting queen for King Richard. After all he, too, was known for personal piety characterised by natural generosity. Perhaps the two would make a fine pair of rulers for England. He remembered what grandfather Cornelius had told him before he left England, that Joanna had acted as Regent for her father, Afonso the Fifth while he was absent from Portugal on one of his military expeditions to Tangier. That was in fourteen seventy-one, the year Edward the Fourth of England won his crown back. She would have been of but twenty years then, just eight months older than Richard, then duke of Gloucester. Whatever her austere aspect now, there was clearly a formidable woman behind it.

The Infanta dropped to her knees before the duke of Norfolk, he being the representative of her betrothed, King Richard the Third of England, her head bowed humbly as if she were penitent. Norfolk stepped down from the dais, nobly took her hands and raised her, his face smiling down upon her in contrast to her own features. She deigned to grant his grace a slight smile while he conducted her onto the dais and her chair beside the king, otherwise she maintained a stoical expression that gave away nothing of her thoughts.

Robert was tiring of the spectacle. Courtiers and others hemmed him in the throng and lord John was with the duke of Norfolk. Feeling a little lost he was just about to push his way nearer to his lord when he noticed Fra Maurice talking to a man who by his livery, had the appearance of a Portuguese servant. Obviously the monk was too lowly to fraternise with archbishops and cardinals, though as lord John's ghostly father he had a natural place by his side. From what he knew of the monk, he was not one to converse casually with lowly servants so this one either had some message to convey to him or there was some business afoot. As the two parted, the Portuguese shoved his way through the crowd in Robert's general direction. Robert placed himself close by a doorway where, he considered, the man might be heading. As he passed he noted the badge of whoever was his master – a gold tower with a blue door. Robert followed him as far as the door and after the man had passed through, shoved it open himself to see what lay behind it. There was a corridor that led to a further door at the far end. Romanesque arches punctuated the wall on one side of the corridor and Robert could see that it opened into a small courtyard where men were grooming dozens of horses. He leaned in casual curiosity at one of the arches and noted the servant as he picked out a horse and mounted up. Soon he was off, trotting through a large gateway that faced the city. Perhaps that was where he was headed. There was nothing particularly unusual in all this, but Robert thought he might manufacture from it an excuse. He still had the letter from grandfather Cornelius in his pocket and he was keen to get into the city.

With this in mind, Robert went back into the great hall. The royals and the nobles were moving off. He knew the duke of Norfolk and probably lord John would soon be in conference with King João and his immediate family so he hurried over to have a word with him before he disappeared into the royal apartments.

"My lord, I would ask leave to go into the city," he begged as he managed to catch up with John of Pomfret. "There is nothing I can do for you here, and with regard to our other business, that to do with any possible plotting by the king's enemies, I might learn something."

Lord John raised his eyebrows. "How would you do that? You have no contacts here." His eyes were constantly flicking towards the royal party and their gradual movement towards their privy apartments.

"My grandfather who, as you know has often acted as an agent for his grace the king, has given me the names of one or two here in Lisbon that I might contact for information. If there is anything strange afoot, I may be able to discover it." He decided after all not to inform his master about the strange behaviour of Fra Maurice, if indeed there was anything dubious about it.

"Then go to it," replied lord John enthusiastically. "I am well attended here, but report back to me tomorrow. There is to be a banquet tonight, which it now appears, you will miss. I hope your contacts, whoever they are, invite you to dinner otherwise it will be tavern fare for you, I fear."

Robert swept lord John a cursory bow, the other being in a hurry to join the royal party and not overly concerned with servile protocol from his squire. Robert made his way into the palace courtyard and decided he would walk down into the city, having no horse allotted to him, though he could no doubt procure one in the name of the lord bastard, John of Gloucester. Making himself known to the sergeant of the palace guard, to ensure his unobstructed return, he walked down the castle hill into the upper town. He followed the route of the procession, that being the only part of the city known to him. Presently he found himself in the *Baixa*, the lower town among the markets and merchants busily plying their trades. There seemed to be numerous spice markets where sacks of pepper, cinnamon, ginger and other exotic condiments combined to swim through the olfactory senses. He knew Lisbon, a maritime city, was a great importer of these expensive goods, more precious, some of them, than their weight in gold. Lisbon was even more cosmopolitan than London, the only other city he had visited where the population was diverse.

Here was a very Babel where, so it seemed to him, every tongue since the dawn of time was being spoken and individual expression was lost in the constant clamour. How was it possible to pick out a single language, one he understood? That was limited to English, French, Breton and a little Latin, though he had small practice in speaking the latter other than its use in a church. French was spoken at court and from infancy his father, when he was home, had insisted he spoke in Breton so he could converse in that language on the few occasions he had visited his father's family in their home country. The native language of Portugal was akin to Spanish and should he have known any he might not have felt so out-of-place. He decided to ask for the man whose name his grandfather had given him. Though his enquiry might not be understood, there was a chance the name would be familiar and he might obtain directions to his house. As it turned out, the first person he asked, a Portuguese baker, was fluent in French and the name was indeed familiar to him.

"Roderigo Anes Pinteado? Yes I know him, in fact I supply his *feitoria*, his trading post, with bread." The man was all smiles and servility as he contemplated the modest richness of Robert's dress. Perhaps he fancied by its fashion and cut, and the fact he was English, that this was one of the nobles who had passed up to the castelo? "You will find him at *Casa dos Escravos*. It is easy to find; merely follow that street until you come to a grove of trees. There is his house." He pointed out a wide boulevard with what looked like the walls of private houses down one side and orchards on the other. Looking along the street he could see it appeared to open up into a green countryside where vineyards and olive groves testified to the peaceful affluence of the city.

The grove of trees turned out to be a sort of perimeter to a high walled enclosure with iron gates where six guards were lounging. What was obviously a guardhouse stood to one side just beyond the gate. It was of simple wooden construction with daub walls washed white and roofed over with plain red tiles. The bottom of the walls was stained brown by dust from the earth and the internal wattle could be seen where bits of baked mud had broken off. The protective walls were extensive and Robert wondered what was behind such a great, enclosed area. It was not fortified and looked as if it was a recent construction. He noted that sharp sticks were set all along the tops to discourage any attempt to do what he wondered -

get in or out? The guards stood across the gates, which curiously were open seeing that the walls were constructed for some sort of security. A motley collection of black-haired, dark-skinned ruffians, shoeless, wearing short breeches of white canvas and dirty yellow shirts barred his way inside. They held short spears and had curtle axes at their belts, heavy scimitar-type weapons sharpened along one edge only, and simple rondel daggers. They might have worn plain iron helmets, but these were on the ground at their feet. Four of them levelled the points of their spears at him while another went off into the guardhouse. Robert stopped and waited patiently.

A man dressed similar in appearance to the guards, but with some authority seeing as he had dusty brown boots on his feet and wore a linen cap, strolled over fixing him with a hard glare, as was the way with minor officials. He grunted something in his native tongue and Robert, guessing it would be useless to try to converse with him, simply showed him the name of Roderigo Anes Pinteado on a document, which he withdrew from inside his doublet. Whether the fellow could read or not was questionable. If Robert had reached the right place it was possible he might at least recognise the name of his master. Whatever the case, the fellow looked Robert up and down and then issued a stream of commands to his fellow guards. He waved Robert through making it plain that he was to be accompanied by two of the guards.

They passed by a garden of large expanse where a variety of crops were growing, mainly some sort of bean and vegetables. A few black children to keep it weed free were hoeing the ground. The guard led him to a mansion, again of recent construction. The house was a large building with a stone colonnade at the front. Just four stone steps led to a marble paved forecourt where lemon trees heavy with fruit provided shade. A Romanesque arch provided the portal to the inner rooms but before then he stopped in front of a servant in light green livery and wearing a brown chapeau.

"I wish to speak to Senor Roderigo Anes Pinteado. Do I have the right house?" He addressed the man in French as he considered it was hardly likely he would understand English.

"You have the right house, monsieur," replied the man. "Who is it calling upon him?"

"My name is Robert de la Halle, grandson of monsieur Cornelius Quirke of England. I have this letter of introduction." He gave the man the letter, which he scrutinised then nodded in satisfaction.

"If you would care to take a seat just here," he replied indicating one of a group of chairs conveniently placed in the shade of the colonnade, "I shall inform my master." He dismissed the guard with a wave of his hand, then took himself off into the house.

As he sat there he looked about and observed that the road from the outer wall let around the front of the house and through another gateway. Judging by the state of the dry ground it was regularly used, there being not a single weed or blade of grass to be seen. Some sort of irrigation channel seemed to be in use as the garden was a veritable jungle of green leaf that only a copious supply of water could produce. He wondered if there was an aqueduct bringing water from the hills that he could see all around. After a short time he heard the sound of shoes on stone as the servant returned along with another – a man of great wealth by the appearance of him. Robert stood as the man came up to him, his arms open in welcome and a huge smile on his tanned face. He was dressed in a red velvet gown chased with intricate designs in gold and silver thread. He was about fifty years or so in age and fine lines were already tracing a record of the years in his face, particularly around his eyes. The lower part of his face was hidden under a long black beard that was braided into separate strands interwoven with scarlet thread.

"Master de la Halle," he gushed in accented English. "Yes, I can see something of your grandfather in your eyes." He took Robert by the shoulders and looked into his face. "Come, let us go inside where we can talk."

By his manner and dress, Robert began to realise that though he had never seen one, here was a Jew, a race banished from England and also Spain, but which lived everywhere else. Fascinated by the manner of the man, he followed him into the house wondering what kind of business he might have with his grandfather.

9 – The King's Bride

Having passed through the house, his host took Robert into a vast quadrangle where large numbers of black slaves were gathered. Some were in lines that were managed by Portuguese guards and others stood or sat in more casual groups. All the men were dressed in identical white, calf-length breeches and simple chemise, while the women were covered in a single white shift. Those children approaching adulthood were dressed as the adults while the younger children ran naked. The quadrangle comprised a series of single story dwellings with palm thatch for roofing. Each had an opening for a door and a single window, though there was no actual wooden door to enclose them. At one corner of the quadrangle was an iron cauldron with a fire under it where something was simmering gently. Stacked next to it were simple clay bowls and drinking cups. A well was located in the centre and two women were busy there winding up the bucket and tipping water into clay water pots.

Those who were arranged in lines were being kept there by guards who prodded and poked at the people with long sticks pointed at the end, such as commanding the obedience of a donkey. A Portuguese who looked to be affluent by his robes was examining each one in turn.

"Recent arrivals," said Roderigo. "They come from down the coast of Africa and though the captains of the ships that bring them attempt to keep them in good sort, yet a sea voyage for people such as these, particularly if contrary winds extend their time at sea, causes weight loss and other casualties. Doctor Lopez, as you can see, is examining them and noting any infirmities among them."

"Are you not afraid they will escape? I cannot see much to prevent them apart from a few guards and a gate."

"Where would they escape to?" replied Roderigo opening his arms expansively. "These people were originally captives of warring tribes within the darkest parts of Africa. Had not the chiefs of the tribes that captured them sold them as slaves they would have been massacred. They are marched from their homeland to the sea, which none of them had ever seen. Next they make a voyage, in our case to Lisbon, where they are housed, clothed and fed. They are already in better condition than when they lived in their original homes."

"What will happen to them now?" asked Robert, intrigued by the sight. He knew that slaves were traded particularly in this part of the world, but had never had occasion to think on it overmuch. He remembered being outraged on hearing stories of Christians being captured by the Moors and put to work in their sea-going galleys, but these before him were heathens taken from a primitive land. Slaves had been used since the Creation of the world and were bought and sold everywhere.

"Most of these will go into the orchards and vineyards around Lisbon," came the reply. "They will stay here for a week or two while they recover from the effects of their voyage, then go to auction. The women make good house servants and the children too. The men will work the land. You will have noticed the gardens at the front of the house where we grow vegetables to feed the slaves – bean crops mostly. You can see the product of their labours over there." He pointed to the cauldron, which was obviously where the food for the slaves was cooked. "I see from the letter your grandfather sent with you," continued Roderigo, "that he wishes me to invest in a voyage down the African coast to purchase more slaves."

"Is that what he wants? He did not confide in me except that I am to have one quarter of the profits," replied Robert.

"Then that should set you up nicely, providing the adventure is a success. I am about to equip five vessels that are to go to Benin and Cornelius has sent a bill of exchange that will let him purchase fifty percent of the capacity of one of them. King João has just caused this casa to be built." Roderigo spread his arms and turned about indicating the house and its other facilities. "It is the *Casa de Escravos,* a department of the royal trading house of the *Casa da Mina* and dedicated exclusively to the African trade."

"Where is Benin?" wondered Robert. "I have never heard of that place."

"It is a long way down the coast of Africa and has only just been opened up as a trading port. The king is encouraging expeditions even further south and entertains the idea there might be a sea route to India and China. If that is ever realised then tell Cornelius he might expect even greater profits. A ship can load far more spices at less cost than those carried overland by pack animals. We already trade in spices from the Orient here, but imagine if we could get there by sea!"

Robert was impressed with the vision not only of Roderigo and his fellow traders, but the king who had the desire to profit from their adventures himself. Already Portugal was the greatest trading and seafaring nation of the century. A sea route to the Orient would increase her wealth beyond that of the legendary Prester John whose fabulous treasure men spoke of in hushed tones. Now Portugal was about to be allied to England whose king was also a seafarer. There looked to be exciting times ahead and already Robert was a small part of it. One quarter of the profits from a half cargo of African slaves! He could hardly believe it.

Roderigo gestured to Robert expressing a clear wish that they might retire inside the house. When they were seated comfortably in a court where a fountain played over a jumble of stones of various hues, a servant brought two goblets of fine wine.

"You should know," began Robert, "that I am here in the entourage of the lord bastard John of Pomfret who is attached to the court of King Richard the Third of England. We are part of the escort of his bride, the Infanta Joanna of Portugal. My grandfather's instructions are a diversionary component of opportunism occasioned by a greater design."

"Of course, agreed Roderigo, "I understand that, but your grandfather would consider it remise of me should I neglect to inform you of other affairs associated with your expedition." Robert wondered at the description "expedition" but disregarded it.

"His grace, King Richard, is aware that there are those in the world who might not wish his nuptials to progress naturally," drawled Robert as if he was a master of diplomacy. Roderigo smiled and sipped at his wine goblet.

"Your king is correct in his assessment and I am sure Cornelius would agree with me. How much do you know of the friction between the houses of Aviz and Castile?"

"Portugal and Spain! Is there friction?"

"You are aware, are you not, that our king's heir, Afonso is betrothed to Isabella of Aragon, the eldest daughter of Isabella of Castile and Ferdinand of Spain and has been since infancy?"

"I had heard something of that, but what is its significance?"

Roderigo tugged at one of his plaited strands of beard as if, had he been Catholic, selecting a rosary. "Ferdinand and Isabella of Spain have but one male heir, Juan, and he is frail. If he were to die, not an unreasonable prospect and with no spare to follow, the next in line would be Isabella of Aragon, their eldest daughter."

"Meaning that should she marry with Afonso of Portugal and eventually become Queen, he could also become monarch of Spain!"

"Precisely, and Castile have been attempting to get the contract annulled for years, without success."

"How would that affect England, when the Infanta Joanna is queen?"

"It means that England, Portugal and Spain would be allies. Of these, Portugal and England would come out as the dominant nations – a formidable combination. Spain is conscious of it and so is France."

"What you are saying indicates to me that Spain wants to be a more influential player in Europe."

"Just so. Ferdinand and Isabella of Spain desire to be free of the Portuguese contract. That cannot be and so another option open to them is to destroy the marriage of Richard of England with Joanna of Portugal. That would remove one of Portugal's most powerful allies. Richard would likely have to settle for another princess, perhaps one of Spain? They have other daughters, though perhaps a little young for King Richard, who must beget an heir as soon as possible."

"You fear then, for the Infanta's life?"

"I do. We have the added problem of France. They are no friend of Spain but are similarly threatened. Imagine a powerful England combined with Portugal, and France with her ambition of annexing Brittany and Burgundy. Their king Charles is but a thirteen years old boy and France is ruled under the regency of his sister Anne, a most capable woman by all accounts. The schemes of France could easily fall into dust and she is surrounded by enemies that would be only too pleased to take advantage of her weakened state."

"The Holy Roman Emperor for one - and the Italian states."

"You have it!" declared Roderigo. "Then there is the position with Ceuta, a trading post in Morocco at the Strait of Gibraltar where caravans bearing gold, ivory and other trade goods come to sell their treasures. At the moment Portugal dominates the town and its trade, but the monarchs of Spain are covetous and there is always the possibility they will try to seize it. An alliance with England and Portugal will make that so much harder to achieve."

Robert pondered on this. Could the Jew be trusted in his opinion? Isabella and Ferdinand of Spain had recently expelled Jews from their lands and were aggravated that Portugal had welcomed them and gave them a place to trade. England, too, had banned Jews from as far back as the reign of King Edward the First. Where did Roderigo's loyalties actually lie? He would have to tread carefully.

"So the marriage between King Richard of England and Joanna of Portugal is the axle around which the world is turning?" said Robert, his heart aflutter with the dreadful realisation of the consequences of the mission upon which he was engaged.

"It is indeed," responded Roderigo, "and so you can see why the Infanta's life might be in danger. You know - of course you do - that the woman dame Margaret Stanley is involved with this?"

"Her name has been mentioned," agreed Robert, "though I am beginning to think events are way beyond her malign scope."

"Never believe it," snapped Roderigo vehemently. "It is through women as her, vengeful and full of spite that dreadful murder might be done and without a blemish on those behind that murder."

Robert at once realised the truth of what he had just been told. Dame Margaret Stanley was a loose cannon, primed and ready to fire at a moment should a Plantagenet float across her sights. Joanna of Portugal was one such and dame Stanley would have no compunction in destroying the Infanta, even at the cost of her own life, if by doing so she brought down the ambitions of the House of York. It only required the direction of the monarchs of Spain or France to set her to it and then stand back, themselves innocent, no matter how foul the deed - it would never be proved to be in their name.

"I am at a loss as to how I might inform the Infanta of her danger," Robert muttered almost to himself.

"A difficult position, I admit," responded Roderigo, "but I might be able to help you. If you are to watch out for her, you must get close and that is going to be difficult for one of your rank, however, you have your years as an advantage."

"My years!" he snorted. "The lady is almost a nun and I hardly think might be attracted to one of my youth."

Roderigo put his head back and laughed until Robert feared he might do himself harm. "I was not thinking you might try to seduce her," he managed between gasps. "You need something to gain her attention - then she might draw you close."

"I fear you are jesting with me, monsieur," he said in an offended tone.

"No, no, monsieur Robert, I am perhaps being unfair with you. Please accept my apologies. I had no intention of ridiculing you; it is just that I have the very thing where you might inveigle your way into the lady's company. You must rely on your own charm to remain there."

* * *

The Infanta Joanna was delighted with Robert's gift. Roderigo had divined her character exactly. Her eyes had opened wide with surprise, then crinkled into laughter when the young squire led the strange monkey into her presence. It had black fur and a black face surrounded by long, white locks of hair. A mantle of white hair adorned the shoulders and its long, thin tail had a white tip. To a woman whose piety inclined her to life in a convent, the animal complimented her persona exactly. Robert handed her the thin silver chain that was fastened to a silver collar around its neck. The monkey seemed not to have the slightest fear and scampered onto the Infanta's chair, taking from her hands the orange she offered. The animal, though, was a messy eater and juice sprayed everywhere as it bit through the peel. One of her ladies rushed forward with a cloth to wipe the juice from the Infanta's dress, though the princess herself giggled with delight as tiny hands stripped the flesh from the orange and threw the peel at a courtier.

"Where has the creature come from?" she asked of Robert as he knelt before her.

"I am informed from way down the African coast, out of the remotest parts that the king's ships have reached," he told her. "There is none other like it in the courts of Europe. The creature is a female I think."

"Why yes, and it has the look of Sister Beatrice," she laughed, her ladies joining in, though a nun standing nearby looked about her guiltily in case the holy sister in question might get to hear of the jest at her expense.

The lord bastard John of Pomfret smiled indulgently close by. He and the duke of Norfolk had been chatting with the ladies of Joanna's court, telling them of the great palace at Windsor and the city of London of which they had heard, but never visited. Soon they were to embark on a sea voyage and though as ladies of a seafaring nation they supposed the ships of Portugal to be the finest in the world, yet few of them were looking forward to it. The Infanta Joanna betrayed no such apprehension at the prospect of a sea voyage, but as to her marriage with King Richard, none of them had managed to define exactly what her true feelings were. Joanna smiled at Robert and indicated for him to rise to his feet.

"We are pleased with your gift, squire Robert, and it gladdens us to have such a gentle young man at our court. Let us hope that the English gallants we are yet to meet are such as you."

"You do me too much honour, your grace," he replied with a low bow. "Yet I fear my countrymen outshine me as the sun does the moon."

"But not in modesty, perhaps? Ladies, we have much to look forward to," she replied beaming at her women. These were studying Robert with a variety of interest in their faces. One of them, a young woman about the same age as he, was particularly studious and Robert could not help noticing her interest. She was small and gracile, hardly measuring to his shoulders, yet with what seemed to Robert a golden complexion where dark brown eyes twinkled as if stars were hidden somewhere in their depths. She was clad in a rich gown of green velvet with an embroidered lining of silk that showed where it was turned back to display something of the yellow shift beneath. Her hennin was in the English style, as were those of the other ladies, but he thought he had caught a glimpse of rich auburn hair escaping beneath it.

"My lord John," said the Infanta addressing John of Pomfret. "It is our wish that squire Robert come with us on the morrow when we hunt."

"He is renowned as a fine shot with the crossbow, my lady. I am sure he will help us enjoy great sport." Lord John bowed to the Infanta and withdrew from her presence indicating to Robert that he should attend upon him. They left the apartment where the Infanta held her court and into the great hall of the *Castelo de* São *Jorge,* mingling with the general mass of courtiers and supplicants always to be found wherever a king was in residence. Lord John found a discreet spot in a corner of the hall.

"That was a very clever move on your part," said lord John appreciatively, "to discover the lady's maternal soft-spot. The king will be pleased, too. It makes things easier for him and smoothes his path to her bedchamber. Some of us have been concerned that she might be frigid, seeing as she had her heart set on a convent life. As everyone knows, a frigid woman cannot conceive and it is vital our King Richard produce an heir, one that has time to grow to manhood before the king's own mortality catches up with him. That animal is as a child to her and can only help to encourage matters of conception."

Robert held his tongue, nodding and meekly accepting lord John's accolade. No purpose could be served by informing him it was actually the guile of the Jew, Roderigo Anes Pinteado that was responsible for the ruse and was devised but to entertain the lady, not present her with a marital aid. Still, the scheme had worked far better than could be hoped. No courtier could get so close to influence Joanna, but the monkey had done the trick and Robert was now her pet, too.

"I have had my spies about," whispered lord John looking around, "and all seems as it should be. My lord of Norfolk reports the same. Did you discover anything while in the town? Clearly you were up to something. Where did the monkey come from?"

"Oh, I was engaged in some business on behalf of my grandfather when I spied the animal in the house of a trader in slaves. I thought it might amuse the Infanta."

"Well, perhaps I have overestimated your guile and you have merely stumbled upon a way into her favour. No matter - what works, works." Lord John gave a casual shrug as if satisfied his squire was not so much of a courtier after all.

"I did discover something that is of concern," said Robert quickly before his lord's elevated opinion of him began to founder. "It seems there is friction between the royal houses of Portugal and Spain resulting in a devil's alliance with England's enemies, chiefly France." He gave a brief outline of his conversation with Roderigo and the possibility that Spain and France might desire the destruction of the marriage between King Richard of England and Joanna, Princess of Portugal. These countries, not wishing to expose their malice, could make use of the woman dame Margaret Stanley where she might be manipulated into doing the deed for them in her own name, thus absolving them of any possible accusations of complicity.

"Yes, what you say makes a lot of sense," replied lord John, stroking his chin. "Our king is vulnerable without an heir and this marriage with Joanna is his best chance of gaining one. With her out of the way the king stands alone. Should anything malign befall him, we shall be plunged back into the darkness of the recent wars."

"We must be vigilant, my lord."

"Indeed, squire Robert."

* * *

A single hair here and there on the chin of a youth is a matter of embarrassment and Robert was engaged in shaving off the few that adorned his chin. He observed with something of relief that the hairs on his upper lip, though sparse, could just about pass muster and he carefully smoothed them each way to encourage the idea they were more luxuriant than they actually were. Lord John was already attired for the hunt and bounding his way down the spiral stairs from his turret room. His squire would have to hurry if he were to catch him in time to help him onto his mount. It was not just the fact that the Infanta Joanna had commanded him to ride close to her and attend upon her monkey that encouraged his toilet, but the knowledge that the donzela Claris de Montanhas was in their company. Enquiries among the servants had revealed the name of the lady that had attracted his notice at Joanna's court. She was from a family that had fallen on hard times and the Infanta, as an act of charity, had taken Claris into her own household to alleviate the poverty of her family. She came from *Tras Os Montes*, beyond the mountains, a land to the north-east either side of the Douro River, and the ladies of the court had named her for that mountainous region. The donzela's family name he had not yet discovered but her epithet, Maiden of the Mountains, though probably intended pejoratively by the other ladies of Joanna's court, to his mind suited her admirably.

The courtyard into which he emerged seeking lord John was stuffed with horses, their riders and those attendants who would run along with them. Dogs were whipped into order and courtiers fussed around King João and the Infanta Joanna as they were settled onto their mounts. Queen Eleanor did not care for the hunt, nor being bounced around on horseback and so kept to her apartments. The monkey that Robert had presented to Joanna was clambering all over the horse upon which the Infanta was mounted making it skittish. While the Infanta was amused by its antics, her ladies were apprehensive that it might cause the horse to bolt, or at least try to dislodge the tormenting animal, the Infanta along with it. Lord John, who was just about to mount up, grabbed Robert by the arm.

"I think you had better offer to take that monkey from our princess before it causes real mischief," he growled in his ear. Robert bowed his assent and, running over to the Infanta made obeisance to her.

"May I help you with the monkey, your grace," he asked her. "I fear you might find its antics distracting during the hunt."

"Ah, squire Robert," she giggled like a girl, "I had wondered where you were. It is my wish you come with us and take charge of Enola."

"Enola, your grace?"

"Enola," replied the Infanta hooking her finger into the collar of the monkey and drawing it around to sit in her lap. "She is named for the mother of our saint of Lisbon, Saint Vincent whose relics are in the monastery of *São Vicente de Fora*." Strangely, as if it understood what was being said the animal put its hands together, not quite as if in prayer, but sufficiently so to cause the Infanta to think it had. "See, she approves her name!"

"If I may mount my horse, your grace, I can take Enola from you."

"Then go to it, squire Robert, and keep close to us. The donzela Claris will ride with us too. She and Enola seem to have formed a bond."

Robert's heart leaped within him. He had not thought too much of being the escort of a monkey, but with the donzela Claris by his side he felt more than compensated.

The hunting party rode out from the *Castelo de* São *Jorge* their hearts light and none more so than Robert de la Halle. The monkey was a nuisance with its constant scrambling and squeaking and must be securely held by its silver chain and a firm hand pressing it against the front of his saddle. He would have been tempted to wring its neck had it not been for the favour of the Infanta, to whom it seemed a child, and more particularly, the laughter of the donzela Claris who was highly amused by his struggles with the beast. She was riding beside him dressed plainly for the hunt, as he was. They followed closely the King, the Infanta and their courtiers who were more flamboyant in their attire than Robert and Claris who both possessed but modest means. The brightness of their faces and the joy in their hearts more than made up for any deficiency of dress and both had the favour of the Infanta Joanna. The English nobles, including lord Robert and the duke of Norfolk, trotted along with King João and his party while Robert stayed close behind the Infanta and her party of ladies and gallants. Huntsmen ran alongside the mounted riders and behind were the dogs and their handlers. These would flush game out of the woods around Lisbon and it was expected that there would be venison on the table after this day's sport.

As they rode out into the country above Lisbon, the olive groves and vineyards that fringed the city were left behind and before them stretched a vista of woodland, pasture, rough grassland and bushes of myrtle. The King's party stopped while the beaters with the dogs got ahead to start the game from the woodland. The Infanta, riding a little way behind stopped also and looked about her for her pet. Robert trotted over and placed his horse close to hers, relieved when the monkey Enola leapt across to scramble about the pouch she carried with titbits for the primate. He was conscious of the presence of the donzela Claris as she sidled her mount close to theirs while keeping a surreptitious eye on the young squire.

"I have been thinking on your Saint Vincent," he said knowing that the subject would be bound to interest the Infanta. "My father has told me about him, but I cannot remember what it was, except it had something to do with regard to Saint Lawrence, his own patron."

The Infanta's eyes illuminated with pious interest. "Yes, they come from the same region of Spain and were martyred in the same manner."

"Roasted on a gridiron!" exclaimed Robert.

"That is correct," she responded. Saint Vincent came from Saragossa while Saint Lawrence was from Huesca both in Aragon by the Ebro River.

"My father has the gridiron as his armoury mark," said Robert. "Saint Lawrence is patron of armourers."

"Saint Vincent is patron of vintners, a more peaceful occupation," chuckled Joanna.

"Yet one whose product stirs men to wrath and war where they might need use of my father's trade." Robert felt a flush of fear as he belatedly realised he was contesting with a royal princess. The lady either had not noticed or was inclined to enjoy the interplay; whichever there was no furious outburst at his temerity.

"Yes, it is an abiding mystery how the saints manage to interact with each other in spite of an apparent disparity of discipline." Joanna was diverted by the furious squealing of the monkey Enola, which had grabbed a nut through a loop in the purse and could not pull free unless it released its prize, something it was not inclined to do. The Infanta, laughing at the primate's discomfiture, attempted to solve the problem by offering another nut as tempting as the one the beast had in its grasp, hoping it would thus release it and get its hand free. The result was the monkey grabbed the second nut too in the other hand and was now unable, its hands being full, to strip either of its shell, nor pull free of its confining purse. "This animal is not unlike some lords I know of whom my brother the king has had to free himself," she observed coldly. "If I didn't know better, I would say these animals, apes and such, might be kin to mankind; they certainly have some of the same attributes."

"That is too deep for me," said Robert, "though I must admit there are some lords in England that our king would say have the same qualities."

The Infanta took a small knife from the purse and slit the silken loop that had the monkey a prisoner of its own greed, thus setting it free."

"A drastic measure, your grace," ventured Robert, "and a lesson not learned I think."

"Yes, squire Robert, I take your point, though it is but a beast." He noted an expression in her eyes that had something of revelation in it.

"I have heard, my lady," interrupted a small, musical voice, "that there are ravens on guard in the Tower of London." The donzela Claris realised the conversation was becoming difficult and feared the young squire would get himself into trouble unless diverted.

"There are, donzela," replied Robert. "I am astounded you know of them. It is said that if the Ravens ever leave the Tower then England shall fall."

"I know what donzela Claris is referring to," said Joanna with sudden interest. "We have spoken of Saint Vincent. Ravens too protect him. When he was martyred, his body was thrown on a dung heap and certain eagles came down to dispose of him. A flock of ravens drove them away and stayed by his eventual shrine to protect him. When his remains were brought here to Lisbon by ship, the ravens followed and are still here, at the monastery of São Vicente de Fora."

"Then ravens are harbingers of good fortune for Portugal and England, seeing as the birds protect us in both our lands." Robert had seen an opportunity to extract himself from his former arguments, which were showing signs of getting him into trouble, while honing his diplomatic skills. He smiled gratefully at Claris, who had been the means whereby he could extract himself. All he had to do now was keep his mouth shut and not voice the thought that had just come into his mind - that ravens were also harbingers of death.

* * *

Under his breath, Robert was cursing the pernicious monkey to damnation. For what seemed to be a dozen or so times, it had snatched a quarrel from the quiver slung across his back and jumped about his shoulders waving it around. Why it should be attracted to the missiles he could hardly fathom, except he fletched them himself favouring a scarlet flight. He had found he could recover them more easily at the butts where they were separately distinguished by colour from all the others. He was struggling not only with fitting a crannequin and winding the crossbows of the Infanta, Claris' and his own weapon, but he had the creature Enola to contend with too. To make matters worse, its distraction at a critical moment had caused him to shoot past a magnificent buck and thus be the only one in the party not to have brought down his quarry. Even the demure Claris had managed to bring down a sprightly doe which would contribute to the table - and he had been boasted of by lord John as being a deadly shot.

They were gathering together now in the centre of a clearing where the carcasses were displayed prior to being carried back to the *castelo* and the kitchens there. Lord John came over to where Robert was standing disconsolately gazing at the game.

"Oh look," he guffawed, "There is a fine buck with a scratch across its back. That must be the one you missed, though I suppose you were leaving it for the Infanta to shoot at." Robert gave a wry smile. If it had been a fellow squire ribbing him thus he would have responded in kind, but he was compelled to endure lord John's tormenting gibe. "Never mind, no doubt the ladies will credit you with a share of their kill seeing as it was you that wound up their bows for them." Laughing uproariously at his own jest, lord John stalked away to join the king's party who were mounting up ready to return to Lisbon.

"Please do not take the words of that lord to heart," said a gentle voice at his elbow. He turned to find the donzela Claris gazing up at him. She was holding the reins of her horse, which stood patiently behind her. She spoke good, though accented French. "You had an impossible task attending on the charging of weapons while managing Enola and two ladies as well. I saw the way you were controlling your horse with only your knees, not an easy task on such a spirited mount. I suppose you were able to do that because of your knightly training?"

"I am not a knight, donzela, but I thank you for your kind words." His voice was hard and cold, which he regretted almost as he spoke. She drew back slightly as if affronted. He cursed himself inwardly for speaking to her thus and bowed respectfully by way of apology. "I beg your pardon, donzela, I did not mean to snap at you so." Claris smiled at once and nodded her head in acknowledgement of his contrition. "I have not done very well today and lord John's remarks disturbed attention on my manners for a moment. Allow me to help you on to your mount." She stood expectantly by the side of her horse. Impulsively, he clasped his hands to her waist and lifted her up onto her saddle, which she rode as all ladies, to one side. Her eyes widened in surprise and her face flushed in confusion while she decided whether to express fury or the pleasure she was feeling. She contented herself smoothing down her dress and arranging it over the horse's croup while she got her emotions under control.

These few moments of confusion might have been noticeable to Robert, were he not going through the same gamut of emotion too. He found her surprisingly light and had no trouble lifting her. Her waist was small and the feel of a firm, lithe young body in his hands had taken him by surprise. He was not used to handling women thus and had never done so before. Ladies used either a mounting block or, as should have happened here, a pair of clasped hands where she could place a foot for mounting, which would have been more appropriate. He had no idea what madness had caused him to act so.

He took a few steps back and swept her a low bow to hide his own confusion, for which the donzela was grateful as it allowed her to acknowledge his gallantry with an inclination of her head.

"When you have finished inspecting my ladies, perhaps you would take charge of Enola," said an imperious voice. The Infanta Joanna had seen everything and now stared down at him, the monkey Enola squealing as if in delight at his discomfiture and bouncing up and down on the withers of her mount. This agitated the horse and the Infanta, who was an excellent horsewoman, was diverted by the effort of steadying it, otherwise Robert might have discovered the extent of her censure. As it was he took the opportunity the Infanta's problem presented to leap into the saddle of his own horse and reach across to take the creature from her. Observing the king and his party setting off back to the city, the Infanta turned her mount and fell in behind him with her ladies, taking the donzela Claris de Montanhas with them while Robert and a boisterous Enola tagged on behind with the huntsmen.

Back in the courtyard, the noisy hunting party was laughing and jesting. Farriers were taking the horses to the stables and as Robert entered the courtyard he saw the Infanta dismount at a stone block before sweeping up the steps to the palace. Of her ladies, only the donzela Claris remained on her mount and she sat there gazing at him, a faint smile at her lips. He jumped down from the saddle and went up to her.

"Seeing as it was you who put me up here, squire Robert, perhaps you would lift me down again," she whispered winsomely. He looked desperately about him to find a means of securing Enola and finding a post, tied its leash and placed the animal there where it screamed and cursed him. As he reached up to her she slid from her saddle, tumbling into his arms with a gasp of apparent alarm, and he had no choice but to gather her to him. He held her there for a moment longer than was absolutely necessary while Claris made no move to free herself. Finally, conscious they were standing among a throng of courtiers, servants and others he released her and she lowered her eyes demurely.

"I think you must free Enola from her perch," she whispered coyly. "Give her to me and I shall take her to the Infanta." The monkey was indeed making much noise and fuss, attracting attention to the young couple that had charge of her. He untied Enola, which creature immediately went to Claris and usurped his place in her arms. His mind reeling desperately for something gallant to say, he found himself tongue-tied and could only mutely hand her the leash with an elegant bow. She dropped him a curtsey and with a winsome smile still at her lips, walked with grace, he supposed upon the ground, across the courtyard towards the palace to attend upon her mistress, the Infanta Joanna.

* * *

"There are plenty of places down in the *Baixa* where you can indulge yourself with a woman. There is no need to pine over this one – a beauty perhaps, but no more so than many you might find in the lower town of Lisbon." John Biggar had been in the courtyard when the hunting party returned and had witnessed the scene between Robert and Claris. Intrigued, particularly as he knew of Robert's former amour, the impossible Alice de Lucy, he had subjected him to an expert inquisition that would have had anyone confess his deepest secrets. "There are women down there from all over the world, skilled in arts that only the nobles of England have knowledge of. There is nothing to compare in the stews of London, unless you have a lord's purse, while here you can purchase paradise for a few Reis."

Robert was beginning to believe John Biggar might be better employed as a priest, so skilled was he in getting a confession. He dismissed his friend's suggestion with an impatient wave of his hand. How could he look Claris in the face if he resorted to such lewd passion, an act of debauchery that could no way assuage his need for her. Both he and John had visited the low houses of London along with the other squires, to gain experience of life, but he had never felt he had hold of a woman until the moment he clasped the waist of Claris de Montanhas and lifted her onto her mount. "That damned monkey is the problem," he snarled. They were seated in a tavern in the *Bairro Alto*, the upper town of Lisbon, drinking wine and getting drunk. "It is there at every moment. The Infanta dotes on it but when it wears even her down, she hands it either to me or to Claris. It will not be petted, even though the Infanta yearns to do so; it is forever jumping around. If the creature would settle in her arms she could mother it. Claris has charge of it now otherwise we might have stolen a few moments together."

"Excuse me, gentles, I could not help but overhear." The new speaker was a merchant by his dress, though neither of them recognised the house his livery displayed. He addressed them in English, the language they were speaking in the tavern. He was sitting at an adjacent table. "May I introduce myself – Hugh Newby, a trader of Lisbon but native of Norwich. It is the sound of English voices that encourages my boldness."

"Then you will know I am poor company today," grumbled Robert.

John Biggar examined the man closely. He was somewhere around thirty years of age, richly dressed in scarlet doublet and white hose with a short black mantle that hung from one shoulder and fastened across by a silver chain into a gold buckle. A black cap with a gold medallion pinned to it adorned his head. Bright blue eyes were set in a tanned face framed by blond hair that descended down his cheeks to finish in a neatly trimmed beard. His belt containing a short sword and dagger was on the bench by his side.

"You are a long way from home, master," said John by way of accepting conversation with him."

"As are you," Newby replied. "I have business here at Lisbon and trade wool into Iberia in exchange for a whole variety of goods. These I sell into the markets of Flanders and England. You do not look like merchants to me. I have seen you, master, at the palace." He nodded at Robert.

"I had not thought to be distinctive there," snapped Robert, still in a foul mood. He felt there was something familiar about the man, but then, he was English in a foreign land and perhaps a familiar accent gave the impression of prescience.

"It would be difficult for you not to be noticed, my friend, especially when you are one selected by the Infanta Joanna to be guardian of her pet."

"My friend bears the burden well, having an incentive other than service to the Infanta," grinned John Biggar.

"Ah, yes, the fair donzela; who would not suffer the torments of an imp for a few moments in her company? I see your wine is almost finished and I have a full flagon here which I will gladly share for the pleasure of the company of fellow Englishmen." John pointed at a vacant place opposite at their table and Hugh Newby joined them. He topped up their wine cups and toasted to a hope for their good fortune. John introduced himself and Robert.

"Here is damnation to all primates," growled Robert raising his cup.

"Excepting those ordained by Holy Church," put in John.

Hugh Newby laughed at the jest and fixed Robert with a sympathetic smile. "It seems to me, my young friend, that your problem is a simple one and easily remedied."

"I have already thought of a remedy, but I fear throwing the beast from the ramparts of the palace might not meet with the approval of the Infanta," replied Robert lugubriously. "I had thought of hanging it by the neck as any other felon, and the creature is a rare thief, then pretending it had caught itself by its own silver chain."

"What prevents my friend from committing murder is the fact that the monkey contributes to the well being of the Infanta and is conditioning her towards the idea of motherhood, which is a duty she must perform in due course," explained John. "There is also the small fact that it keeps him close to the object of his affections."

"Your mention of things maternal provides the answer to your problem," said Newby with a knowing smile. "What does a nurse do when a child is fractious? Why, she gives it something to suck on that has been dipped in an opiate. The child is quietened and peace is restored!" Newby leaned back and opened his hands in satisfaction at his solution.

"Of course," cried Robert, "and then the Infanta can fondle the soporific animal to her heart's content."

"Thus reinforcing the bond between them and inducing a propensity to become broody," said John thumping the table with delight, "which serves the best interests of our King Richard."

"The best ideas are always the simplest," stated Newby with a twinkle in his blue eyes. "There is no shortage of apothecaries in Lisbon and such potions are their main stock-in-trade. I would, however, advise caution. A potion devised to work on a human child may not have the same affect on a monkey. You would not wish to poison the beast, I suppose?"

"The idea, though tempting, would be disastrous and probably lead to our own deaths," said Robert with alarm. "It might even cause the Infanta to become frigid at her loss and thus earn not only her displeasure but that of our King, too. It hardly bears thinking on."

"Well, the situation is not without remedy," said Newby, tugging at his beard pensively. "It merely requires a potion to be tested on a similar animal to observe the effects and get the dosage right – again, a simple matter. There is an apothecary close by here that will be able to help us. I have used him several times and he also serves the *Casa dos Escravos*, which you may know of."

"Yes, I was there myself the other day on some business of my grandfather," enthused Robert. He is an apothecary in London."

"Then you will know how things might be arranged. The man I recommend, as I say, serves the slave markets and provides potions to keep violent slaves docile."

"Then lead us to him," cried Robert, his voice slurred with mild intoxication.

"It will do no harm to see what the apothecary advises," agreed John.

"Let us finish our wine first," chuckled Hugh Newby. "It is paid for."

* * *

Robert's initial enthusiasm for the scheme to quieten the animal named Enola was dampened when he entered the apothecary's shop in a grubby back-street of the *Baixa*. Until then he had thought he might indulge in the familiar smells of home, where his childhood, when not at the forge, was spent in the herb garden and the fragrant mystery of his grandfather Cornelius' shop. There, he recalled, were peculiar objects, stranger than the relics hardly visible inside the reliquaries of many a church. They hung from the rafters, or were displayed along shelves. Herbs and dried plants added to the musty but pleasant smell and shuffling around among these, muttering for all anyone knew blasphemous incantations, was Mother Malkin, his grandfather's ancient assistant, brought there by his own father and the woman Anna Thorne, now dame Quirke, his grandfather's wife. Nevertheless, he had known nothing there but kindness and whenever he was afeared by the terrible sights that a child in London was bound to witness sooner or later, there was always one of them able to calm him.

Here, all was different and he was disturbed as soon as he set foot in the place. The first thing was the smell; rancid, sour with an undertone of the shambles, the slaughterhouse. Objects such as bat wings, dried reptiles, the whole wings of strange birds, animal skulls, a human one, dried intestines of who knows what – interesting and mysterious in his grandfather's shop were here sinister with an air of malevolence about them, instilling not curiosity, but apprehension. Who would come here for a cure? The apothecary himself hardly dispelled Robert's feeling of dread. He was a short, fat, black-robed man whose wrinkled and twisted face would do disservice to a walnut. His cackling speech did nothing to dispel the malodorous gloom of the place.

"What can I do for you, masters?" he grunted in poor French. He gave a nod of recognition to Hugh Newby, then cocked his head to one side and fixed the two squires with an obsequious leer. Newby explained their mission, leaving out any mention of the animal, a monkey, being the pet of the Infanta Joanna of Portugal. All the while the apothecary bobbed his head up and down indicating he had been tasked with similar problems ere now. Shuffling about on an untidy table littered with all manner of animal and dried plant parts, he pulled out a bundle of parchments. Sorting through these he brandished one triumphantly. "I have here a recipe that should work for you with, as master Newby says, a little modification. I shall try it out in various strengths. How big is the creature in question?"

"About this high when on its back legs," said Robert putting one hand above the other. It weighs about the same as a cat."

"Then a cat should do very well to test the medicine," replied the apothecary enthusiastically, rubbing his hands together. Would you attend upon me at the same time tomorrow when I shall have the drug ready for you? It will, of course, not be cheap – there is some experimenting to be done after all . . .?" Robert and John looked with alarm at each other. Neither had much in the way of ready money, being but poor squires dependent for food and lodging on their masters. Robert, unfortunately, looked prosperous but a king had gifted his cloth and his father had paid for the tailoring of it. Apothecaries, he knew only too well, set their price according to the appearance of their clients.

"Never fear the price, masters," interrupted Newby, seeing their obvious embarrassment. "I shall lend you what is required using my credit here with the good apothecary. I have no doubt ambitious young men as yourselves will soon earn enough to repay me and if not, then I shall put it down to speculation and offer it as a good deed to crave an indulgence from Holy Church. I have business nearby tomorrow and I would be glad to bring the potion to you rather than you having to come all the way down to here."

"Oh, many thanks, that would be fine." Neither Robert nor John could be sure when they could get away. If their masters wanted them close by they could be bound up until the day of departure for England. Robert had the additional problem of attending the Infanta with the monkey Enola.

"I'm not happy with this venture," said John Biggar as he and Robert walked together up from the *Baixa* and through the *Bairro Alto* towards the *Castelo de* São *Jorge*. They had said their farewell to Hugh Newby who promised to meet with them the next day at the castle. As a merchant he reckoned to have business there. "We are dealing here with a poison, a benign one we think, but a poison none the less. Our motives are apt to be misinterpreted if we are discovered with such a substance on us."

"The man Newby seemed genuine enough," mused Robert while stepping adroitly around a dump of donkey excrement. "Did you take note of the way he avoided any mention of the Infanta to the apothecary? The man is discreet, you must give him that?"

"Yes, and he did point out the danger of too strong a dose that might result in the death of Enola rather than simply rendering the beast soporific. I would advise caution, though. The court is sensitive to the use of poisons and the Infanta's food is tasted before she is served."

"The business is still under control," stated Robert emphatically. "The potion will only be administered by me with nobody else involved. I think it might be wise, though, to test it before giving it to the monkey. What is the method of use?"

"I have no idea," shrugged John. "I presume the apothecary will send instructions with the potion. In any case the only creature at hazard is the monkey and if it comes to the worst and the creature dies, then we can put it down to its exotic origins, being from a remote region of Africa nobody knows of."

"Then we must wait until the morrow and decide how we are to test it. I would suggest a cat as the apothecary told us. There are plenty of them around the castelo."

The next day Robert was in a court of the castelo tossing around a small lump of wood with a string attached while a cat attempted to catch it. John Biggar was lounging close by on a stone parapet, apparently idling his time. Presently Robert managed to tempt the cat with a morsel of meat, which it was unable to resist. Soon it trusted him enough to let him fondle and stroke it. Though the court was busy with the to and fro of servants and courtiers, nobody paid any attention to the two youths. Nevertheless, John strolled over and stood between Robert and the crowd while he applied to the cat's fur a couple of drops of liquid from a small bottle. Leaving the animal and strolling off they settled down to watch. The cat sat in a patch of sunlight, licking its paws and grooming its fur. Presently it went off, somewhat unsteadily and curled up in a shady corner where it fell asleep.

"What do we do now," whispered Robert into John's ear. "There is no telling if it is alive or dead and if it sleeps, how long for and we can't hang around here much longer."

"At least we know the method of application works well. The monkey is always grooming itself, and searching for whatever lives on its body."

Some hours later the cat was seen strolling about the court as if nothing untoward had happened. That evening Robert placed a single drop of the potion onto Enola's shoulder fur, which the creature was habitually grooming. Sure enough, when they were sitting in the infanta's chamber listening to the chatter of her ladies, accompanied by the melodic sounds of a dulcimer being tapped upon with hammers by a laconic youth, Enola curled into the Infanta's lap and lay there, blinking slowly with no inclination to leap about and squeal. Its mistress was overjoyed at being able to stroke and pet the animal while Robert worried some of the drug might get onto her hands. However, she was unlikely to suck at her fingers so no harm would be done her and the monkey was merely placid, not unconscious as the cat had been. One drop of the potion would be enough for his purpose, he realised.

Robert was just complimenting himself with his success in quietening the monkey when the youthful musician put down his dulcimer and took up a set of what looked like bagpipes. Breathing air into the sack and pumping away, a discordant note disturbed the air followed by a strange haunting sound that had the hairs stand up on Robert's neck. Bagpipes were common at court, but this set was unlike anything he had heard before. There was something unearthly and eerie about the sound. He snapped a quick look at the Infanta to gauge her reaction. Surprisingly she leaned back in her chair with a smile of contentment at her lips while stroking Enola. The monkey had lifted its head at the sound, but then sank back into its now docile state. The player had a single chanter over his shoulder and fingered what looked like a simple recorder. It produced a grave tone and a pitch lower than the pipes commonly heard in the courts of Europe.

Claris was placed at the edge of the circle of ladies sitting about the Infanta and he edged his way towards her.

"A strange instrument," he began. "I am surprised the Infanta does not complain it might disturb Enola." He was about to make some derogatory remark about the sound it produced when Claris placed a hand on his arm and leaned into him to speak quietly into his ear.

"That is because she recognises the music. The *gaiti de foles transmantana* are traditional pipes from the *Tras os Montes* where I come from, along with my brother Anselm, who is a skilled musician, as you can hear."

Robert felt his soul draw in like a limpet that when touched, clamps itself closely to a rock for protection. He gave silent thanks to the Virgin that he had not gone so far as to denigrate the sound of the pipes. Scrutinising the youthful musician, it seemed he did, indeed, have a resemblance to Claris, especially about the eyes. "He is your brother?" he asked rhetorically.

"Yes, Anselm and I came into the household of the Infanta at the same time. In truth, it was he that caused her to take an interest in our family."

Suddenly the sound of the pipes became less discordant to his ear as he took careful interest in the music. "Does he play several instruments? I noticed he had a dulcimer across his knees just now."

"Yes, he plays the lute and also several woodwind. His favourite is the shawm, a double reed instrument brought into Europe by the Moors, I believe, in any case they are common. Anselm tells me he is looking forward to finding a recorder when he comes with us into England."

Suddenly the Infanta declared herself weary and anxious to tell her beads in her chapel before retiring to bed. She beckoned for Robert to take charge of Enola, who was still in a state of quietness. He took the animal from her taking care not to make contact with the area of its body where the potion had been applied and noted how much heavier it seemed when under the influence of a narcotic.

"Master Salgado, you have played well this even', said the Infanta laconically. "I shall be grateful of your music when we set sail for England. There will be scarce any other entertainment on board, I fear." With that she swept the chamber clear of all but her ladies. Standing outside in a small courtyard, Robert went over to the musician, Anselm, who was packing his dulcimer in a woollen bag.

"Give you good e'en, master Salgado." At last he had learned by the Infanta's parting words Claris' family name, having neglected so far to ask it of her. He much preferred to think of her by her epithet *donzela de montanhas*. He spoke in French while sweeping the musician an elegant bow. Claris spoke only Portuguese and French and he assumed her brother would share her linguistic ability.

"Squire Robert de la Halle. I am pleased to meet you at last. My sister speaks fondly of you." His French was good but accented similar to that he had heard of Spaniards.

"You have me at a disadvantage. The donzela Claris hadn't told me of you until just now."

"Ah, but everyone knows the guardian of the Infanta's little *macaco*." He smiled cheerily with no hint of ridicule in his dark brown eyes. Unusually he was bare-headed, his thick black hair hanging in numerous plaits being his favoured adornment. Robert thought this was due to some sort of artistic temperament. A small neatly trimmed beard gave his face a pear-like quality, a feature that in his sister was more rounded and cherubic. Gold rings were fixed through his ears. His doublet was unlaced showing a fine linen shirt

209

beneath and open at the throat where a thin gold chain hung across. He wore breeches rather than hose and his calf-length boots were of black leather. Altogether he presented a strange aspect, which, Robert supposed, was permissible in an artiste. Certainly it must have got him noticed had this been his condition when the Infanta first set eyes on him.

"That is a strange looking lute," said Robert, pointing at another instrument Anselm was just about to put in its bag.

"You have a discerning eye, monsieur. I wonder if your ear is as acute." He held the instrument up before him. "It is presented to me by the Infanta Joanna. I am to play it before King Richard in England. It is unlikely he will have seen or heard one before now. It is a new instrument known only in Spain and now in Portugal. It is a *vihuela de mano*."

"It has a woman's body."

"And like a woman, hard to fathom. I have no music for it and so must make it up as I go along. It has many possibilities."

"Not so those bagpipes, though I must say they are unfamiliar in sound to those you usually hear at court."

"You mean the *gaiti de foles transmantana*. We play them in the mountains where the sound carries a great distance. We have sometimes frightened away our enemies who cannot decide if they are hearing phantoms in the mists. I would not normally play indoors, but the Infanta Joanna enjoys the sound so I play for her."

"Perhaps you might play them when we are sailing to England and keep the sea monsters at bay," laughed Robert. "I wonder if they work on pirates?" He was disturbed by Enola, who was becoming agitated and beginning to jump about. At least he knew now how long the effects of the potion would last.

"The macaco is perhaps nocturnal? She will give you a sleepless night I think."

"Usually she sleeps when it is dark," he responded. He could hardly say the animal was coming around from the effects of a sleeping draught. He would lock the creature in the chamber he had been given, not much more than a crack in a wall but lord John would not have the monkey in his chamber. Claris was out of reach for the night in the Infanta's chamber so he had nothing to look forward to until the next day.

"Let us find a table in the great hall where there is usually something to entertain us," offered Anselm. "The macaco will be welcome sport there. The king has no jester but I can usually find a welcome, especially when I bring a lute with me. Do you sing perhaps and are they lewd songs?" Before he could answer, Robert found himself being led from the courtyard and towards the great hall. Even with Enola in tow, it promised to be a pleasant evening.

* * *

"There is something very wrong with that potion," whispered Robert fearfully. "The bottle is not the same as the original. It is almost the same but there was a chip on the base which has mysteriously gone." John Biggar leaned back against the wall of the great courtyard, concern furrowing his brow.

"Have you examined the contents?" he rasped while examining his friend's face for signs of poisoning.

"Yes, that is the worse part. I put a drop on a crust of bread and left it in a corner of my chamber. Some time later I returned to find a large dead rat there."

"It is well you noticed the absence of the chip. I think we are the innocent objects of a plot to poison the Infanta. What do we know of the man Newby?"

"I thought there was something familiar about him when we first met, but I am unable to recall what it might be."

"One thing is for sure, you cannot leave matters as they are," advised John. "For one thing, if another plot succeeds you might find yourself implicated."

"Then I must inform the lord bastard John of Pomfret. He knows of the risk to the Infanta's life."

"And tell him you have been party to administering a dubious potion around the Infanta? I think you better have a plausible tale ready if you do."

Robert slouched against the wall deep in thought. "I have it!" he exclaimed. "I shall tell him it is part of a scheme to discover the identity of whoever is behind the plot. After all, I have the poison to prove there is deadly work afoot and thereby removed the danger. I have been acting as his agent in this, as I have been instructed to do."

"That is plausible, at least," said John. "It is probably the only course open to you. I can vouch for you where the man Newby is concerned. I shall say we suspected him from the start."

Lord John of Pomfret was aghast when Robert disclosed what he knew. Robert explained that when the man Newby suggested a way of quietening the Infanta's pet they suspected immediately there was something suspicious and thus went along with him in an attempt to discern the extent of the plot. The potion had been tested on a cat before applying it to the monkey. That was sensible and the plotters would have accounted for a modicum of wisdom in the young squire they had selected. Whoever was observing at court would have seen by Enola's lethargy that the potion had actually been administered undetected. It would thus be a simple job to switch the bottles for one containing a deadly content. He could already identify two of the conspirators - Newby and the apothecary, but not who they were working for. He pointed out that the bottle containing the potion could only have been switched by someone here in the castelo and possibly close to the Infanta.

"I'll have this man Newby taken and put to the question along with the apothecary," snarled lord John. "That will loosen his tongue."

"That should certainly be done," replied Robert, relieved that his lord had accepted his explanation, which was probably due more to an onset of panic and the constant worry over the welfare of the Infanta than Robert's ability to tell a convincing story. "However, my lord, I have an idea that might reveal more of the plotters."

"You have done very well so far," responded lord John. "I suppose the plotters thought your youth and inexperience would prevent you working out what they were about. Give me your idea."

"Nobody other than ourselves and John Biggar know that the plot is discovered." Robert lowered his voice conspiratorially even though until then they had been speaking normally in lord John's closet, his servants having been sent out. "The potion seems to be potent and is intended to work by transference on contact. The Infanta, while petting the animal Enola, would transfer the poison to her food, rendering irrelevant the fact that it had been tasted beforehand. It is a subtle way of getting past her poison tasters." A sudden flood of horror swept over him as he realised that the plot to poison the Infanta would probably cause the death of Claris too, seeing as she would take occasional charge of Enola and suffer the same fate. "If I take the animal to the Infanta without applying the potion it will exhibit its normal exuberance and the Infanta will continue in robust health. Whoever exchanged the bottle will suspect I have either lost it or disposed of it. In any case they are bound to check if it is still in my chamber."

"So all we have to do is keep watch," cried lord John enthusiastically.

"You can be sure that will keep any plotters away," said Robert. "The bottle is stowed in a corner of my chest and only myself and the poisoner knows that. I propose wrapping the bottle in a cloth dipped in the poison. Whoever unwraps the bottle will take the poison on himself. Afterwards the plotter will advertise the affects of the poison and then we shall know the extent of any infiltration of the court by the Infanta's enemies."

"And should the villain die before we can question him?"

"At least we will have another link in the chain accounted for and the identity of such a person will probably point to fellow conspirators. To extract information from Hugh Newby first we will have to catch him and I think that might not be easy. The apothecary has a shop in the *Baixa* and should be easier to find but he may not know anything of Newby's contacts here at court. Spies are usually close mouthed on such matters."

"Yes, you may be right. Time is of the essence. We are to set sail for England in two days and we must be sure to have cleared out this nest of vermin before then. There will be enough rats on board ship as it is without adding some of our own to their number. We shall proceed with your scheme. Take great care. I would not have you poison yourself."

That evening Robert brought Enola to the Infanta in her privy chamber as expected. Surrounded by her ladies and a few courtiers and servants, she was relaxing and listening to the plucking of a lute. Anselm Salgado was the lutanist and close by, to Robert's delight was his sister, Claris whose eyes brightened as the young squire entered. The Infanta's eyes brightened, too, at the sight of her pet and the monkey seemed pleased to have her stroke and caress it. Of course it maintained its usual torments on the assembled courtiers, throwing bits of fruit around and they affecting to be amused by its antics. The Infanta was helping herself from a bowl of delicacies, sweetmeats, oranges, grapes and nuts while giving some to Enola and clapping her hands in delight at the sight of tiny fingers, like those of a baby, tearing at the fruit. Robert realised with a feeling of dread how easily the poison might have been transferred to the Infanta's hands. The contents of the bowl had been carefully examined in case there were any foul substances present, but the monkey Enola was exempt from this scrutiny.

The evening passed normally until the Infanta proclaimed herself ready for her evening devotions, when the monkey was transferred back into Robert's care. Once more he passed the remainder of the evening in the great hall where the lively monkey entertained with its mad antics those gathered there. Anselm, sitting by a window, strummed gently on the strange new instrument the *vihuela de mano,* experimenting with new chords and trying to fathom its depths so he could play it pleasantly, when commanded, at the court of King Richard the Third of England. Robert reported to his master, lord John before retiring. All was quiet and when he reached his chamber, there were no signs anyone else had been there.

It was noon the next day before the dreadful climax of Robert's plan was realised. He had risen early as usual to attend upon the lord John and so left his chamber unattended. Enola was set on a perch in lord John's chamber, sullen with the restriction caused by the silver chain attaching its collar to the woodwork. A servant brought food and after lord John was served, Robert partook of his own breakfast. Afterwards the two went down into the great hall where a variety of English and Portuguese nobles were in conference, working on the final arrangements for the voyage to England. There were to be twenty Portuguese vessels in the Infanta's escort along with the original five that had brought the English nobles to Lisbon. It was the beginning of April in the year of Our Lord fourteen hundred and eighty-six and this day, they knew, a similar number of English vessels, twenty or so, would be setting sail from Southampton, bringing the English princess, Elizabeth of York to Portugal where she would marry King John's first cousin, Manuel. The hope was that they would meet and salute each other as the two fleets passed somewhere in the Bay of Biscay.

Suddenly there was much shouting and commotion from the direction of the Infanta's apartments. Female screams could be heard and courtiers dashed up the stairway from the great hall, fearing that their princess was in jeopardy. Lord John snapped a glance at Robert and set off apace with his squire to discover what had happened. On entering the Infanta's privy chamber they saw Joanna standing, her hand at her mouth, staring with horror at a figure on the floor. Her ladies were squealing hysterically. Robert looked for Claris and with great relief saw her standing by, her hand at her mouth and her eyes wide with fear. There, on the floor, clad in the robes of a friar was the body of Fra Maurice, lord John's own chaplain. His face was twisted in a rictus, clearly the result of a sudden attack of apoplexy. Suddenly, Robert remembered where he had first seen Hugh Newby. He had been in conversation with Fra Maurice who, he also remembered was Spanish.

"I shall get my own doctor of physic to examine him," cried lord John, visibly distressed. "I know he has not been well for some days. This is a terrible thing to happen." He beckoned Robert to him and whispered in his ear. "Go and find an English doctor. We must not let anyone else examine the body otherwise poison is sure to be detected. This is too close to me and scandal must be prevented."

Robert hurried away, understanding the peril they faced. As King Richard's bastard son, sent to escort the Infanta Joanna to England, to have his confessor discovered poisoned could have disastrous consequences, and blame might be apportioned to the lord bastard, John of Pomfret, or at the very least, suspicion.

10 – A Perilous Sea

"This matter drinks deeper than we first imagined," said the lord bastard, John of Pomfret. "I have been pondering on it and I believe part of the plot was to destroy me as well as the Infanta Joanna." He was standing by the window in his chamber looking out over the roofs of the *Bairro Alto* and stroking his chin pensively. Robert stood by him, all other servants having been dismissed. Both cast an eye at the door and lord John indicated with an inclination of his head for his squire to go and check who had an ear to it. Robert jerked the door open and seeing nobody there looked out down the passage. Only the usual servants were bustling around carrying out the myriad duties required to get the Infanta installed aboard her ship along with her ladies and courtiers. Closing the door firmly, he returned to his master and stood by him, anxious to hear what he meant.

"I think I understand, my lord," he tried tentatively. "If I had been found to be the one who had caused the Infanta to be poisoned, then it might have reflected badly on you."

"It would have done more than that," snapped lord John, "It was my own confessor who was the main culprit. With the Infanta dead, the alliance would be in tatters and my father's future plans wrecked. Do you realise just how many at the English court would benefit from that? I am one of his closest and loyal followers. If I should be disgraced, even possibly implicated, then I would either be imprisoned or executed for treason. That would deplete around the king those most loyal to him."

"My lord, how could you be blamed for my error, your servant who has been duped by a subtle tongue?"

"I would have been accused of putting you up to it! If my father were to die without an heir then there are several ready to step into that position. It is a matter of the succession to the Crown. We have seen how a bastard usurper as Henry Tudor might claim it – why not I."

"My lord!"

"Yes, the thought shocks you, but there are those who have personal ambition at the backs of their minds. First there is the earl of Warwick. It would be a simple matter to reverse his father's attainder and though still a minor, proclaim him king as some sort of puppet. Next there is Richard of York, bastard of Edward the Fourth. He has no love of my father and believes he had him falsely bastardised and removed from the line of succession. John de la Pole, earl of Lincoln is another – he is my father's heir apparent as it is. Except perhaps for Warwick, these have a claim no better than mine, so you see, getting rid of the Infanta and, though a bastard, King Richard's most loyal son makes the way nearer for all of them."

"You think there is the chance that the king's life is in danger too?" gasped Robert, leaning faintly against the side of the window. "He is not entirely without loyal friends. I would cite his grace the duke of Norfolk and viscount Lovell as two of proven felicity."

"Yes, I agree, yet too many others died at Bosworth Field. Perhaps there is no overt danger, but you know his feelings regarding France. His sister Margaret of Burgundy might call on him to aid her against the expansionist policies of the French court. Duke Francis of Brittany is in a similar position. Remember the king's attitude in fourteen seventy-five at Picquigny, when as duke of Gloucester he urged his brother, King Edward to reject the French king's offer of a pension? Edward allowed himself to be paid off then, but Richard would have gone to war. It would not be difficult to get him at the head of an English army. He came close to death at Bosworth; in France he could do so again and might not be as lucky, his English enemies having no need to raise a finger against him."

"But my lord, until now we have thought dame Margaret Stanley might have designs upon the Infanta's life. It is more likely she is behind it; poison is a woman's weapon, or a priest's. Fra Maurice was a Spaniard, not an Englishman and I seem to remember Hugh Newby had a surcoat showing a golden castle with a blue door, which I since have discovered is a badge of Castile! He told me he had trade with Spain."

"I take your point, squire Robert. There are too many possibilities, so let us fall back on what we know and see if we cannot confound the king's enemies." The lord bastard walked up and down the chamber as he reasoned it out. "So far nobody is aware there has been an attempt on the Infanta's life except you, squire Biggar and myself. Had King João found out about it there would have been hell to pay and us none the wiser. I might have been implicated along with you. For all the plotters know, Fra Maurice either poisoned himself accidentally or really did die of apoplexy. They might suspect we have discovered the plot, but how can they find out without betraying themselves? The doctor I engaged to examine him is sworn to secrecy and has no idea there was malice towards the Infanta. If we proceed as if nothing untoward has happened the perpetrators might be drawn out. We know there is a plot afoot, where before it was only a possibility."

"We are perhaps fortunate that our men, my lord, were unable to take up either Hugh Newby or the apothecary, otherwise the plot would have been advertised causing those behind it to withdraw into the shadows." Robert was proved to be correct regarding his earlier prediction on the arrest of Hugh Newby. The man had vanished probably assuming his part in the plot had succeeded. Disappearing was not a difficult thing to do in Lisbon, where ships were leaving for foreign ports all day long. Neither could the apothecary be found. His shop was shuttered and when broken into by lord John's men was found abandoned except for a few remaining scraps of dried vegetable matter.

"What orders have you given for the disposal of the body, my lord?"

"I have had the foul friar, who died without extreme unction, taken by some Dominicans into their monastery for internment. Having died unshriven he is condemned to eternal damnation and serve him right." The two men crossed themselves.

Robert gave some thought to the slave trader, Roderigo Anes Pinteado. He was the one who had come up with the idea of using the monkey to get close to the Infanta. One point in his favour was his familiarity with grandfather Cornelius and if *he* trusted the trader, then Pinteado was probably innocent. For all he knew the Infanta might have been terrified of the monkey, which made it unlikely that it was a deliberate ploy. Its awakening of her maternal instincts was a bonus nobody expected and probably the plotters had seen that as an additional threat. One thing was clear. Robert realised how duplicitous men were around a Court and nobody could be trusted to be entirely without guile, a prerequisite of ambition. It was the way of the world – the only way to get on in life. Unless born into the nobility, for the rest of humanity it was that or starve. He gave a mental shrug. He was about to leave behind Lisbon and its duplicitous citizens. Was that a relief or were they carrying in their fleet, like plague, the core malignancy? Indeed it could just as well emanate from Spain, France or, perhaps most likely of all, England. Were they sailing from danger, or into it? Questions, questions and too many possible answers.

* * *

Grey and deep green were the dominant colours in Robert's mind as he leaned over the rail of the ship for what seemed the hundredth time in two days. Deep green was the sea and grey was the pallor of his skin, or was it the other way round? He could hardly tell and would have been grateful for the discharge of stomach contents into the sea but the truth was there was none left in his wracked body to expel and all he could do was retch uncontrollably. He pushed himself weakly from the rail when the spasm passed and tried to console himself with the thought that the bouts of sea-sickness were becoming fewer, but nothing could insulate his pride from the glances of the sailors as they went about their business unaffected, with amused smiles ever at their lips at the sight of what they presumed was an English lord displaying his tenuous hold on mortality.

From his position on the deck he could see the captain and his sailing master, along with the duke of Norfolk, Thomas Howard and the lord bastard John of Pomfret. All were looking to windward out from the elevated deck of the after castle over the heaving ocean. Something was engaging their attention and, taking the opportunity of letting his curiosity get the better of him to alleviate his suffering, he staggered across the deck to try to discern what it was. The vessel was on the steorbord tack and all he could see was the other ships in the fleet spread out protectively around their own vessel, a carrack where the colours of Portugal flew from the main masthead and those of England from the fore mast. The sea was running with white tops to the waves, white horses at full gallop. The main sail had been furled and they were running under the fore sail with the lateen mizzen for balance. Even with this reduced sail they were making fast progress. Lord John, spotting Robert on the deck, gesticulated for him to come up onto the after castle. He managed to force his weakened legs across the deck and mounted the companionway, his legs threatening to collapse under him at each step.

"I hope you have had your fill at trying to spot mermaids beneath our hull," jested lord John, seeing the distressed condition of his squire.

"Happily I saw none," came the retort. "If so I would have leapt into their arms and trusted to their tender graces rather than endure another moment on this bark."

"You can still speak, it seems, so your brain is working normally even if the rest of you is not. Look to windward beyond our fleet and tell me what you make of it."

Robert went to the steorbord rail and screwed his eyes up against the strong light that lanced down in spears between the dark clouds. At first he could see nothing other than the ships in their fleet, then, in a shaft of distant light he thought he saw something.

"A sail, I think, my lord – yes, perhaps two."

"They appeared the first morning after we set sail from Lisbon and were closer at first but since have dropped away. It seems to me they are following us."

"Perhaps they are merchants eager to sail in the wake of a strong fleet and thus take advantage of our numbers, which will keep brigands at a distance."

"If that were true, then they would keep closer company, or even ask to join with us. As it is they have fallen back but maintain sight of us."

"I know what you are thinking, my lord; that these might have some designs upon the person of our princess. If so they will have to pass through a line of armed merchant ships and that would mean their certain capture or destruction. Also this ship is crammed with armed men who would not let a mere pirate overcome them."

"I am aware of that," growled lord John impatiently, "which makes me all the more uneasy. If those ships have a malign purpose they will be aware of the difficulties in attacking us, which smacks of the possibility there is a plan to circumvent our power."

"You think there is a fleet at sea that has the intention of attacking us?"

"No, of course not," snorted lord John. "That would provoke war between England and the nation that attempted it – and it could only be organised and paid for by a monarch. No, whatever is afoot is more subtle."

"I think we should not worry unduly, my lord. Things happen slowly at sea and if those ships dare to approach us more nearly then we can think on it. At this distance they can do us no harm."

"You are correct, squire Robert, yet I remain uneasy. I have instructed the lookouts at the main masthead to inform me if there is any change in their course. Keep you close to the Infanta, and vigilant."

"I shall, my lord," replied Robert. The young squire felt his spirits rise at his lord's instruction for where the Infanta Joanna was, so too the donzela *Claris de Montanhas*, his Maid of the Mountains. He made his way down from the after castle and towards the grand cabin below, where the Infanta was installed for the voyage to England. He looked around for sight of the monkey Enola. The animal, being ship bound and therefore not able to get herself lost, had taken to the rigging to the delight of the sailors for whom she had become a sort of mascot, and who had dressed her in a short skirt with a hole for her tail. She was up there now, sitting on the crow's nest with the lookouts. Glad for the moment to be rid of the beast, he turned to the guards on the cabin door who acknowledged him and let him pass.

The cabin was warm and packed with servants, courtiers and the Infanta's women. The Infanta was seated regally in a chair against a petition, which screened off her private sleeping space. The seat was covered with a blue velvet cloth embroidered with holy images. At night, all the others had to find a place on the cabin floor hunched against the wooden walls to prevent them being tossed about in the heavy seas. Anselm Salgado was seated at her feet gently plucking at a lute while Joanna employed her time stitching away with silver thread at a piece of crimson fabric. Her ladies were similarly employed. Sitting close by her side was a priest in the habit of a Dominican, similar to Fra Maurice, which caused in Robert's breast a flutter of anxiety. This man, though, was elderly and a native Portuguese who had been with the Infanta for many years. He was reading to her from a psalter. Robert marvelled at the calm of the scene. The movement of the ship was becoming increasingly violent and he wondered how long the women could continue with their task.

A particularly heavy lurch caused the Infanta to gasp impatiently and put down her work, which was the signal for her ladies to do the same. Some of them were looking decidedly ill except for the Infanta and Claris, who sat demurely, apparently none the worse for her experiences. She gave him a beaming smile as he entered the cabin and made obeisance. Anselm looked up with interest and then, recognising who it was, bent his head down to concentrate on his lute playing. One of the ladies managed to get out "My lady . . ." then with her hand to her mouth scrambled to her feet and scuttled out of the cabin. Two others followed her immediately. If the Infanta was piqued at their hurried and un-ceremonial departure she declined to show it. No doubt she had become used to it in the two days they had been at sea.

Robert had become genuinely fond of the Infanta Joanna. He supposed that was partly because she had the same colouring and voice as Claris, while her manner with her servants was gentle and considerate, as her acceptance of the rapid withdrawal of her stricken ladies had indicated. She was rather plump where Claris was slim, but then she *was* twenty years older, and yet still attractive. He wondered how she felt about her forthcoming marriage? When he first saw her at her brother's Court he had thought her withdrawn and stoically fatalistic as if resigned to an unhappy future. Though a royal princess and thus a marketable and diplomatic pawn, she had resisted many marriage proposals and now, approaching her middle years, she was commissioned by her brother the king to become a brood mare. He was particularly impressed by her generous rescue of the impoverished gentlewoman, Claris Salgado and her brother Anselm. King Richard, too, had similar characteristics, which had brought him near to disaster on several occasions – his refusal in the year before Bosworth to have Margaret Stanley incarcerated for one. Having observed at his Court Joanna's brother, he concluded King João the Second of Portugal and King Richard the Third of England were kindred spirits. Both were munificent but ready to explode into violence at a moment. Rule of law was important to these monarchs and their common people, when unjustly imposed upon by one of the nobility, habitually petitioned their kings with a good chance of success. At the age of eighteen, Joanna had actually ruled Portugal for a while as Regent in the name of her father, so she could only be an asset to a king who had tended to lean on his previous wife, Queen Anne, for support and advice. As a direct descendant of Lancaster united with the House of York, her union with King Richard could bode very well for England.

"Good squire Robert, I wonder where Enola is?" The Infanta handed her piece of fabric to the lady beside her and gazed at him in enquiry.

"She is aiding the sailors, your grace," he informed her with a smile. "I have just seen her keeping good lookout with some of them at the mast head."

"Then get her down, squire Robert. I would have her here with me for the night. I fear for her when she swings about in the rigging."

"You need have no fear in that regard, my lady," replied Robert. "It is her natural habitat – it is the sailors who risk themselves aloft." He had faintly entertained the wish that the animal might lose its grip and fall overboard, but anyone witnessing her scampering about the masts, ropes and tackle of the ship could see there was little chance of that. "The only problem I have is how to get her down if she will not come."

"I am sure you will find a way, squire Robert. Take the donzela Claris with you. Enola might come directly to her and then you shall be redundant."

Claris sprang to her feet and dropped a curtsey to her mistress.

Once outside the after cabin the two young people stood together staring up at the main masthead. Enola, by some prescience realising they were looking for her, jumped up and down on a spar and squealed in excitement as if daring him to come and get her.

"I could climb up there," said Robert apprehensively, trying not to show the very thought of doing so made him dizzy, "but the infernal beast would simply jump away from my grasp. I have had much experience of late in trying to get hold of it, and failing."

"Enola is almost human in many respects, as you have told me," said Claris with a chuckle. "If that is so then greed might be the means of her capture. Simply entice her down with the promise of food. She has not eaten since this morning and is always hungry."

Robert raised a finger indicating he had taken on her idea and now would execute it. He sent a sailor for some fruit from the store and when the man returned with an apple and some nuts, raised the apple visibly in his hand then placed it on the deck. He removed his doublet and pulling Claris back, observed the monkey. Enola's eyes gleamed black with greed as she spied the fruit. Scampering along the spar she slid effortlessly down a stay and dropped onto the deck a short distance from the fruit. Robert readied himself with his doublet. A crowd of sailors gathered to watch the entertainment. Enola eyed him up and glanced at the fruit. He could see her greed was getting the better of her as she began to squeal and jump up and down. Suddenly she shot across the deck to grab the apple while Robert flung his doublet with the intention of entangling her. He was nowhere near fast enough. Before the doublet fluttered to the deck she was away up a backstay and sitting on a spar chomping at the apple. The assembled sailors laughed and cheered the triumph of their new mascot. One of them ran over and placed another apple in Robert's hand, laughing uproariously and hoping for a repeat performance. Already he could see that bets were being laid and he had no doubt the monkey was the hot favourite.

He looked at Claris who was displaying as much amusement at his discomfiture as the sailors were. Not only that but their own men were spilling on deck to witness the spectacle. Robert retrieved his doublet and shook it out while he thought on what to do next. Lord John appeared among them and he was laughing along with the rest.

Robert squirmed with annoyance. He realised the speed of the monkey in what was clearly an environment where its natural condition fitted it, was an advantage he could not overcome. This called for guile and an idea came to him. Turning to Claris he whispered in her ear: "Would you like to make some easy money?"

She looked at him in amusement. "What have you in mind, sir?"

"Simply bet that at the next attempt, Enola will be my captive."

"I am like to lose what little fortune I have," she responded.

"You will not lose, but trust me."

She stood back and studied his face and noted not one jot of doubt there, only a sly smile. He was up to something and she decided to go along with him, after all, if she lost out he would be honour bound to replenish her purse, which would keep him close.

She nodded and wandered off towards where lord John was laughing with his comrades. In the mean time, Robert sent a sailor off for a short length of rope and a selection of empty wine flagons. The man went of greatly amused and shortly returned with four flagons and the requisite length of rope. Robert examined the flagons and selected one with a narrow neck. Next he tied the rope to the bottle so that it could be swung around without slipping free, then he tied the other end to the rail of the ship. Finally, he shook out his doublet once more and having slung it over his shoulder, swaggered with the flagon to the centre of the deck. In his hand he held a fist full of nuts, which he showed to the assembled crew and courtiers. Enola, who had demolished the apple, sat on her spar watching, her tiny black eyes twinkling greedily. He took the empty wine flagon and poured the handful of nuts into it while making sure Enola saw clearly what he was doing. He set it on the deck and then, to their astonishment, walked away and stood idly by, leaning against the main mast as if unconcerned, swinging his doublet in his hand.

Enola, seeing the flagon unattended on the deck slipped down a stay and scampered across to where it rolled to the motion of the ship. She thrust her hand into the flagon and grasped a handful of nuts. At this point Robert pushed himself off the mainmast and strolled casually towards the monkey idly shaking out his doublet. Enola tried to pull her hand out of the flagon but while she clutched a fistful of nuts could not get it clear. She began to scream and jump about hysterically, frantically tugging at the flagon. The crew were in uproar, shouting for her to let go of the nuts but the monkey, once she had possession of her prize, would not let it go for anything. All she had to do to withdraw her hand was to release the nuts, yet she was by nature unable to do so. Robert threw his doublet over the frantic creature and gathering her in a bundle under his arm, used his dagger to cut the rope before strolling off into the stern cabin to the accompaniment of muffled screams, where the Infanta awaited her pet. Claris, quick to respond to the situation went round those who had thought to fleece her of her money and collected her winnings from them. Presently she returned with a fat purse to the Infanta who already had the tale from Robert. It was one of the few times anyone had heard her laugh uncontrollably. They heard her say "a lesson learned," and something about a silken thread.

* * *

The wind went on rising all afternoon until by nightfall a full-scale storm was raging. Robert stood on the after castle with the sailing master, Joel Diaz, muffled to the neck in an oiled woollen cloak. The captain, Michael Storr was with their admiral, Thomas Howard and the other nobles in the great cabin. Robert's head gleamed wetly in the dark, completely enclosed by a leather cap he had borrowed from one of the crew. Storm lanterns gave a fitful light, just enough to identify the location of various parts of the vessel. At the stern, a huge lantern was rigged, tied top and bottom to prevent it tearing away. Every ship in the fleet had a similar lantern to mark their position and to ensure they kept in some sort of order until dawn. They were sailing under a reefed fore sail and lateen at the mizzenmast. Apart from when they left Lisbon and the mouth of the River Tagus, he had seen no more of the main sail, which was furled aloft to its great spar. He had been sent up here by lord John to report on the location of the two sails that were following their course. Now darkness had fallen completely he could gain no further sight of them until daybreak.

His duty done, the thing now was to report to lord John and get off this heaving deck. However, his sleeping place in the crowded fore castle held no attraction for him. The cabin reeked of vomit, which made him retch even though his stomach had settled somewhat. One hundred and fifty sailors were on the ship and a further one hundred soldiers. The Infanta and her entourage were accommodated along with the nobles of her escort, his own master the lord bastard John of Pomfret and the duke of Norfolk among them. Also the archbishop of York and his monks were on board. Some of the soldiers were courtiers, of course, but it meant that any time below deck meant strict confinement alongside unwashed bodies.

"I think this storm will increase in strength during the night, but blow itself out by dawn," offered Joel Diaz. "Your admiral has ordered us to keep in visual contact with the other vessels, easy for him to say." King Richard had appointed John Howard Admiral of the Fleet. The duke of Norfolk was an experienced sailor and now his father was no more, England's chief guardian of the seas after the king himself. Robert looked out over the sea trying to identify the position of the other ships. He could make out perhaps six of them, their storm lanterns appearing every now and again as they plunged in and out of the deep troughs between the waves. Astern there was nothing but blackness. There were at least four ships whose watch keepers no doubt would be following carefully the stern lantern of the Infanta's ship. Below, black water swept the deck spasmodically as waves broke over the gunwales and poured back through scuppers into the sea. He hardly relished crossing to the forecastle and decided to stay with Joel Diaz for a while yet.

They were not alone on the after castle. There were four watch-keepers, one at each corner of the elevated deck under which was the great cabin. Another sailor stood close to the sailing master. His job was to run down and communicate orders to the men working the ship's steering tackle. Below the great cabin, directly under where the Infanta had her sleeping quarters, was the tiller that controlled the ship's rudder, fixed at its extremity by ropes with block and tackle to haul it around to steer the great ship. In front of it was a binnacle containing a compass rose with a pointer of magnetised iron which floated in a bowl containing oil. The needle mystically pointed to the North Star, Polaris, even when that star was hidden behind cloud, or in the day when it was not visible at all. It was a crowded space where, apart from the four men required to man the tiller, other sailors had their sleeping places. Also here were the ship's navigation instruments used by the captain Michael Storr and Joel Diaz to determine their position when out of sight of land. There was an astrolabe and a cross-staff, both for calculating latitude, and a lodestone used regularly to keep the iron needle of the compass rose magnetised.

Robert noted that one of the watch keepers at the stern was replaced, and the man thus relieved gratefully hurried down the companionway and across to the fore castle in which many of the crew had their places. Perhaps it was time for him to do the same. The wind was finding its way through his cloak and vestments and he was of little use here. He was just about to take his leave of the sailing master when the vessel gave an almighty lurch and seemed to turn beam on to the wind. Robert managed to grab a halyard on the mizzenmast while Joel was thrown violently against the ladebord rail.

"Have we struck a rock?" cried Robert in panic.

Diaz waved him away impatiently and dashed down the companionway to get to the tiller. Water was pouring across the deck as the waves struck beam on and it would have been death to try to stand on deck without a lifeline. Robert followed after Diaz. He had to discover what type of peril the vessel was in. He entered the tiller flat to be greeted by a scene of utter confusion and devastation. The great tiller was lying on the deck, broken off at the point just before the pintle of the rudder. Diaz began shouting orders, getting the sailors to their feet and sending some down to the hold to break out a spare tiller. Robert, realising he would be of no use here, rushed back on deck where water swilled knee deep. Michael Storr was there shouting orders to his mariners to get the sail off her. He was desperate to get to Claris and the Infanta who would be terrified at the sudden change in the ship's otherwise controlled passage across the sea.

Sailors were running everywhere and he heard Diaz order the application of a sea anchor. Up above sailors were taking in the foresail and lateen sail, letting the ship drift at the mercy of the storm. He guessed that without steerage the sails would cause the vessel to heel over and capsize. Better to let it run free. He helped fasten ropes to the sea anchor, a sort of sail that would trail behind them in the sea pulling them stern to wind. The danger here was that the ship might be pooped by a huge wave coming at them from astern, but the stern castle on this ship would probably reduce the likelihood of that. As the ship swung stern to wind under the restricting pull of the sea anchor, water stopped sloshing across the deck and he was able to get the door of the main cabin open. As he did so, Thomas Howard and some of his men spilled out onto the deck. Seeing Robert the duke demanded an explanation.

"The tiller, your grace," he managed to gasp. "It has broken and control of the steering has been lost." Thomas Howard understood at once.

"How could that be," he demanded. Robert had no way of answering that question and it seemed the duke regarded it as rhetorical anyway. He shoved past Robert and went up to the deck of the after castle. Robert let the duke's men shoulder him aside then darted into the main cabin. There was consternation, as might be expected. The women were screaming and the courtiers were white faced with terror, not having any idea what was happening and fearing they would be lost. He looked around for the one face important to him and fixed his eyes upon Claris. She was clearly frightened but trying to remain calm, the better to attend upon her mistress. The Infanta was in her sleeping quarters and had not emerged. Claris' eyes met Robert's as he pushed his way through the hysterical throng.

He took her into his arms and cried into her ear: "fear not. There has been a failure in the steering of the ship, which the sailing master has in hand. Soon all will be restored." Already the affect of the sea anchor had caused the violent yawing to subside and Claris let her head rest on his chest for a moment, comforted by his words.

"Thanks be to the Holy Virgin, she whispered. I thought we had struck a reef or been attacked by Leviathan or some other sea monster. They say such creatures lurk in a storm."

"They do, to be sure, but not in this case," he reassured her. "It is a broken timber, that is all. The sailing master has sent down for a spare and once it is fitted we shall be back in trim, never fear."

"I must go to her grace," she said at last pushing gently at his chest.

"Yes," he replied, "and tell her all is well. I must return to the deck and help get the vessel back on course."

On the after castle, Thomas Howard was in conference with the captain and sailing master. Joel Diaz was at a loss to explain how a timber designed to withstand the heaviest usage could have failed so suddenly. The storm was not so great as others he had encountered. The lord Bastard, John was there too, listening to Diaz with concern written all over his face. He was holding a storm lantern to provide a small amount of illumination. When he saw Robert he stood away from the duke and beckoned his squire over to him.

"This was no accident, I fear," he said with deliberation. "There is something else amiss. Do you not see what it is?" Lord John looked astern at the creaming waves; their white breaking tops the only visible sign of the sea around them.

Robert looked about him. All was as it was before the failure of the tiller except the ship was pitching violently due to the affect of the sea anchor dragging astern.

"All looks to be in order now, my lord?" he said in a puzzled voice. Clearly he had missed something.

"Come here," said lord John. He led him to the stern rail and took up the end of a rope, which he examined by the light of his lantern. "This is a lanyard cut cleanly. It was attached to the stern lantern by which the other ships in our fleet could see the location of their princess. Do you see it now?"

Robert looked up to where the lantern should have been. All he could see was the swirling blackness of the storm. They were adrift in the ocean and the only visible means of the others in the fleet keeping station on them in the black night had gone!

* * *

A grey dawn was just breaking which found them afloat and back in trim but as yet with no sight of the rest of their fleet. Robert was in the tiller flat with the sailing master and lord John. They had reset their previous course, beating to windward and expecting that the fleet would be looking for them. The storm had abated just as Joel Diaz had predicted and now they were under full sail at last. A weak sun began to appear every now and again through grey cloud. Captain Storr was up on deck anxious to see where the rest of the fleet might be as the light increased visibility. The broken tiller lay to one side and they bent to examine it.

"You can clearly see where it has been cut into," observed lord John. The tiller had saw marks at a point just inside its socket, which meant the sabotage was hidden from view. "That could only have been done in harbour," he continued. "This vessel was given new masts and rigging before being entrusted with the Infanta Joanna. Any one of the shipyard workers could have done it. This is part of a plan to wreck us. It was bound to fail in heavy weather and the Bay of Biscay is noted for its violent seas."

"How does that explain the disappearance of the stern lantern?" queried Robert. "There must be someone on board who had the job of getting rid of it. He is unlikely to bring down his own destruction, surely?"

"You have a point there, squire Robert. Perhaps some fanatic has been recruited to help confound us in the event the tiller remained intact?"

"In that case the disappearance of the stern lantern, meaning our fleet could not locate us in the night, must be part of some other plan not entirely dependent on wrecking us."

At that moment there came a cry from the deck. Robert and lord John made their way rapidly to the after deck and joined those gathered there. John Howard was there with Michael Storr and Joel Diaz. They were standing at the windward rail staring with great concentration a few points off the ladebord bow. Clustered with them were the courtiers they had in their company. Robert and lord John pushed through the press to see what was so interesting. Perhaps they had sighted the rest of their fleet, which might now be visible in the increasing light of dawn. Unfortunately it was not their own ships; to their consternation three galleys were bearing down on them, their single sails set and oars adding to their speed. It was clear they were about to be attacked by brigands.

"They have the wind gage of us!" cried captain Storr. Thomas Howard bellowed for the guns to be run out. There were two each side in the bow and the same in the after castle. These last were of no use at the moment seeing as the galleys were approaching ahead. Robert and lord John of Pomfret exchanged anxious glances and took themselves to one side.

"Three galleys! I saw but two yestere'en," said Robert, his eyes wide with apprehension.

"It was their sails you saw, the third was probably somewhere astern and may not have had a sail set," replied lord John. "There are three now, that's for sure and they are coming for us."

"I wonder how they know where we are?" said Robert. "We had no steerage for some time during the night and therefore no course set."

"Down wind," replied lord John. "The signal for the breaking of the tiller was the extinguishing of the stern light. Once that happened we could only go in one of two directions, down to the seabed or downwind. All the galleys had to do was steer downwind after us. It is probable their captains knew what our trouble was while our fleet would be left wondering where we were and no idea our steering was lost."

"Then they must have anticipated we would recover from the disaster."

"Yes, we have a well found ship under us and the storm was not that bad to have sunk us. Moreover, we now have to beat slowly to windward to catch our fleet while those galleys have the wind in their favour."

"Effectively between our ship and where we might expect our fleet to be," Robert realised. "Yet if they are part of a concerted plan to capture our vessel then who is paying for it? Three galleys with a crew of say two hundred apiece will not come cheap."

"Huh, that is the easiest question of all to answer – plunder," snorted lord John. "We have in our hold the dowry of the Infanta Joanna, enough to satisfy every man of them, then there is the coin and jewels of our nobles, not to mention the possibility of ransom. Why, the king would pay handsomely to get me back and there is the archbishop of York and the duke of Norfolk, Thomas Howard on board along with a host of lesser nobles, all worth ransom. Be in no doubt, we are a rich prize the like of which none of the felons in those galleys will ever have a chance at again."

"Then if we are captured the Infanta will be murdered and the rest of us taken prisoner?"

"The Infanta will be murdered certainly, otherwise why go to such elaborate lengths to isolate us from our fleet. Whoever is in overall command of those galleys will be the main protagonist and her death will be his only objective. After that the pirate crew can do what they will. As for you, I am afraid you will not survive either, unless your father can raise a king's ransom for you; the same goes for our crew and common soldiers, which is why all of us will fight like the Devil."

"When you have finished discussing the time of day with your squire, my lord, perhaps you might like to get into harness." Thomas Howard was glowering at lord John, ignoring Robert altogether, assuming he would be commanded by his master.

"I was just about to send down to break out our harness, your grace," responded the lord Bastard, jostling Robert towards the steps down into the hold. "We must arm ourselves for the fight," he growled.

Lord John ordered a group of soldiers to stand back while he descended. They were bringing handguns up from the hold. Already these were being attached to mounts on the gun wales of the ship set there for the purpose. The galleys would attempt to come alongside and board, where overwhelming numbers might defeat the ship's company. To do that they would have to approach through the fire of the ship's guns, which hopefully would deplete their numbers sufficiently to drive them off. In addition, archers would fire down on them from the castles fore and aft and platforms in the rigging. Whatever the situation, it was shaping up to be a bitter and savage action. If the brigands succeeded in getting aboard then the fighting would be hand-to-hand with the brigands having superior numbers. Each galley would have at least two hundred fighting men while their ship had perhaps two hundred soldiers and crew. This vessel was carrying the Infanta and her retinue, along with the attendants of high-status nobles, which reduced their fighting capacity.

They clattered down the companionway in to the hold where Robert located their chests. He pulled out lord John's harness and helped him divest himself of his clothes except for his chemise and bries to which he laced his hose. He dug out an arming doublet with its arming points for tying on the plate and helped him into it. Next he knelt down and fitted the sabatons over his shoes to protect his feet then fitted the greaves to his lower legs. Strips of wool were wound around his legs to prevent the leg iron chafing. These were part of an assembly where poleyns provided a protective cover for the knees and connected the upper and lower parts of the leg armour. Cuisses were strapped around his thighs and their tops tied to his arming doublet. A mail coif was draped over his head and around his neck, then the faulds, a series of flexible steel strips, were tied to the waist of his doublet. Robert strapped on the tasset plates, which would protect lord John in the area between the faulds and the cuisses. His cuirass, comprising a breast and back plate was strapped to his body and then Robert found and fitted the rerebraces to his upper arm and the vambraces to his forearms which were connected via jointed couters at the elbow. Pauldrons were fitted over the shoulder completing the arming of his body. All that was required now was to strap on the helm, which lord John wore without a visor for the moment, as he wanted to have a clear view of the coming action.

In full harness, the lord Bastard, John of Pomfret stamped his way back on deck to join the captains on the after castle while Robert found a boy to help him into his own harness. Once armed, he made his own way onto the deck. Men were sighting over the handguns at the gunwales while boys ran to and fro carrying gunpowder charges and ball ammunition. Linstocks for igniting the powder charges were glowing, sending thin wreathes of smoke to disperse in the wind. Halberdiers crowded into the centre of the waist ready to repel any of the enemy that got aboard. He could see men clustered around the cannon in the after castle. In the waist of the ship archers were stringing their bows and Robert had thought to bring his own cross-bow up from the hold along with a quiver full of his scarlet-fletched quarrels. The best position for shooting was on one of the upper decks and so he joined his master, lord John on the after castle.

He gazed wistfully at the door to the main cabin, which now had a guard of six halberdiers. If the brigands did manage to get aboard he would be down there with them fighting for the life of the Infanta Joanna and the donzela Claris Salgado. He imagined the women sitting helplessly in terror, hearing the sounds of battle and having no way of knowing if some pirate might break in and murder them. He determined that would only happen after his death and the brigands would not find his demise easy to achieve. If only a means of preventing the brigands boarding them could be found.

Suddenly he had an idea. He remembered how in the storm the ship's cook had managed to provide hot food for the nobles, even though his fire had been extinguished. Being curious he sought out the cook and asked him. The man was only too willing to show him. He had two pots, one that fitted inside the other. He put the meats inside the smaller pot and sealed the top. The next part amazed Robert. The cook took some quicklime he had for the purpose and placed it in the large pot then fitted the smaller pot inside it, next he poured some water over the quicklime and covered both pots. He bade Robert wait for a short time then told him to place his hands around the outside of the pot. Curiously it was quite warm. The quicklime was producing considerable heat. He knew that slaked lime was used as a wash to whiten castle walls, but had not realised that the process of slaking lime with water produced so much heat.

He made his way down into the hold of the ship and found the cook and got him to break out a barrel of quicklime. Then he ordered some seamen to carefully place a quantity of quicklime in canvas squares and tie them into bags. The cook, an old mariner, immediately knew what he was up to. The tactic had been used in naval warfare in the past, most notably at the Battle of Sluys against the combined fleet of France, Genoa and Castile in the reign of the English King, Edward the Third. There was an attack of galleys against the English fleet at that battle and the English had a novel way of defeating it. Getting the men to bring the canvas bags up on fore castle deck. A company of longbow men were engaged firing at the approaching enemy and Robert found their captain and got his attention.

The sailors had furled the main sail and they were scudding along under a topsail, foresail and the lateen sail at the mizzen. The brilliant banners of Portugal and England streamed valiantly from the two mastheads reaching at their extremities over the sea beyond the after limits of the ship, proclaiming this was a well armed fighting vessel. The full light of day was now upon them and staring forwards he could see the three galleys closing fast. With no colours showing that might identify them, they had taken down their sails so as not to hamper their operation. All hands would thus be available for fighting. Their oars were moving in unison as if three giant insects were crawling across the surface of the ocean. Already he could see rows of halberds arranged upright ready to be grabbed when the time came for boarding their prey. Gunners were levering the cannon around ready to fire once in range.

Just then there was a shout from the main masthead. A lookout was pointing beyond the galleys to the horizon. He could see ships, three, four – five heading their way. It could only be their own fleet turned about to look for them. That was of no immediate help seeing as it would take half the morning for them to get to them and the galleys were now in range of their guns. Two explosions rent the air as the gunners opened fire on the nearest galley. Robert, wreathed in the acrid yellow smoke of the discharge, squinted through the murk and saw one shot go wide, skipping across the sea like a stone on a pond. The other found a mark; splinters flew up from the galley and several oars hung trailing in the sea. It hardly slowed the approach of their enemy and soon the oars were back in action while the bodies of the erstwhile rowers were thrown ignominiously overboard. There was no mercy on that vessel, not even for its own men. As the galley drew near, the after cannon were unable to depress far enough to fire into it but now it was under the muzzles of the handguns and they let off a volley that drew screams and shouts from the galley. It was so near blood could be seen pouring from the deck into the sea but it seemingly had little effect on numbers. They could see at least two hundred men and they were getting the galley ready to run alongside.

Now the archers opened fire and more of the enemy fell to the deck, though others were hidden behind hastily erected pavis. These were no use against the guns, but handguns took time to load and fire. The brigands were gambling on getting close enough to hook on with grappling irons before they were too reduced in numbers. Robert sighted on the man at the tiller, whom he managed to hit, but another ran to take over without much effect on the direction of their collision course. The hand gunners managed to get off another volley while the longbows shot arrow after arrow into the mass of rowers and this time it did have an effect. Half the oars were out of action and the rest were beating the water independently rather than in unison. The vessel began to fall away. Again bodies were flung overboard to clear space while the galley retired to lick its wounds.

Once more the cannon fired and found a mark in the next galley, with a similar result. The progress hardly slowed and this time there were two of them one close astern of the other. It would be difficult to stop two of them and Robert could already see men in the galleys with grappling irons and coils of rope. It became apparent to him that they would come at them on both sides of the ship and their vessel was bound to be boarded. Something needed to be done to reduce the odds. In the confusion of a hand fight it would be too easy for some of the enemy to break through to the main cabin.

"We must go for the galley on the ladebord side," he shouted at the captain of archers. "Ignore the one to windward." The captain nodded his understanding and got a dozen of his men along the forecastle rail to ladebord. Each had three arrows tipped with a canvas bag. The pirate galley began to ship oars ready to board and already Robert could see men swinging grappling irons at the end of mooring ropes. The other archers were shooting down at the men in the galleys but already the handguns were unable to depress far enough to fire into them. As the galley began to ship oars in preparation for coming alongside, Robert gave the signal to the captain of the archers. They came to the side rail and shot down into the galley. The canvas bags at the tips of their shafts burst upon impact and a fine dust of quicklime began to envelop the pirate crew. Firing the rest of their missiles into the boat, the brigands there were blinded and dropped their oars. Those with the grappling irons fell back upon their comrades, clasping their hands over their eyes, unable to see while the oarsmen lost control of their oars and the armed men dropped their weapons. Where the quicklime came into contact with water inside the galley it began to heat up and produce fumes, which added to the confusion. Men were thrashing around, their eyes burning in their sockets and their exposed flesh beginning to scorch. Unable to see or control their vessel, it rapidly drifted astern behind the noxious cloud of quicklime that had been the instrument of their agony.

There was no time for congratulations. A vicious pirate crew was attempting to come over the steorbord rail and already the fighting was becoming desperate. Robert charged his crossbow and fired at one of the brigands, taking him in the chest. Fitting the crannequin and winding it to latch the string he fired off another shot. Some of the brigands had managed to get aboard and thus it became impossible to fire into the mass of fighting men for fear of hitting his own. With increasing horror he saw a tight knot of brigands making their way towards the stern cabin. A moment was all the time he needed to realise their intent.

They were a foul looking crew, the dregs of humanity typical of those to be found lurking in the back streets of any harbour the world over, but one of them seemed to be in command and was clad in good harness. Full of dread for the safety of the women in the cabin, he clambered onto the ladebord rail, that being on the opposite side of the ship to the fighting, and ran along to the stern where he dropped down onto the main deck. He drew his sword and dagger, and placing his back to the cabin doors, stood ready to repel any brigands that managed to get through. Someone dropped down beside him and whipping round defensively he saw the lord bastard, John of Pomfret similarly armed and ready to defend the cabin. The two stood together and faced the enemy.

The duke of Norfolk, John Howard was also on his way, fighting his way down the companionway from the deck of the after castle. The enemy were concentrating on this part of the ship and now some were forcing their way through. One of them was unlucky and tripped as he came at them through the heaving mass only to fall upon Robert's sword. He finished the man by a thrust to the throat with his dagger and shoved him aside to fall writhing on the deck. Somewhere beyond the front line of brigands he saw their leader hacking his way remorselessly towards them. He was clad in black harness helmeted with a sallet, unvisored. The bottom part of his face was obscured by the steel bevoir that protected his neck and chin. In addition, he had a cloth tied over his mouth. Clearly he did not want to be identified. Nevertheless, Robert thought there was something familiar about him. Now they were being attacked in earnest and already Robert had taken a couple of blows that, had it not been for his armour, would have put him down.

Having left his visor off, his face was vulnerable and one man came at him jabbing with the spiked end of a poleaxe. Robert, being lithe and quick, with reflexes fine tuned to the danger of combat, managed to dodge him twice. The third attempt was more determined and the deadly spike grazed the side of his helm. However, it momentarily put the man off balance and Robert stepped forward and butted him in the face then plunged his dagger into his opponent's groin, that part being vulnerable below the breastplate he was wearing. The man screamed and dropped back to disappear into the struggling mass. Lord John of Pomfret was fighting manfully beside him, handing out the same treatment as Robert. One brigand came at lord John forcing his way between him and Robert while another attacked his front. Robert managed to grab the top of his helmet and pulling his head back drew his dagger across the brigand's throat. Bright red blood sprayed over lord John who hammered the man aside with a back swipe of his gauntleted hand.

From that point on it seemed the attack of the brigands began to slacken. John Howard with his men was attacking hard from the rear and so the enemy were forced to retire and try for their vessel to escape. Fighting bitterly, Robert saw the eyes of their captain blazing with a mixture of hatred, fury and frustration as he was forced further from his objective, which Robert had no doubt was the Infanta Joanna. He had seen those eyes before and hopefully, after the fight when he had time to ponder, he might remember who they belonged to.

11 – Saint George for England

As the last of the brigands was driven off, the English and Portuguese began dealing with their own dead and wounded and also those of the enemy. Thomas Howard ordered two of the enemy wounded to be taken below and information extracted from them. The rest were ignominiously dumped in the sea, a treatment they might have expected in any case from their own kind. The duke of Norfolk then entered the great cabin to reassure the ladies and the clergy that the danger was past and five of their own fleet were almost upon them. The monks came out on deck and began tending to the wounded and dying and offering prayers for the dead.

Robert was about to enter the great cabin when Claris appeared at the door leaning faintly on the frame. Her eyes were wide with shock as she looked upon the blood spattered over the deck before the doorway. Seeing Robert standing there, his sword and dagger bloodied and his armour daubed with gore and dented she began to slide to the floor in a swoon. He dropped his weapons and rushed to her, lifting her to her feet and steering her into the cabin. Her eyes opened and gazed into his, flicking from terror to concern. She reached out to his face and brought her hand away bloodied.

"You are wounded," she whispered, her deep brown eyes shining wet with concern. Now his attention had been drawn to it he did, indeed, feel what was a cut in his face. He supposed it had happened in the heat of the battle and therefore he had not felt it.

"A scratch merely," he responded flippantly. "My father will be pleased when I tell him how much I have come to appreciate the protection of his good steel harness." He thumped a gauntleted fist against his breastplate.

"I shall tend it for you," she replied, recovering her composure and patting at his face while examining the wound.

"The Infanta?"

He looked about the cabin and saw the duke of Norfolk was already in attendance upon the lady whose safety was his responsibility. The Infanta Joanna was seated on her chair as if all were normal and a show had just been put on to entertain her during what was otherwise a tedious voyage. If there was any need for female hysterics her ladies were supplying it in abundance and the Infanta seemed content to let them represent her rather than show a degree of panic herself. The Infanta's women were surrounded by men in armour who were making a fuss of them, and had Robert been a few years older, he might have concluded they would continue fluttering for some time yet to get the most out of their experience, now the real danger was over. As it was his breast heaved only with concern for Claris and he led her by the hand to a chair where he seated her.

"You must clean yourself, good sir," she said looking up at him gently. "And I think you have lost your weapons."

He gasped with alarm. His harness was smeared in blood and he had dropped his sword and dagger when he went to her assistance. He bowed to her as elegantly as he could manage in his haste, and went to the cabin door to retrieve them. Lord John stepped past him making his way to join Thomas Howard and the Infanta. His harness, too, was besmirched with blood and his approach provoked a fresh round of pretended distress in the ladies.

The deck resembled a shambles by the presence of blood and the mariners were already swilling it away. He found a scrap of woollen cloth and wiped his sword and dagger before sliding them back into their respective scabbards. The same scrap served to clean away what blood he could see on his armour and he got a boy to clean behind him. Lookouts were shouting down information on the close presence of some of their own fleet and looking out over the sea, the galleys were rowing away. The stern chasers fired after them and managed one strike before the galleys were out of range. Now there were other ships around there would be nothing more to fear from them.

Some hours later Robert found himself commanded to attend upon the duke of Norfolk and the lord bastard John in the captain's cabin, which he had moved with his personal effects into the cabin under the fore castle. They were back on course for England and already other ships of their fleet had been sighted. Claris had washed the cut along his right cheek and the ship's chirurgeon had stitched it together. There would be a scar, not as grand a scar as his father's perhaps, but yet something to show for his martial adventure. They had all changed back into their normal clothes, those of the two nobles being of a quality that would not disgrace the king's court. Robert was plainly dressed in his good doublet and hose.

"Sit you down, squire Robert," said Thomas Howard gruffly as the young man entered the cabin. They were seated at a square table and Robert took the only vacant chair. "You may serve us," continued the duke, "and pour for yourself." He nodded at a flagon and goblets in the centre of the table.

Robert reached for a flagon and poured wine into the three silver goblets on the table. He felt a thrill of excitement being in conference with the duke of Norfolk who, next to viscount Lovell was probably the most prominent noble in England and also the lord bastard, John of Pomfret, King Richard's own son.

"First of all," began the duke, "you are to be commended on your action with the quicklime. It is certain that had brigands from two galleys managed to get aboard us, we would have been overwhelmed. As it is, we have eighteen dead and thirty wounded, some of whom may survive. It was a close and bitter fight in which you distinguished yourself."

"The ship's cook must take some of the credit, my lords," replied Robert jocularly. "It was he that gave me the idea, though I believe my lessons on the Arts of War delivered to his squires by your grace's noble father, telling of the Battle of Sluys, was of proven worth." He remembered with a mental shiver the cold winter days when the old duke, killed at Bosworth, would lecture his squires on battle tactics in the draughty hall of Framlingham Castle. He would particularly favour describing the strategies of King Edward the Third, victor at the famous battle of Crecy, fought two years after his naval victory at Sluys; and his son, the Black Prince's battle at Poitiers among many others.

"You learned your lesson well, it seems. You could make a good captain one day." The duke took a long pull at his wine and placed down the goblet with a thump. "Now, my lord John of Pomfret tells me there is a plot against the life of the Infanta Joanna, that you have both known of it and yet never saw fit to disclose it to me. You were both charged by the King to look for such, but not, I think, to conceal it."

"Your grace . . ." stammered Robert, panic churning his innards.

"Never mind the excuses. I have had those from lord John. Though I have ordered you to serve him, you are still a squire of my house and owe your final allegiance to me."

Robert felt his spirits deflate. In a moment he had gone from elation at Thomas Howard's praise and now he was plumbing the depths of despair as he realised his fault.

"Your grace, I was unsure at first and wished to be certain before putting my suspicions to you." Though unfair to himself, he could hardly place the blame on the lord bastard John of Pomfret.

Thomas Howard waved him to silence and leaned back in his chair. "Had it not been for your actions in the recent fight in this ship I would have had you flogged and sent back to your father in disgrace." He paused to let his words sink in. Robert felt himself shrinking and wished himself anywhere other than here. "Luckily for you the lord John here is culpable too and his father the king will have something to say to him, and to you as his accomplice no doubt. As it is," the duke continued, "no harm is done and the Infanta is quite safe. Had she been poisoned or come to any other harm, you would have been racked and then your head would have been forfeit – do you understand?"

"I do your grace." He could hardly speak and his voice was no more than a croak. It was heady work associating with great nobles, but highly dangerous and not something for the inexperienced or unwary to contemplate lightly. He had got himself into the present predicament mostly by accident rather than design, but the risk to his neck was the same whatever his personal ambitions might be.

"More wine!"

Robert slopped some wine into the duke's goblet, his hand trembling causing a few drops to spill onto the table. The lord John of Pomfret sat silently, not looking at either of them. Obviously he had already been spoken to and was keeping a sensible silence. The duke of Norfolk took up his goblet and directed his attention to the lord bastard. "I shall now take your report, lord John."

The lord bastard leaned forward; pleased the subject of discipline was being dropped, at least for the moment.

"The two prisoners have been put to the question, your grace. They had little to tell us of the actual plan but there is a name you will be interested in. The brigands were assembled at La Coruña with a promise of a great prize. They lurked around the seas near Lisbon and waited for us, fully expecting the Infanta's ship to lose her escort, though not knowing the details of how that would happen. Their captain was a well-known Spanish brigand, though he was not the one in charge of the business with the Infanta; that was an Englishman. Their expectations were largely those that squire Robert and I had already worked out, they would plunder the Infanta's dowry and any other treasure they could rob. The men had guessed the Infanta was to be murdered, but that was no part of their business. Her foul murder was to be done by the Englishman."

"You have his name?" growled Thomas Howard eagerly, his eyes flashing fire.

"I have, your grace and it is one familiar to you."

"Sir Reginald Bray!" cried Robert all of a sudden. He had just realised, while listening to the words of lord John, who the eyes of the mysterious brigand belonged to. He had good reason to despise them seeing as Bray had previously imprisoned him and nearly had him hanged.

"The very same," agreed lord John.

"Then the Stanley woman is behind it," snarled the duke. "Shall we never be rid of her?"

Robert opened his mouth to express relief that at least those great English nobles surrounding King Richard were thus cleared of suspected involvement in the plot, but something in lord John's expression stopped his tongue. Pausing made him recognise just in time the lord bastard's fear that it would be unwise to mention their discussion regarding the possibility of fluid loyalty in certain high nobles. The duke narrowed his eyes suspiciously having noticed the tension between the two.

"You were about to speak, squire Robert?" he intoned.

"I . . .I would say that perhaps this latest failure will discourage her from further attempts," he stammered lamely. "Once in England dame Stanley will no longer be able to bring her malign influence to bear."

"Then let me disabuse you of that idea," snapped the duke. "There are always those whose ambition can make use of a pernicious enemy. I shall advise the king of the danger to his future queen. There had been one attempt at poisoning her before this latest effort, I cannot think that will be the end of it. Indeed, the failure of so ambitious a scheme as that we have just defeated will almost certainly lead to a change in tactics. I can fight a visible enemy and cope with high odds, but it is much harder to defeat a determined and secret assassin." Robert hung his head. The response that sprung into his mind; that the duke had, in fact, little part in the defeat of the plot against the Infanta, remained stillborn.

"Yes, your grace," put in lord John. "That has made me think more on this recent attack. The disappearance of the stern lantern, which caused our fleet to lose sight of us in the storm, was no accident. The lanyard, which secured it, was deliberately cut. Someone on board this ship did that and may still be with us."

"The prisoners did not reveal who that might be?"

"They were not privy to the actual plot, your grace. They were mere churls. I had managed to get out of them all they knew, I believe, before we dropped them overboard."

"We must be vigilant," replied the duke. "At this stage observation might serve us better than attempting to interrogate the entire crew, much as I would like to. Let us wait until we reach England where the Infanta can be taken to a place of safety."

Robert kept silence. The duke's presumption that one of the ship's crew was responsible for cutting the stern lantern free was but one possibility. There was nothing to say that a servant of any of the nobles in the ship might have done it, in fact, it was the most likely.

Now that the plot against the Infanta was more generally known, he thought it time he confided in Claris. She was close to Joanna and therefore in a position where she could observe those about her. Until now he had let her remain in ignorance rather than alarm her. Now, while sworn to protect the person of the Infanta Joanna, it had become necessary to alert Claris to her own danger, which he quietly admitted to himself, was his chief concern.

"Are her women to be trusted?" asked Robert having managed to get Claris quietly into a corner of the well deck. She had responded with a gasp of fear when he informed her of the plot against her mistress. The business with Elona he deliberately left out, confining his tale to that of the brigands and the probable involvement of dame Margaret Stanley. After a while Claris' demeanour took on a certain stiffness and her mouth set itself in a firm line of determination. Princess Joanna had been kind to her and her brother and she would do all in her power to prevent harm coming to her.

"I believe so," she replied thoughtfully, her brow marked with a frown. "They have all been with her for years. Our matron is Ana de Mendonça . . ." Here Claris paused and flushed.

"Is there something about her I should know?" he wondered.

"Not pertinent to the safety of the Infanta, no, but I shall tell you providing you do not go gossiping among your fellows."

"Of course not. Anything you tell me I shall keep close, never fear."

"Well, many ladies have paramours among those at court," she whispered, turning her face away from his and looking out over the sea. She pondered for a moment then turned to face him. "In the case of Ana de Mendonça, her paramour is our King João and she has a child by him – a boy."

"Ah, another bastard – just as my own king, my present liege lord John of Pomfret!"

"Yes, this one is named Jorge de Lencastre. He is five years old and my lady Joanna, his aunt, has taken charge of him from birth. He resides in the Convent of Jesus at Aveiro."

"So this lady, Ana de Mendonça is another who lives by the charity of her mistress?"

"Not in the same case as I," she responded. "Her father was Dom Nuno Furtado de Mendonça, who was Lord Chamberlain in the household of the king's father, Afonso the Fifth. King João has ordered that a convent be built especially for her at Santos-o-Novo and she shall become its beneficiary."

"Is the boy left behind? I have seen nothing of him."

"He is to be placed in the tutelage of Diogo Fernandes de

Almeida, the son of one of the king's trusted courtiers."

"Then we can rest easy; in fact, from what you say her women are her best defence. A problem might occur in England should the king, in all innocence, appoint ladies of *his* court to join them."

"I think we must tell Anselm too," she suggested. "He is close to the Infanta and a man. Although he might not look it, he is a skilled swordsman."

Robert pondered on this. He was not happy at disclosing the threat to the Infanta to another, but seeing as Anselm was as bound to the lady as his sister, her suggestion made good sense. It would be practical to have someone near who might stop an assassin. For sure, her ladies would not be able to do so. Anselm was ever in the Infanta's chamber and well placed to protect her."

"I shall suggest that to my lord, John of Pomfret - and the duke of Norfolk must be informed," he added as an afterthought. "If they agree then Anselm shall be brought into our circle."

* * *

It seemed as if all of England was in Southampton to welcome their new Queen. King Richard had sent half his court to swell the numbers of the burgesses, merchants and dignitaries assembled around the harbour. There was hardly room to accommodate them all on the quay where the Infanta's ship was about to dock. Many were spread along the waterfront and hanging from windows or even sitting on rooftops. Everywhere was festival – jongleurs were singing ballads, tumblers were performing their intricate tricks, all eager to make money from the crowds of common people come here for the spectacle. The king had commanded that the flag of Portugal be flown everywhere beside that of St George and thus dozens were flying in the warm breeze along the quay and in the town. Every building was festooned in colour, and those who had no flag hung strips of bunting to add to the display. All knew of the Infanta's lineage, descended from John of Gaunt, a daughter of true Plantagenet blood that would unite once and for all the noble houses of Lancaster and York. Now she had come to join with their king, there would be no more bastards that might contest for the Crown to despoil the peace of England.

The Infanta's epithet, the Holy Princess of Portugal, was recognised by the large numbers of clergy, priests and prelates standing in prominent positions on the dock. With them were nuns from several London convents and these would take charge of Joanna on the road to her new capital, where King Richard waited eagerly for sight of his intended bride. In the centre, where the Infanta would first set foot in England, stood viscount Lovell with his entourage. Beside Lovell stood John, earl of Lincoln with his party. Thomas Howard's household knights were there, waiting for sight of their liege, the duke of Norfolk who would escort the Infanta from the ship and hand responsibility for her over to viscount Francis Lovell.

Robert stood beside Claris in the well deck of their vessel as the sailors hauled at the halliards to get the sails off. Men in the bow and stern were ready to throw ropes to others on the quay so the ship could be hauled gently alongside. Six boats with oars had taken control of the ship by hawsers and began drawing the vessel into the harbour between the dozens of ships anchored in the approaches and at the quays. These too were decked with flags and banners, their crews lining the rails and rigging to get a view of the Portuguese princess.

"I suppose it will be difficult for us to meet, once you are at court with your mistress?" sighed Robert. Claris leaned gently against him and laid a hand on his arm. The two had drawn close during the remainder of the voyage. Neither had said very much about their feelings for each other, hardly daring to presume a romance between them would find approval, yet an attachment had formed. Normally a youth would declare undying love for the object of his affection while she would feign coyness. He would ply her with compliments and trinkets while she would bestow a favour – a kerchief or ribbon for him to wear. Nothing of this sort had occurred yet the bond between them was palpable. It was as if their growing together had been pre-ordained and being natural, required none of the formalities demanded by society. Perhaps the close confinement on board ship had brought this about and once on land, at least in Robert's mind, he might need to pursue a more traditional courtship.

One thing that encouraged him was her brother Anselm's attitude. When observing them together, he regarded them with something of amusement and a hint of patronage. Was that due merely to the romantic soul of a troubadour? Claris' father and mother were dead and Anselm was therefore her guardian, except brother and sister were in the household of the Infanta who would therefore be the one to decide the fate of her handmaid. His father, Laurence, would have something to say should his son wish to attach himself to an impoverished noblewoman with no dowry. Robert's hope was that his father might consider her rank to be recompense for the lack of any other pecuniary advantage. But in all this he realised he was premature having yet to formally declare his love to the donzela.

"I fear so, sir, since there is nothing between us other than the fondness that fellows in an adventure might naturally find." She turned her eyes upon him, rending him from head to toe. His spirit leaped, as he perceived here was an entrance to her heart.

"Then might I approach your mistress with a request for a more formal arrangement?" he asked, his face shining forth the deepest secrets of his soul. For a moment it was as if her eyes were melting into his and the spheres that he had heard swept the heavens were forming a coronet above them. Then all became dark as she lowered her head and gave it a diminutive shake.

"I fear it is impossible, I have no dowry, no wealth, only a name and that means little in Portugal, nothing in England. Unless you can show how you might support a wife, I cannot see a way forward."

Truly Robert was of tender years, yet to make a place for himself and acquire some wealth and property. Unless his father died, and that was unlikely nor his wish he remained a pauper swain. He gripped her firmly by the shoulders and fixed her with his eyes. "If there is one thing I have learned in these few weeks it is that there is a great world opening up to be explored and I cannot think there is no room in it for us. I shall find a way; by my sword - I swear it! Only declare your love to me and it shall be so."

"I do willingly so swear," she cried, "but I fear, my love, I fear."

He gathered her into his arms and held her close. He could feel her frame trembling against him. To be sure there was much water between them, but not so deep nor far as to be un-navigable.

"If you would unhand my sister," said Anselm, coming over to them, "her mistress is about to come on deck and her women are needed about her."

Robert looked to him for any idea of disquietude, but saw nothing other than an amused smile at his lips. He was not surprised, as he had forged a bond with Anselm too. His liege the duke of Norfolk had agreed to Anselm being included in their secret and the troubadour was more resolute even than his sister. Robert was learning that a man is most happy when acting in the defence of a lady and one such as Anselm, steeped in songs and poetry of chivalric love, particularly so. There was three of them now – the same as the Holy Trinity. Perhaps it was a sign all would be well? He let Claris slip from his arms and with a demure curtsy, she left them to attend upon the Infanta.

Sailors hastily removed the gunwales and planking in the centre of the well deck to let the Infanta walk unhindered from the ship. At the quay men were hauling at the bow and stern ropes bringing the ship with a gentle bump alongside. As soon as the ropes were tied to secure the ship a gangway was pushed from the quay onto the deck. Its rails were decked with red and white roses entwined with woodbine producing a heady perfume for the Infanta to breath in as she embarked from ship to shore.

The Infanta stood aloof with her ladies behind and her clergy before. Robert gazed wistfully at the diminutive Claris who affected not to notice anyone but her princess. The priests paraded from the ship followed by the men of the duke of Norfolk's command. These formed up either side with a passage between where the Infanta might walk. She was dressed in a gown of gold, embroidered with brown silks tracing flowers and birds. Her headdress was tall and similarly decorated, not a hennin as the ladies of King Richard's court wore. The duke came to her side and offered his arm in support. He was splendidly dressed in scarlet and black, belted with sword and dagger each having jewelled hilts. John of Pomfret came and stood behind her, his men falling in behind him. Robert was to join them as they disembarked.

The Infanta Joanna walked slowly forward and with the duke of Norfolk by her side, stepped from the gangplank onto English soil. Clarions sounded a brilliant fanfare and a cheer arose from the throats of the assembled people, so loud that the Infanta seemed taken aback for a moment. The sound reverberated from the surrounding buildings and flocks of gulls arose squawking into the air, alarmed at the noise. Before her the nobles and commons got to their knees, while just beyond them the crowd parted to let another through who would greet the woman about to become England's new queen.

Elizabeth Wydville was resplendent in a white satin gown with a purple velvet gown over, trimmed with ermine. As the mother of Elizabeth of York sent to Portugal to be the bride of the Infanta's cousin, duke Manuel of Beja, it was fitting that she should be here to conduct the princess of Portugal to her new Court. Joanna's women sank to their knees as the dowager queen of England approached. Elizabeth Wydville, though no longer having any temporal power, retained the aspect of a queen, which awed those who came before her. She had lost nothing when it came to making an entrance. King Richard had long forgiven her previous indiscretions and now he had sent her on this special mission to greet the Infanta of Portugal. Elizabeth lived in splendour close to the court but recently had displayed a marked preference for a convent life, a disposition that encouraged the King to send her here today. Joanna, who knew of this, smiled happily when the two came together and as the dowager queen sank to her knees, lost no time in raising her again.

The other nobles each came forward and made their obeisance. John Howard, standing in support of Joanna maintained a stoical mien, his family having a long history of distrust where the Wydvilles were concerned. Today, however, he could find no complaint. He released the Infanta and stood back while Elizabeth Wydville took her arm. The two queens, old and new progressed through the crowd to the town square where the Mayor of Southampton was poised to deliver a speech of welcome from the people of England to their new queen. Afterwards they retired to the house of a prominent citizen, cleared for the purpose, where the royal party would prepare themselves for the journey to London. All along the way people cheered and danced for joy, delighted that their promised princess was with them at last.

* * *

Robert felt himself thrust into the outer darkness. Having spent the last few weeks close on board ship with the Infanta and her entourage, he was now diminished at court among the powerful nobles and rich courtiers. Even Enola was taken from him, which animal was a way to get close to Claris. King Richard, though amused by its antics, soon tired of it and sent it packing to the Tower menagerie. His interview with his father Laurence had not gone well, in fact, he had been told there would be no marriage contract and to put the idea out of his head. He had no property and no wealth with which to support a wife and unless his intended bride had a reasonable dowry as her marriage portion, only poverty could result. He had an allowance from his father and the promise of some small profit from his grandfather's trading venture in Portugal, which was nowhere near enough. Try as he might, Robert could think of no sensible response to his father's interdict. It was pointed out to him that it was his choice to become a soldier and unless he could rise in the household of a great noble, then his future was bleak. Then there was the recrimination - it had been better for him to become his father's apprentice for a surer way to prosper, but he had turned that course down. Even then he would be in his twenties before reaching a state where he could take a wife. High nobles might become affianced in infancy, but for everyone else, people tended to marry in their mid twenties.

Laurence the Armourer, brooking no argument, had taken himself away to his forge at Gloucester and Robert was now sitting disconsolately in the garden of his grandfather Cornelius' house on Wood Street near the Cripplegate area of London. Anna Quirke, seeing him there came and sat beside him.

"It is not much use moping about, Robert," she said firmly. "What were you thinking of raising that girl's hopes the way you have? You must have known you are unable as yet to support her. Did you think that living on water and a crust might sustain you in your love?" He turned his face from her, refusing to speak. She looked at him with some sympathy.

Finally he managed to mutter a few words. "She is all alone in the world – except for her brother," he added. "She would hardly be worse off with me."

"She is in the company of the woman who is shortly to become Queen of England, not exactly a pauper's estate." Anna was relieved that Laurence had resisted the impulse to use Robert's youthful inexperience against him. He might have done so had Anna not privately advised against it. That would have driven the lad deeper into himself and provoked resentment and a dichotomy between father and son that might never be recovered. "You are commanded by the lord the king's bastard to return to court, or at least his company. My advice is to serve him as you have been doing. You are clearly in his confidence and who knows what advantage that could bring?"

"Do you think my father might change his mind if he was to meet her? He has refused to do so. Should he but spend a few minutes in her company, he cannot fail to consider her with his highest regard."

"I am sure you are right, Robert," agreed Anna compassionately. "Remember, he is the king's armourer and is bound to come to court soon, especially for the wedding. He will see her there and no doubt take an interest in her if only to satisfy his own curiosity. Perhaps we should think on that for now and not despair. Sometimes silence can be more eloquent than the declamations of the finest poet."

Robert seized on her words, his spirit taking a leap. *We should think on it and not despair*! Had he an ally in Anna Quirke? She had come from humble beginnings and was now comfortably ensconced as his grandfather's wife. Perhaps she too knew something of the pangs of hopeless love and was thus sympathetic to his cause? He had not dared voice his other concern – that the court ladies were ever the objects of pursuit by amorous courtiers and Claris could be snapped up by any number of them, each having the wealth and property to take her. It was just the lack of dowry that had so far prevented serious competition, but that might not always be the case.

Anna patted him gently on the shoulder. "Your grandfather has sent me to bring you into the house. He would speak with you on another matter."

Robert walked with Anna into the house and found the apothecary pouring some aromatic smelling liquid into a small glass bottle.

"Ah, Robert," he said familiarly as he saw his grandson. "Notice what I am doing here." He held the bottle before a lighted candle. "Observe the colour," he said.

"There is none," replied Robert, slightly perplexed. "It is perfectly clear."

"Just so," replied the apothecary. "Now watch." Cornelius took up a small clay vessel and poured a few drops of its contents into the bottle. The liquid immediately turned a deep green. Cornelius took a wooden plug and wrapping a scrap of linen around it, sealed the bottle. "Here is the elixir I shall send to my client, who is sick with the palsy."

"Which is the cure," asked Robert, "the clear liquid or the few drops you put in afterwards?"

"Why, the clear of course."

"Then why bother with the green drops?"

"Because, had I sent the bottle with merely a clear liquid my client would have felt cheated and any peddler of coloured water would have usurped my fee, and my client all the worse for it."

"I sense there is a lesson somewhere in this for me, grandfather."

"There is, my son. It is this – that sometimes we must colour our real intentions with a falsehood in order to perform our true service."

"I am not sure I follow your meaning, grandfather?"

"Sit down, my son and let me tell you of what I know concerning the court of our good King Richard. You are his dedicated man?"

"I am, sir, as you well know." The two of them sat down by the fire and Anna brought them each a cup of ale before leaving them alone. Cornelius Quirke was beginning to show his years and his black hair hung with streaks of white. It would not be long before all would be as snow. He was fairly wealthy yet he dressed modestly, though the heavy black folds of his gown betrayed him, black being the costliest of dyes. First a cloth was dyed deep blue using woad, then dyed with red madder, then finally cork to deepen the black.

Everyone else wore the cheaper colours of yellow, fawn, blue and green. Other colours denoted rank: prelates of the Church and high nobles wore scarlet and only monarchs, purple.

"In the few months you have been out of England there has been some changes," began Cornelius. "You know, of course, that the lord Stanley has gone and his lands confiscated to the crown. That happened before you left for Portugal. The king has yet to allocate them to his followers and some are becoming dismayed they are not being preferred. Then there is the parliament recently convened. It is the king's second and there he commanded the advancement of law in favour of the commons, with the English language being used so that everyone can understand what is being said. Already judgements are being made in favour of trade where before the interest of the nobles would have been preferred."

"This is not news, grandfather; the king was already bringing in these measures before the battle which did for Tudor ambition."

"Yes, but only now is it having an effect. Men are looking to this alliance with Portugal and the similarities between the two monarchs of these countries. King João the Second had his version of lord Stanley in the duke of Braganza and applied a similar solution. You may know, having travelled in that country, that another traitor, the duke of Viseu, his wife's brother, was killed by King João with his own hand. The king called him into his presence then stabbed him to death."

"Just as with Lord Hastings." Robert had picked up on the comparison.

"Quite, king Richard had him peremptorily beheaded without trial, for disloyalty. Then there is Portugal's mastery of the seas and navigation. King Richard was England's premier admiral in the reign of his brother Edward and his most loyal supporter, then as now is the duke of Norfolk, father and son also sailors. The two monarchs have a lot in common. Richard's brother, King Edward was a merchant king and accrued much wealth, which the Wydvilles got away with unfortunately. He had been the only king in memory who actually left a surplus in his treasury at his death. Our King Richard is cast in a similar mould and would also engage in trade. Moreover, he is interested in naval exploration, just as King João."

"I understand all that, grandfather, but so far as troublesome nobles are concerned he is in no different case to any other monarch in all the countries of Europe."

"Except King João of Portugal is determined to curb the power of his nobles such that they will no longer be able to contest with him, and here in England, I believe King Richard is looking to do

250

the same. It is that which is worrying his nobles here. After Bosworth the king realised he has more security in courting popularity with his people than his nobles, who are liable to change their loyalties at a moment, while the commons are resolute about their king."

"A good point; I saw it at Bosworth. Lord Stanley's men would not readily change sides and attack their king and the earl of Northumberland was unable to order his men to do so either."

"That is it exactly," said Cornelius with a clap of his hands. "Bosworth was a seminal event where the king saw that the old order had failed him and must, perforce, be changed. Northumberland has seen the coming storm and keeps himself to his castle at Alnwick. My information is that others who feel threatened with loss of power are in contact with him. There may well be trouble from there before long. His ancestors all fought in the Lancastrian cause and he, the fourth earl is the only one to come over to York - if he has actually done so. His conduct at Bosworth rather belies that opinion."

"Were I King Richard," said Robert, "I would think the same, but even great lords cannot rise against a king if their own people won't fight him."

"Then you are in harmony with your king – not a bad place to be unless you fall foul of his dissenters, and there are bound to be many of those. His nobles are still powerful, and men incline to the system they know rather than one they have no knowledge or experience of. The king has a narrow path to tread and there are swamps either side of it to suck him down."

Robert had a sudden vision of Henry Tudor caught in the sands of Morecambe Bay, unable to extricate himself and nobody able to help him either. What had seemed to him then the satisfying death of a traitor could too easily be visited upon his own king. Was God playing a game with men, or just those who would contend for greatness here on earth, kings and such, setting themselves as temporal rivals to the almighty himself, only to fail ignominiously?

"The king has added the emblem of Saint George to his own achievement of arms, where he is depicted as slaying the dragon, the said dragon some say being Cadwallader, of course, which Henry Tudor had usurped for his own purpose. Our patron saint is also a principal Portuguese saint and King João has as his motto *For Law and For the People* under the emblem of a Pelican. All this is in accord with the principles of our own king whose motto is *Loyaultie Me Lie* – Loyalty Binds Me."

"A pelican – the emblem of Christ; then the portents are beneficial, are they not, grandfather?"

"Who knows what is awaiting us," sighed Cornelius. "Your own mother was hale and hearty one day and dead the next, along with your sisters. Our king Richard lived in the expectation of being but a northern lord for his whole life with five others between himself and the crown, and then was propelled into kingship beyond all expectation." He stopped and twisted his long bony fingers together for a while in a state of apparent agitation. "I have word that dame Stanley is in France and gathering about her a coterie of traitors and schemers agitating on behalf of both France and Spain along with a few disgruntled Lancastrians, fled after their defeat at Bosworth. France is no lover of King Richard, and Spain is jealous of Portugal. We can be sure they will have agents at King Richard's court. What we do not know is the precise mischief they intend. One thing is certain; your recent experiences do not rule out attempts at bloody murder."

"I have already spoken of this to the lord bastard John of Pomfret, and my lord the duke of Norfolk is also aware of the danger," said Robert.

"Then be sure to speak of it to none other," snapped Cornelius.

Robert nodded mutely, deciding not to let his grandfather know that Claris and her brother Anselm were ready recruits to their cause. As his grandfather had already demonstrated – it was sometimes prudent to keep silence on certain matters for the greater good.

* * *

Robert's inevitable interview with King Richard regarding the attempts on the life of the Infanta Joanna had been strained but was not so traumatic as he might have expected. Perhaps the duke of Norfolk had put a word in for him. Maybe it was because John of Pomfret was involved and his grace thus tempered his ire for the sake of his son. The king had simply listened to Robert's story, all the while studying his face for signs of dissembling, then dismissed him peremptorily.

Robert stood outside the presence chamber in trepidation. There were raised voices to be heard beyond the door and the two guards beside it stood stoically gazing into infinity. Presently the lord bastard John came out and took Robert by the arm, leading him into the great hall of Windsor castle.

"The king has ordered that you remain in my household and he has charged me with the job of discovering any further plots against his crown."

"Why not my lord the duke of Norfolk?"

"Thomas Howard is in overall charge of the king's safety and that of Queen Joanna but he has a wide range of duties that will take him away from court. We are both to remain within the *verge*, that is, within twelve miles of the king's body."

Robert knew that the verge was a constantly moving boundary that travelled with the king. Under its jurisdiction separate law courts tried those matters regarding discipline of the king's subjects within the verge."

"Are you then Marshal of the King's Household?"

"I am appointed such until we can get to the bottom of these plots. I have sent for your grandfather, the apothecary, to advise me. He has agents in France, Portugal and Spain."

"Yes and I have spoken to him already. He well knows the problem we face and his agents are gathering information as we speak."

"Good, I look forward to hearing his report. On a lighter note, his grace the king has seen fit to send you a quantity of fine cloths so that you can attire yourself suitably around his court." He noted Robert's eyes light up at the news. "A delight I know but remember you must pay a tailor to turn the material into clothing and it will have to be the latest court fashion. That should deplete your purse and put you into debt. I hope you are in favour with your father?"

"Ah yes, my condition with him is somewhat strained at the moment but not, I think such that I cannot make my peace with him." Robert was in fact thinking that clad in a fine new fashion he would not compare so badly with the other courtiers and thus gain greater favour in Claris' eyes. Hopefully this would let him keep at a distance any that might have amorous intentions towards her. It had not occurred to him that the intrigues and machinations involved in a complicated courtship was fit training for the life of espionage, which the lord bastard John of Pomfret was plunging him into.

"Make sure your tailor accounts for all the cloth he uses. It is habitual that he will skimp in the cut and reserve the rest for another customer, whom he will charge for *your* cloth. The tailors of London are looking to make a great profit from the king's wedding and afterwards the crowning of his queen."

A few days later his father returned to London, as expected, and after some deliberation took Robert to the shop of his own tailor. Henry Davy was also the king's tailor. It might be thought beyond reason to expect him to attend upon a humble squire personally, but his policy was to greet each new customer himself before passing over the least wealthy to one of his assistants. This had the double effect of flattery on the customer while the tailor could assess for himself the likely depth of his purse. Just as Laurence the Armourer was an artisan craftsman who only worked for those who could afford his prices, so it was with Henry Davy. Both men, however, realised that fortunes at Court could turn on a moment and a courtier low in stature might be suddenly elevated. In that case he was sure to want the best and most fashionable attire and thus the tailor, having greeted him with respect during his humbler circumstances, was well placed to pick up new and more profitable business.

He and Laurence were on good terms. They shared a common secret - the actual dimensions and peculiarities of the king's body. Both men used their skills to ensure the king would always appear straight of limb even though, in fact, he inclined somewhat to one side. For the moment it was the tailor whose skills were most in demand. King Richard had been anxious that on greeting his betrothed he might appear suitably upright, even though the condition of his frame was causing him some distress and tended to make him lean awry. The Battle of Bosworth, and the strain on his frame at the climax around Henry Tudor, had taken its toll. Laurence had confided to Robert that he believed the king's fighting days to be over, but Richard would never admit that and so there would be more business for his armourer as he continually adjusted the king's harness to accommodate a deteriorating body. His tailor, however, could look forward to continuing business with the king whatever the future state of his frame. Robert, of course, had no idea that the king's body was distorted by a worsening spinal deformation. Laurence would never disclose such knowledge even to his closest family and neither would the king's tailor. Both men were as resolute in preserving the secret as any priest, perhaps more so.

Had Robert realised any of this he would have been more tuned to the machinations involving anyone at the royal court. It was a world of secrets which many were privy to but might not speak of except to those in their immediate circle; and most of those could not be trusted to keep silent even to the point of betraying their own family. As it was he was learning discretion and already he possessed secrets of his own, chief among them the knowledge that his father had a love child, a daughter that neither his father nor grandfather Cornelius knew of. He was torn between keeping the knowledge to himself or revealing it to his father. His recent experience had taught him the consequences of failing to reveal what he knew to those affected. On the other hand what could be gained by disclosing what he knew? As his father's son and heir he had nothing to fear by revealing the presence in the world of a sister, and a bastard one at that. The only outcome would be to upset his father's conscience without profit to anyone. Not only that but the dubious loyalty of the mother was a question not yet answered. Did he really want to encumber his father with a situation where a follower of dame Margaret Stanley might have a hold over him? Little did he realise how soon his resolve to silence would collapse, as if a castle had been undermined to tumble into dust, before propelling him into greater and deadly intrigue.

12 – The King's Judgement

Anselm Salgado strummed gently at the strings of a lute while Robert placed himself beside Claris as they strolled casually behind the court, where the king and his betrothed walked together in the grounds of Windsor Castle, their people trailing discreetly behind. Robert was dressed in his new finery, a crimson silk doublet with a tawny gown worn over and his head adorned with a crimson chapeau trimmed with black. The cut of the doublet suited his sturdy frame giving him a lean look in the latest fashion. The troubadour had been singing a song of the mountains where his family had lived before their descent into poverty. The royal couple had taken a liking for each other and walked, their heads inclined close, in private conversation. King Richard was keen to show Joanna the great and as yet unfinished construction of St. George's Chapel, demolished and rebuilt by his brother King Edward the Fourth. Everyone had a good idea as to what they were discussing. King Richard's brother Edward was interred here in a splendid chantry chapel and though the rest of the building was not yet complete, Richard hoped it would be a suitable repository for his own bones and those of the lady walking by his side. He had caused the bones of King Henry the Sixth, the Infanta's relative, to be interred here and he was thinking to have his brother George duke of Clarence's bones brought here too, from Tewkesbury Abbey. The body of his former queen, Anne Neville lay beside the high altar in Westminster Abbey close to the chapel of Edward the Confessor. As it was unseemly to have two queens lying beside the king, he thought it fitting she remain there among a plethora of royal tombs. Shortly he was to commission a suitable memorial to her. As for the chapel here at Windsor, he was planning a magnificent tomb dedicated to the Plantagenet dynasty, which he fervently hoped, they would continue by their union.

Until becoming king he had thought to be entombed at York, or at least in the northern parts of his realm, but as he was now an English monarch, he must be interred close to those other monarchs who went before him. How fitting that a grand chapel, dedicated to Saint George, a patron of both England and Portugal should at the inevitable end, receive their bones where he and Joanna might lie side by side for eternity.

Robert looked down upon his tabard that bore the king's new badge, the image of Saint George spearing a red dragon trampled beneath the hooves of his white charger. The white boar was still in popular use and could be found on tavern signs throughout the realm, but King Richard now insisted the new badge be preferred as it reflected both his success over the dragon Cadwallader at Bosworth and the unification of England and Portugal. Claris walked close enough to Robert so that their hands could brush each other's as if by chance. Presently lady Ana de Mendonça turned around and with a flash of her eyes, informed Claris she should walk with the other ladies. Claris quickened her step and caught them up.

"My sister has not detected anything unusual in the ladies about court," said Anselm as he strummed a few idle chords. "There are a few dubious courtiers, though, particularly among the nobles. Rumour has it that the earl of Northumberland has been spreading stories that there shall be scant preferment from this king."

"He is, no doubt, recalling his own disappointment in that direction. I hear King Richard has strengthened the authority of the Council of the North making the earl of Lincoln more powerful than Northumberland. Add that to the new laws favouring trade and commerce, and placing limits on the influence of the old nobility to use the law for their own profit, it is little wonder there are dissenting voices. The new law of bail, where a man cannot be held before his trial, discomfits those who were wont to use the threat of imprisonment to extort money or property. How often have we heard of a man being imprisoned for months only to be acquitted at his trial? Some innocent men have given up a lawsuit rather than endure it."

"The situation couldn't be more to the king's benefit where trade is concerned and there is great expectation among the merchants now the king is to form an alliance with Portugal. We Portuguese are the leading nation when it comes to navigation and exploration." Anselm played an open chord that proclaimed joy.

"Yes," agreed Robert, "I am hoping for some small profit myself through my grandfather's contacts in Lisbon."

"Your father has not been slow in picking up trade, either," laughed the troubadour. "He is already measuring several Portuguese knights for new jousting harness."

"Which reminds me," said Robert with a frown. "He has asked for my presence at court this afternoon. He knows I shall be there anyway in attendance upon the lord bastard John so it is strange he is particular. It usually means he has something to tell me and, things being as they between us at the moment, it might not be agreeable."

"Then I shall pay close attention. I love a little intrigue and I believe Claris will be listening closely, too."

"You think it might have something to do with her?"

Anselm diverted the moment by pretending to fathom a particularly difficult chord on his lute. He knew of Robert's declaration of undying love for his sister and was yet to pronounce upon it. He had been content to let Laurence the Armourer, as Robert's father, take all the blame for placing what were, after all, reasonable obstructions in their pathway. Had Robert the rank and means of taking a wife, Anselm could have wished them joy, but as her brother he felt himself in *loco parentis* and his brain told him Laurence was right in his interdict. Of course, it was Joanna who had the real say over the marriage of her handmaiden.

"I cannot think what it may be," was all he said.

Ahead the king and the princess were making their way into the great hall of the royal apartments where the king would hear petitions from his subjects. Joanna retired into her chapel, which King Richard had reserved for her use while he conducted his business. The great hall was crowded as usual and outside many more waited hoping for entrance. The king took his place on the dais, above which was the emblem of Saint George slaying the dragon. Viscount Francis Lovell and the earl of Lincoln, who took their places either side of him, joined the king. Seated by a side table with his clerks was the king's new secretary, Thomas Witham who until recently had been the king's Chancellor of the Exchequer. The duke of Norfolk had been sent north on some errand of the kings so would not appear but John of Pomfret was there and was yet to spot his squire in the crowd. Robert looked around to see if his father was there too. After a while he found him standing chatting with a several merchants, wealthy ones by the look of them. Laurence the Armourer beckoned his son to join him and Robert pushed through to attend upon him.

"Now Robert," his father began rather nervously, drawing him to one side. "I have a request to put before the king which may shock you. I wondered if I should have a word with you first, but I think it better if you listen to what I have to say to his grace. Were we alone I fear you might interrupt me before I can tell the full story and you can hardly do that in front of the king. If the king grants me my wish then it will be because he is satisfied that the conditions I shall set before him are no bar, which means you should be satisfied also. If he does not grant my request, then there may be severe repercussions, I cannot tell. Whatever happens I may not proceed without his permission."

Robert stepped back and looked at his father, seeing in his face deep concern. *What could it possibly be?* The prospect of introducing him to Claris for his favourable opinion was fading fast. Whatever he was to ask of the king, it had nothing to do with his relationship with her. "Severe repercussions?" he gasped. "Have you been up to something with grandfather Cornelius?" Involvement in some clandestine scheme of the apothecary's was the only thing he could think of, and Cornelius was firmly on the side of the king. He searched the crowd for the familiar figure of his grandfather, but if it had anything to do with him, then he was not at court to respond.

"No, it is entirely my own business. Be patient and you shall learn soon enough. You should go and stand with your lord. You have a life of your own to concern yourself with."

None of this sounded good, but Robert saw in his father's face a grim resolution that would not be resolved until the king had pronounced upon whatever was concerning him. He stepped back, slow to take his eyes off his face but Laurence waved him away, so he reluctantly turned and went over to join the lord bastard, the king's son."

The day's business ground on tediously as usual and seemed more so as Robert waited while his father would be heard. Presently the time came for Laurence the Armourer to come forward. He made obeisance, knelt before his sovereign and lifted his head. The king leaned forward as curious as everyone else.

"Master armourer," he said familiarly. "What is it that brings you before us here today?"

"My lord king," began Laurence. "I have a request of you and I ask you hear it."

"But of course, man," replied the king looking about him in puzzlement, "but we are surprised you have said nothing to us in private. It is not as if you have never had the chance, serving by keeping us in good harness. You may stand." Laurence got to his feet and swept the king a bow.

"It is this, dread king – I wish to marry!" His voice carried loud and clear across the heads of the assembled courtiers and petitioners.

Robert gasped out loud and John of Pomfret looked at him suddenly. "You know nothing of this?" he whispered to his squire.

"I do not," replied Robert. "I know he has been at his forge at Gloucester rather attentively of late, and I did wonder if he was neglecting the court where he picks up much business."

King Richard sat back in his chair and laughed while his

companions smiled beside him. "Is that all, why, you hardly need our permission for that," he chuckled. Slowly his face became wary as he realised there was something more. "Is there a problem with the lady?"

"You might think so, your grace, but I feel I can speak for her sufficiently to allow you to grant my suit."

King Richard frowned deeply, clearly intrigued. "Then speak up, man, and tell us who the lady is that finds such favour with our armourer."

Robert felt his ears pricking and a tingling sensation fluttered down his spine. Lord John turned his attention to the scene before the king.

"I have brought her here, your grace if you would receive her?"

"Present her to us then," commanded the king.

"Your father certainly knows how to build a drama," muttered lord John into Robert's ear. "I have seen him do this when he is about to uncover a particularly fine harness fresh from his hammer." Intrigued they saw the armourer turn to one side and hold out his arm. The crowd parted to let a lady through. She was veiled in white silk draped over a blue hennin and wore a deep blue velvet gown trimmed with miniver. Here was a mystery to rival those in the legends of the Arthurian tales as could be read in Thomas Malory's book - a haunting damsel and a boon being asked of a king. Robert knew that was his father's favourite study and clearly, as lord John had discerned, the armourer was exploiting the court's fascination with Arthurian romance to some purpose not yet disclosed.

Robert regarded her with great curiosity. She was clearly well born by her walk and the clothes she wore, but not high born. She had a colourful embroidered belt around a trim waist from which hung a chain securing at its end a small book of hours, which she held in her hands as she stopped by the side of the armourer. She sank slowly before the king and raised her head while Laurence reached over to lift her veil and reveal her face.

The king looked upon the woman and slowly sat upright while his face clouded over as he recognised her. Robert, from his standpoint could not see her face, but the king clearly knew who she was.

"Is this a jest?" snarled the king, flicking his eyes between Laurence and the woman. "You wish to marry this woman when you know what she has done?"

"I do, dread king," responded Laurence nervously but with his jaw set firmly. "You have said you would hear me and that is all I ask. You have made laws where your people cannot be condemned before being heard and when you have heard my petition, and questioned the lady, it is my belief you will be merciful and grant her to me."

Robert was hopping about from one foot to the other, craning his neck to try to get a look at her face, but unless she turned her back on the king that would be impossible.

King Richard glowered at the woman, then relaxed and leaned back into his chair. "Let me get this clear," he intoned. "You have declared yourself to be my loyal subject and yet you wish to marry this woman, dame Isabella Staunton!"

"I do, dread king, if it please your grace to hear me?"

Robert felt as if he had been pole-axed. Lord John placed a steadying hand on his shoulder as he swayed in shock.

"There is more intrigue in your family than at court," he said jocularly. "Had you no idea that your father was consorting with a traitor?"

"Not the faintest," replied Robert in astonishment. His mind was whirling with images tumbling over each other to gain first position in his thoughts. He saw his mother's face bending over him when he was a small child, and recalled the family settled around the fire in winter when his parents told tales to entertain himself and his sister. He remembered the day they buried three of them in the churchyard of Saint Michael and All Angels in Gloucester, his mother and two sisters, the youngest less than a year old. His father had been away at Middleham Castle serving the king who was the duke of Gloucester at that time, and Robert had been taken into the care of his father's friends John and Gurden Fisher at their inn. Later he was kidnapped by the aid of Isabella Staunton and imprisoned by her husband before his father managed to retrieve him. It wasn't as if his father did not know what the woman was like! Then there was the business with the attempted escape of Henry Tudor, in which she played her part. Again she had been the one to capture him and although she had contrived to get him away, it was only to serve her own purpose and fool him into diverting pursuit in the wrong direction. Of course, there was the revelation that she had borne a child to his father. No doubt that was the hold she had over him. She had disappeared after Henry Tudor's death and it seems looked to Laurence the Armourer to be her champion. He contemplated with horror the implications of all this. His father was about to bring down the wrath of the king upon his head and that was bound to affect the whole family.

"State your case, master armourer, but be aware I am not disposed towards this woman," growled the king, who sat back in his chair and glowered angrily at his armourer.

"My lord king, I know her history as well as you," said Laurence, "except there are extenuating circumstances which I think might argue for mercy. Though I in no way admit precedence, yet there are those in your kingdom who once inclined towards the traitor lord Stanley, and who now are in favour. This is because the authority of their lord, which I must state devolves from your grace, compelled them. If their liege happened to change sides in a particular cause, they were bound to do so also. It is pertinent to this case that you have recognised that there are limits to that commitment and this became evident at the recent battle now called Bosworth Field."

King Richard leaned forward with interest.

"I believe I know where you are going in this," he said acidly," yet the lady has had no business on the battlefield but in the circumstances that led to that confrontation. It is by such as her that my crown was brought into peril."

"I believe, your grace, that the lady is a victim of that same circumstance. First of all she owed loyalty to her husband, Sir Charles Staunton who leased his lands from lord Stanley and as such was bound by his opinion."

The king acknowledged the point with a slight inclination of his head.

"You will remember the case of her mother, the lady Ankarette Twynhoe?"

"Her mother, you say?" snapped the king, his face showing a keen interest. "This is her daughter?" He stabbed a pointed finger at the woman still kneeling before him.

"She is, your grace, and the brutal execution of her mother was that which turned her mind and let her become the creature of the lady Margaret Stanley."

A murmur of interest arose as a rumble of distant thunder in the assembled crowd. This was a well-known case where the woman, Ankarette Twynhoe was summarily hanged at the behest of George duke of Clarence. The case had been a scandal where King Edward the Fourth had pardoned the woman after her death and was one of the causes of Clarence's eventual attainder for treason and his execution. It had also deprived Clarence's son, Edward of Warwick of his place in succession to the crown of England. Richard had blamed Elizabeth Wydville for the death of his brother George, probably with some justification, and now it was all coming back to him. The woman Ankarette Twynhoe had been caught up in the politics of the time and became one of the victims. Clarence's spite after the death in childbirth of his wife, Isabella Neville, had been vented on an innocent woman, accusing her of poisoning his wife merely because she had been one of Isabelle's handmaidens. King Richard had forgiven Elizabeth Wydville for pragmatic reasons and now, here before him was a woman who had a moral claim on his sense of justice.

King Richard's expression softened as he considered the case and Laurence felt he was making some progress. Isabella Staunton remained on her knees before the king, who now looked down upon her and scrutinised her face. When he had learned of her mother's fate, along with his brother King Edward, Richard had felt keenly the injustice perpetrated against Ankarette Twynhoe. Nevertheless, he was now king and must make judgement dispassionately.

"This woman," said the king quietly so only Laurence and a few near him could hear, "was instrumental in aiding the escape of the traitor Henry Tudor. Her mother has been granted my brother's pardon, a king's pardon, so there was no excuse for her continuing animosity towards our house of York. I have your own son's testimony that she took him prisoner at her house in Lancashire and used him such that she would have had Henry Tudor out of England and to safety where he might further disrupt our realm. Furthermore, she has as her mentor the witch dame Margaret Stanley who even now is plotting against us."

The king leaned back and looking at his armourer, challenged him to confound his statement. Laurence knew that this was the pivotal moment. If he could not get around the king's reasoning then the woman was doomed and so, he expected was he. Robert, who had been attending closely to this exchange, and having heard something of the king's last words fretted uneasily. He scourged his brain for something that he could bring to the discourse in aid of his father but could dredge up nothing other than agreement with the king's assessment.

"May I speak, your grace?" The king's head jerked around as Isabella Staunton spoke. Laurence placed a hand on her shoulder as if to indicate it were best for her to remain silent, but her words had been uttered and it seemed from his expression the king was curious to hear her.

"You may speak, but for the time remain where you are, on your knees," came the reply.

"It is true, my lord king, that I worked in the interest of my husband, who as a vassal of lord Thomas Stanley was his loyal man.

That was fine when he went into Scotland in those latter wars and was there when Berwick was restored to England. Lady - that is, dame Margaret Stanley, was kind to me after my mother was cruelly hanged when she had committed no fault. How could I do other than that which she asked of me? It was a monstrous injustice, which your late brother the king acknowledged when he issued a posthumous pardon. To a young girl, however, who had lost her mother to the hangman, that were small recompense and it was a simple matter for dame Stanley to inculcate in me a hatred for the house of York. It is true that I was caught up in a scheme to discover the whereabouts of the young prince, Richard of York. Lady - that is dame Margaret suspected your armourer, Laurence who stands here beside me, was in some way complicit with getting the prince away from England. I admit that my task was to seduce him while his son was kidnapped with the intention of forcing him to reveal his secret. That didn't work on two levels, your grace. One was that the boy was discovered at the house my husband had taken in London and subsequently rescued, thus confounding the plan. The other is that in seducing master de la Halle I succumbed myself to his charms and later, when I found I was carrying his child I secretly exulted. From that time, knowing the complete loyalty master de la Halle has to your majesty, I began to shift in my former opinion. You know the rest of the story from the account given to you by his son Robert. What you do not know is that I, having nowhere to go, took myself and my child to Gloucester where I knew master Laurence had his forge."

"Wait!" commanded the king. "You are clearly a clever and resourceful woman and I am aware of several holes in your tale, the chief of which is that what you did was engage in treasonable intent towards your anointed king. You paint a picture of a woman with shifting loyalties. Would you have us believe they now rest resolutely upon us and our throne?"

"My lord king," interrupted Laurence, "the lady's loyalties may have shifted but not, I must point out due to personal ambition, but to the complex circumstances she found herself in. There are those in your realm who have shifted so in order to gain some preference for themselves; Lady Staunton was ever the creature of others more powerful than she and thus as a bark tossed on a storm wracked ocean."

"You wax lyrical, master de la Halle," said King Richard with a hint of amusement in his voice. It seems the lady has awakened a sleeping poet. There is a child, yours she claims?"

"Yes great king, a daughter to replace those I lost to sickness along with my wife."

"Ah yes, that is something I know of only too well," lamented the king, his eyes taking on a distant gaze as he pondered on his own child, a prince lost to sickness too and soon after his queen, Anne Neville. Robert wondered if this was another of his father's dramatic devices to gain sympathy.

"My lord king," Laurence uttered in hushed tones, "there is something more I would tell but not within the hearing of this court." He raised his voice so all could hear. "I ask that you give the woman Isabella Staunton into my care and I shall stand surety for her. She has a loyal heart, your grace, which has been turned in a direction she otherwise would not go. I believe she will be true to me, who has always been your faithful servant."

King Richard beckoned to viscount Lovell and the earl of Lincoln to bend forward so he could speak in confidence. This provoked a good deal of vehement whispering and malevolent glances by the two lords directed at the pair standing before the king. Presently they stood back and regarded the petitioner and his woman with grim faces. King Richard scrutinised them with great concentration.

Robert, who had been watching the proceedings with mounting concern, felt his father's case was not getting a favourable reception, nor, in his heart, did he expect it to. It was a desperate and foolish appeal and he wondered at his father's stupidity, to risk destroying his business and family. If he ended by being attainted for treason then apart from suffering an ignominious death, Robert, as his heir would be dispossessed and impoverished with no prospects of advancement anywhere in the realm. The woman must have had a greater influence on his father's heart than he ever imagined.

After a few moments when the whole court was hushed, the king began to give out his decision.

"We shall not pronounce upon this matter for the time being," he began. "There was formerly a miscarriage of justice regarding this woman, her mother to be precise, which we would not wish repeated. However, while we are not satisfied as to her fidelity to our crown yet we do not see her as a threat. We place her into the custody of our armourer master Laurence de la Halle, who shall stand surety for her conduct and answer with his life should she betray our trust. This condition shall remain in place at our pleasure and be it known that dame Isabella Staunton may suffer lawful penalty for treason without appeal should she default on this condition."

A muted discussion rumbled through the hall as those present wondered at the king's judgement. He was known for being gentle where women were concerned; the continuing existence of the dowager queen, Elizabeth Wydville was testimony to that. Here, however, was a plain case of disloyalty where the woman Isabella Staunton had deliberately aided the escape attempt of Henry Tudor after his defeat at Bosworth. Had she been a man her head would be off her shoulders before the day was out.

"We had better have a few words with your father," declared lord John decisively. He too was curious about the affair. The two strode across towards the armourer and his probationer - Robert determined angrily to speak his mind. Before they reached him, however, viscount Lovell stepped down from the dais and conducted Laurence and the lady away into an antechamber. Lord John and Robert could only stand there and watch. Was the couple to be arrested after all?

Presently a servant in viscount Lovell's livery came to them.

"You are required to attend upon my lord Lovell," he said haughtily as if he had some sort of authority. Lord John of Pomfret opened his mouth ready to admonish the man for his arrogance when addressing the king's son, but his desire to discover what was happening with the king's armourer overcame the thought to chastise the man.

"Lead on," he snapped, withering the fellow with his eyes who, realising his error, scuttled before them, bowing and scraping obsequiously.

They entered a chamber where Lovell stood gazing out of a window that overlooked the upper bailey of the castle. Hatless, his blond hair was lit by the sunlight giving him an almost saintly air while the shadow rendered his pale blue eyes as black. Laurence was standing at one end of a large oak table while dame Staunton was seated on a curved legged chair close by him. Anxiety was written in her face as she gazed up at the man who had declared a desire for her hand in marriage. Lovell turned from the window and peremptorily dismissed the servant who had brought them there. Just the five of them remained. Lord John went and stood by viscount Lovell while Robert stood beside his father, his tongue eager to begin remonstrating but being restrained by the presence of Lovell.

"We wait upon his grace the king," intoned Lovell. "I am not happy with his decision to *postpone* sentence upon this woman." He emphasised the word postpone, indicating that she was far from being free and clear of the king's judgement. "You presume upon his grace's charity towards women, but those wives and children of traitors he has let remain on their otherwise confiscated lands were innocent themselves, their husbands being the guilty ones. Here we have a woman who was actually complicit in deliberate plots against the crown of England. She is in a different case entirely, as is her mentor the accursed Margaret Stanley. Be aware, master armourer, that I understand well how you attempted to gain the king's sympathy by comparing the loss of your wife and children to the greater loss of his grace's family."

"I understand your hostility, my lord, but your last point is unfair," responded Laurence. "The same can be said of most families in the realm; all have lost loved ones to sickness. His grace the king has grieved for his own and by extension all his subjects, seeing as he is God's anointed. Just as our Lord Jesus Christ died for us it is something he shares in common with his people. Both of us now wish to marry again and bring up children to replace those we have lost. It is by God's command that we populate the earth to replace those who have gone before us, otherwise Holy Church would prescribe laws against remarriage, which plainly it has not."

"Well said, master de la Halle." Suddenly everyone fell to their knees as the king spoke. He had been listening outside and entered the chamber quietly rather than be conducted inside by a servant and had heard Laurence's outburst. "You state the facts plainly and in our case we have a duty to our realm, to provide a lawful heir to rule after we have departed this earth." King Richard lifted his right arm indicating they should rise. "My lord Lovell is also correct in his assessment and we would not have you think we are so easily duped by a plea on our conscience. I recognise that this woman's closeness to the witch Margaret Stanley may reveal something of the plots against our crown and it is only that which has saved her so far. We would not have her speak of them in open court, so we have you here. Be assured, the woman's fate is not yet secure. You may resume your seat, madam."

Isabella curtsied and arranged herself on the chair she had risen from when the king entered the chamber. King Richard walked around and took a seat at the end of the table, facing her. He gestured for viscount Lovell to be seated and afterwards the lord bastard, John. Laurence and Robert, having been given no instruction, remained standing.

"We have had the tale from squire Robert, here, who you deceived into informing his lord, Sir Ralph de Assheton that the Tudor was on his way to Scotland when, in fact, he was attempting to flee England from Lancashire."

Richard leaned forward and fixed her with steel in his eyes.

"Ah yes, my lord king," said Isabella, resolutely returning his gaze. "That was, in fact, the only way I could get word out as to where Henry Tudor actually was. Until then he was being looked for in Wales. I admit that the messenger being Laurence's son focused my mind somewhat, otherwise the opportunity would not have arisen."

"You are telling us it was a deliberate ploy on your part? That is at odds with the boy's story. Squire Robert, is that not so?"

Robert opened his mouth to agree with the king but Isabella got in before him.

"If you would permit, my king, the boy does not know the truth of the matter. He told you what seemed to him the truth, but had I not arranged matters as I did, the lad would have been hanged out of hand and the Tudors would have made good their escape. I knew Henry Tudor was heading into Lancashire; his plan was to leave from Liverpool castle, but Sir Ralph got there before him thinking he was chasing the lady Margaret alone. I knew that she was to meet with her son and, Liverpool being closed to them, were likely to ride north. Thus I knew Sir Ralph had his men searching for Lady Margaret Stanley somewhere nearby and I considered it would not be long before the Tudors arrived at my house. My husband had been one of lord Stanley's men and therefore his house was considered safe. When the Tudors did, in fact arrive, I hid Robert as best I could but my servants, who had been loyal to my husband and his liege, lord Stanley, soon informed as to where he was. That placed my child and me in peril. I invented the plan to use Robert to divert attention away from the intended Tudor route to Foundray and point pursuit into Scotland as my reason for keeping him alive. Then he was dragged into the house and condemned to hang. At that point Sir Reginald Bray, pretending indifference in front of a condemned boy, let him hear of the plan to ride for Scotland. We had already decided to let him think I had planned with my servant to let him go and that is what happened. I could not tell him of the actual route the Tudors were taking, but I considered that once Sir Ralph knew Henry Tudor was in Lancashire and not in Wales then he would raise the county and track him down. That is, in fact what happened."

Robert clamped his jaws tightly shut as he heard this. It was his overhearing of a certain conversation, through the thin wattle of the wall where he was imprisoned, that disclosed the name of the departure point, the Pile of Foundray. Had he not, by chance heard that and then, again by chance passed it on to Sir Ralph, then the

Tudors would have been across the Morecambe Bay sands and away while the whole of Lancashire searched in vain. Isabella Staunton had no idea of what he had heard, or that he might pass it on to Sir Ralph de Assheton. Indeed, he had no idea of its significance himself at the time and almost forgot about it. He remembered too her vehement declaration of hatred for the House of York, though she now seemed to have recanted if she were to be believed. One thing for sure, if he mentioned any of this now, the woman's fate was sealed. He stood on the balls of his feet and rocked back and forwards in an agony of indecision. For his father's sake, though, he would remain silent, at least until he had spoken to him well away from the ears of the court.

"A pretty tale, madam," declared the king, "and one that relies heavily on chance rather than deliberation. However, the boy *was* permitted to escape, that part of your tale is true and he did alert Sir Ralph de Assheton as to the whereabouts of the Tudors. My other captains were chasing all over Wales looking for him, so I suppose I must own you some gratitude."

"I simply did the best I could in very difficult circumstances, your grace," replied Isabella demurely. "Afterward I dared not linger at my house for fear of retribution should I be taken by Sir Ralph. The fate of my mother, being summarily hanged without proper trial, was in the forefront of my mind. I think I cannot be blamed for hiding myself and only now that matters have calmed down might my story be given a fair hearing. I had with me my child, Laurence's child and squire Robert's sister. I took myself south to Gloucester where I knew the father of my child had his armoury. I arrived there half starved and in a desperate state. Laurence's friends, not knowing who I was except my claim I was the mother of his child, took me into their inn while they got word to Laurence."

"This is true, my lord king," Laurence said in the interval while the king considered her words. "My first instinct was to throw her into the nearest goal, but when I looked upon the infant I could not bring myself to do that. I thought on taking the babe into my keeping and immediately handing Isabella over to your justices. I realise that was the proper course, but the fact is the woman has that about her which endears her to me. Her house and lands are taken from her and her status reduced from the lady of a knight to a poor dame with no substance of her own to support either herself or the child. I informed her that her plight, our plight, must be placed before your grace for judgement."

Slowly the realisation came into Robert's mind that here was an opportunity to gain the upper hand with his father. His own situation with Claris was similar to that his father was now embracing. Just as Isabella, Claris was an impoverished gentlewoman without house nor home, moreover she had nothing of sedition about her while Isabella Staunton was still awaiting the king's judgement upon what Robert knew to be a dubious argument. If King Richard found in favour of his father, then that would place Robert on the moral high ground. Taking upon himself one of his grandfather Cornelius' lessons, he arranged his features to indicate nothing of the possibilities that were racing through his mind.

"There is but one more thing I would say to your grace," said Isabella. "Dame Margaret Stanley, who is now in France, has sworn vengeance upon your house and I think she is resolute. She has no power or money, of course, but there are those in France who would use her to work against your government of England. I know nothing of her current plans, of course, but I can tell you of her longer strategy."

King Richard jumped to his feet, his eyes flashing fire. He stamped about the room and even viscount Lovell was nervous, content to stand back and let the king pace the floor. Robert felt his spirits sink. His own plans began to dissolve while his father stood transfixed with fear. Isabella bowed her head and waited while the king calmed himself. Lord John was the only one to show little emotion, and leaned back in his chair curiously.

"I have been plagued by this woman for too long and I will not endure it any longer. I shall send my agents into France and have her very life before this month is out or I am no Plantagenet!"

"I can make arrangements, my lord king," grunted Lovell dispassionately.

"I fear that would do no good," Isabella interjected. "Dame Stanley is a tool. There are others who would simply carry on without her. She is but a convenience, not an essential part of any plan. The power she might have had fell apart when her son met his doom."

"You know who these traitors are?" snarled the king.

"I was never entrusted with names, your grace," she replied, "but my husband mentioned King James the Third of Scotland and what he was pleased to call *the auld alliance* and before she departed England, I recall dame Margaret saying something about it to Sir Reginald Bray."

"Ah yes, the supposed agreement between Scotland and France where each might aid the other to the discomfiture of England," said the king, calming down now he was on familiar diplomatic territory.

"That was dealt a death blow in the latter wars after which Berwick was returned to England."

"The danger remains, your grace," put in Lovell suddenly. "My own sources inform me that Northumberland is courting popularity with the Scottish court and he is the one who should be our first line of defence along the borders if an invasion of England from there is ever attempted again. If he lets a combined army of French and Scots through, then we could have a fight on our hands."

"That is unlikely," drawled John of Pomfret who, until now, had listened but with apparent little interest. "Your grace is popular in the northern counties, the earl's lands in particular and his people would never attack your throne. Remember the lesson of Bosworth? The English will not attack their own king for the sake of a foreign army and the people of Northumbria are loyal to you, your grace."

"Yes, I think I agree," added Lovell. "Henry Percy might sulk up at Alnwick Castle and seek solace at the Scottish court, but he is devoid of real power and lacks valour. He is no Hotspur, the name by which his great grandfather was known. In any case the Scottish king has problems with his own nobles."

"Let us return to the present business," said King Richard coming to a stop in front of Laurence and Isabella. She rose from her seat and stood meekly beside the armourer. "My nuptials are soon to be celebrated and afterwards the crowning of my queen. I would not have the celebrations marred by this business, though I remain unhappy with it. My decision is that you, master de la Halle, shall take this woman to wife and thus become responsible for her future conduct and loyalty. She has nothing to bring you other than herself and her child. Her husband's lands were forfeit to the crown after lord Stanley's conviction for treason. That is the substance of your request and so I grant it. It may turn out to be a sterner sentence than you anticipate."

Laurence bowed before the king while Isabella sank to her knees in obedience. The king glared at Isabella, nodded for her to stand then turned and beckoned Robert over to stand before him.

"Squire Robert de la Halle; you have served us particularly well these last few months. Had it not been for you Henry Tudor would have escaped our realm. While in Portugal you discovered and confounded a plot to murder your intended queen and then fought bravely to defend her when her ship was attacked at sea. Once more we have discovered the hand of Margaret Stanley in that. As with your father, it appears you too are drawn to the life of this woman Isabella Staunton, almost as if it were God's will. You are due some reward for your service to your king and your queen, therefore I award you the manor and lands formerly in the possession of this woman's deceased husband, Sir Charles Staunton. I need those I can trust in the former Stanley demesnes and so I choose you as one of them."

"My lord king!" gasped Robert falling to his knees. King Richard extended his ring hand and Robert kissed it. "My lord king, I had no thought of reward!"

"Then all the more deserving of it. You may rise."

Laurence the armourer stood as if perplexed, though if he was wondering about his son's reward or if he had made the right decision regarding Isabella Staunton, it was impossible to read either passion in his features. The woman looked at Robert rather than the man she had just been given to by the king. Her face betrayed nothing of her thoughts, which was strange given she had just escaped with her life and been given a new husband whom she declared had her favour. The lord bastard, John of Pomfret smiled munificently at Robert as if he had been the one to grant him a manor of his own. Viscount Lovell scowled at everyone, clearly unconvinced the king had done the right thing while King Richard's features displayed a benign aspect that stopped short of pleasure in his judgement.

"Consider yourself betrothed, master armourer and let there be a marriage shortly." The king turned his attention to Robert. "Thomas Whitham will draw up the necessary documents granting you, Squire Robert, the manor and lands aforesaid," stated the king while indicating with a wave of his hand that the interview was over. Isabella sank to her knees along with Laurence and then rising, the pair backed towards the door. Robert made a low obeisance and moved in the same direction. Lovell and lord John remained with the king.

"That was a close run thing, my dear," said Laurence to Isabella as a servant closed the door behind them.

"It was the most peculiar interview," she responded with her gaze on Robert. "I am thankful my former lands are at least held within my new family."

"It is rather more than you could have hoped for," replied the young squire.

"Well, the manor has become neglected of late," she sighed, "and I think you had better see to its management while there is something left worth the having."

Robert fixed his father with a hard stare. "I think I am owed an explanation, father," he snapped. "You were ready enough to pronounce on the woman of my choice being unsuitable due to

272

having no dowry, and here you are in an even worse case."

"The two are completely different. I have the means to support a wife, you do not."

"Really? The king has just granted me a manor and lands, not a great manor, nor extensive lands, but I am now in a very different position and even you cannot deny a house needs a mistress to run it!"

Laurence tugged at his beard and kept silent as the significance of this change in circumstances descended upon him. "I think we must speak with your grandfather. He knows nothing of this and must be informed."

"Yes, a good idea," said Robert confidently predicting to himself that Cornelius Quirke would be as disturbed by this turn of events as he was.

* * *

"I could get you with child?" suggested Robert to Claris. "That would change things in our favour and now I have a house for you, neither my family nor yours could dispossess us."

Claris giggled and kissed his cheek. They were sitting together in the great hall at Westminster. It was empty at the moment, eerily so as they contemplated on the sumptuousness of the marriage celebrations of the previous week. Then the hall had been a mass of golden cloth and bright heraldry as the Prelates and Nobles of England displayed themselves in their house colours and where a series of gargantuan banquets had fed not only those in the hall, but the people of London too, who had been served from tables set up beside Westminster Hall. The poor had not been forgotten either as a particular field was set aside where bread trenchers soaked in rich sauces and scraps from the tables were taken for them to feed on. Even there the king had provided barrels of ale and the whole of London revelled in the happy occasion.

"It would displease her grace the queen, I think," she grinned.

"Then I shall claim precedence and tell her there is at least one of her ladies who has been in a similar condition, the lady Ana de Mendonça. The queen has ordered the care of her bastard, the son of King João no less. I remember you telling me about it."

"What a brave knight you are – to presume to instruct the queen of England upon the morals of her handmaidens. You have undergone a conversion then. The last time you were in her presence, merely one among a troop of squires, you were on your knees and tongue-tied."

"That was a formal occasion when we pledged ourselves to her service after her coronation. As things stand now, I have leave from my lord John of Pomfret to go into Lancashire to arrange for someone to look to my interests there. The whole thing is unsatisfactory and I am like to be cheated. The house needs a mistress to run it while I am away on the king's service."

"You might ask dame Isabella to recommend someone?"

"You jest!" he snorted derisively. "The place would probably become a nest of spies."

"Then you must demand she suggest someone who is a confirmed Yorkist, or at least whose integrity would not permit disloyalty to King Richard. He is a popular king with the people of England; the matter should not be that hard to arrange? I would gladly become your wife but until my brother Anselm agrees to our union I cannot approach the queen to ask her permission. That is only the beginning of our problem. I have your family to contend with and they are not disposed to taking on another charity case."

"Something must be done," he grumbled. "If I have no clear claim upon your hand, someone else will step forward and steal you away. We dare not disobey the queen and if you are not promised to me in particular then there is no reason why she should not dispose of your hand as she may."

"I have no dowry, remember. Who else would ask for my hand?"

Robert jumped to his feet and stared vacantly across the empty hall. It was not the lack of dowry that worried him, but that other courtiers would see her as a lady that might be easily seduced. There were many of those and it usually ended with the lady retiring into a nunnery her reputation in tatters and never to be seen in the world again. Even if she had a family, most would not accept back into their household a woman whose marriage value was reduced to nothing.

The family conference, provoked by his father Laurence's declaration that he was to marry with dame Isabella Staunton, had not produced the favour for his own case as he thought it might have. It was dame Anna Quirke who had reacted most vehemently against his father's marriage. Unusually for her she actually cursed the woman and stormed at Laurence for his foolishness. Robert supposed that was due to the natural antipathy that was produced by two attractive and indomitable women of a similar age belonging to the same family. Grandfather Cornelius was hardly less furious than his wife and even her son Philip, in London for the king's marriage, had sided with his mother. All were in accord, then, except his father who remained stoically defensive of Isabella. The woman herself kept her own counsel and let Laurence speak for her, realising anything she said might inflame family passions even more and give them the excuse to bring greater opprobrium upon her head. Besides, they were bound for Gloucester soon and she would have Laurence all to herself. She had his child, so let the rest rant and rail how they would.

When he introduced the idea of taking Claris to wife, he had confidently expected some sympathy as a reaction to his father's upset, but the reverse occurred. Everyone repeated their former objections – approaching his sixteenth year he was too young to take a wife and though he now had some property, it was an impoverished manor that was just as likely to plunge him into debt than profit him. The king had been generous, but he was unlikely to grant a mere youth a great manor house, indeed another might consider himself hard done-to at the poverty of the gift. If there was a profit to be made it would be several years in coming and perhaps then the matter of his betrothal might be considered. In the meantime he should look for a woman with a marriage portion of her own to bring him. That would make a great difference to the fortune of his manor. He had responsibilities to his tenants now and could not afford dalliance with a pretty but penniless face. What had begun in his mind as a stroke of fortune, where he might marry the woman he loved, had somehow become yet another obstacle and he was at a loss as to how that could be.

"I must go into Lancashire," he said decisively. "The last time I saw the manor I had no thought of ownership and I have no idea as to the state of the tenantry there. The impression I got was they were loyal to Isabella, but that might have been the residue of her husband's due. When I have seen for myself I shall be in an improved condition to form an opinion as to its profitability. Perhaps I might present a better case when I return."

"That is wise for the moment, I think," sighed Claris. "I have Anselm close to defend me, should it be required so you have no worries there. He too has become a favourite of the king. I still think you should approach dame Isabella. She can give you an introduction to someone local who might properly advise you."

"Yes, you may be correct. In fact, dame Isabella has an interest in maintaining the manor in good order. She is unlikely to want it to fall into ruin now she is in a position where she can keep watch over her former holding."

"You are becoming pragmatic, my love, the attribute of a courtier. I shall strive to keep my virgin status so as not to confound our future plans," she chortled.

"I remain convinced my earlier plan to get you with child is surer for us, but the way things are going, the only happiness for me will be in heaven."

"*Quod felicitas habetur in ista vita, non in alia*," she responded playfully, tapping him gently on an arm.

"There is no happiness save in this life," he translated. "Let us pray that might be so in our case." Her use of the Latin reminded him that though penniless, she was of noble Portuguese blood and educated. She would make him a good wife and the thought reinforced his determination in that direction.

* * *

"I have little alternative but to trust to your advice, dame Isabella, thought I am still not certain whether you entertain thoughts of vengeance if not against my father, then certainly against the House of York." Robert regarded her under a frown. Fortunately I have had some dealing with the fellow Hubert, who seemed a honourable man, so I shall seek him out. Where can I find him?"

They were sitting alone in a chamber within the Peacock Inn close by the Cripplegate. Had he been older he might have wondered how dame Isabella had managed to forge a relationship with him that was independent of everyone else. He would have answered that question quite reasonably by supposing his encounter with her in Lancashire, and the subsequent revelation of his father's child, which he had kept to himself, was the cause, but all this was beyond his comprehension. He had other, more pressing matters on his mind.

Dame Isabella, disdaining the cold atmosphere in the house of the apothecary, had insisted she and her new husband take rooms at the Peacock until they set off for Gloucester. Wisely she did not trust her personal safety in a hostile house replete with charms and potions and by the attitude of dame Anna, it was probably sensible. Whereas the apothecary's wife might not stoop to poison, she could not be sure that the attendant witch, Mother Malkin, might be so restrained. The old woman hailed from the same part of Lancashire as dame Isabella, who thus knew of the strange practices perpetrated in the remote corners of that county. Robert, adopting his father's habit at the thought of the old crone, crossed himself unconsciously.

Dame Isabella, observing this, interpreted it as being directed against her. She contemplated the young squire condescendingly.

"He will be at Staunton Manor," she sighed coldly. "There is nowhere else for him to go. He was a soldier many years ago in Outremer and upon his return was taken into the house of my mother. He has no family in England and he came with me when I married Sir Charles. You can be sure he will do everything he can to preserve the manor."

Robert wondered what words were being left unspoken. He suspected the woman had hopes of regaining the lands once promised to her by the treacherous dame Margaret Stanley. He shrugged off the thought. The decree of the king overrode the claim of an attainted traitor. The Stanley lands were now the property of the Crown. Indeed, the king had acquired numerous lands through the process of attainder and showed reluctant intent when it came to reallocating them. Probably dame Isabella was content that by her marriage to his father, she would maintain some tenuous connection with her former holdings. He smiled to himself. Once Claris Salgado, his Maid of the Mountains became mistress she could kiss any such thoughts goodbye.

"Shall you write to him?" he asked, assuming the woman was literate.

"It would do no good; Hubert cannot read. You may give him this as a token." She took a ring from her index finger. "It was given to me by a friend and Hubert will recognise it."

Robert took the ring and gazed at it in the palm of his hand. It was a simple gold ring set with a single garnet. He knew this stone was associated with Mars and faintly wondered that a woman should have such a symbol on her finger.

"I notice you have picked up a scar, just as your father, except his is rather more pronounced. If yours fades any further it will hardly impress the ladies." She smiled cheekily and he suddenly saw how his father might be attracted to this woman. Whatever her darker attributes she had a bright way with her that overcame whatever traumas troubled her from the past. He felt that he should not respond and encourage what was clearly an attempt to endear him, but her demeanour and natural charm provoked his own natural gallantry.

"Scars do not have to be visible to be potent," he responded.

She gasped in understanding. "Ah yes, you speak I think of the woman – what is her name? Clavis?"

"Claris, madam, Claris Salgado and she is a noble lady fallen upon hard times. For all that she is a handmaiden of the Queen.

"But not a maid for long if you can convert her?"

"She is a virtuous lady who would not permit such a thing outside lawful union" He thought himself somewhat sanctimonious in his response and could not prevent a sly smile at his lips. Dame Isabella noticed that immediately and gave a lascivious laugh.

"Then you should wed her quickly before the Queen finds her a husband out of her charity." She frowned with amusement as Robert's face clouded over at what was a statement of his own fears. "You fear she will be lost to you?" she said quizzically. "If that should happen then let us hope the Queen is wise enough to grant her an old husband."

"An old man!" snapped Robert. "That would be too cruel."

Dame Isabella laughed out loud. "You have not thought it through. I know in my own case, marriage to an old man is not apt to last long and most ladies are excused when they take a paramour to compensate for what their husbands cannot give them. Would you rather her chosen husband be virile and get a swarm of children on her, or bring her to her death in childbirth?"

Robert's expression mirrored his distress and he shook his head before placing his hands over his face. "That thought is even worse," he muttered through his fingers. "You must think me a poor creature to be despised and jested with."

"I am truly sorry if what I have said upsets you, Robert." She spoke to him as if she were his mother, a habit she had of assuming authority in whatever situation she found herself. "It is just that, for women life is full of such disappointments and we learn to deal with them as best we may. Nobody is guaranteed a long or even a good life, not even you, but you only have to look around to see how fortunes change in an instant. Take lord Stanley, for instance. Not long ago he was the most powerful baron in England; now he lies in a traitor's grave and his vast lands confiscated to the Crown. His former tenants find themselves either dispossessed or, as in the case of Staunton Manor, under a new master. I was desperate too, driven from my home with a babe in my arms and like to be taken for treason. Now, by the king's grace, I have a good husband and a bright future."

He though he detected a slight cynicism in her tone when she mentioned *the king's grace*, but perhaps that was due merely to his suspicious nature towards her.

"Not everyone had your guile," he replied, bringing his hands down from his face and glaring at her.

"You do me an injustice, master Robert. Nothing that has happened to me has been under my control – my mother's murder, my marriage of convenience to an old husband, my allegiance to a woman who helped me in my need, my meeting with your father. All these were circumstances by which I was forced to respond. You must do the same and trust to God for any happiness there may be in your destiny."

"Yes, I suppose there is something in what you say," he mused petulantly. He drew a deep breath and took himself in hand. "I shall get me into Lancashire and seek out the man Hubert."

"When you find him, give him my fondest regards and my hope that you find him well."

"I shall do that madam." He bowed elegantly and left her sitting by the inn window, her light brown hair protruding under her crosslet shining in the light while she gazed wistfully into the busy London street below.

* * *

The lord bastard, John of Pomfret insisted he continue with his training to arms, as he was still too inexperienced to take a place in the front line of battle. If he were to go into Lancashire it was necessary his martial skills be enhanced otherwise he would fall prey to the coarsest felon on the long road there from Westminster. He was to join with a troop of soldiers formed to reinforce the garrison at Liverpool castle, formerly a bastion of lord Thomas Stanley. That were fortunate as otherwise he would have had to go along with a cavalcade of merchants with the ever present danger of attack by outlaws. An armed troop was certain to travel unmolested.

Robert had considered himself a mean fighting machine, particularly after his success in the fight with the galleys and earlier at the siege of Pembroke Castle. That idea was being slowly and deliberately beaten out of him by Sir Simon Hartshead who commanded the troop he was to ride with. He was an English mercenary presently in the employ of the king with instructions from the duke of Norfolk through John of Pomfret to ensure his household squire have his interrupted training resumed. It was normal for a squire to train in the household of his lord until around the age of eighteen before being regarded as a man-at-arms. Certain young men advanced earlier than others and Robert had already more battle experience than most of his age. Sir Simon Hartshead had laughed in his face when he boasted of his prowess in the sea fight and at Pembroke. The mercenary pointed out that the heat of battle produced circumstances where a weak and tender youth such as he could, by luck, defeat a better man. He had best not rely on such luck. Sooner or later he would come up against a trained knight where the confusion of a mêlée did not apply, and when that happened he were a dead youth. Sir Simon then proceeded to beat the lesson into him.

At first Robert thought he would do well against the soldier. For one thing Sir Simon was nearly fifty years old and bound to be slow while he was young and agile. This belief was confirmed in his mind as he squared up to the man, both having two-handed whalebone practice batons. These were made heavier than the real battle swords so as to strengthen in practice the necessary muscles but prevented serious injury. Sir Simon stood in front of him not even bothering to raise his guard. Both men were in full harness. Robert circled him, making a few feints with his baton while Sir Simon stepped back from him. Frustrated, Robert decided to go in strong and bring his opponent down. Stepping forward he struck at the steel gorget around his neck, expecting the blow would bruise Sir Simon's collarbone and render his sword arm weakened. Robert staggered forward as his baton swished harmlessly though the air and suddenly a boot in the small of his back sent him sprawling in the dust. He crawled hurriedly away thinking Sir Simon would come and finish him with a tap on his helm, but the soldier merely stood there examining the edge of the whalebone as if unconcerned.

Robert scrambled to his feet and looked around. They were in the outer bailey of Windsor Castle with the great chapel of Saint George behind them. Several other squires and novices were there grinning at his discomfiture. Most were jealous of him, not only for the tales he could tell of his recent adventures and the reward of a manor the king had granted him, but also for the fine steel harness he wore, crafted by the king's own armourer. Few, other than the sons of the greater nobles, could afford such harness. Sir Simon Hartshead had no interest in such pettiness; he had a job to do and as a mercenary recognised that luck had a greater part to play in warfare and the fate of a man than might be expected, and this youth was an example of it. He knew that some lesser men survived battle against the odds while the brave and reckless, those who normally might get the better of their opponents, came to their deaths. Having said that, there was a time for the desperate charge, which the present king of England had proved at the Battle of Bosworth. King Richard was a man who by his build and stature could not be thought of as a robust knight, but still managed to best a stronger opponent.

Robert, thankful that at least the ladies of the castle, principally Claris Salgado were not there to witness his ignominy, attacked Sir

Simon with increased fury striking this time for his legs, the knees and feet being particularly vulnerable. That resulted in Sir Simon lifting somehow the baton from his grip and tripping him so that he once again found himself in the dust. In training, Robert had always fought with squires of his own age and normally got the best of them, even when one might be older. Of course, none could get past their master at arms, but then they were conditioned from boys to being beaten by him and no shame attached to it. Robert had imagined himself a battle hardened veteran and his spirit was being slowly crushed as he fought with Sir Simon, who had no such authority over him. Soon he was hot and tired while Sir Simon seemed hardly warm. Though he affected reluctance to give up, yet Robert was grateful when the soldier suggested they stop for the day.

"We shall practice each day we are on the road," the soldier told him matter-of-factly as they made their way to a small chapel to see to the condition of their souls. "You fight well but too furiously. That is fine when in battle but it only works when practice causes you to react instinctively to your opponent's attaint. If you are lucky and he is too afraid to defend himself properly, or is constrained by a press of men then you might get away with it, but sooner or later you will be confronted by a man who is not subject to panic and then you are undone."

"You may regard me as suitably chastened," conceded Robert who was warming to the fellow. "I look forward to contesting with you again." He had decided a degree of contrition might be beneficial to ingratiate himself with the soldier. It had become clear to him he had much to learn from this man and so it were better to be on his good side.

13 – Lord of the Manor

The grim pile of Liverpool Castle stood overlooking the estuary of the River Mersey, the whiteness of its lime-washed walls hardly diminishing its aura of menace. It was from the port here, mused Robert, that Henry Tudor and his mother would have made good their escape from England had the soldiers of Sir Ralph de Assheton not cut them off inadvertently and sent them northwards by way of Staunton Manor. The troop, headed by Sir Simon Hartshead with Robert by his side, made their way along the dirt approach road, which was deeply rutted with wagon tracks, to where a stone bridge and drawbridge spanned the deep cut moat. The castle stood on what amounted to an island created by cutting out the stone foundation so that the waters of the estuary provided a barrier around and before, making the edifice accessible only by the drawbridge. Beyond was the gatehouse, a square construction, thrusting out from a pair of round towers, crenellated and provided with arrow slits. Behind the towers was a rectangular keep. A crenellated embattled wall swept to the right of the keep to a further round tower suitably placed to defend the entrance to the gatehouse.

The drawbridge was down and the gates open as the garrison having clearly recognised the flag of Saint George and the colours of the king, were in expectation of the troop. They clattered across the bridge and passed through the underneath of the keep to come to a halt in the castle bailey. The lord's apartment block was situated to the right as they entered the bailey and a man in full harness stood there with a few men-at-arms to receive them.

Sir Simon had informed Robert as to his purpose at Liverpool Castle. The present Constable was Sir Richard Strangeways, the heir of a prosperous Yorkshire family and Stanley loyalist, but now careful to declare himself a firm Yorkist. His father, a former Speaker in the House of Commons, had indeed, supported the Yorkist cause, at the battles of St. Albans and later at Towton, but then, lord Thomas Stanley too had supported York in those former days. It had been Thomas Stanley with the present King Richard, then duke of Gloucester who had raised the siege of Berwick and returned that town to England in the reign of King Edward the Fourth. King Richard, wary of one who had been close to Thomas Stanley, had sent Sir Simon Hartshead with additional troops to ensure Lancastrian spies of Margaret Stanley could not use the castle as a point of entry to his kingdom from France. The castle was undermanned as the garrison had not been paid since lord Stanley was gone and those garrison men whose families lived nearby had absconded back to their homes.

Sir Richard Strangeways was a short, stout man with a pronounced paunch and a wizened face - a small part of red flesh which could be discerned within a coarse brown bearded frame - that proclaimed him over fond of his cups. He looked like a bear in harness, an appearance that was reinforced by small, brown ursine eyes that betrayed nothing of the thoughts that lay behind them. His surcoat was white displaying his heraldic device - a sable shield with two white lions passant and three red bands paly. He greeted the newcomers enthusiastically enough, probably in the hope they had brought with them the means of paying the remnants of his garrison. Those of his soldiers who stood laconically around also had a look of expectation about them.

"See to the stabling of the horses and the lodgement of the men, then you may join us in the castle hall," ordered Sir Simon.

Robert, curious to discover the layout of the castle, climbed down from his mount and directed the men to do the same. It turned out the stables were half empty as were the barracks and so his task was easily completed. He left the men with their sergeant and made his way to the battlements to look out over the estuary. Dark grey cloud loured over the murky waters of the tidal estuary; waters turned a muddy brown by the constantly shifting sandbanks while a cold wind blew in from the sea. The town containing the habitations of close on a thousand souls, lay along the north shore, its harbour having but few ships lying under the protection of the castle. It was a poor place that relied mostly on its trade with Ireland. Nearby he could see Stanley Tower, the large fortified Liverpool residence of the Stanley's who had disdained the castle, the constableship which had last been granted to the Molyneux family, deadly enemies of the Stanley's. That house was now inhabited by Robert Harrington, a faithful retainer of King Richard's who along with his elder brother had fought by his side at Bosworth. A long-time rival of lord Stanley, Harrington was enthusiastic in holding the place for King Richard. The Harrington family had been deprived of their own seat at Hornby Castle by Thomas Stanley, which was now restored to them. Edward Stanley, son of Thomas had lived there and was dispossessed under his father's attaint for treason. He was married to Anne Harrington, an unwilling bride who had been forced into the match by Thomas Stanley who had been granted her wardship from King Edward the Fourth, in spite of the pleading of his brother Richard. James, the elder Harrington brother now possessed Hornby

Castle joyously granted back to the Harrington's by King Richard.

He gazed along the estuary to the north where he imagined Staunton Manor stood somewhere close to the sea. Tomorrow he would ride there and seek out the man Hubert but for now he must inform Sir Richard Strangeways of his claim and later perhaps manage to effect an interview with Robert Harrington. Thomas Stanley had disputed with the Harrington's for years over claims to land in this area and he wanted to reassure the knight that he had been awarded the manor by the king in case he had an eye on it himself.

He clattered down the steps from the upper seawards battlements and walked across the small bailey towards the great hall in the Constable's house. He pushed his way past a pair of sullen guards who, seeing his fine harness considered he had some rank; it were better not to contest with him and so he passed through unchallenged. Sir Simon and the Constable were standing by a brazier, ablaze with logs in the centre of the hall where smoke rose to the vents in the roof. Rushes that had been down for some time lay around the stone floor and a pair of ugly hounds got to their feet and bared their fangs, casting truculent eyes towards Sir Richard waiting for the command to attack. Sir Richard hooked a thumb over his belt and placed his right hand on the pommel of his dagger. His pose was habitual rather than threatening though his general mien was aggressive. He pointed at the dogs and grunted something unintelligible, whereupon they settled reluctantly into the rushes and crunched at some bones that lay there.

"I hear you are to take possession of Staunton Manor," he growled, his thick, deep voice entirely in agreement with his grizzly appearance.

"Robert de la Halle, at your service, sir." Robert swept him an elegant bow.

"Fine harness you are wearing," commented Sir Richard. "Never seen a rig like that on a squire unless he be noble."

"My father is the king's armourer," replied Robert defiantly. "Being his son carries little in the way of privilege, but provision of good harness is one he allows me."

"Don't let his fine appearance deceive you, Sir Richard," said Sir Simon. "He is good with that sword and is a renowned shot with the crossbow. He saved his liege lord, Thomas Howard at Bosworth Field with it."

Robert suppressed a gasp of surprise at this accolade from Sir Simon. The knight had driven him hard in the two weeks it had taken them to get from Windsor, going several bouts each day.

Robert had discovered the knight had Lollard sympathies and thought that his fellow squire, John Biggar might have been a better companion, but Sir Simon was content to have Robert with him. He explained that now he was approaching the end of his fighting days he recognised in Robert those skills he possessed himself at a similar age. He too had survived that time more by luck than his own prowess and had he not been mentored by an older knight, would not be here today.

"Well, he better be fiercer than he looks. There are outlaws abroad in Lancashire, bolder since lord Stanley was taken."

"Yes, his grace the king is aware of it and that is why he has sent me here with my men, to keep the peace."

"To secure what are now crown lands is more likely," said Sir Richard cynically. His grace is parcelling out his demesnes piecemeal rather than grant the whole of the Stanley holdings to a single noble. If Sir Richard Radcliffe had survived Bosworth, or Robert Percy it might have been a different matter, but with his closest friends gone the king is not about to restore a great magnate in these lands. He is clearing out the former Stanley tenants and replacing them with his own favourites – less dangerous." He pointed an accusing finger at Robert. "You had better watch your back, squire. There are those hereabouts ill disposed towards your king."

Robert considered the reference to King Richard being *his* king and wondered that here was another of dubious loyalty.

"Not all are landowners and lessees, Sir Richard," he replied. "Liverpool is a guild town and the tradesmen here will welcome the king's law which lets them trade profitably and not be cheated by over powerful nobles. No more may a man be threatened with imprisonment on a trumped up charge while his property is seized in his absence. As for the nobility, the king has abolished the compulsory requirement to provide money to the Crown as a supposed gift, known as a benevolence, which as you know, is rarely repaid in full and not at all in some cases."

"Courting popularity with the commons is what he is doing and that will be his undoing if he continues," replied Sir Richard. "Besides, not everyone is fooled into thinking he is entirely benign. The expectation in Lancashire is that his favourites will occupy the Stanley demesnes and note that Sir William Stanley, who came to King Richard's aid at Bosworth is yet to have his due reward."

"Has Sir William said so?" snapped Sir Simon. The Constable flushed, the small parcel of his face glowing redder than ever. His heavy beard served to hide much of his confusion at the realisation he had said too much.

"No, no, it is just that one in my position hears things."

"That position was formerly in the army of lord Thomas Stanley," growled Sir Simon. "Those in command of it were dubious in their loyalty to the king and failed to come to his aid when ordered. We know of lord Stanley's duplicity, but discovering which of his captains were equally treacherous we cannot yet tell. No doubt any around here that show signs of rebellion might be assumed to have residual sympathy with the defunct Tudor cause." Sir Simon fixed the Constable with a steady stare.

"The matter is resolved," replied Sir Richard pragmatically, pretending insouciance. "There are none in England who would contest the English crown. We are, however, far from the Court here in Lancashire and are a county Palatine, but without a prince to govern us."

"The king will deal with the matter in due course. Normally the County Palatine of Lancaster would be governed by the authority of a royal noble, or one of high status. In the mean time he will not make the mistake of favouring those in the County that were formerly Stanley loyalists."

"I understand that but speaking for myself, there is no doubt as to where my loyalties lie – with the crown, whoever is wearing it. I cannot speak for any other except recognise there may be difficulties ahead."

Robert, listening to this exchange had the impression that Sir Richard was probing the opinion of Sir Simon Hartshead to see if there was any wavering in his support for King Richard. Did that mean the king's troubles were not yet over? Not surprisingly, after the treasonable inactivity of certain nobles at Bosworth, King Richard was less trusting than heretofore and a cautious lack of preferment was apt to produce discontent.

"I think times are changing," Robert chipped in. "Whereas a monarch previously relied on the support of his great barons to defend the throne, recent events have shown this is a dangerous assumption – lord Stanley demonstrated that most convincingly and so too did the earl of Northumberland."

"You are not suggesting the realm be defended by tradesmen!" snorted Sir Richard derisively, looking with scorn upon the young squire.

"I am simply saying that even the greatest general cannot fight if his people refuse to rally to his colours. A king that has the love of his people is not going to be toppled by a jealous magnate or a foul usurper either."

Sir Richard Strangeways clamped his mouth shut, realising that this young upstart might provoke him into revealing too much of his inner thoughts. In these lands and in the presence of King Richard's followers any sign of wavering loyalty to the king would result in arrest and loss of property, if not life itself.

"Yes, squire Robert is correct in his assessment," said Sir Simon. "You of all people should know that lord Stanley, much as he might have wished it, had been unable to order his people to attack their lawful king at Bosworth; neither could his brother Sir William Stanley while Henry Percy could do nothing other than either fight for the king or stay out of the battle. He chose the latter and lives with the shame of it. Sir William Stanley belatedly ordered his men to support their king, which they had no hesitation in doing. It was the great lords that failed the test of Bosworth, not their soldiers."

"As for myself," muttered Sir Richard Strangeways, pretending boredom with the argument, "my only desire is to return to Harlsey Castle in Yorkshire where my wife Elizabeth awaits my coming. I tire of the recent wars and wish to live out the rest of my days in peace."

"You will remain here as Constable until his grace relieves you," responded Sir Simon. There are dues that come with the post and I presume you are content to have them?"

"Indeed, good sir. Be it known I understand well where my interest lies. It is just that my body is in decline and I would spend my remaining time at my home." He indicated towards a bench and a pair of chairs for them to seat themselves while he dropped wearily into his own chair. The hall was rather bleak and though there was arras hanging by the walls, they were old and showing signs of mildew.

"As for that, I have a new home I must attend to," said Robert. "I crave your hospitality for the night, Sir Richard then I shall be on my way tomorrow morning." He supposed the old knight had brought little from his home and not having his lady with him, had no enthusiasm for domestic comforts. The old knight looked dispassionately at Robert.

"You may have a place in the hall and stabling for your horse. As for this evening, I would appreciate the company of you both. I have much news to catch up on and you are fresh from Westminster where the king presently lies. Feel free to remove your harness."

* * *

Staunton Manor was rather more dilapidated than he remembered it. How strange it was, the way in which a building fell into desuetude when there was nobody there to care for it, almost as if part of its fabric depended for health on the living souls of its inhabitants. The drawbridge was down and he noted one of the ropes used to lift it was dangling uselessly by the wall. The gates were closed but offered little resistance to even a casual attacker. The moat was but a swamp, choked with weed and stinking of decay. One of the first things he would order was the cleaning of it. In any case, the manor was his now and he would soon get it into order.

Apart from the anticipation of taking over his property, what cheered him was the weather. It was getting late into the year fourteen eighty-six and the woods that hid the approach to Staunton Manor were resplendent in autumn colour. Today, shortly after the sun had reached its zenith and shadows were lengthening, it was still warm and the tang of the sea came to his nostrils. To the west there were sand dunes and beyond them a shallow beach sloping down to the grey sea between England and Ireland. The great expanse of Morecambe Bay was just to the north. He wondered whom the king had sent over to the Isle of Man, which lay in the sea channel between the two countries? Formerly the Stanley's claimed to be the king's of Man and that was where Henry Tudor had tried for in his escape bid. Whoever it was would have his hands full. The islanders were the remnants of Viking stock and fiercely independent. They would not take kindly to a new lord, he was sure.

The same went for him, in a small way. He was master here now and those who lived and farmed the land would at first be wary of him, if not openly hostile. Still, he was determined that would be their problem. So long as they paid their rents and gave him his due service then he would be satisfied; those who gave trouble would find him a hard master.

There were three companions with him, soldiers of Sir Simon Hartshead. The knight had given them to him as an escort to discourage attack from outlaws or brigands impoverished by the death of lord Stanley. The manor was but a few miles north of Liverpool on the coast immediately west of Ormskirk, and Lathom House, the now defunct seat of the Stanley's. Thus the king had placed him right in the heart of those demesnes distrained by the Crown from the treacherous lord. Robert thanked Sir Simon for his kindness but the knight reverted to his habitual gruffness and growled that he did not want to spend valuable time hunting down felons should Robert be molested on the way to his manor. The intention was the men would spend a night at the manor house and return the next day. Robert was nevertheless grateful. He had in his saddlebags his personal things and hidden in the bottom of one of them, coin for the purchase of supplies for the house, supposing there would be scant comfort there. His coin was small and probably insufficient, but it was all he had until he returned to London. His grandfather had informed him some of the profits from his business venture in Portugal would be available to him by then.

He came to a halt before the drawbridge and called to the house. There was no movement at the wall so he dismounted, not entirely trusting the drawbridge to the weight of his horse, and drawing his dagger stamped across to hammer on the gate with the pommel. He thought he heard voices on the other side and presently a small interrogation flap protected by an iron grill was opened where a face appeared and displayed shock at the sight of a man in full harness. Robert recognised Hubert at once, by his white hair and gaunt features.

"Hubert! It is your master, Esquire Robert de la Halle who demands entrance," he said with all the authority he could muster in his voice. Hubert's eyes widened in recognition and muttering something that sounded like *aye*, closed the flap. The sound of iron grating on iron indicated the bolts were being withdrawn and after which the gates swung open to reveal the courtyard. Hubert stood to one side while Robert walked his horse across the bridge and signalled to his three companions to do the same.

At first the courtyard appeared much as it had the last time he was here. The crutch hall seemed in a good state of repair except he noticed grasses growing at the base of its wall and also around the entrance to the stone tower at one end of it. He couldn't help glancing across at the kitchen block where as her prisoner, lady Staunton had secreted him out of sight. The daub that had been loose then was even more dilapidated with more of the wattle exposed and no sign of servants either. His companions looked about them for someone to take care of their horses.

"It seems we must shift for ourselves," muttered their sergeant, one Nicholas Belward. "The place is all but deserted." He cast a scowl at the man Hubert, who stood stone-faced and mute.

Robert looked him up and down. At least the man seemed in a reasonable state of cleanliness. He remembered dame Isabella Staunton telling him he was a man-at-arms in his youth, a crusader no less in the region known as Outremer, the Holy Land. Thus he preserved the military discipline of tending to his personal condition, at least the captains in an army normally did so.

"This is now the king's manor held by me as his appointed tenant-in-chief. How many people are there here?" he demanded.

"There be just me, Bolly Gent and Agnes Fry. The smith is here. He has managed to find work from the village and the farms. The rest have gone, but they be back soon enow when they hear you are come."

"They know of me?"

"They know you will have a purse with you. They have no money or means to acquire food and are living off their families. Those of us still here are near destitute."

"I expect to collect some coin in the form of rents."

"Coin, you say!" Hubert laughed derisively. "You'll get no coin hereabouts. Folks is too poor to have coin."

"Not according to the manorial court rolls," responded Robert quickly. He had anticipated this sort of problem and made enquiries before he left London. True there was little actual coin, but the rest was paid in kind in the form of corn and other produce. Some of the villains worked land held from the manor but owed service to the tenant for his own upkeep. These were formerly Stanley lands and lord Thomas had not been one to let his tenants live free. "Let me see my barns. The harvest is in and they should be full."

Hubert scowled angrily at him. "There be the barn," he said pointing to a wooden frame with wattle and daub infill just inside the north curtain wall. The door was open and it was obviously empty. The daub needed some attention, too, he noticed.

"According to the manorial records there are two farms in this manor tenanted by freemen who must pay rent. In addition, there are parcels of manor lands let out to villains who must have worked the manor lands in order to keep hold of their own land."

Hubert shrugged as if unconcerned. Robert clamped his mouth shut while he thought this through. He nodded to sergeant Belward who seeing a cold forge and empty stables led his mount and those of his two men to see to their care. Presently he returned and opened his arms helplessly.

"There be no oats or feed of any kind and the stable lacks straw for bedding down."

"I see," said Robert, his jaw set in determination. "Then let us remount ourselves. I shall see to it we are properly fed and our needs catered for before nightfall." The soldier grinned and gave him a bow of obedience. "Master Hubert - point me towards the principal farm of the manor. Who is the tenant there?"

"That be John Formby and he has two burly sons. His house is about a mile north of here."

Robert climbed into his saddle along with the other three. "Let us ride. I would speak with this John Formby. Are you prepared?"

Sergeant Belward slapped a hand on his sword hilt, understanding what Robert meant well enough. The other two grinned in anticipation of some sport. They had thought themselves on a mundane ride through wild country when they could have been in barracks with their comrades, but this promised to be something to make their trouble worthwhile.

The manor farm was a cluster of wood framed and thatched buildings with one of wattle and daub, the habitation of the yeoman farmer and his family. As the small troop rode into the yard before the house, scattering fowl and a foraging pig, a man appeared holding an axe, a wooden head where the edge was tipped with iron. It was not long before two huge fellows, presumably his sons, joined him. These two carried staffs and looked as if they knew how to use them. They probably did, seeing as their liege lord, that would have been lord Stanley, would call upon them to fight for him should the king issue a Commission of Array. It was possible that these two had been with the Stanley army at Bosworth, but that was of little import now. If they were intimidated by the sight of armed men fronted by a man in full steel harness, they showed nothing of it, which rather suggested they had been soldiers ere now.

"Are you John Formby?" demanded Robert.

"Aye, and who be you?" responded the farmer aggressively. He was plainly dressed in a woollen smock and hose with a sleeveless leather jack over. His hair was tied back and although he was a rude yeoman yet he had an air of competence about him. The two with him were similarly clad - one was around Robert's age and the other slightly older, perhaps twenty years or so. Robert had noticed that the condition of the farm and buildings was somewhat better than at his manor house.

"I am squire Robert de la Halle, tenant of the manor from which you hold your farm. I wonder why your rent has not been paid? I have a bailiff at the manor who would receive your payment."

John Formby snorted and guffawed with his sons. "The manor is untenanted, or so we were led to believe. Lady Staunton was our mistress after Sir Charles died and she had to run or be taken as a traitor. That means our land is unprotected by a lord and thus there is no obligation for us to pay anything until we have a liege lord appointed."

"The king has gifted the tenancy of the manor to me and the

rents and other privileges are due. The manor became the property of the Crown when Thomas Stanley was attainted for treason and thus any rents due are payable to the king or his representative, which at this time is me."

John Formby shuffled his feet uncomfortably. He knew well enough that annual rents and taxes could not be avoided but in the absence of any authority considered himself fortunate in having all the profits of his produce to himself. Here was a young upstart, a mere youth demanding his rights as tenant-in-chief of the manor from which he held his farm. He might have contested his right but there were three armed ruffians with him and he was experienced enough to realise he would lose miserably if he resisted.

"It has been a poor harvest this year," he grumbled while he thought on the matter.

"That is the case every year," replied Robert. "I have never heard a farmer enthuse about a grand harvest, but all are ready to elevate the price of their produce when there is a genuine dearth."

"If you would step down, good sir, perhaps we could talk on this over a mug of ale?"

Robert realised that was a good offer. Though he was determined to at least feed and care for the men and horses for the moment, he was at a loss as how to arrange the storage and perhaps sale of any produce he might collect in rent. John Formby had already worked this out and though in the long term he would have to submit to the authority of his master, yet he could perhaps gain some short-term profit.

Goodwoman Formby was a generously proportioned woman who gave the impression she was only too pleased to serve her guests with her best ale. They were seated in the house around a sound oak table with John Formby at the head with his sons on the side bench. Robert realised, once he had seated himself lower down, that the farmer had actually usurped his rightful position, but he decided to let that go. Sergeant Belward sat beside him while the other two soldiers sat outside in the autumn sunshine in the farm yard, each clutching a mug of ale that was regularly replenished by the farmer's wife.

"While we speak I am having a cart prepared with feed and straw for your mounts. It will be at Staunton Manor before your return," stated Formby. "How long do you expect to reside there, good sir?"

"Until I can arrange for my bailiff to look to my affairs while I am away on the king's business," he replied.

"It is my intention to make a home there, but until I can acquire a bride, that will be some time yet, I fear."

"Be there a young lady who you have in mind sir?" piped up goody Formby, detecting by her feminine intuition the young squire's heart. Her husband missed that entirely, being consumed with interest regarding his statement about being on the king's business. This were an ambitious statement for such a youth and unless he were boasting outrageously, something that needed careful consideration.

"There is, goodwoman Formby, but there are obstacles."

"Well, obstacles is God's way of letting us prove ourselves worthy," she replied matter-of-factly.

"The king's business?" said John Formby curiously in a small voice.

"Yes, I am recently returned from Portugal where I was among those bringing our queen to England. I was fortunate in detecting and preventing an attempt on her life, an attempt, I might tell you, that was made through the agency of dame Margaret Stanley, late mistress of these lands."

John Formby glanced worriedly at his wife while his sons frowned with concern.

"I seem to have disturbed you," said Robert with more than usual perspicacity.

"It would be dishonest of me to state otherwise," replied Formby. "Lady . . . dame Stanley was a powerful force in Lancashire and many folk cannot or will not change allegiance casually. Having said that, few would conspire against the Crown of England and I have heard those returning from Bosworth were unhappy to learn they had been thought traitors to their anointed king. My two sons here can testify to that."

"I was there and I saw for myself that lord Stanley was unable to order his people to attack their king. That is why there have been no recriminations against the people here, just those nobles who turned against the English Crown. My own reward is due to that."

"You were at the Battle of Bosworth?" gasped Formby. "Surely . . . your age?"

"Oh, I was not in the line of battle, but with the horses of my liege the earl of Surrey, now duke of Norfolk."

Formby sat back in his chair and stared respectfully at the young squire. He had thought him a simple upstart but now he was beginning to revise his opinion. Young he may be but clearly closer to the king than most. The king himself had granted him the tenancy of Staunton Manor. He needed time to think.

"I shall send a goodly supply of food and kindling for your fire," he said at last. "Once you have made yourself comfortable at the manor, perhaps we can talk again. I have a wealth of local knowledge that can be of much use to you. I am guessing there are some repairs needed at the manor and you can count on me to arrange labour to see to it."

Robert was surprised at the goodman's enthusiastic support. He had come to the farm ready for a confrontation and to take from him that which he required for his immediate needs. Now the yeoman was offering to help with essential repairs. In all this, Robert overlooked the fact that no mention of payment in coin had been forthcoming. His purse, thin enough before, had as yet to find a means of swelling it.

Evening was closing in when they arrived back at the manor. Robert noticed smoke coming from the vents in the one of the buildings, the kitchen. He walked his horse over the bridge and into the courtyard. A forge was alight in the stable block and he could see signs of where fresh straw had been delivered.

"See to our horses, sergeant, then come into the hall with your men. Whatever food is on offer we shall share. I do not anticipate a grand feast."

Entering the hall under the stone tower he found a fire ablaze in the hearth and a stout table laid with wooden trenchers and pewter mugs. Benches were set each side of the table and the rushes on the floor looked fairly new. The place had not been entirely neglected, or was it that Hubert had simply been looking to his own comfort.

Hubert stood by the door as he came in and gave him a desultory bow. Beside him was a boy of about eight years or so, bare footed and dressed in a coarse woollen smock tied with a piece of old rope.

"This be Bolly Gent," explained Hubert, giving the lad a gentle cuff, "who has forgotten his manners." The boy bowed to Robert. "He will serve us until you appoint your own servant. Agnes has the kitchen fires alight and will provide something for us to eat."

A wooden partition divided the room and he remembered this was where the crib for the babe, his father's daughter had been. He went around and found it still there, somewhat forlorn and out-of-place. Here too was a truckle bed and a straw mattress. It was plump and looked to have been prepared for him as a sleeping place. He gave little consideration to the fact that he was certainly shoving Hubert out of his accustomed bed. He called to the boy, who came running.

"Here boy, unstrap my harness at the back there and help me out of it. First though, you can get my saddle bags from the stables and bring them here."

The boy scampered away and returned a few minutes later, hauling with some difficulty the heavy saddlebags. Robert took out his day clothing and once divested of his harness, appeared in the hall as a young courtier clad in a green gown trimmed with velvet.

Robert invited Hubert to sit with the rest of them. Goodwoman Agnes Fry was a thin scrap of a woman, getting on in years but willing enough. She had an ingratiating manner, which belied her former aspect. Robert seemed to remember her cursing him to scorn along with the other kitchen servants when he was hidden away in the larder there. Isabella Staunton had explained it was the servants who betrayed him to the Tudors, while she would have kept his presence hidden. Be that as it may, Agnes was all smiles and bobbing respectfully as she brought an iron pot from the kitchen giving off an aroma of some sort of stew. Robert thought it might be rabbit and wondered which local game he had the right to take. Fish chiefly from the moat and rabbit probably, but certainly not venison. Rabbit took time to prepare and it was hardly likely whatever was in the pot had been caught in the last few hours. That meant the household servants were taking game illegally, which hardly troubled him, but he put the knowledge away in his mind in case he ever needed to assert his authority over them. The three soldiers were returning to Liverpool in the morning leaving him to his own devices.

Another thing for consideration was the quality of the wine he was drinking. The others had ale but Hubert presented a flask of wine, which, he said, was residual stock from the cellar of Sir Charles Staunton. The former tenant had been dead for close on two years and Robert could hardly think his personal stock would remain intact for that long, particularly when the manor had nobody to guard its continued existence. Not only that, but the wine he was drinking was fairly young, so who had purchased it when there was no coin in the house? These things he pondered upon but decided not to mention his suspicions while Nicholas Belward was within hearing. Robert was the king's representative in this manor and could not fail to investigate should he suspect some sort of felony. Once they had gone he might ask a few questions of his servants.

* * *

The winch for the drawbridge was fitted into a platform above the inside of the gate and covered over by a tiled roof; otherwise it was exposed to the weather. It was accessed by a single ladder that itself looked as if it was ready to be replaced. Robert stood looking up at it with Hubert by his side, then watching through the gate the three soldiers riding off back to Liverpool.

"That must be tended to. It is pointless having a bridge that cannot be raised or lowered. I hear tell there are outlaws in these parts?"

"There are certain disaffected men, that's true but they will not trouble us here."

"Why is that?"

Hubert pushed his woollen cap back on his head, his brow wrinkled as if the question was a difficult one. "I suppose it is residual fear of lord Stanley," he said at last.

"That is nonsense," came the incredulous reply. "The place has lain virtually unprotected for months and the Stanley influence is no more."

"Perhaps you are correct," said Hubert laconically. "It will do no harm to get the bridge back into working order." Robert stared at him questioningly. There was something about Staunton Manor that was eluding him and Hubert knew precisely what it was.

"I shall write to dame Isabella. She is with my father at Gloucester by now. She will alert me to the state of the district and no doubt tell me of any nefarious activities I should know of. I believe she still maintains an interest in the manor and would see it properly managed. I am beginning to wonder why she recommended you as my bailiff?"

Hubert turned abruptly aside and walked off a few paces, deeply disturbed and clearly in dispute with himself. Suddenly he turned to face the young squire.

"Let us walk the boundary of the manor house while I tell you what you want to know."

Robert put out an arm towards the bridge and the two men tramped over it and turned back to look at the curtain wall. They set off at a casual stroll while Hubert got his thoughts together.

"You realize we are near to the sea here?"

"Yes, I have yet to go that way but I fully intend to see what lies beyond the dunes which hide it from our sight."

"It is a low flat beach and when the tide is out the sea seems to disappear only to return of a sudden."

"Yes, I have seen that further north, across the Morecambe sands."

Hubert jerked his head around. Clearly he knew how Henry Tudor had met his end there. Perhaps he also knew of Robert's part in it?

"Liverpool lies just to the south, as you know and after the demise of lord Stanley, certain goods that found their way into Lancashire via Stanley Tower are now no longer able to do so, unless they pay the usual harbour dues and landing taxes. Goods such as French, Spanish and Italian wines are particularly costly and the duty on them raises their price even higher."

"So they are coming ashore here?" Robert realised immediately the significance of the good wine he had been drinking the evening before.

"That is so, master. Lord Stanley was one of the main customers for such goods along with other houses in Lancashire."

"You mean he deliberately defrauded the king of his revenue?"

"Only for certain luxuries – the more mundane, wool, hides, that sort of thing coming mainly from Ireland he was content to charge landing dues for, in any case he took some of the tax to himself, for administration."

"I see, and Staunton Manor is placed just so for such clandestine business." Robert felt a thrill of excitement and also a conflict of loyalties. Overturning a smuggling operation would further ingratiate him with the king; however, that would not do him any good locally and if he failed here he would be depriving the king of support far from London. Rather than condemning the activities of the smugglers, it might be better to go along with them, at least for the time being. He was thinking he might profit too. The king had landed him with a poor manor and Robert having no personal wealth, the task of providing a secure home for Claris had seemed daunting. The place was dilapidated and needed some repairs to bring it up to a proper condition. Of course, if he were part of the local business it would do him no harm with the other houses that were also taking advantage of the smuggling operation. Destroying it would have an adverse affect and hamper his task of preserving the king's interests in the region. That is what he told himself and it made good sense.

"Is there a shipment due any time soon?" he asked non-committaly.

"I cannot say, master Robert. How would I know?"

Robert realised Hubert was unlikely to give away anything unless he had some assurances that the business was safe from exposure.

"Was dame Staunton – Isabella, aware of what was going on?"

"It was Sir Charles that organised it," replied Hubert.

"And after his death?"

"My lady had much to contend with afterwards and I do not know how she conducted her business."

"Yet you were her steward."

"But not privy to all her affairs."

"Well she could not have dealt with the matter alone. The wine I had last e'en was not from Sir Charles' supply; it was a young wine. It must have come here after his death."

"I know nothing of that," replied Hubert stoically. "Probably it was bought in Liverpool." Clearly he was not going to get further information unless the man could trust him.

"In that case the manor accounts will show its purchase." He felt the tension in Hubert at that remark. "I have told you that dame Isabella has recommended you to me as my bailiff? She would not have done so had she thought I would be displeased with your conduct here at the manor in the absence of a tenant."

"She is a fine lady fallen on hard times," was all he muttered in reply.

"Well, not fallen any further. She is now my stepmother and I am not inclined to have her taken for a smuggler. She is in enough trouble as it is with the king. A disclosure of felony while she was in charge of the manor would finish her." He let the thought dangle there.

"Here, take this." Robert handed Hubert the ring entrusted to him by Isabella. Hubert took it and gazed at it lying in the palm of his hand. "It is my wish you become my bailiff here and I think dame Isabella might be pleased to know you have accepted the position." Hubert slipped the ring onto the little finger of his right hand.

"There is a shipment due sometime in the next few days. We have no explicit date as the vessel depends on wind and tide." Hubert told him cautiously. "What do you intend, if I might ask?"

"I suppose there is some sort of signal arranged?"

"Yes, a small beacon in the dunes before the beach. We have to wait for high tide. The vessel will anchor in the approaches to Liverpool for the night and a couple of boats will bring the goods ashore."

"And where do we store them? Not here I hope."

"No master, that is only while I get word out then they will be moved inland."

"To John Formby's farm, I take it." Robert had noted the good condition of the farm. The state of the house and furniture was rather better than most habitations of a yeoman farmer, unless he happened to have some other profitable business.

Hubert smiled at him for the first time. "It is fortunate you are with us in this," he grinned. "We were like to be taken had you been of a different character."

"Ah, do not mistake me," came the reply. "I am the king's man and look to his interests. However, I now have a manor to run and scant funds of my own. It would not profit the king to have me fail here and perhaps have someone less trustworthy take my place."

"We shall get along fine," said Hubert pleasantly. "You shall find me a trustworthy and loyal bailiff, one who brings a profit to the tenant of Staunton Manor."

"Yes, I have been thinking on what you have just said – Staunton Manor. I think the name must be changed."

"But everyone in the county know us as Staunton Manor. It would be confusing to alter it," responded Hubert, his mood becoming darker.

"Fortunes are apt to change too, and having a manor named after a defunct tenant is equally confusing. It is better to have a name that need not be changed with the tenant. My father has ever had problems with the dialect around here. It would amuse me to torment him with a new name that might confound his tongue, though not that of his wife who speaks the language."

Hubert's mood lightened again at the idea. He looked about him. The manor was in a clearing surrounded by trees, mainly oak and beech. "Can I make a suggestion, master Robert?"

"I was hoping you might do that."

"Then let us call it Hall I'th Wood."

Robert tried it on his tongue a few times and with Hubert's corrections, soon managed a passable Lancashire pronunciation. They completed the circuit of the Hall I'th Wood and strolled over the bridge into the courtyard.

There were a few people standing around waiting for his return, by the look of them poor villains. They stood together in a group as if for protection. A sudden flash of memory presented a picture of those mercenaries huddled together in the lower bailey of Pembroke castle, just before they were shot down. Some things remained in the mind for life. There were no women with them and they looked at Robert under lowered heads, wondering what sort of man he might be.

"These be they who hold land in tenure from the manor," Hubert informed him. "I sent word yesterday for them to gather here. You were right when you said they owe day labour."

Robert walked over to them. "As you can see," he addressed them, "the manor has been neglected recently and I want you to see to its repair. The first task is to dredge out the moat, at least the part of it that is foul and then I can restock it with fish." Robert had noted that parts of the moat incorporated a series of ponds and these were choked. "Master Hubert here is my bailiff and you will take instruction from him. You have had plenty of time to tend your own land these past months, and neglected mine so tending to the immediate needs of the manor should not trouble you."

The men shuffled their feet uncomfortably but none spoke in complaint. Probably they thought the less said the better.

"I also need some servants to look after the manor in my absence. Look to your women folk, and your sons. Master Hubert will make the necessary appointments. They will be paid wages, but be warned, the state of the manor means there will be small income for the present, so I shall make payment in kind where I can. It is therefore in your interests to see that my manor thrives. I must be away on the king's business at intervals and like his grace, I expect the loyalty of my people."

He looked over them and saw, if not gladness, then a taciturn acceptance of his words. No doubt any grumbles would emerge once they had his measure, but for the moment they were wary of him and that was all to the good.

"There seems little discontent among the tenantry," mused Robert to Hubert. "It seems Sir Charles must have either been a good master or they have been kept under by him – I wonder which?"

"Sir Charles was something of a tyrant, that be true, but his lady tempered him. Shortly after he died the whole country became confused and the tenants here were careful not to cause her any problems otherwise they might have had Margaret Stanley to deal with." He lowered his head and looked at Robert under white bushy brows. "There is something else, of course."

"The matter of imported goods, I take it?"

"Yes, master Robert. Everyone around here has a finger in that particular pudding in one way or another and the tenants are unsure as to how you will respond. When the goods arrive we shall need their labour to get them ashore and away into the countryside."

"One thing - how are the goods paid for?"

"Ah, yes," said Hubert in a crafty voice. "Lady, I mean dame Staunton dealt with that side of it. Let us go into the hall where I can tell you how the business works."

A few minutes later Robert and Hubert were sitting together close to a good fire each with a beaker of wine."

"Rather finer than in most manors, I think," said Robert with a twinkle in his eye as he sipped at his wine. "So how is the business financed?"

"Well, I shall tell you. There is a scheme where several prominent families buy a share in each trip according to their own means. This requires payment in currency, of course, but there is also payment made in kind – specifically bales of wool. Lord Stanley paid his share in this way with wool from his estates. He otherwise would have had to pay export taxes. It was a simple matter for him, seeing as the Custom House is at Chester while Stanley Tower is the departure point for goods from the Stanley estates to the Isle of Man. The Tide Waiter at Liverpool is one of his own people. He also has a share in the venture."

"Tide waiter?" interrupted Robert.

"Yes, the Tide Waiter is the king's official who watches for sail as it enters the harbour and supposedly any landing point along the coast, though that is not easy as you can imagine and neglected in these parts. There is one at Liverpool and others on the Wirral peninsular covering the approaches to the Dee estuary and the Port of Chester. He will board a vessel and examine its cargo before arranging for the place where it must tie up at the quay to be assessed for dues. Now you may know that it was King Edward the Third who first levied tax on imports as well as exports and particularly on the import of wine. This tax is called tunnage and is levied on each barrel. In addition, if a ship carries more than twenty casks, then the king takes two of them as prisage, one said to be taken from before the mast and the other after the mast but only from English ships – foreign ships are simply taxed on the whole cargo. No ship belonging to our business ever has more than twenty casks when it docks at Liverpool or Chester."

"That is not to say there were rather more when it left the continent for England?"

Hubert gave him a wink. "There is a customs house at every licensed port, Chester being the nearest one. Ships landing cargo at any other port may only do so with the permission of the Collector of Customs based at Chester. He is the official charged with collecting the king's dues and is answerable to the Controller of Customs at the nearest licensed port. There are thirteen such ports in England, but nobody has the resources to ensure compliance. Both these officers at Chester are Stanley men, or were. I suppose that with Sir Richard Strangeways at Liverpool Castle and the

Harrington's in possession of Stanley Tower, the present business will be upset. On the other hand, the smuggling operation here might thus become more lucrative."

"When Lord Stanley controlled the Customs House at Chester and appointed the Tide Waiter at Liverpool, there would be nobody looking further afield where a cargo may land without paying the import tax or tunnage. It might become more dangerous now."

"Exactly, lord Stanley took care to appear to be acting properly in the king's interest at the harbour and in any case, he had the income for collecting taxes there for himself too. There might not yet be any suspicion regarding our particular business."

"I see," mused Robert, "and because the whole community is involved there is little chance of an informer spoiling the game. They would have had lord Stanley to deal with in any case. No wonder local people are so nervous now that I have taken over the manor close to where the goods come ashore."

Robert wondered whether his life might have been forfeit had he not declared himself sympathetic to the business. As yet he was a probationer having not actually become involved in the smuggling business. He had a feeling that would soon change.

* * *

Robert was shocked at the sight of so many people on the beach. He could see why that was necessary – the operation would have been impossible if just a few were involved. It was highly dependent on labour if the goods were to be brought ashore quickly before the tide turned and then before daybreak spirited away to certain locations in the hinterland, his own manor being the principal hub. Somewhere out there across the blackness where he knew the sea to be was a vessel anchored. Already the first boats were rowing out, though how they would find the vessel in the dark was something he was pleased could be left to those who knew this shore.

He had gone into the sands with Hubert who took him to where a couple of men were tending a small but bright fire, which, nestling between the dunes, Robert was almost on top of before he saw it. He knew the light, small though it appeared, would be visible for miles out at sea. There was a half-moon lurking behind dark scudding clouds, which spasmodically revealed the beach to be a great expanse of black with sheens of shining shallow water up to the fringe of the tide where waves ran white for the last few yards before merging with the sand. Soon the tide would turn and the vessel must be on its way lest it became stuck and visible in the day.

"Here be the first of the cargo," whispered Hubert as the splashing of oars heralded the approach of a boat. Suddenly a troop of men ran from the dunes and splashed into the shallows. Each returned with a barrel or a crate on his back and trudged off towards the manor. Soon more boats came and men poured from the dunes to carry away the goods.

"The whole country hereabouts must be on the beach," growled Robert. "How much cargo is there?"

"It comes from France where the goods were purchased. The ship will sail from here to the harbour at Walney Island, which is protected by the Pile of Foundray, to take on goods brought there by the monks of Furness Abbey as return cargo. Not every vessel in these waters touches a registered English port."

"I had thought we would be receiving just a few barrels of wine," mused Robert recalling the circumstances that first introduced him to the location of the Pile of Foundray.

Hubert gave a crafty laugh. "The rise or fall of great lords has little effect on the local business. Every habitation around the coast of England is similarly organised. Lord Stanley had things pretty well set up and the people are merely carrying on in spite of his attainder. In fact it has become rather easier now, seeing as lord Stanley's reputation with the monks at Furness Abbey was at low ebb. He *would* continually interfere in their affairs."

"Man does not live by fishing alone," jested Robert.

"He would starve else," replied Hubert. "The folk around here live by scraping up cockles and netting shrimp; a poor fare."

"I think we might return to the manor and see to the disposal of the goods," said Robert. "Neither of us is contributing much here on the beach and the people seem well disciplined by themselves."

"I was just about to suggest it. Normally that is where I would be. It is just that you are new to the business so I wanted you to see for yourself how it works."

Back at the manor, the barn that had previously stood empty was now beginning to fill with wine casks, and crates containing expensive spices. John Formby was there with his two sons along with a wagon and pair of oxen ready to transport some of the goods to his farm. Once there they would be distributed to his customers. Robert had learned Formby was the main agent of the smugglers now that Sir Charles was no more. That was according to Hubert, though he could not help but think Isabella Staunton might have had a hand in it. Formby did not seem like one comfortable negotiating with the local nobility, but Isabella would have been.

It was some days later when he discovered the answer to that conundrum. Thankfully the last of the smuggled goods, except the portion he kept to himself, were away into the countryside and with those who had purchased them when Sir James Harrington with six of his men arrived at the manor. Robert met the knight in the courtyard.

"Sir James," said Robert, sweeping a respectful bow. "Welcome to my home."

"Give you good day, squire Robert," replied Sir James amiably as he climbed down from his mount. "Is that new woodwork I saw on the bridge? You have been busy with more than one task it appears."

Robert wondered what he meant by that.

"The manor was somewhat neglected, Sir James and I have ordered essential repairs."

"So I see."

The knight was a tall man around his mid fifties, but looked to be in fighting trim with little sign of corpulence. Robert knew that he and his brother, also named Robert, had fought beside King Richard at Bosworth and been there in his last great charge against the Tudor. Indeed, Sir James was a knight of the king's body and Chief Forrester of Bowland. He was clad in steel cuirass with mail haubergeon under and a white plumed sallet to his head. He wore a fine wool travelling cloak which opened as he dismounted showing a surcoat with his family arms – a sable field with silver saltire cross and a mascle in the centre. "My men here would appreciate a mug of ale while we speak together," he growled, waving a casual arm at his companions.

Robert gave orders to Hubert who arranged for the horses to be tended while his master and Sir James went into the tower. The boy Bolly Gent was there and Robert got him to rake up the fire and throw some more logs on to get a blaze going. The weather had turned cold and wet. Presently, Sir James having divested himself of his sallet and travelling cloak sat with Robert by the fire, each with a pewter goblet of wine. All the while that Robert was chivvying his servants, he was wondering what had brought probably the most powerful knight in the region, indeed one of an influential few in England, to his humble manor.

"I hope you have reserved enough of this vintage to last until the spring," began Sir James smoothly. "There will be no more shipments until then, the weather at sea being against us."

Robert's heart began to flutter. By his words and tone Sir James was fully aware he was drinking wine that had been brought into

England without the proper dues being paid on it. His mention of *the weather being against us* indicated the knight was involved somewhere in the business. If not, and he was simply playing a game of cat and mouse, all was up with squire Robert de-la-Halle and was like to have a capital charge brought against him. Sir James leaned forward and looked him in the face.

"Thomas Stanley, of foul memory, certainly spoiled things for many of us in these lands. Now he is gone we can establish proper government again."

What did he mean by that? Proper government – the strict application of the king's writ? His grace the king was determined on the rule of law in his realm and here they both were drinking illegal wine.

"The traitor disturbed many in this region. People around here have all been cheated by him at one time or another. His henchmen had more authority over them than the king himself. My family have been maligned and dispossessed and we are not the only ones."

"I have heard of it," replied Robert injecting a sympathetic tone into his voice. "Happily, his grace the king has restored Hornby Castle to you and Thomas Stanley's progeny, Edward Stanley is cast out."

"Yes, he is and good riddance. Our king is full of good grace and knows how to reward those true to him. Edward Stanley would have been taken for a felon had he not fled. I hear he is somewhere in Northumberland, probably ingratiating himself into the favour of that dissembler Henry Percy."

"I expect the son of a traitor will find small comfort there."

"Not at all, but more of that later. First I would have you know that any matters regarding the importation of goods into the king's realm must be passed through me. It was ever my business and Thomas Stanley disturbed it, just as he interfered with everyone else in these lands." Harrington spoke authoritatively and assumed no contradiction. "In future I shall inform you, or in your absence, your bailiff, who I know and trust, as, I presume do you . . .?"

"Indeed, Sir James," stammered Robert, labouring somewhat out of his depth.

"Yes, of any shipments that are to be unloaded here in these discrete domains, I take it you understand me?"

"I do, Sir James."

"You shall profit by it, of course. This is otherwise a poor manor, made all the more so without a certain understanding of how business is conducted in these parts."

"You need say no more, Sir James."

"Good, I hoped that would be so, in fact, your bailiff advised you were of an adventurous nature. I must say I am most impressed by your reputation. I was one of those who chased after Henry Tudor in Wales while you discovered him here, at this very manor and close to my own home. I see something of fate in this."

"There is a divinity that shapes our ends, rough hew them how we will," replied Robert unconsciously."

"There is something of a philosopher in you, my young friend. Perhaps some vagabond poet might pick up on such thoughts at some future time and make his fortune by them. But we digress; there is something of greater import I must tell you."

Robert, relieved he was not to be taken for cheating the king of his proper dues, visibly relaxed. Sir James, noting the young squire's relief smiled and, leaning forward, patted him on the shoulder.

"I am eager to hear it," declared Robert enthusiastically.

"I have mentioned the earl of Northumberland, Henry Percy. The king's spies inform him that there is a plot afoot to foment rebellion against his grace King Richard, and it centres on that particular lord."

"I find that hard to believe, Sir James, if you would pardon my presumption in saying so."

"I understand why you should doubt it," responded Sir James. "After all, the earl's own people despise him for not entering the Battle of Bosworth on the king's side and thus rendering them the jest of all Englishmen. That is part of the problem for Henry Percy. It is a matter of shame for him that his considerable power cannot be used as influence at the court of King Richard. He does not have his people behind him and the king knows it. Thus he is being left out when rewards are being granted. Take this region for instance, the Palatine County of Lancaster. I can tell you now that control of the county will be granted to John Scrope, fifth baron of Bolton. As with my own family, he has a consistent record of loyalty to the House of York. You may rest assured that we shall all profit by his appointment."

"I shall be guided by you in this," said Robert, who had little personal knowledge of these great lords.

"That would be well, and you will not lose by it. There is something more, however, and you must ready yourself. It is likely there will be a call to arms in the near future, probably early next year and you will be required to muster your people to the king's cause."

"A call to arms! Surely all that is past?"

"You might have hoped so, and did we all, but the matter with the earl of Northumberland confounds us. He is at present in Scotland at the court of King James the Third."

"This is strange to me," cried Robert. "I cannot comprehend what you are saying. I know you and baron Scrope were with our king, when he was duke of Gloucester, at the war with Scotland in fourteen eighty-two. Lord Stanley was there too, and if what my father told me is true, you were allies then?"

"Aye, fortune is a strange and frail woman," sighed Sir James. "I was knighted banneret there, after the taking of Berwick.

"I believe King James is not popular with his people," said Robert.

"He is not, partly due to his reluctance to apply justice fairly, unlike our own king, though he does wish for an alliance with England, which isn't helping him either."

"Yet sensible," commented Robert. "An alliance with England would prevent a great deal of unnecessary bloodshed and improve the condition of the common Scots."

"Except prejudice gets in the way of reason," continued Sir James. "But why should we care? The main concern is that Scottish prejudice leads to danger for England. You have heard of what Scots are pleased to call *The Auld Alliance*?"

"I have, where some Scots think that an alliance with France, an old enemy of ours, would bring them benefits should that nation manage to successfully invade England."

"Well, they are mistaken in that, but let their prejudice blind them. They still burn for revenge after Berwick was ceded to England again. That does not diminish the danger, however. You may have a house that can be rendered secure except for a careless churl who leaves a door unbolted. Scotland is the back door to England. France knows that and the Scots are too simple to comprehend how they might be used, or else French gold had bought them. As usual, the common people will pay the price in blood."

"The Scots cannot hope to defeat England especially now that King Richard is on the throne," considered Robert, "but with help from France, and the earl of Northumberland's compliance, they might be tempted to try. What I cannot understand is why France would want to become involved?"

"You were too young perhaps to remember, but your father knows of the Treaty of Picquigny back in fourteen seventy-five. King Edward invaded with what was the largest army ever to cross into France. Louis the Eleventh, the Spider as he was called, rather than fight a war he would probably lose bought off Edward with a pension. Richard of Gloucester opposed the pension, considering it to be shameful when the English people had paid with their taxes for the war. When Edward died, that pension was already in default. Neither had Edward repaid parliament the taxes he had levied."

"I remember my grandfather telling me the tax raised at that time by King Edward for the invasion was an additional one tenth of all land incomes, which caused a deal of trouble when it came to collecting it."

"That is correct," said Sir James. "While the high nobles benefited from the pension, the ordinary soldiers had just their pay with no prospect of plunder or profit from ransom. Many starved when they returned to England. It is one reason why King Richard has abolished the forced payment of benevolences, used by his brother King Edward to extract loans from the people. The whole system brought Edward into disrepute. King Richard, however, is planning another invasion of France and this time there will be no payment of pensions. His grace is out of countenance with the French due to their part in the Tudor invasion and they continue to protect English rebels, Margaret Stanley and her minions being principal in plotting against our realm."

"But the finance – how will the king raise so great a force especially now he has abolished his own method of benevolences?" Robert, a tenant of the king, began to worry about how much would be levied on him.

"By the help of his allies, of course. He has at least tacit support from King João of Portugal while the dukedoms of Brittany and Burgundy will join if England leads the way. The Holy Roman emperor might also be persuaded to add his weight to the project. If he does, then the monarchs of Spain will enter the fray."

"So if the French can encourage rebellion in the north of England, it will prevent the possibility of them being invaded by King Richard, who must send his army north?"

"That is so." Sir James drained his goblet and placed it on the table after which he got to his feet. "I think I have said enough for now. If you wish to buy a share in a future cargo, I shall be pleased to accept your coin. Our local business need not be impaired by national events, but be prepared to bring some of your tenants should the king issue a Commission of Array."

Robert stood under the gate watching as Sir James Harrington rode off with his men. Sir James was a loyal subject of King Richard, a quality that was not compromised by a little dealing on the side. He knew now who was financing the clandestine operations centred on his new abode. If so powerful a knight saw nothing wrong in making a profit from the business, then neither should he.

14 – The Assassins

"It is called The Hall I'th Wood," said Robert with an amused grin on his face. Claris frowned, unable to comprehend what he had said. He had pronounced it with a distinct Lancashire accent knowing full well she would not understand.

"Allishwod," she tried, her features screwed in concentration.

Robert laughed and she glared angrily at him. "You will have to learn to speak the name of your own home," he informed her. Both of them sank into melancholy at these words. Their suit had not progressed any further since they had last met. He had left Windsor in the autumn of fourteen eighty-seven and now it was late spring the following year.

They were standing just outside the great hall, in the bay window of Kenilworth Castle that looked down into the inner court. To their right they could see the oriel window of the queen's presence chamber. King Richard had brought Joanna here for a variety of reasons. The castle had been on the site since the twelfth century but had been extensively remodelled by John of Gaunt, Queen Joanna's great ancestor from whom she had her Lancastrian heritage. That alone made it somewhere she might be happy and where better than to give birth to her child, expected in the summer.

Then there was the word from the North. A great force was being assembled in Scotland and the earl of Northumberland, Henry Percy, was showing no signs of opposing it. His demesnes were the main buffer between Scotland and England so his recalcitrance, a repeat of his tardiness at Bosworth, boded ill for King Richard. The king had formally ordered him to take an army to the borders to threaten any invasion but no reply had been returned.

The king's choice of Kenilworth from where he could command the assembly of an army was sensible. Situated just a few miles north of the great castle of Warwick, it was positioned suitably as a rallying point. Robert remembered the region well. Just a few miles to the northeast was the Redemore Plain, that very battlefield men were now calling Bosworth. The king, it seemed was fatally drawn to this spot and Robert crossed himself as he thought on it.

"I must return to her grace," said Claris reluctantly. "She is taking her court to the *Pleasance* by boat. She has developed a love for the house and the king will not have her take horse in her present condition. It will be her last visit there. Soon she will go into her confinement and not emerge again until forty days after the hoped for prince is born."

Robert had heard of the *Pleasance in the Marsh*, a mansion built by King Henry the Fifth away from the castle at the far side of the expansive castle lake. Henry had used it for feasting with his friends rather than in the great hall of the castle.

"Is Anselm going with you?" he asked casually. "If he is, then perhaps I could join him. Besides, if the queen is to venture out of the castle defences she will need some protection. Anselm knows of the potential danger to her grace while the rest of the court does not."

"Anselm will go too," she informed him. "With his lute and minstrelsy he is a favourite of her grace. Perhaps you should approach my lord of Norfolk. He is responsible for the queen's guard. There is always a goodly number of armed men close by her when she leaves the castle. Your previous experiences are invaluable I think."

They turned from the window and walked into the queen's presence chamber, the guard there letting them through upon recognising the lady and the young gallant. Queen Joanna was sitting on a chair while her ladies fussed about her in preparation for their jaunt. One of them was fitting slippers to her feet. The duke of Norfolk was close by chatting amiably with her while her confessor sat reading from a Holy text by a window. The room was large and well lit with windows looking over the inner court. Brightly coloured tapestries depicting scenes of forested nature and pleasant greenery adorned the wall and a pair of brachet, pets of the Queen, sniffed the air and regarded the newcomers nonchalantly.

"Ah, here is the *donzela de Montanhas* fresh from a tryst by the look of her," she giggled. Fortunately Joanna was in a happy mood at the thought of her little sojourn to the *Plaisance* and not inclined to chastise her for absence. "And she has her leman with her, I see." The duke looked at them with casual interest. Robert and Claris sank to their knees before the queen, who bid them rise again. Robert wondered about the queen, a pious woman of great virtue but who seemed to delight in the love affairs of her ladies. Her care for the child of her matron, the lady Ana de Mendonça, Jorge de Lencastre was testimony to her tender interest. He supposed it was due also by her marriage to King Richard, which seemed a happy one – his grace was certainly pleased with his new wife. Perhaps that was because she was a lady previously unknown to him and thus rare. His first queen, Anne Neville had grown up with him at Middleham Castle and therefore had no particular mystery to haunt him. Joanna was able to advise him wisely, having ruled as Regent of Portugal from the age of nineteen for two years while her father was away with his army in Africa. Her brother King João the Second had similar problems with his nobles as Richard, so her advice was invaluable and safe. King Richard had nothing to fear from her, unlike his brother King Edward with his queen, Elizabeth Wydville who had a self-seeking family in her train ever clamouring for royal favour.

"I was about to order you to go to the *Plaisance*," said the duke of Norfolk, looking worriedly at the queen while he spoke to Robert. "I dislike that place. It is not fortified, except it has a moat, and has too many possibilities for mischief, having been built for that purpose. His grace the king is presently at Warwick with Sir William Stanley and will not return here until tomorrow. I have the care of the queen until then and she has cast aside my request for her to stay in the castle until he returns."

"The house in the marsh is built for pleasure, your grace – not the kind of mischief we fear."

"Well you are wrong there," snapped the duke. "The requirements for clandestine amoral activities are no different to more deadly ones. You must be vigilant. I have my spies there, of course, but it does no harm to have another close to her grace and you seem to have a gift for discovering plotters which confounds reason."

Robert felt uncomfortable being described as a spy, though in this case he supposed that is what he was. "How am I to go there?" he asked. "There is scarce room in the queen's barge.

"There are two following with the queen's guard. Others are already at the *Plaisance*, having ridden around there. You can find a place in one of the barges. I shall be there with the queen."

Robert bowed respectfully to the duke and hurried off. Claris would be with the queen in her barge and he could hardly believe his luck in that he had a place in one of the escort barges. It was but a few minutes row to the *Plaisance* and that meant he would land at the same time as Claris and be in close company. The ride there took a great deal longer than the short row across the lake.

There was much fussing and courtly display involved in getting Queen Joanna through the water gate of the castle and into her barge. The eight rowers were splendidly clad in green and brown doublet and hose and wore scarlet gloves. Joanna was clad in a blue mantle trimmed with ermine under which could just be seen a yellow silk gown, voluminous enough to hide any sign of her pregnancy. She wore a necklace of pearls around her throat and her head was topped by a hennin in the English style. Her ladies were dressed in fine silks, coloured peach with matching hennin. Claris was one and as she took her turn to get aboard, Robert watched as she stepped daintily from the quay by the water gate into the barge. A canopy in the Yorkist colours of murrey and blue covered the centre part of the barge under which the queen was seated on a chair elevated above the others. Anselm was there, seated at the queen's feet and reclining on the cushions placed around her. He strummed gently some tune or other on his lute while the queen waited for the bustling to stop to let the rowers begin their work. This would have taken no time at all were it not for the courtiers coming aboard, each one insisting on genuflecting to her grace before vying for a place as close to her as possible. The last to embark was Thomas Howard. The duke of Norfolk had stood by scrutinising all those coming with the queen before stepping into the barge and giving the order to cast off.

The lake at Kenilworth had been formed when a dam was constructed to provide a long narrow entrance road across the top of it to the castle. Not only did this form a substantial defence, and supply water for the moat around the rest of the castle walls, but being well stocked with fish, it was a valuable food resource too. Castle servants licensed to take fish were dotted about here and there in small boats, each with a rod and line. As the queen's barge slide past they stood and bowed as best they could. Joanna and her courtiers laughed at the antics of one man who, having hooked a large fish, was trying to control his rod while bowing to the queen. This he contrived to do, depriving her of the expected spectacle of him falling into the water.

"Had the fellow any sense, he would plunge in. Her grace would have sent him a purse in payment for the amusement his discomfiture brought her." This came from Abel Mostyn. Robert had been delighted when he found the ancient in the barge he was in. Sir Ralph de Assheton was with the king at Warwick but he had left his trusty ancient behind to command this part of the queen's guard. "Why have you brought your crossbow?" he asked with a puzzled frown. "There will be no hunting, not with the queen in her condition."

"Shooting at the butts," Robert replied. His bow nestled at his feet along with the crannequin to wind it and a quiver containing a dozen of his distinctive, red-flighted quarrels. "The queen will not hunt, obviously, so entertainments are put on for her, including an archery contest."

"Yes, I hear you are a good shot with that machine," came the unenthusiastic reply. "I prefer the long bow. It can shoot six to one over the crossbow."

Robert grinned and patted the stock of his weapon. "That is so, my friend but not everyone can draw a war bow; this takes practice to shoot but not muscle training from youth, as with the long bow." He decided not to state the obvious and offend the man – that a long bow was the weapon of the commons and shooting before the queen, the contest would be between courtiers, many of whom could not draw good English yew."

"Here are some other fellows out to entertain her grace," noted the ancient, nodding towards the shore.

Across the water a boat was being rowed with a crowd of courtiers in it. Clearly there being limited room in the royal barge they had made their own arrangements. There they were, perhaps a half dozen, waving and bowing while their rowers were pulling frantically to get close to the royal barge.

"Cheeky buggers," muttered Abel Mostyn. "Who do they think they are? Why not get in line and follow on, or wait to greet her grace as she lands at the *Plaisance* harbour."

Robert could not help but agree with this opinion. He was amazed at the sycophancy of some courtiers and it was a wonder the king patiently tolerated it at court. Of course, those closest to him were rather more familiar in his presence, while such display tended to increase the further down the social scale a courtier happened to be. It was more pronounced around the queen. Many saw her as a way to the king and thus tried continually to ingratiate themselves with her. Monarchs were well used to this and probably inured to it, though they generally appeared to accept it as their rightful due and it did serve to provoke a feeling of awe in the observer. Would he be content to stand in line to present himself before God when his time came, or rather be pushed aside by other souls clamouring for preference?

The thought of his inevitable doom caused him to darken his mood and suddenly it seemed there was something not quite right with the intruders. For one thing, where had they come from? Appearing as they had from behind a promontory of the lake was suspicious. For one thing there was no landing stage there and so must have been lying in wait. They should have come out of the water gate with everyone else and clambered aboard their boat to follow on. Better still, they might have ridden around to the *Pleasance* and displayed themselves at the harbour with the rest when the queen landed.

All seemed frenetic gesticulation in their boat and those in the queen's barge had noticed their approach. They seemed harmless enough except Robert saw one of them kneeling down in the boat fiddling with something. He was mostly obscured by the activity around him but why was he not enthusing with his fellows?

"I think there is something wrong over there," he said, jabbing Abel Mostyn in the ribs. The ancient stood up and looked across. After a moment he stepped forward between his men to stand in the bow, shading his eyes with a hand.

Robert, a feeling of dread coming upon him, reached down and fitting the crannequin to his crossbow, wound back the prod until it latched under tension.

"What be ye doin' wi that?" growled one of the guards. Some had their back to the bow and could not see what was happening.

"Just a precaution," replied Robert, never taking his eyes off those in the strange boat. Just then he saw the man who had been kneeling get to his feet. He was still obscured by his companions but Robert thought he saw the shape of a crossbow in his hands. The boat was close to the queen's barge and the courtiers there were gazing at the strangers wondering what entertainment they had in mind. Robert thought he knew what that was. Reaching down to his quiver he withdrew a quarrel and getting to his feet, fitted it to his bow. The boat was in range but if he had to fire it would be a long shot.

A series of things happened at once. Those standing in the strange boat suddenly sat down while the man in the centre remained on his feet with a crossbow coming up ready to fire.

"Murder! Save the queen!" The cry of alarm sounded across the water as the courtiers in the queen's barge saw the intent of the assassin. In front of Robert the guard who had his back to the danger scrambled to his feet and lunged at him. Clearly the fellow thought he was going to shoot at Joanna. Ancient Mostyn, seeing the danger turned towards Robert screaming something unintelligible, his face a mask of horror. There were just a few yards between the assassin and his target, the queen, and it was unlikely he would miss at so short a range.

Robert brought up his weapon. He would have no time to sight it and must fire on the upswing and even then he might be too late. He pulled the release and heard the snap as the quarrel sped away. Then there was a bright flash followed by blackness.

* * *

Robert began struggling as if he were drowning. A brilliant light hurt his eyes and he could hardly tell if its sharp brilliance or the clattering of hammers within his skull caused the pain. He tried to put his arms out to save himself but felt restrained and unable to move. A babble of excited voices came to him and somewhere above him a mist-shrouded face was trying to swim into focus. A groan sounded in his ears and he realised it was the sound of his own voice. He decided the effort was too much and let himself sink back into darkness. Someone was calling his name – a familiar voice, that of Claris! Once more he struggled to wake and this time her face resolved itself from the darkness. She was leaning over him, encouraging him to look into her eyes and in spite of the pain in his head, this he managed to do. She looked away for a moment and he thought he heard her speak to someone else close by. A croaking sound came from his throat as he tried to call her name in an attempt to get her to return her gaze to him, which she did.

Slowly he became aware of his surroundings. Claris was here looking down on him, concern and relief lighting her face. He seemed to be in a small chamber and the restraint that had caused him to panic was nothing more than a blanket covering that prevented him raising his arms. Shadowy figures became clear and he was surprised to find his half-brother, Philip, gently leading Claris to one side while he examined his face.

"Do you know me, Robert?" he asked quietly. Robert managed some sort of groan, which Philip interpreted as an affirmative and looking around at Claris, gave a brief nod. He bent over and looked into each eye separately with some care then stood back. "Rest is all he needs now. He should soon recover what few wits he had," he said jocularly by way of reassurance.

Claris returned to his side and placed a cool hand upon his brow. "We have been so worried for you," she whispered tenderly. He noticed her eyes were moist and the rims reddened as if she had not slept for some time.

Philip returned to her side. "Do you remember how you came to this state?" he queried. Robert struggled with the question. He could faintly remember being in a boat and charging his crossbow, but the reason why escaped him. He tried to shake his head but the blinding pain caused him to close his eyes. "Talk to him, donzela and tell him what happened. It will help him to recover his thoughts."

Claris told him how they were rowing across the castle lake when a barge with what appeared to be courtiers approached, waving and generally looking as if their intent was to attract the notice of the queen, which they did. It was just when they got to within a few yards of the royal barge that the danger to her grace became apparent where an assassin armed with a crossbow was about to transfix her. The guards shouted out the danger but had no means of preventing the attack. At the same time as the assassin fired, a quarrel released by you, my love, struck the man in the temple and although he shot away, his own quarrel sped harmlessly into the air, after passing through the fabric of the canopy directly above her grace's head. Unfortunately, the cry of danger from the queen's barge caused the men in your boat to think it was you who would murder their queen and one of them dealt you a blow just as you fired."

"Had you been wearing harness, your head would not have been cracked," put in Philip, "though probably then your throat would have been cut. Dressed as you were for the court, all that came between the blow of a cudgel and your head was a thick woollen cap. We think the knotted mantling attached to it saved you from instant death."

"The assassin is dead, of course," continued Claris, "but some of those in the boat were eventually taken and put to the question. They had horses on the lakeside and rowing desperately for the bank, managed to mount up and ride off. There were eight of them, counting two who were with the horses. The assassin, of course, would have made them nine, but they left him lying in his own blood in the bottom of their barge. My lord of Norfolk, however, had taken the precaution of having a troop of prickers patrol the fringes of the lake. They soon caught up with them and after a fight, managed to capture two of the murderers. The other six were killed in the fight rather than be captured."

"Those who were taken have revealed the source of the plot," said Philip. "When you are improved and come to yourself, we shall discuss it. I might say that you should not be surprised to learn the woman Margaret Stanley was behind it all."

"You should also prepare yourself for a visit from the king," gushed Claris. "He has instructed he be informed the moment you are come to your senses. Her grace, my lady the queen is now confined ready for the birthing but also wishes to reward you for saving her life, which you undoubtedly did. She has given me leave to attend upon you rather than her."

"Yes, and now I must away," said Philip, rubbing his hands together, "and make myself available should the queen's women need my advice on the forthcoming birth. I shall have a message sent in to her grace. Her joy at your recovery, and the omen it portends, will greatly enhance the chance of a safe delivery."

It was two days before Claris pronounced Robert well enough to get out of bed and into a chair by a small fire. He was comfortably lodged in a chamber in one of the castle towers with a small window looking out over the surrounding countryside. Early on this second morning, just after Claris had stood over him while he consumed a concoction of oatmeal she had decided was good for him, King Richard arrived. Robert tried to scramble to his feet but the king waved him back down again. A chair was brought for his grace by an attendant courtier, on which he sat with a grateful sigh, as if he were in pain. Claris was on her knees and a smiling king, too, raised her.

"Once more, squire Robert de la Halle, you have managed to place yourself just so when our crown is in jeopardy," intoned the king. "Not only have you saved our queen but our unborn child also. Apart from our own grief, the consequences for England would have been dire indeed if what the murderous traitors planned had come to pass."

"I did no more than any other in the same circumstances," Robert replied modestly.

"Yet there were many others around the queen while only you saw the danger in time, small time though that appears to have been." The king clasped his hands and gave Robert a benign smile. "You are due reward for your action, squire Robert. We shall think of something suitable. I have it from Sir James Harrington that you have managed to put your manor in Lancashire in good order. The queen also informs us that you are enamoured of this lady here. Is that so?"

"It is, your grace," he replied. Claris moved to his side and clasped his hand.

"We see the lady is in like mind?"

"I am, your grace." Claris could hardly speak and her face reddened fit to match the glow of the fire in the chamber.

"The queen informs us that the impediment, apart from that of youth, is in the matter of a dowry?"

"Both my parents are dead, your grace. There is just my brother Anselm and I. We have no property of our own and it is only by the good grace of the queen that we are in our present state."

"That is a matter easily settled," smiled the king. "Her grace intends to provide you with a dowry, and we would wish reward for good service could always be so simple. Squire Robert, your manor has need of a mistress and I understand your father has counselled against a marriage with this lady due to her having no dowry. Well, that matter is now resolved."

Robert and Claris could hardly believe what was happening. One moment their situation seemed hopeless and now, without any premeditation or planning on their part, their lives were transformed. Claris gave a cry and falling on her knees before the king, kissed his hand before standing and taking her place by Robert's side, who managed to get to his feet. The young squire was beyond words. He had been brought up to attend a royal court, but for the moment he could think of nothing to say.

"One thing more," said King Richard, easing himself to his feet. "Your family has served us well and loyally for many years; indeed, your father is to attend upon us here at Kenilworth on another matter. Your grandfather has also served us faithfully and thus we have entrusted the care of our queen in her pending travail to his grandson, your cousin Philip, as one of her physicians and watchman advising her women. There is that afoot which smacks of treachery and seems to dog our footsteps. We would have those around us who not only have proved worthy of trust, but have the ability to ride on the back of fortune in our service. You have shown yourself to be such a one. We have no perception as to the mind of almighty God, only that he works through his instruments here in the world. As we trust in God so we must trust in those he has sent to preserve our crown. We shall speak further on this. For the moment, get you well again. We think there will be more work for you before your service to us is done."

"That would be a willing labour, your grace," was all that Robert could say.

With those final words, the king turned and left the chamber. Afterwards Robert and Claris dared not speak. They looked at each other in wonder.

"Does this mean I can take possession of your body, having the king's blessing?" asked Robert cheekily at last.

"It is probably so," replied Claris, "but I should wait awhile lest the taking become the leaving of this world.

"I am feeling better already," laughed Robert. "I believe my convalescence will not be prolonged."

* * *

At the age of seventeen, Robert had barely become a man, but having lain with his love there was no further rite of passage he could take. He had fought in more than one battle, confounded the king's foes and twice saved his queen from death. In all this he considered the conquest of Claris' virtue his greatest triumph, even though the battle had not been a hard fought one, rather chasing after a retreat, though her rearguard action had proved exhausting. A contract had been drawn up between them to which his father, nor Anselm could hardly object, seeing as how the monarchs of England had both favoured the match, and the queen given Claris a dowry. She had been generous indeed and Robert was already planning some improvements to the Hall I'th Wood.

Claris, too, was overjoyed at the prospect of having the ordering of her own home, even if it was in a remote part of England replete with strange hauntings, so she had heard. Well that hardly bothered her; there were similar creatures and demons lurking in the mists of the mountains of her birth, the *Tras os Montes* of Portugal, and she considered the spells and talismans that protected folk there would work just as well in Lancashire. Anselm had taught her some songs that would keep foul spirits at bay and one in particular that a mother might sing over a sleeping babe to keep it from harm. Already he had taught it the queen. It was too soon for Claris to discover if she was with child, but she knew that if she and her betrothed continued the way they had been of late, that condition might not be too long in coming.

A few weeks after the incident on the lake the whole court at Kenilworth was in a state of expectation. The queen's labour was imminent, according to the messages sent out of the lying in chamber by her women. Philip and the other physicians were lodged close by and though as men they disdained attending upon a woman in labour, yet they had plenty of advice to give her midwives. The king kept himself busy with affairs of state and the increasing alarms coming from the north, but was never more than a few steps away from where his queen lay in her darkened and quiet chamber. Apart from her confessor, the only man allowed in there was Anselm, who was provided with a corner where he could sing and play when the queen commanded. He sang songs of Portugal interspersed with those court favourites of Languedoc, the land of troubadours to calm the woman who lay in her bed attended by nuns and her gentle women. The midwives were there, too, clucking and gossiping quietly together, waiting for the time when a royal birth would occur.

Splendidly attired in red pleated doublet trimmed with blue velvet, to demonstrate fidelity, both to his king and his lady, Robert attended upon the lord John of Pomfret in the great hall of Kenilworth Castle. His head still had a bandage over the torn area of scalp, which remained tender. He was glad that there was to be no immediate call to arms as he would not welcome the pain a head wound confined within a steel sallet would cause. The king was sitting elevated on a dais, while before him was a table where his secretary, Thomas Witham, had neatly arranged parchments and papers. With the king were the archbishop of York, Thomas Rotherham, Sir William Stanley, lord Thomas Howard the duke of Norfolk, viscount Francis Lovell and the earl of Lincoln, John de la Pole. Also close were Sir Ralph de Assheton and Sir James Harrington. These were the ones immediately familiar to Robert, though there were others who, by their dress and manner, were of equal knightly status. He looked around for his father, whom he knew would be there somewhere, and so he was, talking amiably to a stout, dark visaged and fierce-looking man he faintly recognised but could not, for the moment, place in his mind. Laurence the armourer looked across at his son as if he expected him to come over. Robert asked lord John for leave to attend upon his father and the king's bastard son, all his attention on the king, impatiently waved him away.

"Ah, Robert," said Laurence. "I think you know Sir James Tyrell?"

"Of course," replied Robert as he recognised the man by his name. He was stouter than the last time he saw him and more swarthy in appearance.

"Squire Robert, you are become famous since we last met. I believe it was around the time of Buckingham's rebellion, fourteen eighty-three?"

"At my grandfather's house," agreed Robert. "Just before I left to go to his grace the duke of Norfolk at Framlingham."

"Yes, the lamented John Howard. I wonder that if I had been at Bosworth whether I too would have been killed; yet we have Howard's son in that title now."

"We lost many friends to the king there, for sure," said Laurence, "and this present business with Northumberland could yet deprive us of others we can hardly afford to lose." He directed his words and his gaze to his son. Tyrell smiled and jovially slapped Robert on the shoulder.

"I believe fortune shines Her face on you," he chuckled with an undertone of profundity. "Even the plotting of dame Stanley cannot breach the defences you erect before her."

"Do we know for certain the recent attempt was yet another of her schemes?" said Robert. It was incredible to him that dame Stanley would go to such extreme lengths to revenge herself on King Richard.

"Yes, I am afraid it is true," replied Sir James Tyrell with a sigh.

"The woman is quite mad and thus a useful tool for others who plot the destruction of our realm. If it were not so she would hardly have the means of prosecuting such endeavours. The usual practice is to shut such as she in a convent and forget about her. The fact she is still free and living close to the court of France is a thorn in the side of our king."

"Who were the men that would have murdered the queen?" asked Robert

"English Lancastrian exiles brought here for the purpose," said Tyrell. "They had escaped back to France after Bosworth and were smarting for revenge. The plan was for them to take themselves into Wales and from there to France. We know now who recruited them." Tyrell eyed them meaningfully. "Sir Reginald Bray."

"That man is a curse upon our family as well as this land," snarled Laurence. "I suppose he was not one of those taken or killed?"

"Unfortunately not," sighed Tyrell, flapping his arms in frustration. "We know, however, where he is headed - into Scotland and the earl of Northumberland. One of the prisoners disclosed that after some *persuasion*." He laughed, being cognisant of the method used to extract the information.

"Then we can assume he is injecting residual Lancastrian venom into the situation," replied Laurence.

"There will be a purpose in it, you can be sure," said Robert. "The man is devious in the extreme." He was recalling the duplicity by which Bray tricked him into thinking Henry Tudor was heading for Scotland rather than the Furness peninsula. "I would have definite word of his presence there before being sure of him."

Just then a courtier came over and informed Laurence that the king commanded his armourer attend upon him. Robert stood with Tyrell watching while his father bustled away.

"I suppose the king must have his harness in battle order," said Tyrell laconically.

"Yes, but my father has already attended to that. There is some other work the king wants from him but I have no idea what it might be. Have you, Sir James?"

Tyrell looked at Robert as if he would disclose a dread secret before arranging his features into a condescending smile. "The king entertains his court generously and thus his body is rather stouter than when he first took his crown. I suppose there will be a few minor adjustments required to his harness."

Robert knew that Tyrell was a favourite of King Richard and privy to that which was denied everyone other than his closest squires of the body, his tailor and his armourer. His father had a forge here at Kenilworth, requisitioned for his especial use while the king was here and the king's armourer worked secretly within it. The only other person allowed in there was a woman brought from Windsor Castle, a labourer who worked the forge bellows and who was dedicated to his father's service. She was a fearsome-looking woman, large of frame and built for aggression, but meekness itself while at the forge. Her name was Maud Mudd and she had been the first to storm her way into the house in London where Lady Isabella Staunton, as she was then, and her husband Sir Charles was holding Robert a prisoner. She had received the king's personal accolade for that exploit and his father trusted her discretion implicitly.

As if prompted by his recollection of that time, dame Isabella de la Halle appeared from among the throng of courtiers and knights milling around in the great hall and, spotting Robert, came up to him.

"I must beg leave of you, madam," said Tyrell bowing gracefully, yet disapproval of her showing in the firm set of his lips. He turned to Robert: "and of you, young sir." Turning swiftly on his heels, he stalked off to where viscount Lovell was engaged in conversation with Sir Ralph de Assheton.

"That man's charity does not extend to me, is appears," she commented wryly.

"He knows your history, madam," responded Robert.

"I had hoped that were behind me, at least so far as you are concerned," she sighed. "Your betrothed is not as cold."

"You have not displayed a propensity for taking her prisoner and locking her in a cellar or a larder; she might have a different opinion else."

"Those matters were expedient, which you know full well. It was by my good offices that you survived both of them."

"I suppose things might have turned out worse," he was forced to agree.

"You are fortunate in your betrothed," she said, her beautiful face lit by her inherent charm, or was it the skill of a seductress? He could not tell. There were many such about a court and they were all adepts when it came to ingratiating themselves into the hearts of gullible men. "To marry for love at your age is a blessing given to so few. I count myself fortunate that your father and I are reconciled to each other. He, of course finds nothing particular in that; he loved his wife, your mother and now he loves me. I, on the other hand, had first to endure the travails of an unhappy marriage and shift as well as I could."

"You were not faithful to your first husband, as we know," he replied coldly. "How is the product of that encounter? She cannot be here with you?"

"Isolde is with dame Fisher at Gloucester. The child is but two years and well cared for with her. Fortunately the good woman does not take out her dislike for me on the child. As for myself, I could not endure the atmosphere there when your father is away, so I have come to him at Kenilworth."

"You will fit in here, madam. Intrigue is ever haunting a king's court."

"Then count yourself fortunate any intrigue I discover will be to your father's benefit, you may depend upon it."

Her continued declaration of fidelity towards his father was beginning to have an affect on him and he found himself warming to her. Indeed, it was difficult not to like her. She was beautiful, charming and witty with an undercurrent of danger that Robert was becoming mature enough to apprehend. He had wondered at her involvement in the smuggling business at the Hall I'th Wood and grudgingly admired her for the way she had managed the enterprise in the absence of male protection. He was still uncertain about her relationship with Margaret Stanley – the woman was, after all, her former patroness. Hopefully her marriage with the king's armourer was testimony to her acceptance of King Richard's crown, but a niggling doubt nevertheless remained like a worm hibernating in his brain.

"There is a matter I think you must address. It concerns your betrothed, Claris Salgado."

Robert bristled at this. "Leave that lady out of your scheming, madam," he snarled. "She is not to be trifled with nor, indeed am I."

Isabella was taken slightly aback by his aggressive response and flapped her hands at him in confusion. "You mistake me, young sir. It is her interest that concerns me if you would let me speak."

Robert eyed her cautiously but nodded his assent for her to continue.

"It is just that I think it would be wise for you to wed her before the conflict that is bound to occur soon with Scotland. You are a squire in the service of a high lord and also, as tenant of your manor, must bring to the king three archers and ten armed men. If you were to fall, heaven forbid but you know the dangers of battle," they both crossed themselves at the thought, "the lady will be bereft not only of her love but her protector too. As your wife, any property you have will naturally come to her. Her position merely as your betrothed provides small security. I speak as a woman who understands these things."

While delighted at the prospect of sealing his contract with Claris by marriage, the thought of her left alone by his death in battle upset him and he had to drive the thought down lest it unman him. Then there was the lurking suspicion that Isabella might have her own agenda. She had befriended Claris and should she be left alone by his demise then Isabella might manage to manipulate affairs where she could wrest her lost manor back. If that were the case, though, surely Claris in not being Robert's wife would make that task easier, so why recommend immediate marriage? Perhaps he was misjudging her, but the woman was an expert dissembler and proficient at playing the long game.

"I take your words to heart, madam," he said firmly. "Claris is to return to the queen's chamber now I am sufficiently recovered, so the business must be managed swiftly. There is the collegiate chapel of Augustinians in the grounds here where our union may be solemnised. You and my father are at Kenilworth and there is no shortage of other witnesses."

"Then I will inform your father while you make the necessary arrangements with the priest. What is the matter? You look as if you had been banished the court." Robert stood as one struck suddenly dumb. Isabella scrutinised his face curiously, then looked to where his glassy gaze was directed. At first she saw nothing untoward. A group of ladies and knights were entering the great hall. Most of them drifted into the crowd but one elderly knight stood as if considering his next move. Beside him was his lady, a diminutive young woman many years his junior. Isabella's heart went out to her. It had not been so long ago that she had been in a similar state. She realised that it was to these two that Robert was directing his attention.

"The lady is known to you?" she asked, her intuition homing instantly onto the lady rather than her husband.

"Yes, I know her. She was at the siege of Pembroke Castle, taken with her parents and held there by the Tudor traitors."

"She has a pretty mien," said Isabella switching her gaze alternately between the two before settling on Robert. "Were you . . . friends?"

"We hardly spoke to each other," he replied distantly. "When the siege was raised and the castle returned to the king she was restored to her betrothed. That is Sir Piers Pellingham. Her name is Alice. Her father is Sir Hubert de Lucy, castellan of Pembroke Castle.

Isabella returned her gaze to the lady. She was expensively dressed in the latest fashion and her husband kept her close.

She knew the feeling only too well. An old husband with a beautiful young wife on his arm to display his wealth and demonstrate, somewhat unconvincingly, the possibility that he yet maintained the stamina to do good service in the marriage bed.

"Now the lady is married she is free to pursue an illicit amour," Isabella said with a mischievous smile. "If she happens to fall with child she can heap congratulations upon her husband who will no doubt think or deceive himself into being the father. I note she is not showing yet. Perhaps she is recently married? If not she probably has no lover to provide for her, in which case there might be a vacancy." She raised her eyebrows archly and smiled sweetly.

"You presume too much, madam," said Robert disdainfully. "Do not apply your farmyard morals to one who is undeserving of your opinion."

"It is not my morals I describe but those of the court," she replied, unaffected by his tone. "Remind me - who is it that you went into Portugal with - the lord bastard John of Pomfret was it not, the king's illegitimate son? I seem to recall you saying that the queen has the care of her brother's bastard, George of Lancaster. Then there is your father's other son."

"You dare impugn my father!" snapped Robert taking a pace back from her. Isabella gave a short laugh.

"Ha. Don't tell me you are unaware of your half brother, Philip, got on the woman Anna Quirke, your grandfather's wife, and she nearer to your father's age than that of her husband."

Robert gasped at the woman's temerity. Truth to tell he had suspected something of the kind. Philip was the image of Laurence and anyone seeing Philip and Robert together might easily observe a blood relationship. He had refused to consider it and neither his father nor dame Anna had sought to enlighten him. He had come to the conclusion that some things were better left, but now Isabella had brought it into the open. What more might this woman discover? Perhaps she was a witch? This revelation was bad enough and now she had worked out his previous desire for the lady Alice.

"I see your father beckons me," she said, amused at his confusion. "Perhaps now you will be less severe when discussing my character." She dropped him a sanctimonious curtsy and swept away.

Robert looked over to where the lady Alice was standing beside her husband. The old knight was engaged in conversation with a courtier and ignoring her, which let her turn her face on him. Had that happened before his adventures in Portugal his heart would have leapt for joy, but now he found he was merely curious to see how she fared. He wondered if he should approach and make polite conversation, after all he had helped restore her to her betrothed at Pembroke and it was a simple matter to presume upon that acquaintance. Something told him that were unwise. In spite of his fury at her indiscretion, Isabella's words regarding the lady's possible availability for an illicit amour held him in check. There was that in Alice's face that told him his presence would find favour should he presume upon their former friendship. Claris was soon to be confined along with the queen and would remain there for forty days after the birth.

The heaviness in his heart as he swept lady Alice a cursory bow and turned away, both surprised and disturbed him. Better he get himself into Lancashire and muster some of his men to the king's service, than stay a moment longer at Kenilworth.

* * *

Robert stood beside his horse among the smoking ruin of his manor house, his brain whirling in a mixture of fury, disgust and disappointment. Thank God his new wife had remained at Kenilworth with the queen. Imagine if he had brought her here sooner and then left with his yeomen under commission of array issued by the king. Emerging from the surrounding woods, they found poor Hubert hanged and still warm in the centre of the gate and had to cut him down before it was possible to cross the drawbridge and enter within the walls. Most of the servants had fled and those who were caught lay where their throats had been cut. Agnes Fry, the scrawny old woman who could not possibly have resisted any sort of assault, lay with a crushed skull outside the door to her kitchen, which was now a smouldering and roofless wreck. As for the main building, wood and wattle being the main material in the construction of the crutch hall, meant it had gone up like tinder and while the stone tower remained, its column had acted as a chimney and funnelled flames upward to consume entirely the interior. The only human survivor was the boy Bolly Gent who had hidden behind a heap of manure in the stable. Happily for him the rebels were intent in getting the two horses away rather than engage in a diligent search for more servants.

He had arrived with ancient Mostyn, who had been lent to him along with half a dozen men to get him into Lancashire and form up the men from his manor. They discovered a band of skirmishers had come down from Scotland and pillaged the surrounding countryside. It was led, he had soon learned, by Sir Reginald Bray, which rebel was now installed in Lathom House, the former Stanley residence. The garrison at Liverpool was depleted by the king's call to arms and the Harrington servants and womenfolk at Hornby Castle were assuming a state of siege, most of their men having departed to join the king who was assembling his army at York. The rebels did not have enough among them to prosecute a siege, but they could rampage around the countryside disrupting the recruitment of men for the king and provoking the diversion of soldiers to oppose them.

"I knew that traitor would not simply have gone into Scotland," he spat at Abel Mostyn angrily. "He works his mischief by subterfuge and according to the interests of that devil's dam, Margaret Stanley. I have no doubt it is why he occupies Lathom House. It is a gesture of defiance."

"Cool yourself, young sir," advised ancient Mostyn. "You must consider the best course to take from here. As for your house, that is a great loss to you for sure, but a house can be rebuilt. There are those around here who will have suffered such losses that cannot be restored to them." He looked around at the dead servants.

"You are right, my friend," said Robert. "We should muster as many men as we can, just as we were going to do anyway for the king, then drive out this nest of vipers."

"Before then we must gather to ourselves an idea of how many we are dealing with and here is someone who might be able to tell us." As he spoke John Formby strode into the courtyard. The man was somewhat bedraggled and hatless.

"I thought we had seen the last of Scottish reavers this far south," he gasped. "They attacked my farm and fired it as they have here. My cattle and livestock have been driven off and all my seed corn stolen. Fortunately, we had warning of their attack – the pillaging of your manor was the means of that, and hid ourselves in the woods. My wife and my boys are trying to restore some order but I fear we shall sleep under the stars for a few nights."

"The rebels have departed then?" asked Robert.

"No, they are encamped around Lathom House, near Ormskirk, but will probably head back to Scotland with their plunder, raping, murdering and pillaging as they go. That is the usual pattern with such as they."

"I doubt that," said Robert. "If it were just the Scots, that might be so. Bray's purpose is to disrupt the country around here and thus disturb the king's Commission of Array. He is a powerful knight and would not stoop to mere banditry. Fighting men will not willingly leave their families and property undefended. Bray must be dealt with. His force might be small but its effect is out of proportion to its size."

"There is always the possibility he might manage to recruit disaffected nobles to his cause, then we would really be in trouble," offered Mostyn. Robert had not thought of that and considered it unlikely. The country hereabouts, however, was former Stanley territory and Sir Reginald Bray was Margaret Stanley's creature. Some might be tempted if not to join a rebellion, at least to stay out of it and deprive the king of vital support. Lord Stanley had encouraged that particular strategy and Bray had been complicit in it.

"The first thing to do is turn this enclosure into a camp where we can be relatively safe from further attack. The walls still remain as a defence and the place provides a rallying point for what fighting men we can find."

Ancient Mostyn nodded in agreement and set about with his men to get the dead away to burial outside. John Formby slapped a bare hand on the armoured spaulder over Robert's right shoulder.

"I shall get my two sons here along with my wife for safety. I cannot leave her alone at the farm and with the boys away it is too dangerous for any of us. Will and Gilbert owe the king service as archers and there are others around here that you can call on."

"Let us about it then," said Robert decisively. He ordered ancient Mostyn to clear up as best he could while he took two of his men to go along with John Formby. As the king's tenant at the Hall I'th Wood he had some authority to recruit men to England's cause and that was what he intended to do. For the moment he walked beside his mount with Formby until they reached the farm. The road there was clear and safe so he ordered goodwoman Formby off to the hall while he took her husband and sons with him to find some more men. He mounted his horse so as to give the appearance of martial confidence. He rode in full harness, armed with sword, dagger and a war axe at his saddle. He worried about how to arm his men. The reavers knew the value of iron weapons and farm implements and had taken these along with everything else of value they could plunder. John Formby was not so despondent and led Robert down a track by his farm to an outcrop of stone. He pulled back some dry bracken to reveal a wooden door that seemed to close off the entrance to a cave. Formby tugged at the door while Robert dismounted, alive with curiosity.

"One of our temporary stores," grunted Formby as he hauled the door open. Inside was a small vault of natural rock with an upward sloping floor that ensured it remained dry in wet weather. The place was empty of the smuggled goods it temporarily protected but there were three curtal axes – curved heavy swords having single edges, two hand axes and most importantly of all three long yew bows in good order and a tub of arrows. The strings for the long bows were in leather pouches laid on top of the arrows.

"A poachers hide too, I suspect," grinned Robert indicating he was not about to complain about the poaching of the local game.

"The arrow flights are distinctive and quite different to those we have at home," said John.

"So anyone finding wounded game with an arrow in its hide cannot identify the hunter?"

"Quite so. I hope I am not doing myself a disservice in revealing this to you, squire Robert?"

"Oh I think you understand enough about my involvement in the clandestine activities of the hall to know my mouth will remain tightly closed. Besides, in these times we never know when such secret stashes become useful. The present business is proof of that."

It was not long before Robert returned to the hall with a company of about thirty men. Some had longbows and the others a variety of farm implements that would double as weapons. Robert knew that iron bladed implements, though designed for peaceful agriculture could, in the right hands, become fearful weapons. Indeed, the armies of the king habitually contained levees composed of such and though vulnerable to armoured men-at-arms in open fight, were deadly in close combat and many a noble had met his end by the blade of a common English villain.

Later that day Robert was surprised by the arrival of a contingent of women. These were the wives and elder daughters of some of those who had joined his small martial band. Having nobody to protect them at their homes, they had come to join their men-folk and share in their fate. He had no idea what to do with them and worried that the increase demand upon whatever food resources they could muster might impair his fighting efficiency. There was nothing he could do about it for the moment and dare not order them away for fear their men would go with them.

He called over Bolly Gent, who he knew was adept at catching rabbits and small game. He ordered the lad to take the younger lads and girls and catch as many of the animals as he could, otherwise there would be scant feeding this eve. He had noticed that the nearby sand dunes were riddled with rabbit warrens.

The men got a fire going and retrieved a cooking pot from the wreck of the former kitchens and placed it over the flames. The women skinned and prepared the rabbits brought in by the youngsters and everyone there raised their noses as the smell of rabbit stew wafted through the compound. Robert looked about him with some feeling of satisfaction. He had mustered a small but determined force in the name of the king and managed to feed them. They had some arms, not of the best quality, but serviceable. The next task would be more difficult – that of expelling the Scots invader and getting the better of Sir Reginald Bray.

He turned and looked at the forlorn stack of the stone tower that had once been the principal strength of his manor. It stood stark black against a dark blue sky in the decaying light of day while a single rook fluttered at it uppermost walls as if it knew to reclaim an ancient habitation no longer relevant to mankind. One or two stars twinkled in the heavens, impassive as always. Sometimes he wondered if God had placed them there as a kind of mockery, stoical reminders that eternity obliterates all ambition and by their constancy declares human dreams to be impotent. The moon was risen - a pale orange disc with strange hieroglyphics upon its face. Had God scribed a message there, though no man could tell what that might be? He knew the moon had turned to blood when Christ was crucified and he wondered if its eerie colour now was a washed-out comment upon heaven's indifference to his fate.

* * *

Lathom House lay deceptively quiet, its walls bright under the moonlight shining down on its place within the encircling woods. Lord Stanley, secure in his tenure as England's most powerful magnate, had given small thought to the defensive difficulties of having a house in a clearing circled by forest. It had a moat with drawbridge and protective walls, but the surrounding trees might easily conceal an enemy whose numbers could not be defined. Robert would use this to his advantage, though if the knight, Sir Reginald Bray rode out with all his puissance, his men would have small chance of survival. Bray had thought of this and thus had stationed the bulk of his Scots outside the house, in the clearing, so that they could attack anyone approaching through the woods and give Sir Reginald an idea of his competition.

Lathom House had no legitimate master because the king had not allocated the house to a person of rank. It was almost as if he was reluctant to place a noble lord in a habitation that had been the centre of conspiracy against his throne. So it was that Lathom House retained a few servants and no lord to command it, until Sir Reginald Bray took it without, it would seem, any resistance. The servants should have closed the house, raised the drawbridge and waited for the king's men to come to their aid. The fact they had not done so testified to the direction of their loyalties. These were the residual servants of the Stanley family and had yet to concede the overwhelming victory of the king against his enemies.

"We must reduce the odds if we are to stand a chance against this lot," whispered ancient Mostyn. The soldier was lying on his belly with Robert beside him, looking between the trees over the camp of the Scots. They estimated there was about one hundred men or more against their thirty.

"They are careless," replied Robert. "Consider how we easily worked our way to within sight of the house." The two men, rather than clatter about the countryside for everyone to hear, had divested themselves of harness and wore their travelling clothes; plain brown doublet and hose under dark green riding mantles. The rest of their men were waiting in a grove nearby. In an adjacent pasture they could hear the sounds of the plundered cattle and horses. There were camp fires in the clearing that was the approach to the house. Most glowed a sombre red as the night deepened. A few remained bright and these, they concluded were being tended by the watch while the rest slept. They could see their farm wagons containing stolen grain and Robert hoped his men would not lose control and attempt to get them back. That would have to wait, but it did give him an idea.

"When there are reavers about folk tend to take precautions to protect their goods and stay close to defend their homes," muttered Mostyn. "With the real fighting men away at the king's command they probably think they are safe from attack. If we could get word to Liverpool, the garrison there might send some men, but even they are severely diminished."

"Penrith and Carlisle garrisons will have plenty of men but they await attack across the border by the Scots army along with, so we hear, French mercenaries. If they were to send us help, for all we know to weaken garrisons along the borders chasing reavers might be part of Bray's strategy. In any case, the presence of an armed force at their backs in England, though small, will provoke nerves and confuse matters. No, we must deal with this ourselves, and quickly. Most importantly, if we can destroy Sir Reginald Bray it will be a severe blow to the earl of Northumberland who, no doubt, is in league with Margaret Stanley and the French."

"You have a plan, squire Robert? We are greatly outnumbered and completely unable to take the house by storm."

"Let us turn their own tactics upon them," replied Robert while sidling back from the fringe of the woods overlooking the house.

The two men made their way back to where the rest of their men were waiting.

"Here is what we shall do," said Robert as he gathered the more able men around him. "From what I remember of the layout within the walls, the kitchens and stables are built along the south range. You archers will go with Will and Gilbert Formby and get yourselves within bowshot. You will use fire arrows to ignite the buildings. Wattle and daub lights up very nicely especially when there is a goodly supply of straw and kindling around, such as in a stables or beside a kitchen. The house has few to tackle a blaze so practically everyone in there will be forced to fight the fires. You will continue firing until the place is well alight. If you can manage to shoot into the house itself, so much the better. The walls are richly hung with arras as I remember. They have burned us out so we shall return the favour.

Robert could see that his men received this part of his plan with enthusiasm. "Before the fire attack, I want a dozen or so to get among the livestock and drive them off. Make sure you panic the beasts to make them run. If I understand the nature of Scottish reavers, they will think you are trying to retrieve them and chase after rather than lose their plunder. Once the beasts are away get yourselves back here. I am counting on the fact that Bray and his captains will be in the house and therefore unable to get them into some sort of order; the fire should hamper them in that respect. The remaining Scots, seeing their animal plunder being taken from them will probably form up close to the carts where the rest of it is stored. When the fire attack begins, some of them might break away in an attempt to attack the position of the archers and that is where some of you will be waiting. When you attack they will have no idea of your numbers, simply that there are fighting men on three fronts.

"As for the main action in front of the house, I shall lead that along with ancient Mostyn and his men," declared Robert. "We are mounted and once clad in our harness will further discomfit the reavers. The sight of steel clad mounted soldiers bearing down on them will be entirely unexpected and induce panic. We shall be among them before they know what is coming. Those of you with curtle axes and hand axes will run behind us and deal with those that manage to get out of the way of our charge. Everyone else will use his weapon as he knows best."

"Hopefully we can get the better of them, providing they are split into small groups and dealt with individually," ancient Mostyn informed them. "If we are unable to defeat them we can retire into the trees. At least they will be shocked by the unexpected attack and thus reduced unable to ride freely to further plunder our homes."

"There are a few armed men inside the house," said Robert, "but they will have no idea of the size of the force confronting them and their instinct will be to attempt to lock themselves in behind the walls until they can discover our numbers and our quality. If they do that, and once we have disposed of those outside the house, we shall have them."

"One more thing," growled ancient Mostyn. "Take no prisoners. Any that are merely wounded apply your knives to their throats."

* * *

Robert sat upon his horse waiting patiently for the fight to begin. The eagle tower stood tall at the centre of the house and if there were lookouts there they had seen nothing untoward. He could see the sleeping forms of Scots around their camp fires and one or two sentries stepping from one leg to the other and leaning on their staffs. Suddenly the quiet of the night was disturbed by a clattering and banging over by the pasture. The beasts began to move restlessly and dark shapes could be seen moving amongst them. The men had been told to prick the beasts with their daggers if they refused to run. Bellowing with the sudden pain, first one then more began to move. The men ran behind them thwacking them with switches cut from the woods. Soon the whole mass of them, cattle, oxen and horses were stampeding away into the darkness, their hind legs kicking at the tormenting devils that were running behind them.

The effect on the camp was immediate and entirely as predicted. Seeing their plunder galloping off across the countryside, and fooled into thinking a few villains were trying to get them back, the Scots began to scramble furiously after them. At first, rather more than expected gave chase but Robert saw that some of them had stopped and were looking back at the grain wagons. Then the fire arrows were unleashed on the other side of the house. Those Scots who were not away after the livestock came back and assembled in the centre of their camp. This was the moment for Robert and the main force to attack. Raising his sword above his head he cried out for his men to follow his charge. The Scots were treated to the sight of horsemen in full harness bursting from the trees and bearing down on them, while following were others running at them on foot. The reavers had small time to gather their wits, let alone their weapons before they were trampled on and put to the sword. Robert with ancient Mostyn by his side, was laying about him, either cutting or stabbing, but taking down the rebels. He had but sixteen men with him, yet already there was a greater number of their enemy lying dead or injured and the business had only just started.

It was not long before those Scots that had chased after the livestock, realising they were being attacked by a seriously armed force, returned to the clearing. Robert ordered the farmers to deal with those reavers still fighting while he and the horsemen drove into the returning Scots. He saw John Formby run up and cut down a huge Scot with his curtal axe before the man could get at his claymore, which was entangled in his cloak where he had been sleeping on the ground. Having had no warning and unable to form any sort of defence, the reavers were cut down or trampled while the farmers on foot, enraged at the pillaging of their homes, made short work of dispatching any still alive.

Soon the fighting slackened as the surviving Scots, unable to gain the sanctuary of the house, the bridge being raised, ran for the cover of the trees. Robert waved for Mostyn to join him in riding them down. One thing he could not afford was for a band of them to reform. As it was, barely a dozen reached the trees while the course of their rout could be identified by the dead and wounded they left behind.

As Robert turned, the sight that greeted him both thrilled and awed him. Lathom House was ablaze at one end and the flames were being blown by the light breeze towards the eagle tower, the oldest part of the former Stanley home. He knew the house was crammed with expensive hangings and furniture as this was an opulent house whose owner never expected to be attacked. Normally an army of servants, along with the baron's followers would be able to stifle any fire that started. As it was, the house was staffed by but a few old retainers whose main job was to protect the former Stanley property from plunder. Had they not done so, the place would have been bereft of that which now provided food for the flames. By the time they had mustered to fight the fires it was too late.

The archers returned, trotting into the clearing and gasping at the sight of the dead reavers. Robert had no idea how many armed men were in the house or their quality, except Bray was their chief while Robert's own men were still so few and no match for trained men-at-arms. Quickly he ordered them to withdraw into the woods and wait for him. Hopefully the house would have been too busy with the fire to take note of their actual numbers and the amount of dead they left behind might cause the enemy to think there were more of them than there actually was. Robert drew ancient Mostyn's mounted men up in a line at the fringe of the trees and placed himself at the front of them in the centre. Here was a visible band of steel and who across the way could know what lurked behind in the screen of trees, except it was likely to bring death to those remaining in the house.

Anyone standing behind the curtain walls of the house would look across a litter of dead reavers to see this band fronted by a solitary horseman clad in fine steel, reflecting blood red in the light of the leaping flames to supplement the real blood splattering his leg armour. Bray, he knew, would be regarding him now and wondering who he was and how many men he had with him.

The flames reached the eagle tower and soon the embrasures in its walls were leaping with gouts of flame. One of the floors had glass windows and these burst as the intensity of the fire behind them shot white flame into the air. Robert smiled with satisfaction. His own home had been treated thus and though it would have caused less of a sensation in its burning, yet it had been as valuable to him as this once powerful house was to Margaret Stanley. One thing was certain, whatever the future held, she would never live here again. A great crash rent the night air as the roof of the eagle tower fell inwards. As a child, his father had taken Robert to see a blast furnace operating in the Forest of Dean, where iron was extracted from stone. In front of him now was a similar sight, though much larger where the smoke above the house was lit red by the conflagration below. He almost thought he could see faces formed in the billowing smoke, devils that looked down smiling on what was for them familiar handiwork.

Sure enough, after a few minutes the drawbridge was lowered and a single mounted rider came out holding a white flag of parley. He walked his horse across the bridge and into the clearing, weaving a way slowly through the dead before coming to a stop a hundred yards or so from Robert's position. Beckoning ancient Mostyn forward, Robert gave him his orders.

"Ride over and see what this fellow has to say. On no account tell him who it is confronts him. I am known to Bray and would have him in ignorance of my identity. If you refer to me at all use the title *my lord*, presumptuous I know but it will instil a fear of authority that can only help us." Robert, in fact, knew that were Bray to discover a seventeen years old squire confronted him he might be persuaded to fight his way out with a good chance he would succeed.

"Rather say that if he surrenders, only then shall it be revealed who has defeated him. It is best to keep him in a state of uncertainty. Tell him we know his master is Sir Reginald Bray and here we are in the king's name. Sir Reginald can be assured he will face the king's justice. If there is any further resistance then he can remain within that ruined pile until it is taken by storm, and tell him to look around outside those walls to learn what that would mean for him and his men. My cry is Havoc! If he resists further I shall complete the work I have already brought down upon him."

Havoc, the cry that proclaimed no quarter would be given. That was a bluff, of course, but Robert needed to give the impression he had enough men with him to make storming the walls a practical proposition. Now the conflagration had spread to the rest of the house. Flames were leaping above what remained of the roof and a few shadowy figures could be made out along the curtain walls, silhouetted against the fiery backdrop. The fact the house had burned so furiously meant there were not enough people in there to contain it, and no help from the surrounding country either.

Ancient Mostyn saluted histrionically, playing the game to perfection. He trotted his horse over to the enemy horseman and the two engaged in animated conversation. Presently the two turned their horses and retraced their course, the enemy to the burning house and ancient Mostyn to Robert's side.

"The man was more concerned in discovering your identity than arranging a truce," he reported. "I gave him your message, which he will relay to Sir Reginald. He mentioned they are a body of men-at-arms, but as with us, gave no indication of numbers."

"Then let us stay awhile as we are. I want him to respond quickly before he has time to think and start hatching a plot to get away. The sight of us in martial order and ready to fight might provoke him into surrender. It is a small chance but until I know his real strength I cannot tell what to do next."

"It might also provoke a sudden attempt to escape, squire Robert," replied Mostyn. "In that case we could be in trouble, but let us not dwell on it."

Just then the horseman with the truce appeared again and once more ancient Mostyn went out to him while Robert sat aloof in lordly disdain. After a few moments the ancient returned while the horseman remained in place, clearly waiting for some sort of answer to whatever message he had delivered.

"Sir Reginald Bray challenges you to mortal combat!" he exclaimed worriedly. "He says that if you are slain then he is free to go, along with his men. If he is beaten then his men will surrender in the expectation of mercy."

15 - Settled In Blood

Robert felt his face drain of colour at the thought of mortal combat with a fully trained knight. Bray had fallen for his pose as a high noble; he would never condescend to issue a knightly challenge to anyone beneath the dignity of his rank. If he had known it was Robert de la Halle who confronted him, he would have laughed with contempt at a mere youth whom he had played games with in the past and recently condemned to hang, before manipulating his innocence in an attempt to dupe him into deflecting the pursuit of Henry Tudor. Robert now had the problem of how to deal with this new situation. Sir Reginald Bray had been a champion jouster, one of the finest in England. True he was now past his best years but that was likely to avail an opponent very little. He was battle honed and deadly in combat. He had survived and escaped the Battle of Bosworth when most of the Tudor knights were either killed or later captured.

It was unthinkable that a noble knight would refuse combat when challenged thus and should he do so, Bray would at once understand that the martial state of the men facing him, and that of their leader, was not as robust as he might have previously thought. He might well decide to fight his way out of the ruined house; indeed, he could hardly stay behind its curtain wall for long as the house behind it was descending into a glowing wreck within the crucible of its walls. Bray had no way of knowing what further help might be on the way to reinforce his attackers and though he could not know their true numbers, yet it must have been apparent to him they were relatively few.

In spite of his fully justified fears Robert began to wonder at his chances. All his training up to this time had been towards a moment like this, where he might contest with a man-at-arms unto death. Tales of chivalry and knightly duty had been all his education at Framlingham under the old duke of Norfolk and everything he believed in rebelled against declining Bray's challenge. His favourite reading had been from Sir Thomas Malory's book *Morte D'Arthur,* a gift of his father, where bold knights fought each other until one cried for quarter, except when the combat was specified as being to the death. He was not a knight, though, and realised the challenge was fraudulent in that Bray was unaware of his true identity, seeing only a man clad in the finest armour, the sort of harness only a high noble could afford. It was by the advantage of his father being the king's armourer, and thus his own, that had him clad so. His fellow squires had often tormented him about it, themselves sporting but plain and visibly poor harness that Bray would have immediately identified. He had thought himself clever in posing as a noble knight and completely overlooked the possibility that his subterfuge would result in a serious challenge to single combat.

Into his mind came the glorious spectacle of King Richard's charge against the Tudor position at Bosworth with just his few household knights. The king, though diminutive by comparison to his fellow knights, had seen an opportunity to defeat his foe and avoid severe casualties in his soldiers. Richard himself had brought down John Chaney, a jouster of the same stamp as Sir Reginald Bray then killed Tudor's standard bearer, William Brandon, also a champion jouster. Had it not been for the intervention of Sir William Stanley, no matter how well intentioned, he would have destroyed his enemy there and then. Could he do less than follow the example of the king he served? How might he hold up his head before his sovereign knowing that when tested he had proved unworthy?

The previous testing of his prowess with Sir Simon Hartshead on his way to Liverpool castle stiffened his resolve. That knight had taught him how a less experienced or disadvantaged man might overcome a more powerful opponent. It was all in the mind. Sir Simon had told him to assume an aspect of invulnerability, that there would, not should, which promoted doubt, but *would* be no question in his mind of defeat. At first Sir Simon had easily defeated him, but under his instruction Robert had finally managed to defend himself against the more experienced man. True, he had not managed to overcome him, but neither in the end had Sir Simon easily beaten him, as at their first encounter.

"Ancient Mostyn," said Robert with quiet resolve. "I am inclined to accept Bray's offer of combat."

"Are you sure?" gasped the soldier, his eyes wide with concern. "You do not have to do so. Simply reveal your identity and the man will decline to fight you, it being beneath his dignity."

"But then he will know we are few and not backed by strong authority. He and his followers will charge upon us and I would not wish to have you and our few men slaughtered as he makes his escape. That were ignominy indeed; to have so many deaths and the traitor freely abroad in the land to work against our king."

"I take your point, squire Robert, but you are likely to pay a high price for your chivalry and afterwards we shall be in no better case."

"But no worse case than that in which you already find yourselves. I see no other way forward from this impasse. Sir Reginald Bray, an old enemy of mine, my family and my king, has offered combat and I can do no other than accept. My mind is set upon it."

"Then take my sword," said Mostyn. It is a longsword. I *found* it on the field of Bosworth. You will not be able to make an impression with your own arming sword. Only the swing of a two-handed longsword has a chance against an armoured knight. Offer combat on foot and you might win through."

Robert considered the ancient's advice. Bray's armour was as fine as his, and no mere arming blade would make an impression upon it. The long heavy blade that Mostyn was offering might break apart the iron of his opponent if he could get a hard enough strike.

"Then get you to yonder fellow and tell him I shall fight on foot trusting in my sword to destroy the traitor and carry his head back to my king."

Mostyn grinned at Robert, his former doubts swept away by the excitement of the moment and the forthcoming combat. He might have advised against it, but now the soldier within him thrilled at the prospect of the contest. As Robert, he was burning with a passion to destroy his enemy. This was how he understood it should be, two strong men contesting with each other in a desperate cause and let God decide who was worthy of victory! It was the code of all soldiers, even those who fought for money, mercenaries without, it seemed, conscience; but even such as these thrilled at a battle between what everyone understood as being two principles – good and evil – a traitor and the champion of his king.

* * *

If Robert de la Halle had stopped to consider but for a moment that he was going into combat as the champion of his king, the responsibility might have unmanned him. As it was, he believed his victory would prevent the deaths of his own people, those who farmed the land in these parts and were innocent of the machinations of higher politics. Whether this lesser consideration would find favour with God he could not tell, but then time was not on the side of intellectual debate. Blood was what was at stake here and the matter between him and Sir Reginald Bray must be settled in it.

Ancient Abel Mostyn made a final check over Robert's harness, ensuring his helm, an armet, was strapped down properly and the rest of the armour adjusted to allow him a fluid freedom of movement. Mostyn's men remained mounted while those hidden in the trees came out to witness the combat. Robert placed the archers ready to fire upon anyone who might charge upon them both as an act of treachery or afterwards should he be beaten.

Striding out into the clearing before the smouldering house, with the longsword resting over his left shoulder, Robert hoped his aspect was confident enough to dispel any suspicion that he was not a knight, merely a squire. He stopped, and placing the point of the weapon into the ground stood patiently, his hands resting on the cross-guards. He offered a prayer to the Holy Virgin and also to Saint Adrian, his own patron. Finally he finished with a prayer that proclaimed him to be a warrior of Christ: *Beatus Omnipotensque Armati Christi*.

The gates beyond the drawbridge opened and Sir Reginald Bray strode out armed as Robert with a longsword. Six men-at-arms followed behind but these arranged themselves in a row just beyond the fringe of the moat while Sir Reginald came to a halt a few feet from the anonymous knight who had destroyed the house of his mistress, Margaret Stanley. He was fully harnessed, but unlike Robert, he had his visor raised to show his face. Robert dared not show his.

"Who are you, sir, that deigns not to show his face? Identify yourself," he barked. "I see you wear no livery." Bray slapped his chest where his own device was displayed on his surcoat: a sable fess surrounded by three eagle's legs on a field argent. "You know me, I think?"

"I come to destroy a traitor," came the muffled reply, "*à outrance pas à plaisance*." Robert described the terms of the tourney where *à plaisance* was a friendly combat while *à outrance* described a vicious fight to the death. He lifted his sword and took a stance with his legs apart and his blade angled upwards. Bray muttered what sounded like a curse and slammed down his visor before taking up his stance.

Robert kept telling himself to keep a cool head; he must fight with his brain as well as his muscle. His opponent was older, getting close to fifty years while he was bound to be more nimble and probably his equal in muscle power. The two men circled each other waiting to see who would attack first. This, Robert reasoned, was a crucial decision. If he attacked first then Bray would have an idea of the physical strength and speed of his challenger while Robert would still be ignorant of Bray's puissance. On the other hand, if he delayed too long, Bray might consider him the weaker man and thus gain an important mental advantage. He decided on a feint to get an idea of Bray's speed. He lunged at him with a trial blow. Bray, simply parried the stroke and remained stoically where he was.

A point to Bray then, here was a fighting knight who knew the importance of a first attaint and how it could tell much about an opponent. Robert also discovered that Bray was not easily intimidated. That meant his next attack must be in earnest or Bray's first opinion would be confirmed. At all cost he must keep his opponent guessing. Bray might be content to let Robert initiate the first few blows giving him valuable insight into his opponent's style and strength.

Robert's next attack would be a hard swipe at Bray's head. He knew what the response to that would be – to step forward under the blow and swipe at his body. Swinging the heavy sword around and down Bray stepped forward as expected, his sword already beginning its course at his body, but Robert changed his angle of attack, sweeping past Brays face and across throwing his sword clear and getting Bray off balance. The traitor took a couple of involuntary steps backwards while Robert, letting the circle of his sword continue brought his blade up and down with the intention of cleaving Bray's helm. His tactic was only foiled by Bray taking a quick jump backwards, unable for the moment to parry with his sword. That would unsettle him, thought Robert as he brought his sword back to the defence position.

Bray too stood at the defence, by his manner rather more cautious than before.

His mind moving fast, Robert immediately went into the attack raining blows at Bray that while easily parried, yet pushed him back as Robert drove at him in fury. Then suddenly he stopped and stood at the defence again. He had felt the strength of his opponent in his moves to parry each stroke and reckoned him to be his equal in power but not in speed. Bray, however, was obviously letting Robert attack in the expectation he would tire himself and thus slow down, whereupon Bray's opportunity to respond might succeed. Perhaps he could turn the tables on the older man and let *him* wear himself out? When Robert suddenly stopped his onslaught and took up the defence, it put Bray in an awkward position. Until this moment he had given ground, but would his martial pride let him continue thus? Robert was guessing that Bray, concerned with losing face before his own men, would now go on the attack. While Robert had gained some small advantage, Bray too had learned much about him, how he was obviously pitched against a young man whose speed was the greatest danger to him.

Years of combat, however, had taught the traitor knight a thing or two about fighting. As Robert predicted, Bray went into a hard and furious assault that had the young squire giving ground. Their blades rang loud in the clearing as they parried each other's strokes. Bray, having more experience than Robert managed a few strikes at his body armour, which so far, had stood up well. However, the younger man's speed served to keep him out of serious harm. Bray's surcoat was showing cuts and tears, which served to encourage Robert. If he could have seen his own harness he might not have been so confident. There was a great deal of difference between a mere tear in a linen surcoat and a dent in fine armour. Robert could not see what inroads he was making against Bray's iron while the battering his own was taking was all too apparent to the observers.

They had been fighting hard for some time when, by mutual agreement that only fighting men understood, they stopped and leant on their swords to rest.

"You fight well, young sir," panted Bray, raising his visor.

Robert ardently wished he could raise his to get some cold air into his lungs. His felt his face was flushed red, glowing with effort made worse by the confines of his armet. Yet he dare not let Bray know his identity. Apart from considerations of rank, the knowledge he was confronting a mere youth, a squire he thought to be hapless and clumsy, would give him a mental advantage that might make all the difference. Robert, to keep Sir Simon Hartshead's lesson in mind to believe in his own invulnerability, maintained by subterfuge the mindset of a noble knight. Bray's opprobrium on discovery of his true identity would destroy his confidence in himself and might well lose him the fight. Bray, on the other hand, in ignorance could well be discomfited by uncertainty as to the rank of the man he was fighting. It might be somebody with a name he would not like to destroy. All he knew was that here was a man who could possibly get the better of him, and to his mind that meant someone of high birth.

"I have right on my side, Sir Reginald," he replied, trying hard not to give an indication of his discomfort. "I fight for my anointed king and thus God will decide the justice of my cause. You need only know your inevitable fate is the death of a traitor, whatever the result of our present encounter."

"As for my predicted death as a traitor," said Bray, "I thank you for relieving me of any anxiety in that respect. Yet I find I am in no hurry to stand before the final judge, even though I expect to clear my name on that day. I believe it will not be long ere Dickon is deprived of his stolen throne and then I shall be redeemed."

Robert felt the anger rise within him at Bray's remarks but the voice of Sir Simon in his ear calmed him. *Remember the first principle is to think and fight. Once fury gets a grip, while it might fit you well in the heat of a battle, when combating a single and determined foe it will do you no good."*

"There is no more we can say to each other, Sir Reginald. Let us set to again and this time there will be no quarter."

"Brave words, young sir," responded the traitor. "They shall be poor meat when I make you eat them."

Thinking he might take his anonymous opponent by surprise, Sir Reginald leapt forward, his sword aiming for Robert's helm. It was all the young squire could do to duck out of the way. Even then the tip of the blade scraped across his steel armet. Robert struck back even faster and for a moment Sir Reginald gave ground. The two exchanged blows and while Sir Reginald was battle hardened, yet he found himself unable to get the better of his foe who always managed to avoid his more deadly blows. Robert, for his part, was at once encouraged and frustrated by his inability to get in a decisive strike, one that would either incapacitate his enemy or at least slow him. He kept recalling Sir Simon's words advising him never to lose concentration either through fear or false exuberance. But now there was another difficulty. His breathing was becoming laboured not due to lack of physical fitness, but lack of air. His visor, essential to protect his face and in this case obscure his identity was causing his face to glow hot. Sweat was running down from his brow and he unable to wipe it from his eyes; the problem was getting serious.

A visor restricted vision, which was not too much of a problem when fighting a single foe in the same condition. In battle, it was essential to avoid an arrow in the face, or a pike thrust, but now his eyes were in danger of the stinging effects of his sweat. Again Sir Reginald tried for his head and though he managed to move out of the way, yet the traitor knight did manage a glancing blow. That was entirely due to Robert pausing to shake his head in a vain attempt to clear the sweat running into his eyes.

Now Sir Reginald, sensing there was something wrong with his adversary, began increasing his blows, his blade slashing and cutting at Robert who was only saved from serious injury by his armour. How long his harness would stand up to the pounding it was taking he hardly knew, but it could not go on this way for long. There was only one thing for it. If he were to come back into the combat with a fighting chance, he would have to get his visor open if only to get his breath. The decision to do so was confirmed by Sir Reginald who was having the same problem and had lifted his.

Indeed, Bray now had a real advantage due to his vision being clearer, which helped him judge where Robert's next attack would come.

Bray was now circling his foe, crouched and ready to spring. Robert took the opportunity to raise his visor and wrench it from its clasps. Throwing it to one side he at once felt refreshed. He shook his head to clear the sweat from his eyes, while the heat of his face dissipated in the cool air. The effect on Bray was as if he had been struck by lightening. It was a few moments before realisation as to whom the familiar face belonged and his features twisted in fury.

"You!" he spat. "A churlish boy not yet a man and no knight nor ever shall be. You are a false dissembler that dares challenge one whose rank you can never aspire to."

"Yet I have the better of you," responded Robert.

"You fooled me into thinking you were of noble blood otherwise I should have dispatched you in a moment. No more the niceties of chivalric combat, I shall finish this now!"

With a sound something between a snarl and a scream, Sir Reginald Bray launched himself at Robert. At first Robert gave ground. It was apparent that Bray had lost control of himself in his anger and humiliation at having contested with a mere squire and unable to best him in front of his men. The squire soon realised he could tell where Bray's blows would strike next and easily parried them. He laughed at one particular thrust, deliberately enraging Bray to a state of incandescence. Next Robert began to taunt him.

"Come on old fellow, I have some words to eat, remember. Feed them to me if you can." He blocked a thrust towards his face then followed up by flicking his blade in Bray's face, which caused him to step back. In a flash Robert was on him. Bray, exhausted by the combat and the toll taken on his strength expended by his fury staggered back. Robert thrust his longsword between Bray's legs and shoved a shoulder into his chest. Bray tripped and crashed to the ground, his arms splayed out. Before he could gather his wits, Robert was over him and without a single thought, plunged his sword into Bray's face, driving the point through his skull and the back of his helm until it embedded itself into the ground. He could feel through the steel the tremor of Bray's life departing his body. He tugged at the blade but found it would not come free. He placed his foot on the dead man's throat and hauling by the cross guards, managed to pull it out.

Robert looked to where Bray's men were laying their swords on the ground in surrender. The cries he heard, but could not at first identify, were coming from the throats of his men as they surged forward to congratulate him. It was not the shouts of acclamation that dominated Robert's mind at that moment; rather it was the words of Sir Simon Hartshead. Sir Reginald Bray had lost the fight because in his pride he had forgotten those first principles he would have taken to heart at the beginning of his career – never lose control when in single combat with a deadlier foe. Robert, at the start of his career still had that fresh in his mind. A sound of thunder reverberated across the clearing. The walls of the house were collapsing inward while flame, and sparks of red-hot ash shot skywards. Were those ashes conveying Bray's spirit towards purgatory, Robert wondered, or was his soul destined to plunge straight into the smouldering fires of Hell below?

* * *

The roads south into England were crowded with men returning from the great battle that had been fought by the English under the command of the duke of Norfolk against Scottish and French forces somewhere just north of Alnwick. Robert and ancient Mostyn questioned those they met and though the reports were garbled and overblown by braggarts and men wondering if their plunder was in danger, it seemed there had been a severe defeat for the enemy forces. Here they were with Abel Mostyn's troop of six, along with the Formby boys and the rest of the archers, ten of them, intending to join the king's army and it looked as if it was all over.

"We must find someone with authority to discover the true nature of events," said Robert. "I would not return the archers to their homes in case they are still required."

"Yes, the words of men returning from battle cannot be relied on," replied Mostyn. "There are many examples of false report. I remember after the Battle of Barnet, certain of King Edward's men that had fled the battle prematurely, rode into London proclaiming all was lost when, in fact, the king had won."

"We are close to Pontefract, I think. The road to London is not far off."

"I wonder if the king himself might linger at Pontefract?" said Mostyn. "His father, Richard of York and his brother Edmund were interred in the Priory near there after their deaths at the Battle of Wakefield back in the year fourteen sixty. I know they now rest at Fotheringhay, having been re-interred there by King Edward, but the Priory did care properly for the duke's body, less the head of course."

"I wonder if the head was ever recovered?" mused Robert. "All I remember from my lessons is that it was displayed above a gate in York wearing a paper crown."

"I have no idea," replied Mostyn. "I think I can see the castle of Pontefract in the distance. We should head there in any case and find out what the actual situation is."

Robert looked out across the Yorkshire landscape to where the white gleam of the castle could be made out below a tumble of low, pale grey cloud. The weather was turning cold and already a damp chill swept across the land and trees were showing the first signs of autumn. Hopefully, the king's victory had been conclusive. It was miserable indeed campaigning during the onset of winter.

Their display of Yorkist colours on their surcoats and the badge of St. George newly adopted by King Richard gained them pass at the outer and inner gates of the castle. As they trotted along the road bridge between the two gatehouses they marvelled at the power of the great donjon to their left, towering skywards and unusually thrusting out from the curtain walls rather than standing wholly within them. Robert had seen an almost similar donjon at York, though that was in the centre of the castle there, not part of the walls as at Pontefract. He knew that one Roger de Clifford was executed and hung in chains from the York donjon. It served York as an exchequer, royal mint and a goal. He had been to that city as a child with his father and mother and remembered being impressed by the recently completed Minster. The magnificent cathedral dominated even the castle and was rival to any in the whole of Christendom.

Crossing the outer bailey, their passage beyond the inner gatehouse and into the upper bailey met with some resistance. It was ancient Mostyn, using his authority as a captain in the house of Sir Ralph de Assheton, who got them through. Fortunately it was Sir Ralph who was presently in command at the castle, the king having hurried on towards London eager to greet his newborn son and heir, the coming into the world of whom being the dominant topic of conversation at the castle along with the recent battle. The lord bastard John had gone with the king; so too had the duke of Norfolk, leaving Sir Ralph to deal with the aftermath of war.

Entering the inner bailey, Robert and Abel Mostyn left their horses and men with the castle ostlers and farriers while commanding the archers to stay together while arrangements were made for their needs. Sir Ralph de Assheton was in the great hall within the Royal Apartments of the castle and that was where they directed their steps. There was a good number of soldiery in the great hall, most of them clamouring for some sort of remuneration for their part in the battle. Sir Ralph was at the high table with a bevy of clerics busily sorting through the lists of dead and wounded so he could give a final account to the king. It was with some relief that Sir Ralph noticed the return of his ancient and used it as an excuse to dismiss those petitioners vying for attention. He turned to one of his attendant knights and instructed him to carry on with the task while he had the report of his ancient, Abel Mostyn.

Robert and Abel Mostyn knelt before Sir Ralph in his privy chamber, who got them to their feet and immediately asked for their story. Abel Mostyn told how they had come across a party of Scots raiding into west Lancashire and attempting to divert the king's forces there. When they discovered Sir Reginald Bray was with them, they understood that he was there to foment rebellion among discontented Lancastrians in the region, either to directly turn against the king, or to keep themselves and their vassals out of the conflict and thus sow confusion and deprive King Richard of much needed men. He was particularly descriptive when it came to Robert's fight with Sir Reginald and the manner of the traitor knight's death. Afterwards they were surprised that so few men were in Lathom House and they surrendered after Sir Reginald Bray was slain. All were prisoners incarcerated in Liverpool Castle.

Sir Ralph gasped when his ancient told him of the challenge to single combat with squire Robert and was incredulous that a noble would issue such a challenge to a mere youthful squire of no rank. Mostyn explained the subterfuge and although Sir Ralph was clearly perturbed by it, yet he was relieved that Bray was removed permanently and could no longer work his treason against King Richard's crown.

"Bray is but one of many traitors who have departed this world and are now lingering in Purgatory," growled Sir Ralph. "Northumberland is slain along with the Scottish King James. We have their king's young son a prisoner and more than half the Scottish nobles dead or injured. The French mercenaries are mostly slain and at sea the French fleet, which was bringing more mercenaries into Scotland, is defeated such that they will not think to attempt an invasion from the north again. France had schemed to use the Auld Alliance with Scotland against England to divert us while they deal with the problems they have in their own lands. They will not do so again."

"So the earl of Northumberland actually joined with the Scots and the French against King Richard?" Robert had never been entirely convinced that Northumberland would turn traitor in that way; rather he thought the earl would merely stay out of any conflict as he did at Bosworth.

"Yes, the whole thing was a fiasco. He attempted to raise an army from his vassals, but they mostly refused to rebel against their king, in fact they joined us in great number. Many were still smarting at the ignominy of staying out of battle at Bosworth and, in any case, prefer the rule of King Richard to that of their liege lord. Henry Percy was expecting to compensate his loss by obtaining discontented men from across the north of England and it sounds as if Bray was a part of that."

"We believe that is why he had landed in the former Stanley lands in Lancashire," said Robert, "hoping the residual influence of that particular lord and his lady, dame Margaret, still plotting in France, might raise men against their king. Is the king well? I take it he has taken no injury in battle, Sir Ralph."

"For once he kept out of the fight," answered the knight. "He says little but I think he is troubled with pain in his back. His grace has difficulty mounting his horse and has taken to using a mounting block. The duke of Norfolk, your liege lord squire Robert, led the vanguard while viscount Lovell had command of the left wing and I had the right wing. The lord bastard, John of Pomfret commanded the reserve, which were also committed later in the fight and did good execution among the highlanders. The enemy had the advantage of high ground when we came upon them, so my lord of Norfolk made a forced march around and attacked from their rear. The Scottish and French guns were all pointing south while we managed to get ours into action and destroy theirs before they could turn and deploy them."

"That is unusual, a gun battle," put in Mostyn. "Usually it is the archers that bring down the enemy in large numbers."

"It was so in this case," replied Sir Ralph. "The highlanders charged at us along with King James and were destroyed by our archers. They thought our lesser numbers would be overwhelmed, but they became bogged down in the ground between and stood little chance. That is where King James, the third of that nation died along with many of his nobles. At the end it became a debacle. The border reavers on both sides, English and Scots began plundering the battlefield while the rest of the rebels tried to flee. Many were cut down in the rout and there is much grieving among new made widows in Scotland."

"The queen is well?" asked Robert expectantly. He exulted in the knowledge that Claris would be released with the queen when she eventually came out of confinement. Forty days was the term and he wondered how many days had already passed.

If he could get himself to London and the Court, she might be free about the same time as he arrived there.

"News came some days ago – we have a Prince, which was another reason the king kept out of battle. He would not risk his life now that he has an heir. He must live until the boy is grown if England is to be secure in its future monarch. His grace is overcome with double joy. He has won two victories – one over his enemies and one against the malign fate that robbed him of his first heir."

"And the queen," Robert repeated.

"She is said to be well, God be praised. Apparently the birth was easier than might have been expected, given the age of her grace. At last heaven shines upon us."

"Then, my lord, you will be returning to Court very soon?" Robert was hopeful that he would accompany Sir Ralph to London.

"Not for a few weeks yet. There is work to be done here accounting for our losses. War is costly and the king must know the state of his exchequer. Now that you are here you may attend upon me. I need to send out prickers to keep order on the roads where armed men are returning to their homes and liable to plunder the land as they go. You will take my ancient Mostyn with you on patrol to keep the king's peace."

"Very good, my lord," replied Robert attempting to keep disappointment out of his tone.

* * *

"I thought I might never return to London," said Robert joyfully as he embraced Claris. They were standing beside a bay window in a corridor leading from the queen's apartments at Windsor Castle. The late autumn sunshine illuminated her that she might almost be a fairy nymph in her green dress where the voile wrapping around her headdress drifted about her face as mist in a sacred glen. He held her at arms length and gazed into her eyes. "Sir Ralph de Assheton had me patrolling most of Yorkshire to little effect. We slapped some heads and shoulders with the flats of our swords occasionally, but there was no fighting to be done, merely a few felons to be hanged. England is restored to peace now."

"God be praised there was no fighting," cried Claris, her face showing stern disapproval. "I suppose you now disdain combat with mere villains after engaging in single and mortal combat with one of the most powerful knights that England has produced."

"Ah, you have heard of that. The fellow was elderly and it was no particular feat to get the better of him." He released her and grinned, hoping that would assuage her obvious concern by making light of the exploit. "Besides, he was a traitor and everyone knows that God guides the sword of any that fight against such as Bray."

"Yours is not the story I have heard," she replied, unconvinced by his manner. "Indeed, I hear the king is to speak to you about it."

"I have been summoned to court, that's true," he said brightly. "But in the company of Sir Ralph. No doubt his grace wants to be assured all is well in the country and I can inform him that Lancashire is loyal in spite of a large part of it once being Stanley demesnes."

"You must interrogate ancient Mostyn and his men. They have a different version of what happened between you and Sir Reginald Bray."

Claris frowned up at him. When she first heard the story that was going around, embroidered by Abel Mostyn's men, how Robert de la Halle had challenged Sir Reginald Bray to mortal combat and after a long and hard fight, finally struck him down, she almost fainted. The story had improved in the telling, with no mention of the part about the subterfuge where Sir Reginald was duped into believing he was facing a noble knight, not a youthful squire. Assured that Robert lived and had no serious hurt, she had been torn between the horror of what might have been his death and the frisson of pleasure brought by being the wife of a squire famed for his martial prowess. The queen's ladies were green with envy and she would have to watch one or two of them should they manage to manouvre themselves anywhere close to her husband.

"How is her grace the queen?" he asked, anxious to change the subject.

"In good health and spirits. She came through the ordeal of childbirth easily to everyone's surprise, which was a blessing. The infant Prince Richard is a lusty babe which augers well for the future. The king has had the babe's horoscope cast and it appears the prince can look forward to a long life."

"I expect there will be another pregnancy soon," he mused. "A healthy heir is wonderful news, but the tenuous hold that any infant has on life cannot guarantee his survival to adulthood never mind what his horoscope tells us."

"Yes, such predictions are notoriously deviant. I hear another prince is predicted, but the next child might just as well be a princess, that is if there is another. Matters of conception are not certain." She looked at him with eyes that had suddenly become a soft brown. "I have yet to conceive and it is not for want of trying. We almost wore ourselves out in the few days before you left for

Lancashire. I wonder that you had the strength for combat."

"I think, my love, that God must have plans for us, otherwise I would not have triumphed in my fight with Sir Reginald. Perhaps the delay is due to us having no home, our manor house being burned out."

"We shall rebuild it," she declared resolutely.

"I am to attend upon Sir Ralph after the noon bell along with my lord John of Pomfret. In a few days, the king is to remove to Westminster where there is to be a gathering of parliament. We can take a chamber at one of the better inns here at Windsor until then. Afterwards, when in London, we can move to my grandfather's house. I hope to have some news regarding the business venture he arranged for me in Portugal. With luck we shall have enough money to begin rebuilding our manor house."

The corridor in which they were standing was busy with servants scurrying to and fro. Nobody paid them any attention, it being common for men and women to meet anywhere there was a niche or corner where they could pursue their amours with some small discretion. Standing in full daylight, all that passed was conversation. Things were rather different at night when the same niches were obscured by darkness. They withdrew further into the recess of the bay window as a dozen or so nuns trooped past, their faces obscured by the style of their white wimples, these being folded into cornettes to which black veils were pinned.

"That would have been her grace the queen's fate had she not married our king," said Robert as though the idea was somehow repugnant.

"Her grace would have taken the veil gladly had it not been for her being a Princess of the House of Avis, and thus an object of diplomacy." returned Claris. "She is still favoured by the people of her native land who refer to her as their Holy Princess. I had considered the life myself, there being little choice for a woman with no dowry and therefore no prospects of a decent marriage. If it had not been for meeting you, I might have passed by just now in that company and we two never knowing each other."

Robert gave an involuntary shudder at the thought. "I cannot imagine you as a nun," he laughed at last. "You are simply not cut from that dark cloth." He nodded towards the nuns as they disappeared through the doors into the queen's apartments.

"They are as shadows of another life," she mused, "just as phantoms are and we all may end thus."

"Your thoughts are dark as the tunics of those women. It is almost as if the shadow of death had graciously passed to allow us a few more years of respite to love in before our inevitable plunge into eternity. Let us get into the great hall. Everything is bright with colour there, with no grey thoughts to trouble us."

It was but a few days before the celebration of the Christ Mass in the year fourteen eighty-eight and the highest in the land were at Windsor in the expectation of a great celebration. And there was much to celebrate. King Richard with his queen, Joanna had produced a male heir to the throne of England. The last of the rebels had been defeated and the only enemy that remained to England, France, sulked mightily across the narrow seas. Indeed, France now had much to think on as King Charles was embroiled in disputes with Italy, Spain, Brittany and Burgundy each of which countries, amalgamating in a Holy League under the Holy Roman Emperor, was looking to England to join them against his ambition. After the recent invasion from Scotland, that was something King Richard was more than willing to contemplate.

Robert and Claris entered the great hall arm in arm. Robert had to break away to join the lord bastard, John of Pomfret and the Vice Constable of England, Sir Ralph Assheton. These lords had nothing to say to the young squire, but kept him close along with their other followers. Looking around he saw his father was there, not far from the king who was sitting on one of a pair of regal seats underneath a canopy displaying the royal arms of England and France, the land to which the king claimed sovereignty. Queen Joanna was sitting on the other listening attentively to the Archbishop of York who had his clerics and a few nuns standing in close attendance. Claris was there too, with the queen's ladies. The duke of Norfolk, Thomas Howard, had the king all to himself at the moment and Sir William Stanley was standing in the monarch's line of sight, as always, desperate to be noticed and ever ready to push forward at the slightest excuse.

"Sir Terpsichore looks as if he is at a dance," chuckled John Biggar who had joined Robert among the throng of squires and followers of the nobles. "See how he skips about whenever a courtier moves to block his view of His Grace. His footwork is admirable."

"I hear he acquitted himself well in the recent battle," said Robert. "No doubt he will consider himself now to be in a better position to seek favour. His behaviour at the Battle of Bosworth has not turned out quite as he hoped. The King told him his decision to involve himself was rather late in coming and the confusion it caused nearly cost him the victory, perhaps even his life."

"Some say he was coming to the aid of the Tudor," replied John Biggar quietly.

"It serves him right for prevaricating in the days before the battle. He could not have ordered his men to attack their king no matter what his own intent, so we can discount those sorts of rumour as being merely mischief."

"Give you good den, brother."

Robert turned to the speaker, Anselm Salgado who was carrying the strange stringed instrument he called a *vihuela de mano*. Of greater surprise was the woman he had in his company.

"Maud Mudd!" exclaimed Robert. "What are you doing here?" Robert knew the huge woman with the large bright face from the forge at Windsor Castle; she was his father's preferred labourer when he worked there. In fact, recently she had been closeted in his father's private forge where he fashioned the king's harness so she was highly trusted. Even Robert had no idea why his father worked so secretly. She was dressed in a plain but decent gown and was glowing, no doubt from the application of a stiff brush to shift the forge grime from her hands and face.

"I be workin' for master Anselm here," she informed him. "Just for t'day."

"Aye," said Anselm fondly. "I am to play on the organ for the king and queen, and mistress Maud is to pump the bellows for me – a lighter task, so she tells me, than her usual work in the forge."

"Then why are you porting that instrument?" Robert tapped the sounding board with his finger.

"Her grace the queen has asked me to play it for the king. It is a new instrument, popular in Spain and Portugal but new to the English ear. I consider it particularly fine when used to serenade a lady. I would teach you a few chords but as you have already won my sister's heart it would be pointless labour."

Anselm was clad in a white linen shirt with a varicoloured silken cord sewn around the neck. His doublet, open in casual disorder to proclaim his bohemian nature, was pale blue with yellow showing through the slashes in the sleeve; his hose was striped brown and yellow. Bare-headed, he wore his dark-brown hair longer than the fashion with coloured ribbon braided here and there while golden rings were fixed somehow to the lobes of his ears.

Suddenly the gathering was distracted by the sound of clarions and all attention was drawn to the doors at the entrance to the great hall. Liveried servants opened the massive carved oak doors and a troop of courtiers entered followed by a regal-looking woman accompanied by a richly clad youth who, by his bearing was of high noble blood.

"Who is this?" wondered Robert aloud.

"Ah yes, I forgot you have only just arrived at court," said John Biggar. "Here is the duchess of Burgundy, the king's sister, Margaret. The youth with her surely you recognise?"

"I seem to find something familiar . . . Is it Richard of York?"

"Indeed he is, though he is now Richard of Tournai, come to make peace with his uncle we are told, yet seeing as the youth was bastardised and thus removed from the line of succession then I would not be surprised if he harbours resentment. Were it not for *Titulus Regius*, the document agreed by parliament that proclaimed him and his brother bastards, he would be the rightful King of England."

"I remember impersonating him some years ago when we got him secretly out of the Tower of London to prevent him being murdered by the Tudor faction," recalled Robert. "That was shortly after his brother Edward died, having never recovered from the malady that afflicted him before he entered the royal apartments in the Tower. Prince Richard dyed his hair to my colour so we could switch identities, he being fair as we see him now."

"So that was how it was done," gasped John Biggar, his curiosity satisfied at last. "A simple substitution."

"Yes, I went into the prince's chamber with my father, who was pretending to measure him for harness. We dyed his fair hair black as mine then he left with my father leaving me behind. Everyone knew the prince was fair and so, seeing but a dark-haired boy the same as had gone in with the prince's armourer, nobody bothered them and they simply left quietly together. Some days later, nobody being the wiser, my father returned, ostensibly for another fitting and after an interval where the guard was changed, left with me. The new guard who recognised me assumed I had gone in there with my father, so I departed, leaving behind a chamber with just the prince's two former attendants. It was weeks before anyone realised for sure Prince Richard was no longer there."

"I am amazed that the subterfuge worked so well," said John. "And here he is, having spent the last few years in exile under the name of Perkin Osbeck, a boatman's son at Tournai. I hear the duchess is petitioning King Richard, her brother, for help in combating French ambitions regarding Burgundy. Her step-son Philip is now duke of Burgundy and France is claiming suzerainty over those lands. Her idea is to recruit an English army under the command of this youth to join with King Richard in an invasion of

France. That way the lad can be allotted captured French territory and thus be recompensed for the loss of his legitimacy."

Robert thought the idea had merit. "It seems a sound strategy for the king. It removes, or at least diminishes the possibility of another bastard claimant to his throne raising an army against him."

"Which leaves another free to pursue his ambition here in England." John Biggar looked over to where the earl of Lincoln, John de la Pole was chatting to viscount Lovell.

"You think Lincoln has aspirations for his own elevation to the throne?" Robert was shocked at the suggestion but not, in his heart surprised. Recent years had shown that anyone with a tenuous claim to the throne of England might make a play for it. Henry Tudor had educated everyone in that respect and monarchs everywhere in Europe were beginning to become wary of those nobles closest to them. Take, for instance, the queen's brother, João the Second of Portugal. He had to deal with the treason of the duke of Braganza, a powerful magnate who thought he could take the crown off the rightful king. In England, uncertainty regarding the sanctity of the crown began when King Edward the Third deposed his own father, Edward the Second and began the present Plantagenet dynasty, descending from the House of York. Then there was the Lancastrian Henry Bolinbroke, who usurped the throne to become Henry the Fourth by deposing King Richard the Second. It was the weakness of King Henry the Sixth that provoked the latter wars, restoring the fortunes of York when Edward the Fourth deposed King Henry giving England a Yorkist monarch again. King Richard the Third is about the only one of them all whom it could truly be said has legitimately inherited England's crown.

John Biggar held up his right hand. "Just look at possible contenders. He looked around to ensure nobody was listening to their conversation. It was treason to talk about the deposition of a monarch. "The earl of Lincoln was King Richard's heir presumptive before Bosworth. That became defunct when the king won and survived the battle, more so now he has a legitimate heir. How does the promise of monarchy that is then snatched away affect ambition?" He ticked off a finger. "Then there is that fellow over there with duchess Margaret. Were it not for his bastardy, he would be the rightful king." He ticked off another finger. "The youth Edward, earl of Warwick is another. He is no bastard but is barred by his father's attainder, no fault of his. Of legitimate Plantagenet blood, he would stand before the other two if that attainder were removed." He ticked off a third finger. "Finally we have the lord bastard John of Pomfret. He is King Richard's natural son but not legitimate, which is a legal bar but not necessarily a definite one if, like King Edward the Fourth, whose own paternity was unsure, he can take the throne by force. That is what Henry Tudor was about, after all." He ticked off a fourth finger. "Past monarchs have had to deal with but one contender at a time, and most of those succeeded in dethroning them. Here we have four who can, with some justification, make a claim sufficiently robust to garner support if the political situation can be manipulated to allow it."

"Then the survival of the newborn prince is even more precarious," mused Robert. "I had thought the dangers of disease worse enough – now we must consider a host of possible usurpers such as no English king has ever had to deal with."

"His Grace is aware of it and that is why he was content to let the duke of Norfolk command in the battle with the French and Scots. If the king were to take a mortal wound, which of these could be trusted to bring up safely his infant prince and assure his right to the throne? The king's brothers, George of Clarence and King Edward are gone so, apart from the new babe, he is the last of the royal house. We would be back to the situation that started the dynastic wars between the houses of York and Lancaster. Henry the Sixth was but a few months old when his father died and a regency had to be formed, which started the whole sorry business."

"I believe that is why Sir William Stanley lacks the rewards he expected," said Robert. "The king has not promoted any of his followers to anything like the power that the lords Thomas Stanley and the earl of Northumberland once enjoyed. He has spread his awards sparingly among his high nobles and rather more generously among a host of lesser ones – none have the capability of raising a force that might threaten his throne."

"But there are many in the lower orders who have reason to be grateful to their king," muttered John Biggar conspiratorially. "That might help preserve the peace; however, the higher nobility might well become persuaded that deposing this king might earn them the rewards they crave from a grateful usurper who would be indebted to them. Henry Tudor's policy again."

"Curse the man!" spat Robert. "His malignancy continues to plague the Crown of England even from the grave. Truly I believe he was a creature of Satan and the mother who bore him a witch."

The two squires crossed themselves and turned to face the dais where the king was beckoning for Sir Ralph de Assheton to approach him. He spoke to the knight who looked around searching the crowd until his glance fell upon Robert. He pointed at him, then by a gesture, commanded him to come forward into the royal presence. As Robert walked somewhat apprehensively towards the king and queen, Thomas Howard stepped down from the dais and stood next to Sir Ralph. Robert swept the queen what he hoped was an elegant bow then went down on his knees and looked up at King Richard. The king returned his gaze plainly with no hint of what the summons was about.

"Sir Ralph de Assheton," intoned the king, never taking his eyes from Robert's face, "I understand this squire had the temerity to challenge a noble knight to single combat."

"It is true, your grace." Sir Ralph fixed Robert with a steely glare that chilled him to the core.

"Of course, such a condition could not arise except for a deception," continued the king. "Had Sir Reginald Bray known he was facing a mere stripling as we have before us, he would never have consented to the contest. It is a slight upon the laws of chivalry and we expect the instruction a squire is given would have taught him that. His education was at first your responsibility, Norfolk, was it not?"

"It was, your grace," replied the duke, "and my blessed father's before. I can assure your grace that all the chivalric protocols were beaten into him, as indeed with all those who come to train in my household."

"We doubt you not. It is the case everywhere." The king paused as if wondering what punishment to bring down upon the unfortunate squire's head. Robert understood that the laws of chivalry were inviolable and he had seen enough courts martial to know that there was no defence that could be offered against violation. He was entirely at the king's mercy, a soldier king who had instituted the College of Heralds and sternly resolute in attending to matters of knightly protocols, as his brother King Edward had been before him. "I wonder what you can say for yourself?" The king said at last.

"Dread king," began Robert tremulously, hoping that the king's words were in the nature of an invitation to speak. "I only saw before me your grace's pernicious and treacherous enemy who was determined to interfere with your commission of array and spoil the gathering of men to your army."

"Truly the man was a bitter enemy of ours and though we are pleased to have him out of this world, yet you issued him with a challenge that you know full well you do not have the rank for."

"Your grace, it was Sir Reginald who issued the challenge, I merely responded to it. Of course I understood he would not fight if he knew my identity. As your grace might remember, I am known to him."

"We remember right well," replied the king. "Knowing your previous history with him, what made you think you might overcome him? A traitor he might have been, but he was still a noble knight and battle hardened, too."

"I felt I had to do something to stop him getting further into England. I had no idea what mischief he was planning against your throne. He mistook me for a noble knight due to the condition of my harness, which was made for me by my father, your grace's own armourer, and thus of high quality, as is all his work."

"Yes, yes, this is not the time to promote your family business, squire Robert," snapped the king. "I hear you did not disabuse him of his error?"

"I did not, your grace. I confess that I deliberately concealed my identity from him. I did not know how many men he had with him in Lathom House . . ."

"A property that had devolved to the Crown and which you burned to the ground, but do go on."

Robert felt that every word he spoke was digging his grave ever deeper. It had ever been thus. He had discovered Henry Tudor in Lancashire, but had small recognition. At Pembroke he had managed to get the mercenaries to turn against their masters, only to witness death as their reward. He had discovered a poisonous murder plot against the queen and saved her life only to be berated for dereliction of duty for not reporting it earlier to a higher authority. His saving of the queen's life a second time had brought him some small reward but that had been snatched from him when his manor house was burned by Sir Reginald Bray and his marauding Scots. Now here he was being condemned for the death of a traitor knight, the king's sworn enemy and he his most loyal subject.

The king turned to Sir Ralph de Assheton. "Sir Ralph; you have told us that your Ancient, his name is . . ?"

"Abel Mostyn, your grace."

"Yes, Abel Mostyn; you say he explained to squire Robert that he need not take up Bray's challenge due to his deficiency in rank and that his advice was overruled?"

"That is correct, your grace."

"And that this ancient, Abel Mostyn, though in command of your own men, yet deferred to the assumed authority of squire Robert de la Halle?"

"He was at a loss as to how the situation could be resolved, your grace. They were few in number and lightly armed while Sir Reginald was a fully harnessed man-at-arms along with an unknown number of his companions. As it turned out there were but six of them, though ancient Mostyn, nor squire Robert knew that at the time. Squire Robert, no doubt due to his splendid harness, overawed the man and my ancient, having no plan of his own, followed his direction."

"And helped squire Robert fool Sir Reginald Bray too."

"He did, your grace."

"Tell me - your fight with Sir Reginald squire Robert. It was long and hard fought we are informed. I wonder you did not sustain serious hurt?"

"That was largely due to the quality of my harness, your grace, though I must say that had the fight lasted much longer, it might have begun to fail, but so would Sir Reginald's iron."

The king stared at him for a few moments. The whole of the hall at Westminster had fallen silent. Everyone knew of the deadly fight between this stripling of a squire and Sir Reginald Bray, a famous jousting knight, and many there refused to believe the lad had won the contest honestly. The contest had taken place in Lancashire and that was a land where witches and foul spirits abounded. Perhaps the squire's harness was enchanted?

"Squire Robert de la Halle," said King Richard at last. "You have come to our notice previously where you have, either by luck, subterfuge or mere chance served our crown. This is the first instance where you have actually demonstrated a prowess that has relied more on your fighting skills rather than fate. We cannot, however, have a situation where a low ranking youth can take on a noble knight irrespective of whether he manages to destroy him. I am not prepared to tolerate the chance of your repeating the offence."

Robert felt his bowels turning to water. It seemed he was at the end of his career, one that had been beset by error, the product of immature stumbling. He should have known that the completion of his term of training would not be for a few more years and he should have done what the other squires do, fight with one another and leave their masters to their own devices.

"Norfolk!" called out the king. Thomas Howard bowed before the king. "You are Earl Marshall and as such have command of matters pertaining to the martial disciplines. Before the Yoolis feast this year we are to raise to knighthood several of lower rank who fought well for us in the recent war. You will add the name of squire

Robert de la Halle to the list. He has shown a natural command of men and in defeating a stronger opponent in Sir Reginald Bray, has won his spurs. We might add that his personal loyalty to us has been a consistent feature of his history. This device assures us that any challenges he issues in future will be legally contested. You may stand, squire Robert. The next time you kneel before me you shall rise as Sir Robert de la Halle."

Robert remained where he was for a few moments, frozen at the shock of his sudden elevation when he had expected dire punishment. The king's face finally broke into a smile and the queen leaned across to speak into is ear. Clumsily he scrambled to his feet, unconscious of the hubbub that reverberated around the great hall as word of the king's pronouncement spread.

"One moment, squire Robert," said Queen Joanna imperiously. I think his grace has something more to say." She leaned back and smiled at the young squire.

"I am informed that your manor house is burned. That matters little now. Her grace our queen wishes me to grant you holdings nearer to London. It is convenient to have so virtuous and brave a knight within easy call, so she reasons." King Richard turned to his queen and smiled at her. "There is a manor in the demesnes of the duke of Norfolk that is vacant and it is yours if you would take it. It is larger than that in Lancashire, which we are minded to allocate elsewhere. I take it you are amenable to the change?"

"More that I can tell," gushed Robert, hardly believing what he was hearing. "Your grace is most generous."

"Understand that there is an obligation to provide us with archers and armed yeomen for the statuary three months per year at your expense. My lord Norfolk will tell you what that obligation comprises when he tells you of the rent you will pay him. Our future plans might mean the offer is not as generous as you think, however, we are confident you will prosper in our service one way or another."

"My lord king," said Robert, gathering his wits. "There is something I would say regarding the lands in Lancashire."

"Then tell us," replied the king.

"I have learned much about the people there, who can be trusted and who might vacillate when the wind blows in a different direction."

"There is still a residue of treason there?" King Richard's face suddenly became dark.

"No, dread king, no treason, but some are more capable and worthy of trust and others less so, that is all I meant."

The king's features softened. "Well, the manor we gave you there is again vacant and we would have someone take possession who is worthy. You have a name?"

"Yes, your grace. Along with ancient Mostyn, John Formby was foremost in helping me defeat the raiders and in tracking down Sir Reginald Bray. He is a yeoman farmer already on the manor and he has a wife and two sturdy sons, archers, your grace. He would be an ideal tenant and his loyalty in that remote part of your realm is beyond dispute."

"Has the man sufficient means to run a manor?"

"I believe he is well thought of in the merchant community of the region, your grace." Robert made a silent promise to pray to the Virgin for forgiveness in not mentioning the smuggling operation of which Formby would now become the principal. One thing he had learned, it took money to run a manor and in years of poor harvest rather more than rents alone might bring in.

"We thank you for your council, squire Robert. We shall make enquiries and if all is as you say, John Formby might find our favour should he apply for the manor. Now, we dismiss you before we give any more of our realm away."

"And you may tell my handmaid donzela Claris de la Halle," inserted the queen, who was now beaming munificently, "that ere the Yoolis feast is ended, as the wife of a knight she will be *lady* Claris de la Halle."

Standing to one side of the hall, Robert found himself being congratulated by his fellow squires, grudgingly for most but right gladly by John Biggar. They were joined by Anselm, still porting his strange stringed instrument and with Maud Mudd in tow. For a few moments Robert found himself lost between her ample bosoms as she embraced him in a grip of steel. Had Sir Reginald Bray managed to get such a hold on him he feared he might have been torn asunder and he was grateful when she released him.

A hardly less strident grip, but a welcome one, was that of his wife. Claris had been released by the queen to attend upon her husband and she flung herself at him to cling to him, her arms around his neck and her feet kicking well clear of the ground.

"For a moment there I had hopes that you might put in a word for me," said Anselm jocularly. "I had you as a candidate for the rank of Lord High Chancellor. I am sure his grace would have granted that too had you thought on asking for it."

"You sit at the feet of the queen and have no need of favour from me," said Robert gaily.

"It is well that there is at least one woman in our family that can rightly claim the title of lady." Dame Isabella appeared from the mass of courtiers. "Our fortunes are on the rise and perhaps I too might have that same distinction returned to me. My husband is even higher in the king's favour than his son." She directed her gaze to where Laurence de la Halle was standing behind the duke of Norfolk, conversing with one who Robert recognised as the king's tailor. It was true the armourer had been particularly close to his grace lately, which was strange as the king's harness was in perfect condition and had small need of the armourer's art. His squires of the body kept it burnished and ready for instant use even though the recent war was finished with no prospect of a further conflict in the near future.

"If, as it seems, madam, you are lamenting the permanent loss of your erstwhile manor," snapped Robert impatiently, "you may console yourself with the contemplation of the profit my father's forge will bring you at Gloucester. I have no doubt you will be dressed at court as fine as any woman that your rank might allow. Indeed, that is how you are displayed now." Isabella was clad in a grey velvet gown trimmed with black fur and her hennin was roped around with pearls. A gold chain girdle surrounded her waist and the tassels were of golden thread. Robert thought he had never seen so beautiful a woman, and could hardly blame his father being in thrall to her. She could not, however, compare to his own Claris who was her equal in beauty and only lacked the confidence in her femininity that was the hallmark of the older woman, who used hers as currency.

"You are too cruel to dame Isabella, Robert," admonished Claris. "She has been badly used and does not deserve to be spoken to thus."

"Whatever use she has been subjected to has not diminished her ability to gain advantage for herself."

"Robert! That is the sort of language I might expect coming from the acid tongue of your grandfather's wife, dame Anna Quirke. It ill becomes you, and even less a man who is about to become Sir Robert. I think your promoted calling demands better treatment of women, does it not?"

"I stand rebuked," replied Robert sulkily.

"Then let that be an end to the enmity between you two."

"You have a good wife in donzela Claris," intoned Isabella. "Let us put our differences behind us and start anew."

"I suppose it is wise to do so," said Robert resignedly, seeing as his wife had commanded it.

"Then I shall join my husband," said Isabella suddenly.

Their attention was disturbed by the entrance of a parade of nuns. Isabella, seeing their progress towards the royal dais hurried behind them to join Laurence, who gave her an elegant bow as she took her place by his side.

"Is that not the same group of nuns we saw earlier going into the queen's apartments?" said Laurence half interestedly.

"I think so," said Claris "but they have gained one. She in front is probably their Mother Superior - see how she walks, much older than the rest, I would guess."

The nuns approached the royal dais and began to move across to form up by the queen, who was ever ready to have the Holy Sisters about her court. They were clad in black habits with white wimple and cornettes wired high above their faces, which were hidden from the sight of men as usual with black voile.

Suddenly, with an agility that belied her supposed years, the leading nun sprang towards the king. The courtiers close to him could do no more than shout a warning while the high nobles close to the king obscured the vision of the halberdiers of the king's guard. There was a flash of reflected light on steel as the woman lunged at the king with a murderous long dagger that she had concealed beneath her habit. King Richard, seeing the danger, got to his feet only to present a better target for the assassin. The woman plunged the dagger into the king's chest whereupon, with a look of utter shock in his features, he tumbled back onto his throne.

The duke of Norfolk, having at court just his dagger at his belt, drew it and thrust it into the woman's body. She turned and cried out something unintelligible before collapsing onto the steps of the dais. Thomas Howard thrust his dagger into her once, twice, then assured that she was killed, stood and looked down while others rushed forward to rip the veil from her face. There, lying across the steps of the royal dais was exposed the face of dame Margaret Stanley, erstwhile duchess of Richmond and mother of Henry Tudor. Her claw-like hands were raised upwards, as if her nails were about to rake her prey while her face, fixed into a manic rictus of hatred was framed with pure white hair which tumbled down the steps. Slowly her life's blood, flowing from her wounds, dripped into the red velvet there to be subsumed in colour and, just as her son in Morecambe Bay sands, disappeared as if it had never been.

Robert stood as the rest, frozen for the moment in time. Afterwards he would remember the sight of the faces in the great hall on that day. Queen Joanna threw herself across king Richard's body as if to protect him; the duke of Norfolk looked on, horrified.

Viscount Lovell was there, his face displaying shock while John of Pomfret was merely interested. Margaret of Burgundy clasped her protégé, Richard, once of York, as if he were a precious casket while that youth seemed to smile in satisfaction. The lord bastard, John of Pomfret's face was alight with the idea of possibilities while the earl of Lincoln, John de la Pole tugged at his beard pensively. More particularly, Robert would have cause to remember the expressions on the faces of his own family - Claris had her hands over hers in fear while curiously his father was looking upon the king with a kind of satisfaction while his wife, Isabella, had a glow of triumph about her. Robert remembered, to his shame, his sudden shock at the promise of his knighthood falling to dust. So it was on that the fateful day, when a woman, maddened with grief for a dead son and the destruction of her heartfelt ambition threw herself upon the king that had confounded that ambition, his death and hers being the only recompense she had left to her.

Epilogue - England Present Day

Robert Hall stood, his binoculars at his eyes, looking out from the promenade at Arnside in Westmorland. Annie, his wife was busy with young Bob who *would* insist on buying a map of the area. At twelve years of age, his son had developed a strong sense of history, the product, no doubt, of his schooling where the historic culture of England was woven among the fabric of learning. Wherever they went in the land Bob would acquire a local map and scrutinise it for topography and historic landmarks. They had come to Westmorland to visit the great monastery over at Furness, an edifice located in The Vale of Nightshade that went back to the twelfth century and which was still allowed to practice Catholic Rites in spite of England being Protestant. It, along with a host of former monastic houses, was part of the fabric of England and with Maypole dancing and the Morris, one of the things that endeared him to the country. The quaint stained glass and defunct stone statues, formerly saints, coupled with a grand sense of primitive antiquity inexplicably thrilled him, his wife and his son to the heart.

So deeply embedded was the spirit of England within him that he could almost feel he had been here before, that he was a part of this landscape. The great sands of Morecambe Bay stretched away before him and the soughing of the wind seemed to bring to him a language of its own, doing nothing to dispel a sense of *deja vu*. He sighed for the loss of something he could hardly recall and put down the glasses.

"Are ghosts here, father?" asked Bob. The lad had run ahead of his mother and now was brought up suddenly at the wall by the shore side.

Robert laughed. "There certainly are," he replied. "See that place over there?" he pointed to a pub where the sign identified it as The Howling Man. "That is called after Henry Tudor, who was trapped in the sands five hundred years ago and drowned. It happened in the reign of King Richard the Third."

"Was he Richard the Good?"

"Indeed, that is the popular name he is known to history."

"But who was Henry Tudor?"

"Ah," replied Robert. "Few know the name now, except he is remembered around here for his death in the sands, and the cries of his mad mother."

"Are you filling the lad's head with nonsense again," said Annie as she came up.

"No, my love, just with good English history."

Annie snorted indulgently.

"Just around that headland there," he continued, pointing across the sands towards Cartmel Peninsular with the distant and as yet invisible sea beyond, "you will find Humphrey Head. It is the place where the last wolf in England had its lair and was killed by Sir John Harrington. After slaying it and saving his ladylove from its jaws, the two married. They lie to this day in effigy at Cartmel Priory. If you go there and look up, you will see the weather vane shaped as the head of a wolf. It is famous today as a metaphor for the death of Henry Tudor, as a predator after the English Crown, who had attempted to take the throne of King Richard the Third. Having been defeated in battle, I cannot remember the name or the place, he fled north and was cornered here trying to escape across the sands to Furness, there to take ship at what is today named Piel Castle. He was trapped in the sands and left to drown in the incoming tide."

"And is his ghost seen here?"

"Well perhaps: it is said that if you listen carefully when the tide turns, you will hear his howling across the sands; also, mingled with the cries of the seabirds as they follow the tide, the screaming of his mother, who witnessed her son's doom."

"Did she drown too?"

"No, she was dragged away by those few left that had fled the battle and spent many years in France. Her mind deranged and consumed by absurd plots against King Richard, she came to England disguised as a nun and gained access to the king through his queen, a pious lady who trusted too much. She attempted to stab the king to death, but unknown to anyone he was wearing an iron corset beneath his robes which saved him. The king had a condition which we today would know as scoliosis, where his spine was deformed causing him much pain. In his later years the condition worsened so his armourer fashioned a lightweight iron support for him to wear discreetly beneath his robes. Until Margaret Stanley's attempt to stab him occurred, nobody other than his armourer, his tailor and perhaps one or two of his closest body servants knew of his condition. His portraits show him quite straight of stance."

"King Richard the Third? Was he the one that walled his queen up in the Tower of London?"

"Of course not – that was King Richard the Fifth. If you remember your lesson, queen Catherine was a committed Catholic and King Richard was under pressure by his people for England to embrace the Church reforms that had spread across the continent of Europe."

"And he had her walled up then later married another."

"So the story goes. Her body was never found but then the Tower of London was burned and demolished in the wars of 1605."

"What caused the wars?" Bob was ever asking questions, having learned at school something of the fifth Ricardian Age and was old enough to understand the answer.

"The origins were in the reign of King Richard the Third – the Good as he is now known. His policy was to strip the nobles of their power and rely on the goodwill of his people for security. He made a series of laws, some of which we still have today, that benefited commerce rather than landed interest. The noble families tried to rebel against him but were unable to rally the people to their banners, as they would have done in previous years. King Richard founded the Empire of England by his alliance with Portugal, the greatest maritime nation at that time. His ships brought gold from the country we now call Joland, named after the king's queen, Joanna of Portugal. He still lies, as you have seen, with his queen in the world famous Golden Tomb in Saint George's Chapel at Windsor Castle."

"The one that was plundered by the Spanish invaders of 1605?"

"Yes, in the reign of King Richard the Fifth. The English Crown and the country's merchants wanted to keep the new wealth to themselves and used the reforms of the church as a reason for distancing the country from Rome. The Pope had demanded a share of English gold. That was when the Spanish invaded from what was then Scotland, just as the earl of Northumberland had attempted in fourteen eighty-eight. They were expelled ten years later after much bitter fighting up and down England. It was the Spanish Invasion that afterwards provoked the establishment of the Protestant Church in England, the Spanish having been sponsored by the Pope, who was lamenting the dearth of gold tithes coming his way."

"Was that when the Golden Tomb of King Richard the Third was restored?"

"That's right, and it has been a symbol of England's power and wealth ever since."

"And Caledonia became a province of England, too."

"Yes, it was once a sovereign nation. Its former name, as I said was Scotland, but King Richard the Fifth gave it an even older name – Caledonia after his army defeated that of the last Scottish king, James the Sixth in 1618. It was the culmination of the Scots readiness to aid and support the Spanish invasion. Raids from Scotland had plagued England for centuries. The king felt he could no longer tolerate such an enemy on his borders. Caledonia was colonised by the English and served as a penal colony where certain English felons escaped a hanging by working the conquered land. There are few native Scots there today."

"It is strange that of all the countries in the world, we are the only one to retain a monarch," said Bob.

"A wonder when you consider how close we came to becoming a republic after the excesses of King Richard the Eighth. He was a drunkard and a fool whose military blunders almost brought us to ruin. We no longer let the monarch interfere with the defence of the realm."

"Yes, I know that King Richard the Third was the last to lead his soldiers into battle. That is something everyone learns at school."

"Wisely he stopped doing so after the battle with Henry Tudor," said Robert Hall. "He lived for another eighteen years and produced two male heirs and a female. Unfortunately, Queen Joanna, the Holy Princess of Portugal, died some years before him and he refused all further offers of marriage. His son succeeded him as King Richard the Fourth and the line of the English Crown is unbroken down to the present, where we have the tenth of that name on the throne."

They lifted their heads as a klaxon sounded somewhere in the far distance, its strident tone sounding across the sands.

"Here it comes," said Robert Hall as they all hurried to stand at the wall fringing the shore. "It is the second largest bore in England – see, already the birds are following it in."

Handing his binoculars to his son Bob, he pointed across the sands to where a thin grey line sparkled with the silver reflection of the sun on tumbling waters. Seabirds were darting about landing before the wave, taking flight as it reached them. Soon the sandbanks before them were surrounded by water and began reducing until they became inundated. The bore came racing across the sands and up the estuary of the River Kent. Bob put the glasses on the boiling edge of the flood and stood in silence contemplation as he thought on the story of the poor fellow, Henry Tudor, trapped in the sands as the waters rose around him and no possibility of help. He imagined as his father had described in the call of the gulls, the distressed cries of the mother, a woman driven mad by the passions that had been part of her soul from the day she gave him birth.

He put the glasses down from his eyes as the waters calmed and just a few wavelets slapped dispassionately along the fringes of the shore. Robert Hall with his son Bob and wife Annie stood for a few moments as if they wanted to say something, a prayer, perhaps; such was the effect of the sight that untamed nature brought into their minds. They turned and all three felt compelled to stare at the pub opposite. The painted sign, swinging gently in the slight breeze, pictured in harsh, garish graphics a howling man, his head back and his hair as seaweed floating in the running tide. His hands were reaching up from the water, clawing at the sky as if beseeching a Divine aid that would not come. The mouth was gaping open and his eyes stared wide in terror as they looked upon the waters rising inexorably around.

END

Web Site - www.quoadultra.net

Printed in Great Britain
by Amazon